This is a work of fiction. Names, characters and places, and incidents either are the product of the author's imagination or used fictitiously. Any resemblance to actual persons, living or dead, events, or locations are entirely coincidental.

Text copyright © Eirelyn Kentner 2021

All rights reserved. No part of this book may be reproduced or used in any manner without written permission of copyright owner expect for use of quotations in book review.

Self-published by Eirelyn Kentner with Lulu printing.
www.lulu.com

The Library of Congress has cataloged the hardcover edition as follows:
Author: Eirelyn Kentner
Title: Sweet Little Lies – first edition 2021
ISBN 978-1-257-63243-5
1. Mystery-Fiction 2. Teen Fiction

For Tiggy
My Twin

Trigger warning
(spoilers)
During certain chapters sexual assault/rape are alluded to.
Below are chapters these triggers are specifically mentioned heavily
Chapters: 22, 24, 46 48, and 50

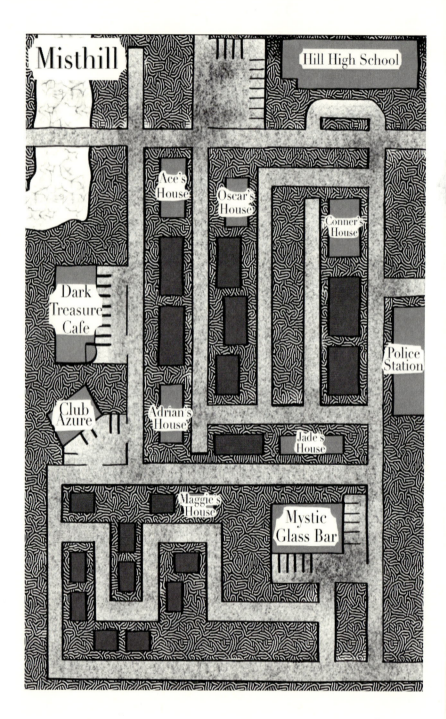

CHAPTER ONE

Maggie Snow
<u>Monday, September 2nd, 12:00pm</u>

Two Years have passed since I've stepped foot into Misthill.
Two Years have passed since I've been home.
"Get off of me!"
"I'll tell everyone."
"Leave this town, tonight!"
I don't know if I'd call it my home anymore.

The hallway in my mom's house is always dark, the only time it's ever bright is if the bedroom doors are open letting the light from the windows shine through into the hallway.

I pull my packed bag off my bed as my mom screams in my ear, "You can't just get up and leave. You're not going back there Maggie! I won't allow it."

I walk into the dim lit hallway and to the front door. My small bag drapes over my shoulder as I push open the screen door. I begin to make my way down the small cobblestone path. My mom, still yelling at me.

"Maggie Dawson Snow! Get back inside this house right now!" You know it's always a bad thing when your full name gets yelled at you. But I need to leave, I technically don't have a choice in the matter.

I sit down on my very dirty black motorcycle. "Bye, Mom."

I pull down on the throttle and I'm out of the driveway. As I ride down the street, I can still hear the faint ring of my name being yelled by my mom.

Time to go home.

Welcome to Misthill, the sign reads as I wiz past it into town.

I ride through the wealthy neighbourhood, not much has changed, all the houses are still big and fancy. All of them have two floors and probably pools in the backyards.

My dad lives on the broken side of town, as most people would call it. The only difference between the broken neighbourhood and the wealthy one is the house sizes.

I stop my motorcycle out front of the house. I slowly get off and step onto the curb to take it all in. The house hasn't changed from its baby blue colour, the only difference is a lot of the paint has chipped off. The grass clearly hasn't been cut, it's almost up to my waist.

I quickly step off the curb and onto the road after the thought of how many ticks could be hiding in that grass right now.

I walk up the driveway and to the small pathway leading up to the front door. It's hard to find at first glance since the grass has grown into it blocking a clear path.

I knock on the door and take a small step back. I'm not expecting anyone to answer. My dad was never home.

Unless things changed when I left.

The door opens to my surprise, "Mags?"

"Hi Dad..." I smile with a hint of guilt.

"What- What are you doing here? Is your mom here too?" My dad leans out the door to look around.

"No just me... Can I come in?"

"Yeah- yeah of course."

My dad step's out of the doorway so I can enter the house. Once inside I look around, a sigh escapes my mouth as I notice the small piles of beer bottles all around the kitchen floor. I walk more inside and into the kitchen to see the piles of the takeout container stacking up on the counter.

I didn't think it would be that hard to take out the trash.

"Sorry that the house is a bit of a mess. I wasn't expecting anyone."

"Do you ever." I mumble.

I quickly turn around, "So is my room still standing?"

"Oh yeah," He nods, "There's only a mattress in there now. Why? Are you planning on staying?"

"Uh, yeah, I was hoping that I could. I'd like to." I lie through my teeth. This is the last thing I wish to be doing right now.

"Great, the gang will want to see you again. I think everyone has missed you. Oh, and I can help decorate your room again."

I hadn't expected him to be this excited about me being back. When I left, I had asked him not to call me, or ask why I was leaving. I thought that he would resent me for it, but clearly not.

"I'm not a big decor person, as long as I've got a blanket. I'm fine."

"Right... Well let's go sit in the living room, get all caught up."

I nod and follow him towards the living room. It's worse than the kitchen. Beer bottles sit all over the couch, the chair, by the tv. On the table and under the table. I can't comprehend how he has lived like this for two years.

I sit down on the couch; dust flies up into my face making me cough.

"So, the gang is still alive and running then?" I ask as I place my bag on the ground beside me.

"Yeah, and I'm still the proud leader. You still have your tattoo, right? You didn't get it lasered off, did you?"

"No, I still have it." I pull up the sleeve of my jacket to show the bow and arrow tattoo on my forearm before quickly pulling it back down.

"Your leather jacket is still in the closet, so you can start to wear it again."

I nod holding in a sigh.

Nothing has changed since I left, the only thing my dad still cares about is the stupid gang. Don't get me wrong it was fun to be in, but not really what I wanted.

"How's your mom?"

"She's good, probably still fuming at home."

Whenever I use the word home, it's mainly because I don't know what else I should say. I don't feel like I truly have a home anymore.

The door to the house swings open, "Yo, Rick!"

I look to my left to see Jade standing there, "Jade?"

"Maggie, what the hell are you doing back here?" Jade asks.

I stand up from the couch dusting off my pants, "Just... thought it was a good time to come back."

Jade pulls me into an awkward hug. I wasn't expecting this to be her response to seeing me. She is much shorter than me even with her platform boots on.

"Are you coming back into the gang then?"

"Wouldn't have it any other way." I lie through my teeth again. I begin to wonder how often I'm going to have to do that.

Jade has hardly changed since I left. Everything about her style is the same even down to the way she ties her leather jacket around her waist. Not to mention the proud way she stands, almost like how an Olympian would stand after winning gold.

I would say that Jade and I are opposites with most things, I'm one of the palest people in town and she's one of the darkest. She can stand confidently because she is, and I can stand confidently because I must.

"I hope you still have your knife."

I nod, "Always keep it in my boot."

"Are you enrolling at Hill High again?"

"Why so many questions Jade? But yes, I'll be going back there."

"Good, it sucks hanging out with all the guys alone."

I scoff, "And you're just learning this now?"

Not to offend any of the guys, but I hardly remember their names, I was only in the gang for a couple of weeks before I left town.

Jade laughs and makes her way to sit down on the couch, she looks over to my dad, "So we found those kids that kept sneaking in and out of the meeting place."

"Did you tell them off?"

"Of course, we did. Clark and I gave them a little scare. Doubt they'll be coming back anytime soon." Jade laughs.

Jade and I were never truly friends. I hung out with her because she was the only person who would talk to me. But I never formed a full connection with her. She was just always... there.

"I'm just gonna go check out my room." I pull my bag up over my shoulder and head towards the room.

The hallway is littered with bottles, I reach the end of the hallway where my room sits. The door is closed and right beside it sits a picture frame with a photo of my family inside, "What went wrong?" I mumble to myself as I push the bedroom door open.

My dad wasn't lying when he said there was only a mattress. He must have sold my bed frame and night table along with it. I would think he used the money to buy more beer.

I step into my room and close the door behind me. I don't think I should classify it as my room anymore, nothing about it is the same.

Placing my bag onto the ground, I take a step towards the closet and open it. It's completely empty to my surprise, the only thing in it are two small cardboard boxes on the floor.

In my bag I packed a small amount of the clothes, mainly my two favorite shirts and another pair of pants. I can easily go to one of the small shops outside of town to get more clothes if I really want to.

I hang the shirts up in the closet and fold the pants on top of the cardboard boxes.

I make my way to the mattress in two steps and sit down. Dust flies up in my face, once again making me cough. I open my bag and pull out my notebook. I flip to the very back where a small pocket sits, it's where I put the letter.

I reach for it when I stop myself and look around. I have so much paranoia when it comes to being alone, I never feel like I'm alone, probably because I never was alone the last time I was here.

I close the notebook and shove it back into my bag. I quickly stand up and walk out of my room.

As I'm walking I almost trip over the many beer bottles that are on the ground. I make my way through the hallway and into the kitchen. I glance into the living room through the small cut out over top of the counter.

My dad is passed out asleep on the chair with a beer bottle already in his hand. I didn't think I was in my room for that long.

I slowly open the front door and walk outside. The sun has begun to set making the night sky begin to shine. I know that once I reach Dark Treasure Cafe, I won't be able to see any of the stars because there will be too many bright lights shining.

I reach my motorcycle and pull the other strap of my bag over my shoulder.

Dark Treasure Cafe is the one place I know I'll be safe to read the letter over again. I just know that it's safer in public where more than one person can see me.

CHAPTER TWO

Maggie Snow
Monday, September 2nd, 6:00pm

     The Dark Treasure Cafe, one of the most common hangout places, at least that's what I remember it as. Always filled with life, and loud music playing once it was past eight.
     I park my motorcycle out front of the Cafe and make my way inside and over to the front counter.
     The Cafe is mostly filled with families and the elderly. I would take a guess that they'll be gone before eight.
     It looks the same as it always has. The brick walls, black tables and chairs. The low hanging lights from the ceiling, the only different thing is the employees.
     "Hi, what can I get for you today."

My attention is brought back to the tall blonde standing in front of me.

"Just a hot chai tea."

"Okay, that'll be $5.99." The girl gives an obvious fake smile. I wonder what her day has been like.

I slide a ten-dollar bill onto the counter, "Keep the change."

I walk down to the other side of the counter to wait for my drink.

Right beside the small counter is a bulletin board littered with random coupons and news about the town. My eyes slowly shift to the top right corner.

Kian Turner. Missing. 18 years old. If found, please call.

"Sad, isn't it?"

I look to my left to see a guy probably in his early 20's, "Uh yeah, it is. When'd he go missing?" And why'd they use that photo of him?

"Since the 29th I think... here's your drink."

"Uh... Thanks."

I turn away and walk over to the small table in the far corner. It's the only table left in the whole Cafe.

The bell sounds from someone walking into the Cafe, I set my bag onto the ground beside me and grab my notebook and the book that I'm currently reading.

I set my notebook off to the side. I don't think I'm fully ready to re-read that letter yet.

I open to the last page I was on in my book.

The words start to flow into my mind and off the pages. When I was younger my dad would always say I should enter one of those fastest reader contests because of how fast I would finish books.

I glance outside. The night sky is fully dark now. No oranges or pinks making it bright or fluffy. Just darkness with the streetlights being the only light.

"Hey."

I turn to see a boy my age standing at the edge of the chair that sits in front of me.

"Hi?"

I look him up and down, the way he's dressed tells me he lives on the wealthy side of town. His bag is literally Louis Vuitton.

"All the other seats are taken… except for the one in front of you." He taps the seat with his fingers, "I was really hoping to sit. Would I be able to sit? I won't disturb your reading, I promise." The boy flashes a smile. How can someone's teeth be so white?

I glance around the Cafe to see if there really aren't any more seats.

There isn't.

"Sure." I smile uncomfortably.

The boy pulls out the chair and sits down in front of me, "I'm Adrian by the way." He smiles and puts out his hand for me to shake it.

"Cool."

I look back down at my book, "Are you going to tell me your name?" Adrian asks.

"Nope."

"Why not?"

I close my book and cross my arms over top of it, clearly, he's not going to leave me alone like he *promised*, "I like the mystery."

"I can tell, you're reading... *The Bone Collector*?"

I take a sip of my tea, "Yup. It's not the best, but the only one I've been able to find to read."

"Well, if you're into mysteries, maybe you'd be interested in what happened to Kian Turner." Adrian says while thrusting his head towards the missing poster on the bulletin board.

"Probably just another kid looking for attention from mommy and daddy or running from something."

"What makes you say that?"

I shrug, "Why else would someone in a small town go missing when they have everything?"

"Did you know him?" Adrian asks.

I shake my head, "I just read a lot, that's what I would think is happening, coming from an avid reader."

"Really?"

Clearly, he didn't hear the sarcasm in my voice, "No."

"Then why? Or wait is this another mystery like your name too?" Adrian smirks.

"Take a guess."

"A mystery."

"Bingo." I actually smile. Not a fake one. I don't know the last time I really smiled.

Maybe I judged this Adrian too quickly, or maybe I judged his Louis Vuitton bag too quickly.

He pushes his brown hair back with his hand, "So how old are you? It's a small town so I know that you're new."

Actually, he's the new one in the town. I'm just an old ghost here for a visit.

"17, you?"

"I'm 17 too," He glances out the window as a car drives by, "Will you be going to Hill High?"

"Well, it is the only high school in town so... I don't really get a choice."

I lean back in the chair once I realize how tense my shoulders are.

I look out the window, the streets are still the same mostly empty streets I remember them to be. Maybe this town truly is a ghost town?

My eyes shift back over to Adrian and notice a small leather backed book on the edge of the table, "What's in the book?"

He looks down at it and back to me, "Uh nothing."

"You can't become the mysterious one now. That's my thing."

"Fine. It's just poems."

I lean forward onto the table, now this is something interesting, "Really? Poems?"

"I know, cringey."

"No, it's just. You don't look like the type to write poems."

Adrian scrunches face, "It's the bag, isn't it?"

I nod, "Yeah it is."

"My mom bought it for me. I never wanted it, but if I don't use it, she'd be pissed."

"Makes sense… So, what type of poems do you write?"

"Poems about life."

"Well, that's what most poems are about, so specifically."

He shakes his head, "No, that's too much to tell someone when I still don't know their name."

"Well take a guess, what do you think my name is?" I smirk.

"Kelly?"

I'm offended, "Seriously, you had to give me one of the bitchiest names to mean girl stereotypes?"

"You asked." He puts his hands up in defense, "But I'm going to take a guess and say that I'm wrong."

"Far wrong." I purse my lips and nod.

"But, so, you're a writer then?"

"I wouldn't say writer." Adrian says.

"Well, I bet your poems are good."

"Why? You haven't even read them."

I shrug, "You have that presence about you, I can sense it. Plus, you have a way of talking that makes me think you're a good writer."

"Really? I never thought you could tell that through someone's way of talking."

"Well meeting new people can make you view things differently."

"So, you just go around talking to people, telling them if they're a writer or not? And that's how you view things?" Adrian chuckles.

"No." I roll my eyes.

"Then how do you view things?"

"If I told you that, we wouldn't have anything to talk about the next time we see each other."

"Next time?"

"We are going to the same school, are we not? I think we'd run into each other at some point, right?" I shrug, "So you'll know the way I view things soon enough."

"How?" Adrian asks.

"I make an imprint everywhere I go."

Adrian tilts his head, "You think that highly of yourself?"

"You have to when no one else is going to."

"Woah." Adrian stares at me, "That was really deep."

I shake my head. I can't tell if he was trying to be sarcastic or not.

Most of the time I try to bite my tongue when saying things, I never want to give too much of myself away to someone. I don't want someone to hurt me again.

"You might be the most interesting person I've ever met in this town." He smiles.

"Trust me, I'm not." I'm just a broken girl who still has no control over her own life.

"I think you are."

As the night ran on, the Cafe gets more and more empty, and the music slowly gets louder and louder.

Adrian pulls his phone out of his pocket, "Oh holy shit, it's 9."

"Really?"

Time really does fly by when you're having fun. I guess I was having fun.

"I should probably get going, first day at school tomorrow and my mom will be pissed if I'm home late." Adrian says.

"I should actually get going too."

I put my book and notebook back into my bag. I never got around to the main reason why I came here in the first place.

Adrian and I walk out of the Cafe together.

I turn towards Adrian, "It was nice meeting you, Adrian."

"You too... uh... I still don't know your name."

"You'll know soon." I turn around and start to walk towards my motorcycle.

"Really! That's all I'm going to get?!" Adrian yells.

"See you around, Adrian!"

I get onto my motorcycle and drive off down the street.

I pull up out front of the house. All the lights are out, the only thing lighting up the house is the flash of the TV.

I get inside.

My dad hasn't moved since I left the house three hours ago. I make my way to my room. I turn on the light. I'm honestly surprised the light bulb isn't burnt out.

As I sit down on my bed, and I pull out my notebook. I flip to the last page and stare at the date on the letter that is sitting in the small pocket.

"*Since the 29th I think...*"

I stare at the letter.

August 29th... from Kian Turner

Did Kian sent me this on the day he went missing? I didn't know that he was missing.

CHAPTER THREE

Adrian Fisher
<u>Tuesday, September 3rd, 7:25am</u>

 I walk down the spiral staircase that sits in the center of my house. The number of times I've almost slipped on these stairs in the morning is unexplainable. I keep telling my mom we need those stair rug things.
 I walk through the doorway to the kitchen. The whole kitchen smells amazing, "Eggs and Bacon to keep the brain charged for the first day back." My mom smiles as she places a plate filled with food onto the island countertop.
 "Thanks, Mom." I smile while sitting down at the island.
 "Are you giving your friend a ride to school this morning?" My dad asks while he walks into the

kitchen holding a coffee and the newspaper that he published last night.

"My friend has a name."

"Oh right, what was it again?" He asks while taking a sip of his coffee.

"It's Oscar, dad. And I have given him a ride to school every day basically since we moved here." I say while taking a bite of bacon.

My dad sits down at the small round table behind me and flips open to the first page of the newspaper, "You know, Honey, I think this is one of our best papers yet."

Two years ago, when I moved here, the main reason was so my parents could become the writers for the town newspaper. To be honest I didn't think newspapers were still a thing, but I tend to follow in their writing footsteps and now write for the school newspaper. Which I also didn't think was a thing.

"You say that every time Matthew." My mom says.

I always get confused when I hear their names. I'm so used to it being mom and dad not Linda and Matthew.

"So, Adrian, you'll be writing on the paper again for your school?" My mom asks.

"Most likely, I don't think Oscar would let me leave." I chuckle.

"But you'll also be trying out for the basketball team again, and keeping up your grades?" My dad asks.

"Of course." I nod.

I reach for my tea and take a slow sip.

I hate the basketball team, my parents made me join it so I could be more active. But this is my last year, so it'll go by fast, and it's only one season of basketball so it'll be fine.

I glance over to the clock on the stove, *7:40*.

"I have to go get Oscar."

I grab my backpack off the chair beside me.

"You've hardly had anything to eat." My mom says as I'm walking out of the kitchen.

"I'll eat more at school!" I yell when I reach the front door. I pull on my running shoes and grab my car keys off the hook.

"See you after school!" I yell to my parents while opening the front door.

"Have a good-"

I hop down the steps of my porch and make my way to my white convertible. I got it last year for my birthday, not really the car I wanted, but I'm saving up to buy my own for when I move out. Hoping that I can stop being labeled as the kid with mom and dad's money.

I throw my bag into the backseat and back out of the driveway, making my way to Oscar's house. He doesn't live that far from me. The whole neighbourhood is small, yet big at the same time. Everything is compact.

I pull in front of Oscar's house and honk the car horn.

Oscar comes running out of his house, his curly hair bouncing up and down with every step.

24

"Morning Bud." I smile as he gets in the passenger seat.

"No, *morning bud*, I asked you to stop honking and just text me when you're here. You almost gave my mom another heart attack." Oscar says while putting on his seat belt.

"But it's fun." I laugh while driving off down the street.

"Anyways are you ready for our first last day of school?" Oscar asks, with a little too much enthusiasm.

"I mean, bittersweet, but yes. And we've got a lot of Black Clover to catch up on tonight."

"Well personally, all of that is unimportant right now because Maggie's back." Oscar says.

I quickly look over to him confused before pulling into the school parking lot, "Who?"

"Oh right, you just moved here when she left."

"Right?... So, who is she?" I ask.

I pull into a parking spot and look over to Oscar, "She's just someone you don't want to mess with."

"That's very helpful, Bud." I purse my lips together before grabbing my bag from the backseat and getting out of the car.

Oscar frantically gets out of the passenger seat and walks over to me, "Well she left two years ago, and she would always get into fights with anyone, and everyone soon started to avoid her."

"Okay?" I fold my arms and lean onto my car.

"Just... It's a big deal that she's back. No one thought she would ever come back. No one even knew why she left, some people say it's because she didn't want to be in her dad's gang anymore, some think that someone made her leave, some even think she just got sick of how small the town was." Oscar explains.

"Bud, I just asked who she was, not about theories to why she left."

"Sorry, but Maggie can't be described by one word, she's a complex being that scares the shit out of me at certain times."

I sigh and start to walk towards the school, "Everything scares you."

"True, but she really scares me. So, some advice, just stay away from her, especially because she's in a gang."

"Bud, all I'm hearing you say is she's in a gang and has a bad past, I don't see anything scary about that." I shrug.

"Hey boys!" I'd recognize that loud deep voice anywhere. Conner moves in between Oscar and I throwing his arms around us.

I met Conner on the basketball team when I moved here. Him and Oscar don't really get along that well, but they try to be civil with one another.

Conner's grip tightens on my shoulder. I don't understand how over one year he could get so big. I truthfully don't remember him being this strong. I feel like he's breaking my arm.

Conner looks over to me, "Adrian, you better be trying out for the team again this year, we need you."

"I am don't worry."

"Conner, did you hear Maggie's back?" Oscar asks.

Conner's face immediately drops, "Are you joking?"

"No, it's been the main talk around town since yesterday."

"I got to go." Conner turns around and walks into the school.

"What was that about?" I ask Oscar.

"Well Conner and Maggie used to date and-"

I stop walking and fully turn towards Oscar, "You're telling me Conner dated someone in a gang. Do you know how many times I've heard him talk about how he hates anyone from that gang?"

"They dated in grade nine before Maggie joined the gang. He started to hate all of them right after they broke up. Maggie basically became a completely different person, she even stopped talking to Ace."

"Ace Turner, Kian's sister?" I ask.

"Yeah, "Oscar nods while we start to walk into the school, "They were best friends, but that was also when Ace was still Alec and hadn't become a girl yet."

"Okay? Wait! Ace is transgender. I'm really lost now."

"Did you not know that?"

I shake my head, "No she just, she's a girl. I never would have known she was a guy."

"Well, she is a girl. But the important thing is that all you need to know is to stay away from Maggie. Because in a gang, will punch you in the face if you are anyway getting on her nerves and I find it pretty convenient she comes back right around the time Kian goes missing."

"You love gossip, don't you?"

"Duh, that's why I write on the school paper. Wait you're still writing with me, right?" Oscar asks in a panic.

"Yes, of course. I wouldn't leave you hanging."

"Thank god."

The newspaper was the first place I had met Oscar. I feel like if I left the newspaper, I'd be leaving our friendship in some way.

Hill High has this thing where once you get assigned a locker, you keep that same locker until you graduate. Oscar and I's lockers are right beside each other which is an awesome coincidence.

Oscar and I reach our lockers. I lean up against mine right as the hallway gets progressively quieter. Whispers begin to fill the air.

"And here comes Maggie." Oscar gulps as his whole body becomes rigid.

I turn and look over my shoulder.

How did I not put that together sooner?

Maggie. The girl from Dark Treasurer Cafe.

She looks different from last night. Showier. Last night she was wearing a baggy sweater with

28

jeans and today she's basically just wearing a bra, those same jeans and a leather jacket.

"So that's what your name is." I mumble.

"What?" Oscar asks.

"Oh uh... just- I've already met her."

Oscar's eyes go wide, I'm suddenly nervous that a reflex is going to kick in and he'll punch me, "How?!"

"Last night, at the Cafe. There was only one seat left and it was at her table, so I asked to sit and-"

"Adrian!! Are you an idiot you could have died!"

"Now I think that's a bit much, Bud. She didn't seem anything like how you 'explained' her."

"Probably because she realized that you had no clue who she was!!"

I place my hands on Oscar's shoulder, "Breath, it's fine. It's not like I kissed her, I just had... a three-hour conversation with her."

"That's worse."

"How is that worse?" I stare at him confused.

"She's mind controlling you with her words." Oscar says while wiggling his fingers in my face.

I swat them away, "Well, I mean if she was, I wouldn't really care, she is hot."

Oscar shakes his head and throws his hands up in the air, "She's already doing it, you're already lost."

"Bud, I'm just joking around, everything fine. I'll try and stay away from her as much as I can if you promise to calm down."

He nods, "Fine. deal."

The warning bell for the first period rings. "I'll see you at lunch." Oscar says before scurrying off down the hallway.

Before going to my first period class, I look down the hallway to see Maggie, that name fits her, much better than Kelly. She's standing with people from the gang. From our conversation last night, it doesn't seem like she'd fit in with any of them. But I guess what she said last night was true, she does seem to make an imprint everywhere she goes.

Oscar and I walk into our fifth period science class. We make our way to the back of the classroom.

I like to think I'm good in school and at answering questions, and I'd normally sit near the front of the class. But I hate science, especially with Mr. Gibes.

"Welcome back everyone-"

Mr. Gibes gets cut off by the loud squeak coming from the classroom door opening, "Miss. Snow, welcome back, you're late." Mr. Gibes glares as Maggie walks into the classroom.

"By, what a second?" Maggie smiles.

"Take a seat in the back, beside Mr. Adams."

"Glady." Maggie gives a snarky smile as she walks over towards Oscar and me.

Oscar looks over to me repeatedly mouthing out, *"Save me."*

Maggie sits down beside Oscar and leans forwards onto the table resting her chin on her arms.

I'm honestly glad to be sitting on the other side of Oscar; I have no clue if she's noticed me yet and I don't know if she'd even say anything to me. She does seem different at school, compared to last night when we were alone.

Mr. Gibes hands out two worksheets after talking for a bit about how the school year is going to work.

"You have the rest of the class to finish up these sheets and hand them in tomorrow."

The classroom fills up with chatter. I glance over to the clock on the wall, only 15 minutes left of class.

I shift my view to the paper in front of me, I write my name and my grade before looking over to Oscar, "What should I put down for interests?" I ask.

Oscar looks up at me, "Writing, basketball, being good at everything."

"I'll just stick with writing and basketball." Mainly because I'm not good at everything.

Oscar was about to say something when slightly loud scratching comes from beside him. Oscar turns to look over at Maggie. I lean forwards onto the table to look past him.

"What are you looking at, Adams?" Maggie asks not even looking up to us. Her tone is much different from last night, more abrupt.

"Uh... just-"

Maggie looks up at Oscar, "What are you trying to say?"

"Nothing." Oscar shuts his mouth and looks forwards.

Maggie looks back down at her paper continuing to scribble a big black circle over the whole page, "Right... You know I missed you... you got a boyfriend yet?"

"No-no." Oscar stutters.

So, Maggie must know that Oscar is gay, but why'd she ask him if he had a boyfriend? And why'd she ask him in such a weird way?

Maggie shrugs, "Guess the right one just hasn't found you yet."

Oscar nods and quickly looks over to me, his eyes popping out of his head, *"help"* he mouths out for the second time in an hour.

"Don't think I forgot about you Adrian. I bet you know my name now, right?" Maggie glances over to me and back at her paper.

"Yeah... Maggie."

"Bingo." Maggie sets down her pencil and fully turns to face Oscar and I, "So are you two going to the back-to-school party in the woods tonight?"

"We don't party." Oscar says.

"Oh, come on, I know you party Adams, and Adrian, I know you can probably party too. So, I'll see you two there." Maggie smirks as the bell rings. She picks up her bag from the floor and walks out of the classroom with the herd of everyone else.

Oscar looks over to me, "We have to go now."

"What?"

"I don't want to defy what Maggie says so we're going." Oscar stares at me with wide eyes.

"Can you at least promise you'll stop with the bug eyes?"

Oscar blinks back to his normal low get eyes, "Fine."

I scratch the back of my neck. There go our plans for binging Black Clover all night.

CHAPTER FOUR

Maggie Snow
Tuesday, September 3rd, 2:15pm

    Hill High is one of the worst places in this whole town.
    All anyone ever does is whisper and gossip.
    The moment I walked into school this morning everyone was whispering, *"Is she really back?" "Why'd she leave in the first place." "Bitch."*
    I walk out of the side entrance of the school. Finally unclenching my fits. Having to resist the urge to punch everyone at this school was harder than I thought.
    I make my way to the back parking lot; my motorcycle is sitting beside a very bright pastel yellow bike.
    A tall girl with long black hair stands beside the bike looking down at her phone. Something

about her is familiar, even though I've never seen her before or even remember her. Her white flower tank top and blue jeans remind me of someone.

I approach my motorcycle and the girl looks up at me, "Maggie?"

"Uh... yeah... Do I know you?" I look into her eyes, they're a familiar almond shape that I've looked into before.

"Right, I look different." The girl sighs, "It's Alec, I go by Ace now."

Holy shit.

"Holy shit... God I shouldn't have said that out loud... sorry... uh wow, you, did it? Congrats. You look great."

"Thank you." Ace smiles, "I thought I heard people saying that you were back, but I didn't believe them."

"Uh yeah... we'll I'm back." I laugh awkwardly.

"Why are you back?"

"Just thought it was time to come back." I give my best fake smile in hopes that Ace can't still read when I'm lying.

"Cool." Ace smiles.

I can remember when we were in grade nine and she had talked about wanting to transition, I gave her some of the clothes I didn't want any more that my mom bought me for Christmas. That's how I recognize the shirt.

She truly looks great.

"I saw the poster of your brother. I'm sorry to hear he's missing." I try to be sympathetic.

"Thanks." She looks down at the ground.

"You look really different." I try changing the subject, "In a good way! Like you look great. This suits you."

"That means a lot... My parents are still trying to get used to it, mostly my mom. But everyone at school is used to it, sometimes there's the weird look, but nothing I'm not used to."

"That's awesome." I nod and smile, "We'll I should get going."

"Yeah, me too- wait are you going to that party?"

"Yeah. You?"

"Yeah, I'll see you there."

"Okay." I nod and smile.

I get onto my motorcycle and make my way out of the parking lot.

I knew I was going to run into her at some point, I just didn't think it was going to be today. It was less awkward than I thought it was going to be. I'm glad she still talked to me and that I didn't fully ruin any connection we once had.

The sun has set by the time I arrive at the dead-end road by the woods. The back-to-school party has always been held here. I'm surprised that not much has changed since I left.

I get off my motorcycle and make my way to the clearing in the forest. I can see the large bonfire in the distance.

There's a table set up with a bunch of drinks and random snacks. I still never know who brings them here.

I grab a beer from the table while walking past. I move my way through the crowds of people surrounding the bonfire.

The sky is surprisingly clear tonight. The stars are bright, and the moon is full lighting up the night sky. These are the night's that I love, the sky is clear, the air is fresh. I feel like I could take on the world.

I was about to lean up against a tree right as I notice Adrian and Adams standing off to the right of the bonfire.

I didn't think they were going to come. I was joking when I said I'd see them here.

They both look like lost puppies as I make my way over to them.

"Hey."

"Hi." Adams eyes go wide.

"Adams you good?"

"Yeah." He nods.

"I don't think he's good." Adrian chuckles, falling back into the tree behind him.

"I'm fine, I'm just enjoying my water." Adams says while slightly moving his head up and down to the music.

I stare at him, "You're at a party just drinking water?"

"I couldn't convince him to have a beer." Adrian gives a sideways smile. I glance down at the beer in his hand wondering if this is his first or second drink and how much of a lightweight, he is. Since he seems drunk already by my judging.

"Try this." I grab Adams water and pass him my beer.

"No."

"Oscar it's just beer, try it." Adrian says.

"I can't"

"Adams, I've seen you drink beer before just fucking try it." I sigh.

Adams peers down at the beer in his hand before taking it up to his lips, taking a small sip. He squints his eyes, "Nope, I'd like my water back."

"Okay fine." I pass him his water and he passes me back my beer.

"So, I'm surprised you two actually came. You don't seem like the party type, especially you Adrian."

"We thought why not." Adrian smiles.

"You should have brought your notebook; some great poems could have been written tonight." I smirk before walking away from them both.

I walk back over to the tree I was originally going to lean against.

"Hey." I look to my right to see Jade walking up to me.

"Hey."

"How was your day back?" She asks.

"Normal for the most part, I'm gonna have to get used to the stares."

"It'll probably only happen for a couple more days."

"I doubt that." I think it'll happen for longer.

I look over to Adrian and Adams talking, Adrian glances over in my direction. I give him a smile; he gives a small smile back before going back to the conversation he's having with Adams.

I shift my foot in my right boot and feel something poke me, "Hey can you hold my boot for a second."

I take off my boot and hand it to Jade, I lift my leg up so I can see my foot, a small pine needle is stuck in my sock.

"Ow." Jade says.

"Yeah." I grunt while pulling it out of my sock and throwing it on the ground.

Jade hands me back my boot and I put it back on, "Thanks."

"How would that even get in there?"

"Great question." I sigh.

"I also just saw you staring at Adrian, I wouldn't if I were you."

"Wouldn't what?"

"Go for him."

"I'm not going to; I was just looking at him." Why does she even care why I was looking at him?

"I'm just saying, he's the perfect guy with the perfect life and perfect grades and perfect everything. He's all mom and dad's money. He's not your type."

That really sounded like a backhanded compliment.

"I'm going to get another drink." I smile while taking the last sip from the beer in my hand.

I walk away and over to the table full of drinks. I stare at the drinks; I'm not really wanting anything else.

"Hey." I glance to my left to see Ace standing beside me.

"Hey."

"Getting a beer?" She asks.

"Maybe." I shrug, "I don't know if I want another one tonight, but." I grab a beer off the table and turn towards her, "This one's still your favorite right?"

"Yeah." Ace nods smiling at me as she grabs it from my hand.

"So how are you parents?" I ask while leaning up against the table.

"Good. Well frantic since they're worried about Kian. I mean I am too, but he was pretty distant this past year other than when mom would say rude things about me."

"I'm sorry to hear that. But of course, they'll be worried about their baby boy." I say sarcastically.

"Yup, always the favorite." Ace sighs.

"Personally, I think you're their favorite and Kian is just the jackass brother."

I see a smile come to Ace's face before it slowly fades away, "Maggie can I-"

Ace gets cut off by screaming coming from around the bonfire. A crowd has formed around two people.

"What's going on?"

Ace and I make our way through the crowd to see what's happening. I look down to see Conner Martin pinning Jacob Ross to the ground.

Everyone around us is chanting *"Fight! Fight! Fight!"*

Sure, I've had my fair share of beating people up, but having people cheer it on is stupid. Conner is being stupid.

I walk into the middle of the circle and pull Conner from Jacob.

"You wanna fight too, Maggie?" Conner asks, his words slurring.

"You're drunk, go cool off before I beat the shit out of you and Jacob for both being stupid drunk asses. You'll both regret it in the morning."

Everyone slowly moves out of a circle and goes back to doing their own thing.

Conner glares at me before walking past me shoving his shoulder into mine while doing so. I know he won't believe it, but I do still care for him, but I also understand why he wouldn't believe anything I say.

I sigh and walk back over to Ace, "Still holding up the tough girl reputation I see."

"It's more complicated than that, Ace."

"You can tell-"

"I'm just gonna go on a walk, I'll probably see you later." I bite my bottom lip before turning around and walking away.

I walk further and further away from Ace and deeper and deeper into the woods, making my way down to the river.

The blasting music and chatter coming from everyone soon fades out and all I can hear is the stream of water coming from the river and the wind blowing what's left of the leaves on the trees.

I stop at the edge of the river; I sigh and look up at the sky and all the stars in it. Sometimes I wish I was one of the stars up in the sky. Just sparkling and getting stared at for its beauty and not it's danger.

I close my eyes and drop my arms to the sides of my body. I let the wind blow through my hair. I let myself fall away into the world for one small second, and one small second is all I need before I open my eyes again.

I turn away from the river and start to make my way back to the party.

I only take a few steps before I trip and fall onto the ground, my knee hitting a rock.

"Fuck." I mumble.

Of course, the rock had to hit right where the rip in my jeans is. I pull out the flashlight in my pocket and shine it at my knee to see a deep cut gushing blood.

"Just perfect."

I shine the light forwards to see what I tripped over.

A shoe, which leads to a leg, and then a torso and then a face. The wind blows the leaves from the face.

I crawl backwards in fear, my back hitting a tree. My hands rushing over my body as I pull myself into a hug, "Holy shit." I breathe out as my hands rest over my chest and lower stomach.

My breathing speeds up as I quickly grab my phone and dial 911.

My hand is shaking as I stare at the body.

"Hello, 911 what's your emergency?"

I stay silent, "Hello?"

"Hi- hi." I stutter.

"What's your emergency miss?"

"Uh the party that's happening in the woods, by the bridge into town. Umm I just found a dead body by- by the river."

My eyes are stuck focusing on the body. What I think to be dried blood on half of his face, "Can you recognize the body by chance?"

"It's Kian Turner." My eyes begin to water from blinking so much.

"Help is on the way; I'll stay on the phone with you until the police arrive."

"Okay." I breathe out.

Soon the Police arrived.
Soon everyone began to gather around.
Soon everyone knew what had happened.

I slowly stand up from the ground when one of the paramedics asks me to follow them so they can look at my knee.

Ace runs over to me, "Maggie what happened?" She reaches out to touch my hair pulling a leave from it. One of the many reasons I don't like having curly hair all the time.

"Ace-"

"What is it?"

I look behind me to see Kian's body getting covered by a blue tarp.

"No-" Ace's voice broke.

"I'm sorry, he's-"

"No! No! NO!" Ace cries out as tears form in her eyes.

I pull Ace into a hug as she cries into my shoulder. I look up to see Adrian and Adams staring at me, I give them the best none worried smile I can before looking down at the ground, holding Ace tight in my arms.

I sit in the back of an ambulance. My knee is wrapped with gauze. I sigh and look down at the ground.

"Excuse me, you were the one to find the body, yes?" A Male Officer asks while walking over to me.

"Uh yeah." I nod, crossing my hands in my lap.

"I just have to ask you a few questions."

"Okay."

"Why were you down by the river?"

"I don't like crowds, I needed to step away to decompress." That's not a full lie.

"And you tripped over his body, yes? That's how you cut your knee?"

"Yes. I tripped over his legs I'm pretty sure."

"Did you ever know the deceased?"

"He was my friend's brother, so yes."

"Did you talk to him much?"

"Not really." I lie.

"Was the deceased ever a violent person that you know of?"

"I don't think so." I lie, "Why?"

"We need to make sure this wasn't a crime of passion." The Officer explains.

"Oh okay." Does crime of passion mean love? Or hatred?

"Well, that's all I'll be asking for now, but we'll follow up in a couple of days. Thank you for your time, you can leave now."

"You're welcome and I hope everything turns okay."

The Officer walks away as I get out of the ambulance. I limp my way over to my motorcycle. I sit down and slowly bend my knee, pain shooting through my whole leg as I do so.

I look over to the Police carrying Kian's body into the back of an ambulance.

I take a deep breath holding in the small tears that want to escape from my eyes.

Why'd it have to be my luck, that I found him.

CHAPTER FIVE

Maggie Snow
Monday, September 9th, 7:00am

It's been five days since I found Kian's body in the woods.

School got cancelled for the rest of the week to let everyone decompress from what happened. Personally, I find that stupid.

I understand why Ace got the rest of the week off, but the whole school didn't need the week off.

I walk out of my room after getting dressed. I've hardly left my room the past couple of days. I went to Dark Treasure once for tea.

A small part of me was hoping I'd run into Adrian again so I could have someone to talk to even if it was just for an hour. But that never happened.

Right when I open my bedroom door my nose fills with the scent of bacon and eggs, "What the heck?" I mumble to myself.

I limp down the hallway to the kitchen. My knee has healed well. I had to change the gauze two times since it started bleeding through. But it's been better since yesterday. I'm kind of glad we didn't have school only because it would have been hell walking up those stairs.

I get to the kitchen still littered with beer bottles, but for the first time since I came home there's breakfast on the table and less take out containers on the counter.

"You made breakfast?"

My dad looks up at me, "Yeah, I went to the store last night and picked up some things, I thought I'd give making breakfast a try... I hope bacon and eggs is still your favorite."

"Yeah," I nod, "Thanks."

I pull out a chair from the table and sit down. My dad places a plate down in front of me.

"Eat up. You've got school today, how's your knee healing up?"

"It's getting better every day." I smile.

I think me getting hurt really scared my dad, I've never seen him act like this around me, at least not for a long time.

He sits down across from me and starts eating his eggs, "I just want you to know that if you ever get in any danger, I'm always here for you, the gang is too."

"I know dad and I'm fine. Just because someone dies doesn't mean you have to start being a good dad all of a sudden." I take a bit of bacon.

My dad's knife hits the plate.

Shit did I say that out loud.

"Mags-"

"I should get to school; I don't want to be late." I stand up from the chair and limp my way to the front door and grab my bag from the ground, "Thanks for the breakfast."

I quickly limp to my motorcycle. I hop on and make my way towards Ace's house.

Once I'm there I get off my motorcycle and make my way up to the front door. Nothing has changed about her house, maybe the inside has changed, but the outside hasn't.

I knock on the door; I tap my foot up and down while I wait.

"Hel- Maggie?" Ace's mom stares at me.

"Hi." I smile.

"What are you doing here?"

"I'm back in town."

"I can see that, but I mean what are you doing at my house?" Ace's mom asks rudely.

She hasn't changed much since I had seen her last. She looks a bit older, crinklier; her eyes have narrowed more and if it weren't for her eyebrows, she'd always look angry.

"Um... I'm sorry for your loss." I gulp.

"What are you doing here Maggie?"

"I was wondering if Ace was home?" I ask.

"Yes, *Alec*, is home."

"Is she going to school today, I was wondering if she'd want to come with me." I smile, even if Ace's brother was the spawn of Satan. Ace was still my friend and I want to be there for her, even if it is awkward.

"No, *he*, isn't going today." Her mom smiles.

"Okay, got it." I nod and slowly turn around.

Ace was right when she said her mom wasn't taking her transition well, I mean I thought it was bad, but not this bad. She still called her Alec. That must suck for Ace.

I get back onto my motorcycle and ride to school.

I pull into the parking lot and right as I'm about to get off a white convertible pulls up next to me. I glance over to see Adrian and Adams. Adrian in the driver's seat, of course. I could never see Adams driving this type of car. He's more of a blue punch buggy kind of guy.

I get off my motorcycle and limp over to the passenger seat, "You! Adams. Have any news on Kian?"

He blinks at me, "Why would I have news?"

"Because you love gossip, so I just thought you'd know something?"

"Oh yeah right, well I haven't heard anything."

Adrian and Adams get out of the car and start to walk towards the school. I limp after them, "Are you positive you haven't heard *anything*?"

"Positive, and shouldn't you know more since you're the one who found him?" Adams asks.

I glare at him, and he quickly goes back to his turtle shell self.

"I should actually be getting praised for that, because if I didn't go down by the river trip over his body and basically crack my knee open, his body would be decomposed by now... or eaten by a deer." I glare. Maybe I'm being a little dramatic, but I don't care.

They both smile and nod.

"Okay fine I guess no ones in the mood to talk today, like seriously Adrian you even talked more at the Cafe, and now you haven't said a word."

"I didn't feel like I had to talk." Adrian shrugs.

"I'm leaving." I roll my eyes and limp off into the school.

Neither of them were any help.

I round the corner by the main office and run into Conner.

"Why'd you break up my fight at the party?" He asks, almost as if he's been waiting to ask me that since the party.

"Why not." I shrug, "You were being an idiot."

"You're not in my life anymore, Maggie, you haven't been for two years. I don't need your help; I was going to win that fight." Conner scowls.

"I'm sorry I was just trying to help. You would have regretted it in the morning. Now move out of my way." I try to move past him, but he steps in front of me again.

"You don't need to care about me, you made that pretty clear when you broke up with me after joining that gang you said you would never join."

Conner runs his hand through his hair, it's darker than it was in grade nine. No longer a light brown, more of a dark brown, it could almost be back.

"Things change idiot, and I hate you, and I don't care about you. I was doing it for my own reasons. And yeah, I joined the gang, things change, rapidly, with no reason. Now get out of my way before I punch you into the ground." I flash an annoyed smile while pushing past him.

Why can't someone just accept kindness without needing an explanation. Clearly, he's still butt hurt over the fact that I broke up with him.

I make my way down the hallway to the gang.

"You look pissed." Jade says.

"Yeah."

"Want to get more pissed." Clark asks. I'm pretty sure that is his name, he's one of the only guys that Jade is closest to. I look over to him as he blows his bleach blonde hair out of his face.

"Sure, why not." I sigh while leaning up against one of the lockers.

"People are blaming the gang for killing, Kian." Jade says.

It takes everything in me not to make my jaw fall open, "Are you fucking kidding me."

"None of us ever talked to him." Clark says.

"People will think what they want to think, and they'll blame the gang of course because a gang always has to be filled with bad people. No one even knows how he died yet. That hasn't been released to the public so how in the world is anyone to blame yet." I rant.

I run my hand over my face and sigh.

"Everyone in this town is an idiot." I mumble.

I sit at the very top of the gym stands. There was an impromptu assembly that I didn't want to be in and was hoping to sneak out of at any moment.

"We assume that you all know what happened last Tuesday. That one of our past students has passed." I don't think he just *passed*; he was obviously murdered. "Due to this we gave the rest of last week off, this pushed a couple of things back." Principal Galilean says.

"With this happening we pushed back our back-to-school dance, which will now be happening this Friday. We are also setting up meetings with the guidance counsellor for anyone who would like to talk about anything, especially if you have been feeling overwhelmed or effected with the recent events that have happened."

I look around at everyone in the stands. Everyone looks sad. Did Kian really mean this much to so many people? Did he only ever hurt me?

"The Police have asked that if anyone knows anything to come forward, even if it's the smallest thing. Anything can help. Also, for all your safety we ask you to keep your eyes open and keep a lookout, don't stay out too late and stay safe most importantly."

Does she really think anyone is going to do that? And since when did this school start caring about its students? The last time I was here they didn't even blink an eye to the things that were happening right in front of them.

I walk into science class at the end of the day. I'm surprised that I'm on time today, especially with me having to limp everywhere.

I sit down beside Adams and lean forwards onto the desk crossing my arms, resting my head in them.

Mr. Gibes begins to talk about the periodic table, which I already know all about. I had to help Ace memorize it in grade nine, so in return I memorized it too.

I start to trace a figure eight on my arm out of boredom.

"Miss. Snow," I look up from my arm, "Can you please tell us what type of gas Argon is?"

"Uh... it's a noble gas, and it's the third most abundant gas in the Earth's atmosphere." I say, slowly leaning back in my chair.

Out of the corner of my eye I can see Adrian and Adams both staring at me. They clearly didn't think I would know the answer to that question.

"That's correct. Now assuming that you know other elements what's Tungsten?" Mr. Gibes asks.

I shrug, "It's a rare metal, found on Earth and normally is combined with other chemicals." I explain.

"Correct again, now please pay attention."

I scoff, "Seriously, I'm pretty sure I just proved that I know all this bullshit already, plus you don't need to be watching to still be listening."

"Do not swear in my class or you're going down to the office."

"Oh, a great threat. I bet they'd all love to see me." I smile.

"Maggie, stop talking." Adams whispers to me.

"Just pay attention in my class, Miss. Snow." Mr. Gibes says.

"Fine."

I glance over to Adams, he's looking forwards, his right hand is shaking and he's clearly avoiding my eye contact.

I limp after Adrian and Adams once class ends, "Adams why'd you tell me to stop talking in class?" I ask.

"Jeez, don't sneak up on me like that, there's a killer on the loose." Adams says.

"I don't kill people. Now answer the question."

"You were going to get in trouble." Adams says as they round the corner and start walking down the stairs.

"What if I wanted to get out of class? Being in the office is better than being in that classroom."

"But you still listened to what Oscar said." Adrian points out.

"Just don't tell me what to do."

Adams nods as we all get to the bottom of the stairs, they both turn to the left and walk into a classroom.

"Where are you guys going?"

"This is the school newspapers office." Adrian says as I follow them into the room.

I stop in the doorway, "Wait really?" I look around in shock, "Why'd it move here?"

"I don't know, it was… Kian's idea." Adams says as he places his bag down on one of the chairs.

"Of course." I mumble.

"Why are you so shocked?" Adrian asks.

I step farther into the room, "I used to run the paper, before I left."

I walk over to one of the shelves filled with boxes, all of them labeled with different years and months, "Can I join again?" I turn around and ask.

"Why?" Adams asks.

I shrug, "Why not, it's only you two working, and maybe it'd be good to get a girl's point of view on things. Plus, I know how to take good photos." I smile.

Adrian and Adams look at each other from across the big table that sits in the middle of the room, "Sure why not, you can join." Adrian smiles.

"Great." That was easier than I expected.

Adams looks around before glancing back at me, "So we were going to start doing some cleaning since it's pretty dusty in here from over the summer, so you can help with-"

"I'm actually going to look in these boxes right now, I'll leave the cleaning to you two."

I turn around to all the boxes and pull out the box from the year after I left. I place it onto the small table beside me.

Adams wasn't lying when it said the place was dusty.

I take the lid off, "Holy shit."

"What is it?" Adrian asks.

I pull out the newspaper sitting on the very top of the pile. I turn around holding up the paper to show them, "This is the worst photo ever taken of Connor." I chuckle.

"Hey... I took that photo." Adams says.

I scrunch my lips, "Well it's a bad photo of him... Sorry."

I look down at the newspaper and read off the headline, "Another Amazing Win at Hill High School's Basketball Game. The Winning goal from Connor Martin... The jackass himself."

"I don't think that was part of the article." Adams says.

I look up at him, "No shit."

I turn back around and start to look through more of the old articles.

There must be something about Kian in one of them. He was one of the best on the basketball team, he had A's in every class, and everyone in town knew who he was. I'm surprised I haven't found anything yet.

"Maggie- What was it like when you found Kian's body?" Adams asks.

I freeze and stare down at the newspaper in my hand, "What do you mean?" I ask.

"Like... were you scared?"

I turn around and look at him, "I found a dead body in the woods, Adams. Of course, that would be scary, but it actually wasn't as scary as you'd think." I lie, "But what is scary is that whoever killed him could be walking past us every day, but if you show weakness, whoever killed him could kill again."

"What makes you say that he was killed?" Adrian asks.

"That's what it looked like to me. And no killer just strikes once for the hell of it. There is always a second murder if the killer is never caught within a couple of weeks. So, I bet there will be another death."

"That's not unsettling at all." Adams stares down at the ground.

I throw my hands up in the air and shrug, "I could always be wrong though."

Well on that awkward note for saying what I think... I think it's probably time to leave.

"So, I'm going to leave now, see you two tomorrow."

As I'm limping out of the newspaper, I notice a box on the top shelf titled *un-published work*.

Maybe that box would be the one to have something about Kian in it. Adams did say Kian was the one to move the newspaper to this room, so it would make sense that he wouldn't want to publish anything that gave him bad press.

I walk to the side exit and stop as I'm halfway out of the school. In the middle of the door there is a big poster for the back-to-school dance.

"Looks like I'll be going to this dance." I mumble to myself.

CHAPTER SIX

Ace Turner
<u>Tuesday, September 10th, 7:10am</u>

    I stare up at the records I taped to my ceiling during summer. Kian had to help me put them up since I couldn't reach even though I was standing on my bed. He was only an inch or two taller than me. *Was.*
    That was the day right before he went missing, at least our last conversation was a good one, right?
    My mom made me stay home from school yesterday. She said that I needed one more day to *heal*. I don't exactly know why she's using the term heal, but I think she underestimates how long it takes someone to heal.
    She wasn't the one who had to see his body getting covered.

I roll out of my bed and make my way downstairs.

I've been mentally preparing myself all yesterday and all this morning to get asked a million times if I'm okay. I still haven't figured out how I'm going to answer the question yet.

But I have a plan. I'm going to channel all my energy into something to keep my mind off everything. I bet it'll work... for the most part.

"You know that you don't have to go to school today." My dad says as I sit down at the table across from him.

"Of course, she does, she was off all last week and yesterday, she needs to go back." My mom says before I can even answer.

I'd love to stay home again today. To *heal* longer. I need more time to wrap my brain around everything that has happened.

"Maggie stopped by yesterday. You didn't tell us she was back." My mom glares at me as she brings over breakfast.

"I didn't think it was important." And I didn't think I had to tell you that she was back.

"Well, she was the one to find, Kian, wasn't she? So, what's to say she didn't kill him." My mom sits down at the head of the table.

"She wasn't even in town when he went missing in the first place." I say, and I wouldn't think Maggie would do that, even if she does have a reason, she's not the kind of person.

My mom started to hate Maggie when she joined the gang and started getting into fights. But

I know why she did it all, Maggie just doesn't know that I know.

"You should get to school, Alec."

"It's Ace. Mom you know this. It's been two years now." I stare at her as she doesn't make eye contact with me.

"Just get to school."

"I haven't even had breakfast yet."

"You can bring a granola bar."

I stand up and walk over to the front door. I sit down at the small bench we have so I can put on my shoes.

My dad walks over to me and places his hand on my shoulder, "Don't be mad at her, she's just sad and doesn't know how to deal with it."

"We're all sad, and her calling me Alec still, it's nothing new, so it's fine." I stand up from the bench.

"Just try and have a good day at school, Ace."

"I'll try."

I turn and open the front door. My bike is at the side of the house chained to the fence, so no one takes it.

Kian got me this bike once Maggie left. Since he knew I wouldn't be walking to school with anyone anymore.

I unlock my bike and start on my way to school.

Time to put on the best fake okay face I've got.

I walk into school and try to keep my head down for the most part. My mom having me leave early for school just means not many people are here yet.

Which is lucky for me because I can avoid as many people asking me if I'm okay as I can.

I walk up to the desk in the main office, "Oh hi Ace, I wasn't expecting you to be back in school for another while. How are you feeling?"

"I'm good. I was wondering if I could talk to Principal Galilean?" I ask. I'm more okay then good, I guess it's a natural response to say I'm good when people ask how you are. And the fact that I don't want to trouble anyone with talking about how I feel.

"Of course."

I get led to the principal's office where I sit and wait for her.

I've always hated the principal's office, I've had to come down here many times, not because I was in trouble or anything, mainly because Maggie had just left and there were people who would start to pick on me for the most random things. She was my protective shield in a way.

Soon after she left Kian became my new protective shield. But now he's gone too. And even though Maggie is back, I don't think we'd ever have the same friendship we once had.

"Ace, how are you?" Principal Galilean asks as she walks into her office and sits down at her desk.

"I'm good. I was just wondering if I'd still be allowed to sing at the school dance on Friday?"

"Well of course, if you're up for it, we don't want you to push yourself to do anything."

I nod, "I would like to do it, I think Kian would want me to do it too."

Principal Galilean smiles, "Well then yes of course, and if you ever need to talk about anything we can set something up with the guidance counsellor."

"Okay, thank you." I stand up from the chair and turn to leave the office.

"And Ace, one more thing. I'm sorry for your loss, your brother was a very bright kid."

I nod with a smile, and quickly walk out of the office. I go to round the corner as I run into someone, "Watch where you- Oh... Hey Ace." Maggie smiles.

"Hey... my mom said you stopped by yesterday."

"Uh yeah... I did, she's... very-"

"Rude, pushy, a straight up bitch." The words fly out before I have the time to stop them. I don't know if I mean them or not. I'm only angry that she still hasn't accepted me yes.

"You said it, not me." Maggie says quickly.

I start to walk down the hallway towards the computer lab.

"So how are you doing?" Maggie asks while walking with me.

I understand that she's trying to be nice, but she doesn't have to be, I know what happened and I don't want her to have to fake her sympathy.

I'm still trying to get used to her being back, I guess. I feel as if she's trying to act like the Maggie I knew at the beginning of grade nine compared to the one I knew before she left. The distant Maggie.

"I've been better." I answer and glance down at the ground.

"Yeah, makes sense."

I look down at Maggie, "Do you still know how to edit together good posters or photos?"

"Uh, I haven't done it in a while, but yeah, I guess. Why?"

"Would you like to help me make a poster?" I ask. If Maggie's going to talk to me, I might as well try to make the most of it. I won't lie when I say that I have missed her, so if there is any chance of getting the best friend I once had back. I'll take that chance.

"For what?"

"The back-to-school dance, I'm singing at it. I need someone to play the drums while I sing and play the guitar. So, I thought I'd make a poster so I can find someone quicker." I explain.

"You're going to sing in front of the school?" Maggie says shocked.

"I have before... you just weren't here."

"Oh," Maggie looks forward, "Well then yeah I'll help. Are we skipping first period to do it?"

"I was planning on doing that, yeah."

"Huh. You have changed since I left." Maggie mentions.

The only thing that has changed is my appearance, I just don't want to go to class and have everyone ask how I'm doing.

I drag a photo of a drum set onto the blank page.

"So... your mom isn't that accepting of you, huh?" Maggie asks. It's painfully obvious that she's trying to force a conversation.

I look over to Maggie and shrug, "Yeah, she isn't, but my dad is, we've gotten closer over the past two years, than the many years I was a boy. It's weird, but nice."

I avert my attention back to the computer screen; I begin to write out what's going to be on the poster.

Can you play the drums? Meet in the music room after scho-

"That's a good thing at least, how are they dealing with everything that happened with... Kian?" Maggie asks, interrupting my typing.

"My dad better than my mom, it's almost like she expected it, she seems so unfazed."

"Do you think she...?"

My head jolts towards Maggie, "Gosh no!" I look around and quiet my voice, "She wouldn't."

"Okay, I just wanted to ask."

I turn back towards the computer and continue typing, I add a background colour and some final finishing touches, "So what do you think?" I ask.

"Perfect." Maggie says.

"Great, so just to print them, then want to help me hang them up around school?" I turn to her and ask.

"Su-" Maggie pauses and looks down at her phone, I can't believe she still has that flip phone, I could never convince her to get an iPhone, "My dad's calling me, which means it's something important. Do you think you can handle putting up the posters by yourself?"

"Oh yeah, I got it. You go deal with your dad." I smile.

Maggie gets up from her chair, "Thanks. Good luck." She smiles before walking out of the computer lab.

I look down at my lap. Back to being alone.

Once I've printed at least 30 posters I grab a small roll of washi tape that I carry around in my backpack with me. I begin to tape the posters on classroom doors and random lockers.

The bell rings and the hallways get flooded with students. I walk down the hallway passing out the posters to random students. Keeping my head down as much as possible so no one asks how I am doing.

I finally make my way to the second floor and reach my math class. It's the one class that I know everyone will try to pay attention to, so I won't have to talk to anyone as much.

I sit down in the very back, where I normally sit in most classes.

I glance up to see Oscar walk into the classroom. I forget he was in this class. We never talked much, I had one conversation with him in grade nine I think, and I think this is our first class together in all of high school.

He walks all the way over to the back and sits down beside me.

"Hey, Ace." He smiles.

"Hi." I smile.

"I'm sorry about your brother, him and I had a few conversations over the years. How are you doing?" He asks cheerily.

"I'm good."

"Well, if you ever need anyone to talk to, I'm always here, and I know we aren't really fri-"

"Thank you, Oscar, I'm going to pay attention to class now." I don't need someone telling me that they'll be my friend if I need to talk to anyone. I would have rather had a friend before Kian went missing and turned up dead.

"Yeah. Yeah of course." Oscar smiles.

I bring my attention to the front of the classroom where the teacher begins to talk.

I'm confused as to why Oscar was so cheery when asking how I was. I mean he is weird...

At the end of the day, I make my way to the music room. Hopefully someone will come to the music room and will want to help me with the back-to-school dance.

I sit down on the ground and pull out my notebook. While I wait to see if anyone is going to show up I might as well work on an English essay that is due. I'm still surprised how early we've gotten assigned an essay. It's technically only the third day of school.

I pull out a small bag of cheese and crackers that I didn't end up eating at lunch.

A faint knock comes from the door as I'm about to start writing. I look up to see Jade leaning in the doorway. I used to have a crush on her in elementary school before she joined the gang in grade eight. I only stopped liking her because I saw less of her around school. Not because she joined the gang.

"Hey. You're Ace right?"

"Uh... yeah that's me." I smile.

Wow she's pretty.

"I found your poster asking if someone could play the drums." Jade smiles while holding up the poster in her hand.

"You did?"

"Yeah." Jade chuckles.

"Really?! Do you want to play me like the drums? I MEAN!! Can you play the drums?"

I can feel my face turn red as she steps into the room. Why did I say that? How did I actually say that? "Yeah, I can." She laughs.

God, I really need to think before saying things out loud, how red is my face right now? I shouldn't even be that embarrassed. I've never talked to Jade, and I haven't liked her in four years. So, why are my insides twisting in a circle?

"Wait really!? That's great, would you want to maybe play them in the back-to-school dance?" I ask.

"Sure, I'm Jade by the way."

"I know. I mean yeah hi I'm Ace." I give a small wave.

"Yeah, I know. It says on the poster."

I nod, "Right... Well, do you want to sit? I can show you the song I was thinking of and maybe we can practice since the dance is on Friday and that's coming up quick."

"Sure." Jade walks over and sits down across from me on the floor.

"There is a chair if you don't want to sit on the floor."

"I like the floor, there's more room to stretch... Also, I'm sorry to hear about your brother, but we don't have to talk about it. Know it might be hard to talk about and stuff."

"Oh, thank you." I smile.

Jade clears her throat, "Anyways, what song are you thinking for the dance?"

She leans forwards resting her chin in her hand. Is she actually interested? Well obviously, she is, or she wouldn't be here right now.

"I was thinking Don't Stop Me Now. I'm going to be singing and playing the guitar and I wanted to add drums to the song, hence you being here. Do you know the song?"

"Of course, by Queen, right? That sounds like it'll be cool." Jade says,

"Really? Not many people like my ideas."

"Well, I like them so far."

I watch as Jade tucks one of her curly hairs behind her ear. I smile awkwardly at her, "Anyways, do you want to maybe practice, now?"

"Sure." Jade nods.

"Cool."

Jade and I ended up staying at the school until eight practicing. My mom has a rule that I have to be home by seven on school nights. The only reason I got to go to that party in the woods last week was because I said I was going to the Cafe to work on school.

I lock my bike up to the fence and make my way to the front door. I slowly open it and step inside, slowly and quietly closing it behind me.

"Where were you?" I jump around to see my mom standing on the stairs with her arms crossed.

"At school, I was in the music room. I lost track of time, I'm sorry."

"You shouldn't be out late, especially now when a murderer is out there." My mom glares.

We don't know that he was murdered yet, but it seems likely.

"I know. I'm sorry." I look down at the ground, I hear my mom move off the staircase.

"I can't have anything happen to you Alec." My mom says lifting my chin.

"Mom, it's Ace. How many times do I have to tell that?"

"You are Alec, that is the name I gave you."

"I don't know if you're pushing this on me more now that Kian is dead, but I just want you to respect me and my choices." I begin to raise my voice.

"I lost my son."

"And I lost my brother!" I shout.

"What's going on." I shift my view to see my dad standing on the staircase.

"Nothing. I'm going up stairs." I push past both of them. I get to the top of the stairs and lean up against the wall beside my bedroom door.

"Faith, you need to respect her choices, she wants to be a girl. And we all just lost Kian, we need to be here for each other." I hear my dad say.

"He's gone Richard, he's gone." My mom cries.

I run my hand over my face, leaning my head against the wall behind me. I turn and walk into my room. I lean up against the door once it's closed.

My room has always been filled with positive quotes. I have to stay positive for my sake... and my families.

It's what I know Kian would want... even if he was one of the worst people I knew.

CHAPTER SEVEN

Adrian Fisher
Friday, September 13th, 6:45pm

    I lean up against my car outside of Oscar's house. I sigh and look down straightening my tie. My mom took ten minutes tying it before I left. She always likes when I get dressed up for things. Even if it is only a back-to-school dance.
    I feel as if I'm picking up Oscar as a date. No offence to him, but he's not my type.
    Oscar walks out of his house followed by his mom, "I have to get a photo of you two handsome boys."
    "Mom no." Oscar mumbles as he walks up beside me.
    His mom pulls out her phone to snap a couple of photos.

"Lorna hurry up the boys want to leave." Oscar's dad yells out from the porch.

"Shut up, Hal! They'll want to remember this moment."

"We need to get going, mom." Oscar says pushing me away from the passenger seat door.

I walk around and get into the driver's seat.

"Drive. Please." Oscar stares at me with a clear vision in his mind.

"Okay, I'm going." I say as I drive off down the street.

I turn the corner, "So your parents seem happy."

"They've been fighting non-stop for the past two months, my only escape has been work and now school."

"At least you like working at Club Azure and school." I point out.

"Yeah... I just wish they'd stop yelling."

"I'm sorry, but you're out of the house tonight so it'll be a good night." I smile while turning into the school parking lot.

"Yeah." He nods.

Oscar and I get into the school and walk down the hallway towards the gym.

"How many people do you think are going to show up?" I ask.

"Half the school. The other half is probably at home, or drunk, or high, or asleep. There are many possibilities." Oscar says.

"Yeah..."

We turn into the doorway of the gym and stop. It's surprisingly really crowded.

"Hey boys!!" Conner yells while walking over to us with a drink in hand.

"Hey." Oscar and I say in unison.

"I didn't know you two were coming."

"We didn't know either until last night." I say.

Conner glances behind him, "Well half of our grade isn't here, and it's mostly the niner's."

"I see that, but that gives for some good gossip." Oscar says looking around.

Conner and Oscar begin to have a disagreement that I tune out. It's most likely something they've already disagreed about; they disagree way too often for me to comprehend. I've gotten pretty good at blocking it out.

I look around the gym as my eyes catch onto Maggie standing by the punch bowl. I slowly move away from Conner and Oscar and make my way towards her.

Both of them would most likely get mad that I'm going to talk to Maggie; Both for different reasons.

As I get closer to her I realize she's wearing a dress, it's pretty on her. Short and black. Not what I expected.

I stand beside her and start to fill up a cup with the punch, "I wouldn't expect you to be here, based on how you view the world." I secretly still have no clue how she views the world. I just thought it would be cool to say...

I look over to her as she looks at me.

"Dances are not my thing; I was forced to come."

"Who forced you?"

"Myself."

"That... That doesn't make any sense."

"I know..."

"Well at least-"

I feel a tap on my shoulder, "Hey Adrian." I turn around to see Jessica Falice standing behind me, she's Oscar's cousin and the same age as us. And talks to almost every guy in the school.

"Hey... Jessica." I give a friendly smile.

Last year Jessica was in my Math and English, she was constantly flirting with me and making it obvious. For the most part I just let it slide and never gave into it. But she kept trying and became so overbearing that by the next semester I avoided her at all costs. I haven't talked to her since last year.

"I didn't know you were coming to the dance."

I open my mouth to respond when Maggie laughs, "That's a load."

"What is Maggie." Jessica asks looking over to her.

"It's obvious you're lying, the way you walked up here tapped on his shoulder, tucked your hair behind your ear, smiled with a bit of a smirk. You obviously knew he was coming and you're just trying to get in his pants."

"You're coming off a bit too desperate if you ask me." I can ~~imagen~~ *imagine* Maggie throwing an imaginary piece of popcorn into her mouth right about now.

I stand awkwardly between them. Now I'm wishing I had stayed over with Conner and Oscar.

"Seriously, no one asked for your opinion."

"Yeah, but I love to give it." Maggie smiles.

"You tried this act with Conner, and even Adams once. Oh, and I think you even tried it with Kian. Ha! Now I've got a theory, what if you killed him because he didn't like your nudes."

Jessica walks over to Maggie and gets inches away from her face, "I could end you."

"Oh, I'm so scared, Jessica. The worst thing you could do is cartwheel right at me and I'd still be standing. Don't try to be tough or sexy when you can't be. Because all you are is petty."

Oh. *Damn...*

"I am pretty, thank you."

"I said petty." Maggie glares.

Jessica rolls her eyes before stomping away.

After a few seconds of awkward silence, I finally say something, "Sooo... I'm guessing you two don't like each other."

"You've guessed correct. She's a bitch and trust me I've known her since kindergarten. If I didn't say anything I would have flipped this table because I cannot stand her faux high pitch bitchy voice."

"I could have handled her."

"Could you? You're like a stick with one muscle yet everyone looks at you like you're a God."

"Did you just call me a God?"

"Don't let it get to your head pretty boy."

"And now I'm a pretty boy?"

"I can't say anything sarcastically around you, can I?" Maggie asks.

"I don't speak sarcasm."

Maggie laughs.

"You cannot leave me alone when I'm in an argument with Conner!" I look to my right to see Oscar standing beside me, "He obviously knows I'm right and that doesn't make him happy, and he could squish me like a bug so you can't leave me!"

"Jeez, Adams, calm down you're going to pop a blood vessel in your neck." Maggie says.

"You came over here to talk to her when I could have been squished like a bug!!!" Oscar yells.

"Bud, I'm sorry, I was bored, and look. You're fine. You didn't get squished." I smile.

"You don't leave your friend to talk to a girl." Oscar leans in and whispers.

"Adams, I heard that." Maggie says.

Oscar tenses up and slowly moves behind me so Maggie can't see him. Even though she can obviously still see him.

I haven't been able to understand why she's calling Oscar by his last name.

"Well, I have to go, so I'll talk to you two later, and don't drink the punch is disgusting."

Maggie moves off into the crowd of people dancing in the middle of the gym.

I look down to the cup in my hand that is filled with punch, I slowly lift it up to my lips. Right as the drink hits my lips I gag. "What the hell did they put in this, poison?"

I place the drink on the table and turn to face Oscar, "You for sure came over here to flirt with Maggie." Oscar glares.

"No, I-"

"I literally told you that she's dangerous, and you clearly aren't listening to me. She's like the fly swatter and YOU are the FLY!" Oscar yells.

I place my hands on Oscar's shoulders, "One: I wasn't flirting with her, two: she's not a bad person bud, yes she can be a little passive aggressive, but she's still funny... and nice... and cute-"

Oscar throws my hands off his shoulders and grabs my shoulders proceeding to shake me back and forth, "YOU TOTALLY HAVE A CRUSH ON HER AND YOU'RE GOING TO DIE FROM IT!" Oscar yells in my face.

"I don't have a crush on her." I say once he stops shaking me.

"You just called her cute, what kind of spell does this woman have over you?!"

"Oscar, calm down, we're just friendly people to one another."

"That's another way of saying you have a crush on her. You've only known her for a week, Adrian! A week! She's in a gang and for all we know she could have killed Kian." Oscar says whispering the last part about Kian.

"Yet she has a nickname for you, bud."

Oscar purses his lips together and sighs. He knows I'm right.

"She's not what you remember, and I don't have a crush on her."

"I believe you." Oscar says sarcastically.

"Believe what you want, but I know that I don't like her, we are just two friendly people."

I don't know if I can truthfully call Maggie my friend, I feel as if we're still strangers since I don't know much about her, and she somehow guesses a lot of things about me by just observing. Most of the time she's right, but that's beside the point.

"Attention everyone!!"

Oscar and I turn towards the stage to see Jessica standing in the center with a microphone.

"Welcome to the back-to-school dance, I hope everyone is having a great time so far! I am Jessica, head cheerleader and I am pleased to announce the main entertainment for tonight, Ace and Jade!!"

I look around the gym as everyone begins to clap. I spot Maggie in the far corner by the doors, not clapping or paying attention.

I turn back to look at the stage, "Let's give them a warm welcome as they sing one of my favorite songs!!" Jessica says.

I know for a fact Jessica only listens to pop music and Ace and Jade don't seem like the type to play pop music.

I've never had a conversation with either of them, but they both seem like nice people. Even though I'm pretty sure Jade is in the gang, but none of them seem that intimidating to me.

Ace begins to sing while Jade sits in the back playing the drums. I glance over to Oscar who's in a complete daze. I shift my view over to where Maggie is standing, she quickly looks around before slipping out of the gym.

I sneak past Oscar and make my way over to the gym doors and out into the hallway.

I'm not following Maggie because I like her, I'm following her because what if Oscar is right about her? What if she did have something to do with Kian's death. It would be good to know where she's going, to be one step ahead.

And I don't really want to stand awkwardly in the gym.

Maggie makes her way down the hallway, she walks fast, and quiet, I feel as if I'm being so loud.

I watch as she walks into the newspaper. "Why would she need to go there?" I ask myself while sneaking a little closer to the door.

I peer through the small window on the door, Maggie walks over to the tall shelf filled with all the old newspapers. She grabs a box and places it on the table.

The room is dark, so I have to squint to be able to see what the box is labeled, *Un-published*.

I can see her mumbling stuff to herself, but I can't hear it. I lean a bit closer to the door making it creek open. Quickly, I throw myself up against the side wall.

"Hello?" She calls out.

"Well, if someone's there I'd love to know if I have a stalker." She says sarcastically.

My hand quickly covers my mouth to hold in a laugh that was about to escape.

I duct down and quickly run down the hallway and around the corner. Maggie wasn't saying anything else, and she wasn't doing much so there was no point in sitting around waiting.

I make my way back into the gym and over to the punch table where Oscar is still standing.

"Where'd you go?" Oscar asks.

"The bathroom."

"You missed Ace singing, it was really good, and I had no idea that Jade could play the drums."

"I bet it was really good. You should have recorded it for me. Oh, wait you were in a daze when I left."

"Hey! It was a really cute guy."

"And I'm not allowed to stare at Maggie if I wanted to?" I ask.

"That's different."

"Sure, it is bud." I roll my eyes.

After I drop Oscar off at his house, I drove back to mine. I walk in the front door and kick off my shoes.

The kitchen light is glowing from the hallway. I slowly make my way over there making sure I don't step on any of the creaky floorboards. I've memorized where they all are.

I turn into the kitchen to see my mom sitting at the kitchen table on her computer, she glances up at me. "Hi honey, how was the dance?"

"Good." I smile, "Why are you still awake? Where's dad?"

"Your father is passed out asleep, I just finished up on the next print for the newspaper. We've got the autopsy report for the town to see." My mom says as her fingers move quickly across her keyboard.

I lean against the doorway into the kitchen, "Mom..." I bite back on what I want to say, "You look exhausted, you should go to sleep, you've got the whole weekend to get the newspaper ready for Monday." I explain.

"I can't do it this weekend; your father and I have to go out of town for business and the town needs this paper."

"Mom, go upstairs and sleep, the town can wait a couple of days." I cross my arms over my chest, she glances up at me and sighs

She scratches the back of her head, "I guess you're right." She closes her computer and rubs her eyes before standing up. She walks over to me and places her hand on my shoulder, "You get to bed soon too, okay?"

"Okay, mom. Goodnight."

"Goodnight, honey." She walks through the hallway and up the stairs. Once I know she's gone I rush over to her computer and open it.

I sigh when I realize the computer is already logged out.

I get up and go grab a glass of water before heading up stairs to my room. Along with the hallway floor, I also know where all the creaky floorboards are on the stairs.

As I get into my room, I unbutton my shirt and sit down on my bed, I pull my phone out of my pocket and open Instagram. I got to the search bar and type in *Maggie Snow*.

Only a couple accounts pop up, none of them being her though.

I fall back onto my bed. I close my phone and place it beside me. Now I find it suspicious that she doesn't have Instagram. It's uncommon for someone our age to not have social media.

Maybe Oscar was right about her hiding something, or being suspicious, but I won't fully know anything until I see that autopsy report.

CHAPTER EIGHT

Maggie Snow
<u>Monday, September 16th, 7:00am</u>

 I lay awake staring at my ceiling, wondering, did I miss something on Friday night when I looked through those boxes. Was a paper stuck to another paper, so I didn't see it.
 There was nothing about Kian in any of them, and I find that shocking.
 I walk out of my room and into the kitchen, I quickly glance into the living room to see my dad still passed out asleep on the couch.
 Last night when I came home from the Cafe, he was there asleep, in the exact same position.
 I place a piece of bread into the toaster and wait for it to pop up. Once it does five minutes have passed and I'm still surprised when my dad hasn't woken up yet.

I butter my toast before sitting down at the kitchen table.

A loud noise comes from the living room as I take my first bite. I get up from the table and walk into the living room to now see my dad laying on the ground face first.

"Dad!" I shout.

"Dad!!" I yell again, making him jolt awake.

"I'm awake!" He yells.

"Are you sure, you just fell off the couch."

He stands up and rubs his head, "Shouldn't you be off to school now?"

"Yeah... I was just leaving. See you later?"

He rubs his head even more, "Uh, yeah."

I grab my bag from beside the front door, I glance back over to the toast sitting on the table with one bite taken out of it. I'll get something to eat from the vending machine at school.

Arriving at school is my least favorite part of the day, mainly because I have to find a parking spot. Today I got stuck by the *Welcome to Hill High School* sign that flashes the date and time across it.

Once inside I make my way over to the vending machine down by the cafeteria. I stand in front of it looking at what I want to eat, I guess goldfish sounds fine.

"Maggie!!" I turn to see Clark and Jade walking down the hallway towards me, "Did you know Rick, your dad, is making an announcement tonight?" Clark says while leaning up against the vending machine. I finally figured out his last name, Clark Parker, he sounds like a Peter Parker's long-lost cousin. It would be cool if that was the case, but no superheroes exist in this world. Only in the movies.

I press number 5 on the keypad, "No, and I doubt anything will actually be said tonight. He'll probably be drunk out of his mind, and we won't be able to hear him, let alone... understand him." I say while leaning down to pick up my goldfish from the bottom of the vending machine.

Jade laughs, "Sounds like Rick."

"Does anyone even know what this announcement is about?" I ask.

"No, but I bet you 20 bucks it has to do with Kian and all the blame that the gang has been taking. It's stupid the whole town thinks we killed Kian, just because we're a gang." Clark growls.

I have never been able to see Clark as someone tough, I don't know if it's the fact that he's a year younger than me or if it's because of his blond hair and blue eyes that make him look too much like a rich kid.

"They only blame us because they don't want to think anyone rich would be capable of killing someone. So, they use the poor and run down as a scapegoat." I explain, "The rich have more money, they can cover it up quicker."

"Yeah, you're right about that." Jade says, I look over to her confused.

"Don't you-" I get cut off by the bell ringing.

"Guess we'll see what it's about tonight, see you two later." Jade says quickly walking off down the hallway.

Clark and I look over to one another, "That was... different."

"Tell me about it." I shake my whole body before opening my goldfish.

I sit in the back of my English classroom.

"Today in class we will be starting *The Book Thief*, has anyone ever read it?"

I raise my hand and slowly realize that I'm the only one who raised their hand.

"Perfect, Maggie. Would you like to give a brief description of what the book is about?"

"Uh..." Everyone in the class turns around to look at me, most people are glaring, I clear my throat, "It's about a girl named Liesel living in Germany during World War 2 and the whole book is told from the point of view of death." I explain.

"What are your thoughts on the book?" My teacher asks.

"It's a good book, it challenges your mind, um it makes you think of the relationships people have between friends, family, people who aren't even friends, just anyone in general. The book just makes you think about people and what drives them to be them."

"Beautifully said, Maggie."

I smile awkwardly and nod as everyone in the class turns to face the front again.

I bring my arms closer into the sides of my body, I can be confident, but God do I hate public speaking, especially when it has something to do with school.

During lunch I make my way to the library, the gang normally hangs outside during lunch, but recently they've been meeting in the lounge.

As I walk over to the gang, I notice Adrian and Adams sitting in the corner along with Conner and a couple of other guys I would assume they know from the basketball team.

"So, what was with you rushing off at the bell this morning? You never do that." I say to Jade as I walk up beside her.

"Yeah, it was weird." Clark chimes in.

"I just didn't want to be late to class today, not a big deal." Jade shrugs.

I glance around the library when my eyes stop on Conner who is intensely staring at me, "The fuck you want Conner?"

"Nothing." Conner smugly shakes his head and leans forwards, "It's just... I bet you're the one who killed Kian."

"Excuse me." I fully turn towards him, now everyone in the lounge is staring at us. It's not many people, but it's enough eyes for it to be a crowd.

"I mean you are the one who found him after all."

We don't even know if he was killed, but it is obvious. I think to myself.

Conner's friends laugh.

"Fuck you."

"What? I'm just telling the truth, aren't I, Maggie?" Conner smirks with satisfaction, he's clearly trying to start a scene. Probably as some sort of revenge for me breaking up his fight.

Clark gets up from his chair, but I push him back down.

"No, you're not." I shake my head and slowly walk over to him, "You're just mad, that I broke up your little fight at the party. What? Did you really think you were going to win? You were drunk and would have passed out before you could have gotten Jacob into a chokehold."

Now I'm standing right in front of Conner blocking his view from anyone else.

Conner stands up and his now inches away from my face, "You're a fucking bitch."

"Oh, bad boys got a temper now does he? Maybe you killed Kian. Because you were always threatened by him." I smirk before turning around, walking back to the gang.

"Your dad should have sent you to that psych ward instead of your brother!" Conner says harshly.

I freeze, the whole room does too. The silence echoes as everyone waits to see what's going to happen next. "The fuck did you just say." I slowly turn around and clench my fist.

"You heard me loud and clear." Conner says taking a step towards me.

Without a second thought I walk so close to him I can feel his breath on my face, "Maybe whoever killed Kian should have killed you too because you're just like him." I forcefully bring my knee up to his groin making him fall to the ground. I kick him in the gut and punch him directly in the face.

No one moves, and no one makes a sound, not even the gang.

They all know there's no stopping me. Before I left town, I think I got into about five fights, people were staring and whispering things. Making assumptions about me and I got fed up, I was needing to make a new life for myself before it was made for me. Even if that meant punching people.

I crouch down on the ground, Conner's nose is now bleeding, "Don't... ever fucking mess with me again. Because next time I will break something more than just your nose and that's a promise."

I get up and walk away from Conner and out of the lounge. I can't stand another second with that idiot of a brain. Who the fuck does he think he is? Blaming me for Kian's death and then bringing up my brother like that.

No one is allowed to talk to me that way, no one should be allowed to talk to anyone that way. Did he not learn what I was capable of the last week before I moved away?

I was just standing up for myself.

I turn out of the library and run into someone.

"Maggie- Hey are you okay?" Ace asks.

"I'm fine, Ace. Just leave me alone for once!" I move past her and down the hallway.

I reach the newspaper, once I get inside, I slam the door behind me and sit down at one of the tables trying not to scream at the top of my lungs or put my fist through a wall.

I can feel my blood boiling in my veins.

My leg bounces up and down with anticipation.

I don't know if I should be mad at Conner or mad at myself for letting his words get to me. I made a promise to myself before I came home that I wouldn't do anything like that again, but I've gotten so used to my temper that nothing can be the same. I need to control myself better.

My leg bounces up and down faster and faster. I finally decide to pick up a random book and throw it at the wall.

"Woah."

I turn to see Adrian and Adams standing in the doorway.

"What are you two here to take a rip at me too?"

"No." Adams shakes his head.

"We came to work on the newspaper before lunch ends." Adrian explains as he walks fully into the room placing his bag down on the chair across from me. I'm surprised that he doesn't seem fazed by anything that just happened.

"What are you doing here?" Adams asks kindly as he steps fully into the room closing the door behind him.

"I joined the paper, didn't I?"

"I actually have a question." Adrian says.

"If it's about what happened in the library, save it" I glare.

"NO! No, it's not. I was actually just wondering why you wanted to join the paper, I mean I know you said that you used to work on it, but there has to be more."

"What do you mean?" I ask.

Adrian sits down across from me and folds his hands together on the table, "It just seems like you'd want to join the paper for another reason, especially knowing how you somewhat view the world."

Why does he keep saying that? He literally knows nothing about me.

"Okay, so what if there is another reason... it's not any of your business." I say crossing my arms while leaning back in the chair.

"No, it's not. But Oscar and I run the paper now, so we decide who works on it. So how about you tell us, and you can stay on the paper." Adrian smiles.

"Huh, you do have a devilish side to you."

94

As those words come out of my mouth I watch as Adrian tenses up. I clearly made him uncomfortable.

"But fine I'll tell you… I want to find out who killed Kian. And I think this is one of the best spots to do so."

"What?!" Adams says in shock.

I honestly forget he was here with us; he was so quiet.

"Yeah." I nod.

"Why?" Adrian asks, "We don't even know if he was killed."

"Why not? Kian had enemies, and the newspaper is the best place to figure them out. Plus, I've got my own… *other* reasons. That! You two don't get to know." I explain to them.

"Are we allowed to help you at least?" Adams asks.

I shift my attention over to him, "Really? Shy and nerdy, Adams. Wants to help *me* solve a murder."

I do have to admit I am shocked.

"You haven't been here for two years… we know what Kian was like when you were gone, we can be a big help." Adams explains quietly.

"So, this means I can stay on the newspaper then?" I ask.

"Yes." Adrian smiles.

I smirk, "Perfect."

Once I park my motorcycle out front of my house, I make my way up to the front door. As I open the door, I hear a beer bottle roll across the floor.

"I got a call from the Martins," I pause in the doorway and stare blankly at my dad standing in the kitchen, "They said you beat up Conner."

I fully step inside and close the door behind me before turning to face my dad again, "He deserved it."

"He's your ex-boyfriend, Mags. You can't do that."

"Once again... he deserved it." I shrug.

My blood begins to boil.

"You broke his nose, Maggie!" My dad yells.

"Don't start fucking scolding me now." I roll my eyes.

"Maggie, you have to stop this! What are people going to think about you?"

"I don't fucking care, dad!! And neither should you, because you're always passed out drunk on the couch!!" I yell.

I move through the kitchen to the hallway, "What if people start to think you killed that boy?"

I sigh and turn around, "I know I didn't and that's all I care about. Now I'm going to get ready for the gang meeting."

I begin down the hallway again, "You're not going."

Anger looms over my body, "Why not?" I turn back around to face him.

"I don't want you randomly beating people up, that's not what the gang is about." My dad says.

"None of this is about the fucking gang dad!!" I scream, "I had a reason for breaking his nose, sure it was a little extreme, but I had a reason!"

My dad shakes his head, "Still. You're not going until you get your act together. Beating people up isn't how you get what you want. You're not going to any meetings until you smarten up."

"Don't try to be a fucking parent now!!"

"Then why'd you come back!" My dad yells.

I untense my shoulders and take a deep breath, "Make yourself dinner." He says before walking out the front door slamming it shut behind him.

I stand alone in the house.

The silence fills my ears as the only thing I hear becomes my heartbeat, which slowly becomes quicker and quicker as I walk down to my bedroom.

I resist the urge to slam the door behind me.

The gang was the only thing I had as protection and my dad took that away from me within seconds. Maybe I should be honest with him. Maybe that would help smooth out the situation. Maybe I should be honest with everyone. But how can I be when I haven't been honest with myself in two years.

Do I even need the gang's protection anymore?

I take my jacket off and throw it onto my bed before sitting down. I rest my face in my hands before pulling my phone from my jacket pocket.

"Hello?" Ace says once the call connects.

"I wanted to apologize for earlier, I was in a bad mood, and I took some of it out on you... I'm sorry... It's Maggie by the way."

"Thank you for apologizing, are you okay?" Ace asks.

"Oh, you know, I've been better, but you don't need to worry about any of that." I look down at my legs and take a deep breath.

"Are you sure, I'm able to listen if you need to talk, I heard about what happened with Conner, I'm sorry about what he said."

I clear my throat, "Uh, yeah, but no I'm good. I just... wanted to say sorry... I'll see you tomorrow?" I ask.

"Yeah." Ace says cheerily.

I quickly hang up the phone and set it down beside me.

I don't know if I'll ever be able to be open with anyone ever again, let alone be honest with them.

CHAPTER NINE

Maggie Snow
Tuesday, September 17th, 7:00am

    Leaving my room this morning is harder than other days. I don't want to face my dad.
    "I made you some tea." He says as I reach the kitchen.
    "I'm good."
    I stare at him for what feels like five minutes. Did he forget all about last night? Or did he get so drunk last night that he's hungover and doesn't want to think about it?
    "So how did the meeting go last night?" I ask as I slowly sit down at the table.
    "Good." He answers shortly.
    "I still don't understand why I couldn't have gone."

My dad places down the milk on the counter and takes a minute to respond, "Because, Maggie, you need to learn that beating people up isn't something you have to do to get your way."

I sigh, "That's not why-" I pause, I know that I can't explain it to him in a way he'll understand, "I've beaten people up before, I don't understand what the difference is now."

"By you coming back here it shows me that you want to make a change. I am just trying to help you." My dad explains.

"Help me? Says the dad who's 'trying' to be sober but failing by being drunk every night!" I yell as I stand up from the table.

He stares at me before sighing, "I'm trying my best. And you know I want what is best for you."

I know he does; I know he's trying his best, I know that, but for some reason I can't just say that out loud. "I'll be at school."

I stumble on beer bottles around the table as I make my way to the front door, I pick up my bag, pull on my boots and head for my motorcycle. Slamming the door behind me.

Imagining a world where I told my dad the truth from the beginning seems so far out of reach. But if I had told him everything that happened in grade nine, so much of this could have been saved.

I get off my motorcycle after parking in the school parking lot. The air has begun to get crisp as fall is right around the corner. I'm going to have to start wearing a better jacket while on my motorcycle.

"Hey!" I spin around to see Jade heading my way, "Where were you at the meeting last night? I couldn't find you anywhere."

"Well. My stupid dad didn't let me go because he wants to teach me a lesson about punching Conner." I explain as we start to walk towards the front entrance together.

"Seriously?"

"Yeah, and he thinks he's helping me by making me realize my actions because apparently the whole reason I came back here was to become a better person. Bullshit! I can punch whoever the fuck I want to punch!"

"How long have you been wanting to say that?" Jade asks.

"Almost all night."

I stop walking and take a deep breath before turning to face Jade, "How was the meeting anyways?"

"Just wanted to tell us that if the town is going to keep blaming the gang for killing Kian, we need to stand our ground and don't retaliate since people could call the police, more fingers will get pointed and then some of us could get arrested." Jade explains.

"And how long did it take for him to say all of that?" I ask.

"Maybe five minutes."

I shake my head, "See bullshit, I could have just come."

"Hey gals!" Jade and I look over to see Clark walking up to us, we both raise our eyebrows, "Yeah I'll never say that again... but have you guys seen it yet?" Clark asks.

"Seen what?" Jade asks looking over to me and then back to Clark.

"The newspaper, not the school one."

I close my eyes and take a deep breath, *no losing your temper today*, "Dude, be more specific."

"Kian's autopsy report was released to the public today. Everyone knows how he died now."

My heart drops, even though I was the one who found him it was too dark to see how he possibly could have died. I wasn't that serious when I thought that he might have been killed. I know I saw blood, but my main thought was that he drowned, maybe hit his head on a rock, but then again, his body was a far bit away from the water.

"I don't know, I didn't look. I just heard two guys talking about it at the Mystic Glass this morning." Clark smiles.

"And you didn't hear them say how he died?" I asked.

"Nope, just heard the words newspaper, Kian and autopsy, and I think murder. Then I came to school and saw you two and now I'm telling you two." Clark's smile widens.

"I can't comprehend why you told us then." I sigh, turn on my heel and walk into the school.

By the time the end of the day rolls around the last class I want to be in is science.

"You're on time for once." Adrian says.

I shrug, "I tried."

Adams looks up from his book and glances over to me, "Did you hear about Kian?"

"That he's dead? Yeah, I'm the one who found him idiot."

"No, not that, how he died."

"No, I haven't read the paper yet, and frankly I don't care how he died, I just want to know who killed him." I explain.

Adrian's head pops out from behind Oscar's back, "But if you find out how he died it might help find out who killed him."

He has a point, I think to myself, "Fine, I'll read it later."

Mr. Gibes turns on the projector to show the periodic table, "We're going over the elements again today, because it seems that no one in this class, except Miss. Snow, knows what they're doing." Mr. Gibes says spitefully.

I look down at the table awkwardly, I hate it when people point out that I'm smart. When people know you're smart they can take advantage of you. It's easier to play dumb and then surprise people when you're actually brilliant.

"Let's start." Mr. Gibes says as he begins to point out different elements on the board.

I scan my eyes around the room and begin to block every noise out. I never realised how big this room really was, there are ten rows with three tables in each row. Along with that there are eight lab tables closer to the classroom door, which not until now, I realise that it's made of steel. Why would they make steel doors for a classroom?

My attention is brought back to the front of the room when I hear Adrian's name, "Adrian, can you tell us what Nb is?" Mr. Gibes asks.

Adrian doesn't say anything. I watch as he stares blankly at the board, "Uh... I don't know." He finally says.

"Just give it a try, I want to see what you know." Mr. Gibes says.

I thought Adrian would be good in science, but the way he's acting tells me otherwise. His shoulders have become tense, he looks like he's sweating a lot and he hasn't stopped scratching his arm. He seems like Mr. Smart guy, but I guess not.

"Uh... is it Neon?"

"No." Mr. Gibes says coldly, "Nb is Niobium. Ne is Neon. Let's go to the next one."

Mr. Gibes continues with the lesson. For the rest of class Adrian is quiet. He only nods whenever Adams asks him a question or saying something in general.

I trail behind Adrian and Adams as we make our way down to the newspaper. It boggles my mind how slow they walk, they're both like sloths trudging through the jungle, but in this case, it's a hallway.

"Dudes can you fucking walk faster!"

"What do you mean, we're walking at normal speed." Adrian shrugs.

"No, you're walking like sloths and it's annoying." I walk around them and speed down the hallway. I'm not walking with sloths today.

I arrive at the newspaper. I quickly sit down, pull my notebook out of my back and flip to some of the back pages. I'm wanting to start a log for all the information I find about Kian's death so it's all in one place and I'll never lose it.

"We weren't that slow, we only got here two minutes after you." Adams says as they walk into the newspaper closing the door behind him.

"Two minutes too slow, now show me this newspaper." I demand as I lean back in the chair.

Adrian walks over to a pile of newspapers stacked by the window, "We grabbed a bunch." Adrian blushes as he places all of them down in front of me.

I reach out for the top one, "Wait before you read it, I want to show you both something I made after school yesterday." Adams beams.

"Okay." I say flatly letting go of the paper, crossing my arms.

Adams walks over to the chalkboard and flips it to show a bulletin board with a paper pinned to the very top saying, *Murder Board*.

"I made this so we can put all over our findings on the board and flip it over so no one else sees it if they come in here." Adams smiles.

"Why do we care if anyone knows?" I ask.

"The murderer could walk in and take the whole wall down." Adrian suggests.

"Okay, that's fair."

Adrian walks around to the other side of the table to stand beside Adams, "We're going to start on next week's paper while you read through that." Adrian explains.

"Okay, call my name if you need help." I smile. I don't fully intend on helping with the school newspaper though.

I grab the paper, fold it open in front of me and begin to read.

Due to recent events regarding the death of teen boy, Kian Turner. The autopsy report has come back saying that there was foul play in his death ruling his death a homicide. The autopsy shows that Kian was murdered 3 days before being found in the woods.

That confirms what I've been saying to Adrian and Adams this whole time, even if I didn't believe it myself it made sense. Why else would he have gone missing if someone wasn't trying to kill him? And it seems as though the whole town believed he was killed too, now it's confirmed.

My eyes wander over to the photo of Kian's lifeless body from the autopsy photo. "Okay, what kind of sick person would add the photo of his autopsy report into the paper?!" I ask in disbelief.

Adrian sighs, "Um... that would be my mom's doing."

"Oh I'm-"

"It's fine, it is very *sick*. I don't really understand it." Adrian says.

I scratch the back of my head before looking down at the paper once again. I glance over to the photo of Kian's body. That whole night flashing before my mind, and not the night where I found Kian's body in the woods.

The autopsy shows that Kian was brutally stabbed several times. Many in the chest and in the legs. This caused his death to be due to loss of blood.

I must have been in so much shock that night that I didn't realize Kian had stab wounds all over his body. To be fair there were lots of leaves covering him. Or maybe I did notice but blocked it out of my mind because it was too gruesome.

I look up to Adrian and Adams who are now sitting across from me. "So, he was stabbed to death."

Adams looks up at me and nods, "Yup, very gruesome."

Ace must be trying to avoid this as much as possible. Her whole family must be.

I look back down at the photo and notice the stab wounds are all made from a small blade, I can't tell how deep the wounds are, obviously, but I know that size and shape.

Out of impulse I rip the photo of Kian out of the paper and grab a small piece of paper. I get up and walk over to the bulletin board, pinning the photo up.

"Why's that going up there?" Adrian asks.

"Because Adrian." I grab his pen and quickly scribble onto it the other piece of paper I grabbed, "The murder weapon was a pocketknife." I pin the piece of paper onto the board right beside the photo.

"Uh... how do you know that?" Adams asks.

"Because I have one of my own."

"Uh" Adams blinks at me.

"God! I didn't kill him, Adams. He died three days before I was even in town. If anything, you two are more likely suspects."

Adrian turns to fully look at me, "What!? Why us?"

"Everyone talked to Kian at least once in their lives, and if you didn't talk to him then he talked to you... Just all that matters is Kian was killed with a pocketknife, all we need to do now is figure out who owns a pocketknife." I explain.

"What does a pocketknife even look like?" Adams asks.

"I'll show you."

I go and reach into my right boot where I keep my knife in a small pouch. "Well, that's a problem."

"What is?" Adrian asks.

I walk around the table and over to my bag. I begin to go through it hoping that I possibly took my knife out of my boot and put it into my bag. But that isn't like me. "Fuck." I mumble.

"What's happened?" Adams asks.

"My knife is gone."

"What do you mean gone! That shouldn't be a thing! Someone could try to frame you!" Adams gets up and starts to pace back and forth.

"Bud! Calm down!" Adrian yells before looking over to me, "Did anyone know where you kept your knife other than you?"

"I don't know, maybe."

"Maggie, think this is serious, because even though you weren't here when he died someone in this town was, and that knife probably has all your fingerprints over it and could be used to frame you."

"Yeah. I get that Adrian." I say flatly.

"Okay, my dad knew, but he doesn't touch my shoes they're always in my room or by the front door, um... and-"

Shit, *"Hey can you hold my boot for a second."*

"Jade."

CHAPTER TEN

Jade Button
Tuesday, September 17th, 3:10pm

    I lean up against the fence outside the Elementary school. My parents are working late tonight and had to go to a meeting, so I was assigned with the task of picking up my little sisters from school. It's an easy task.
    The bell rings and a flood of students come running out of the school doors. I watch as a group of ten kids run over to the playground. I wonder if my sisters will ever do that one day, I wonder if my parents will ever allow them too.
    "Jade!!" I turn to my left, right as two bodies slam up against mine. I wrap my arms around the two girls in front of me.
    "Hi, cookies." I smile.

I gave them that nickname after we snuck five boxes of cookies into my room when they were four.

"Hi." Sam smiles up at me, her curly brown hair falling in front of her face before she pushes it out of the way.

"Do we have to walk?" Jamey asks.

"Sadly yes."

The only way I've ever been able to tell my twin sisters apart is their hair. Sam's is short and curly like mine, while Jamey's is long and wavy like mom's.

"But while we walk, you two can tell me all about how school was." I smile as they each grab one of my hands.

We begin to walk down the sidewalk towards our house. It isn't a far walk from the school, but it's a decent one.

"During school today I saw a Morpho Achilles." Sam smiles.

"Oh, and what is that?" I ask.

"A butterfly! You should know this Jade!" Sam yells.

"Right, right sorry. I don't know as much about butterflies as you do." I explain.

Sam is a butterfly expert. She could talk about them all day, every day. Sometimes I can tell that Jamey gets tired of her talking about them all the time. But I think that's mostly because they share a room and Sam's side is covered in all butterfly things.

"Jamey, did you see any butterflies today?" I ask.

"No. While Sammy was off running around chasing them, I was practicing my dance routine for Friday."

"That sounds fun. I can't wait to see it!" I smile.

For as long as I can remember, Jamey has been doing dance. Mostly Hip Hop sometimes, Jazz and Ballet. But every once and while she brings up to me how she wants to join the gang. Which I won't allow, and neither will my parents, it was hard enough for me to join in grade eight. I'm still surprised I'm not disowned yet. But Jamey and Sam are only eight years old. It's too dangerous for them.

We arrive at our house; I look behind me as my sisters run up to the front door. I always make sure that no one has been following me. No one knows that I live on the wealthy side of town. The only person who most likely knows is Maggie.

Once we're in the house, Sam and Jamey run into the kitchen dropping their bags at the front door. I pick them up and hang them in the hallway closet. I know our mom will have a fit if they're left on the ground.

I walk into the kitchen to see Sam and Jamey with a bag of Doritos already opened. Our parents never let us have snacks before dinner, if anything chips are for dessert if we're lucky.

"You better make sure those are put away before mom and dad get home." I say as I walk around to stand on the other side of the island, across from them.

"Of course, we will." Jamey smiles while popping a chip in her mouth.

"So do you think both of you should get started on some homework?" I question.

Both freeze and stop eating the chips, "What homework?" Sam says.

"We don't have homework." Jamey adds.

I tilt my head and raise my eyebrow, "Really?"

They both sigh, "Fine we have math."

"Okay, tell you what." I place both my hands on the island and lean closer to them, "How about we do some training again, and then I help you get your homework done before mom and dad get home?"

"How about you tell us about the girl you looove instead." Sam giggles.

I roll my eyes, "I don't love her." I look down at the ground, then back up at them, "But we can talk about her after we train."

"Why are we training?" Sam asks.

"Because someone was murdered, and we need to know how to defend ourselves if something bad happens!!" Jamey yells.

I really hate how much Jamey knows about Kian's death. Both of them do, they're way too advanced for their age.

I stand in my backyard facing the tree that is in the middle of the lawn. I turn around to face Sam and Jamey. They're sitting on the small picnic table we have on the patio. "So, you have to focus, you won't always have a knife, but you'll always have other objects to throw." I explain.

"But knives do more damage." Jamey smiles.

I nod, "Yes they do." I spin to face the tree again, "You're going to look at your target, squint if you have to," I pull my arm back, "Once you're ready, throw and let go." I lunge my arm forwards, releasing the knife from my hand. It goes flying and impales the middle of the tree.

When I turn around Sam and Jamey have their mouths wide open with shock, "My turn! My turn!" Jamey says as she jumps up from the picnic table.

"Okay, okay, come stand where I am."

I jog over to the tree and pull the knife from it.

I arrive back beside Jamey and hand her the knife. "I'll guide your arm, so you know the motion." I explain before grabbing her arm.

"Ready?" I ask.

Jamey gives me a small nod before turning to look at the tree.

"Okay, focus on the spot you want to aim, and take a deep breath." I pull back Jamey's arm and I'm about to help her throw the knife when my name gets called.

"Jade Madgory Button! What do you think you're doing!"

I take the knife from Jamey's hand and slowly turn around to see my mom standing in the patio doorway.

"Hi, Mom."

I could have sworn they weren't supposed to be home until six.

"Why are you teaching your sisters to throw knives?" She glares.

I can feel Jamey hiding behind me, "To protect themselves, since someone was murdered." I smile, hoping that's a good enough explanation even though I already know nothing's going to be a good explanation for my mother.

My mom sighs and crosses her arms, "Samantha, Jamey get inside and go do your homework."

Sam and Jamey run inside the house, "I'll be right in to help!" I call after them.

"No. No. No." My mom says shaking her head while walking over to me, "You're grounded."

"What!?"

"I don't want you showing your younger sisters your *gangways*. Just because someone died, doesn't mean someone is going to kill them."

"The newspaper, literally, said that Kian was murdered! Don't you want Sam and Jamey to be able to protect themselves?" I ask.

"This isn't up for discussion; I don't want them turning out like you."

"Wow." I scoff.

My mom places her hand out in front of me, "Give me the knife."

"I can't- It's my friends. She uh, let me borrow it."

"Well, you give it back to her tomorrow. Now go to your room. I don't want you helping your sisters with their homework. I'll have your father do that."

"Glad to see you still don't care." I brush past her and walk into the house. I run up the stairs and into my room.

Once I get to my room, I slam my door behind me. I pull my leather jacket off and throw it onto my bed. I grab my guitar which always sits at the bottom of my bed and sit down on my beige bean bag chair.

The first song that comes into mind is the one Ace and I played at the back-to-school dance. I begin to strum the cords that she played to calm my nerves.

I hear a small creek making me look up to see Sam and Jamey peeking their heads into my room. "Come on in." I smile placing my guitar on the ground beside me as they both come running in.

"Did you get in trouble?" Jamey asks as she sits down on the floor in front of me, Sam sitting beside her.

"Nothing that I'm not used to."

"We're sorry." Sam looks down at her lap.

I lift up her head, "Don't be sorry, it wasn't your fault. It was my idea. I should have known that mom and dad would be home sooner." I give a sympathetic smile.

"Did you two finish your homework?" I ask, changing the subject.

Jamey nods, "There were only two questions."

"Buttt, can you tell us about that girl now?" Sam asks.

"Sure, what do you want to know?"

"Everything!" Sam beams, "What does she look like?"

"Well... she has perfect skin; I don't think there's a blemish on her face. Long dark black hair. She owns a bike, just like mine, the only difference is the colour. She can sing, and play the piano and the guitar, like me."

"Wow, she sounds amazing." Jamey smiles.

"She is." I smile.

"You must be in love." Sam smiles.

I blush, "I'm not in love, it's just a crush."

"What's her name?" Sam asks.

"Ace. Turner."

"OH, that's the guy who died, that's his sister right?" Jamey says.

"Yeah, how- how do you know that?"

"The last name, from the newspaper." Jamey explains.

My heart skips a beat, "Wait Jamey you read that!?"

"Yeah?" Jamey looks over to Sam then back over to me.

"There was a really grown-up picture in there... are you okay from seeing that?" I ask.

"Yeah, I'm fine. It's just real life, isn't it? People die every day." Jamey looks at me, I can see the innocence flash before her eyes.

"Yeah, but Jam, not everyone dies like he did. Someone did that to him. Can both of you not look at the newspaper again until you're older? For me, please? I don't want you two seeing those images."

Sam and Jamey both nod.

"Good... do you two want to go downstairs to see if dinner is ready, and I'll meet you two both there." I smile.

"Okay!" Both of them say as they get up and run out of my room.

I lean my head back onto the wall. I run my hand across my forehead and let out a sigh.

I can't have my eight-year-old sisters looking at photos of people stabbed to death. Why of all places for this to happen it had to be our town.

I walk downstairs and sit down across from Sam like I do at every dinner. Jamey sits beside her, my dad and mom always sitting at either end of the table.

"How was the day for all of you?" My dad asks.

"Amazing!" Sam smiles as she begins to tell the story about butterflies, the same one she told me on the walk home. Soon after Jamey begins to tell her story about dancing.

I stare blankly at the food in front of me. I poke around the mashed potatoes on my plate with my fork. The only time I ever feel welcome in this family is when I'm alone with Sam and Jamey, but with everyone I feel like an outsider.

I've never truly been in this family, and I felt more like an outsider once I joined the gang, but they became my family.

"And Jade," I look up from my plate to my dad, "How was your day?" He asks.

"It was good dad." I flash a smile before looking back down at my plate.

"Why aren't you eating, Jade?" My mom asks.

"Not really hungry right now, I'll eat something later."

"Well food is in front of you now, so eat it. You will eat the food we made." My mom says.

The whole table is now silent, everyone looking between my mom and I.

"Fine." I scoop up mashed potatoes and take a big bite, eating it while staring right at my mom. "Happy?" I ask once I'm finished.

I push away from the table and stand up, "I'll be in my room."

When I'm in my room, I close my door and lock it behind me. I grab my jacket from my bed and walk over to my window. I lift it up before slowly crawling out. I close it just enough so I'm still able to get back into the house.

I walk up to the clearing behind Mystic Glass, it's the place the gang always meets up, except for inside the bar.
"Hey. Your parents let you out tonight?" Clark asks as I walk up to him.
"No, I snuck out. Do you want to come get a drink with me?" I ask gesturing towards the bar.
"Of course." Clark smirks.
"Perfect." I grab his hand and drag him towards the bar. I need to let loose for tonight.

CHAPTER ELEVEN

Maggie Snow
<u>Wednesday, September 18th, 7:30am</u>

    I saw Jade last night at Mystic Glass. I was all prepared to ask her about my knife, but then realised that her and Clark were both drunk and stumbling. I think Clark had to walk her home once he sobered up a bit.
    I plan on asking Jade about my knife at school today, but for the time being I have other things on my mind.
    My dad walks into the living room holding a beer, "Morning."
    "Morning, a bit early for that isn't it?" I ask.
    He sighs, "I don't think so."
    I watch as he walks over and slumps down into the chair in the corner. "So," My dad looks up at me and raises his eyebrow, "I had a question."

"Okay?" He brings the bottle up to his lips and takes a sip.

"I was wondering. If... I could maybe, possibly. Go visit Caleb."

"What?" My dad stares blankly at me.

"It's just, I haven't seen him since I was six and I want to catch up. Do you know where he is? Like where he's staying?" I ask.

My dad stands up and starts to walk towards the kitchen, "I think you should get to school."

I stand up and follow him, "I still have ten minutes until I have to leave. I just want to see him, maybe this weekend?"

"No!" My dad doesn't turn around to face me, "Drop this, Maggie. Please."

"I just want to see my brother."

"Yeah, and I said drop it, now!"

I stare at my dad's back, his breathing heavy. "Glad to know you've gotten over me punching Conner, and now you're just mad that I want to see my brother. Great father figure."

I walk out of my house and passed my motorcycle. I'm going to walk today. Clear my mind. Plus, it's a far walk to school, and I don't care much about being there today.

There's a lot of fog outside today, which is surprising since it's still technically summer. I almost don't notice that I'm walking past the police station until I hear my name getting called.

"Maggie Snow?!"

I turn around to see a lady standing behind me, "Uh yeah, who are you?" I ask.

The lady is tall, formal, she's wearing a dark blue pantsuit and a golden badge over her right breast.

"I'm Detective Lana," She reaches out her hand to shake mine, I don't reach out my hand. She stares at me for a second before pulling her hand back, "I am assigned to the Kian Turner case, I saw a photo of you when I was looking around the Turner household. I was informed that you were the one who found him that night."

I nod and move my hand to rub the back of my neck, "Yeah." Why was there a photo of me in their house?

"I will most likely be doing more follow up questions with you later in the month." Detective Lana explains.

"I already answered questions."

"Yes, you have, but now that the whole town knows that this was a homicide, we need to ask you different follow up questions."

Am I the only one in the town that assumed and yet not assumed it was a murder before the newspaper came out, or is that just my brain jumping to conclusions because murder seems like the main reason for finding somebody in the middle of the woods with stab wounds?

"Well, it's nice meeting someone new in town that will be helping, but I need to get going or I'll be later for school." I put on my fakest smile possible.

"It was nice to meet you too, Maggie. I hope we can be a big help to each other." Detective Lana smiles at me before I turn around and walk down the street.

I don't know if she could notice, but I walked away fast. Feeling like you're being interrogated without even being interrogated sucks. It's not that I was lying about anything, it just feels like everything you've ever done wrong in your life is going to get spued out and somehow, you'll end up in jail for something you did when you were six.

By the time I arrive at school it's already the end of the first period. I would have gotten to school halfway through the period if I wasn't stopped to have a conversation.

I wait outside the math hall, tapping my foot up and down as I wait for the bell to ring. Once I see the girl with curly brown hair walking down the hallway I charge.

"Hey." Jade smiles as I walk up beside her.

"Hey." I walk in front of her and put my hand out, "My knife please."

Her mouth parts slightly, "I wasn't planning on taking it, I just wanted to borrow it, I wanted to help protect my sisters."

"From what? You didn't know Kian was dead yet." I whisper.

"If anything, I knew Kian was missing, I was assuming someone kidnapped him." Jade explains.

"You could have just fucking asked to borrow it. Everyone knows that Kian was stabbed to death, and it was obviously a pocketknife, so give it back to me so I don't get framed for this shit." I grumble.

My hand is still held out in front of her, people moving in every direction around us as we stand in the middle of the hallway.

"You saying that, corroborates why I shouldn't give it to you in the middle of the hallway. I'll give it to you at lunch." Jade says.

I pull my hand away and put it into my jacket pocket, "You better."

"I will. Meet me in the back, by my bike, at lunch." Jade says.

"Fine." I brush past her and down the hallway to my second period, arriving right as the bell rings.

I walk into the lounge at the beginning of lunch. I notice Adrian and Adams sitting in the corner. I would have sat with them before going to meet with Jade, but I need to talk to someone else.

"Hey, can I sit?"

Ace looks up at me, "Sure!"

I sit down across from her on the small red chair, "I met Detective Lana today."

Ace's eyes widen, "You did? What did she say?"

"Mainly that I have to have a follow up interview because I was the one that find Kian."

"She creeps me out. She was looking around my house the other day and I found her in my room. She was only supposed to be looking in Kian's room for clues." Ace explains.

"Why was she in your room?" I ask.

Ace shrugs, "No clue, but she was looking at a photo of us from grade nine, the one from the first day of school. The one my mom took of us. It started a very awkward conversation."

Ace still has that photo.

"Isn't that an invasion of privacy, she can't do that without a warrant right?" I question.

"I don't know, I think my mom gave her the right to look anywhere." Ace sighs.

"I'm sorry, but I have to say this. When did your mom become such a bitch?"

Ace shrugs, "Good question."

"But all things aside, just know that I think the Detective is weird too. So, if you need help with anything, I can beat her up." I smile.

"Yeah, like Conner?"

My body tenses up, "You broke his nose, Maggie."

I swallow the lump in my throat, "I know, I feel bad, I just... I'm not going to admit it to him. I've already gotten a bunch of shit from my dad."

"What do you mean?"

"I've been banned from all gang meetings, and now he won't even let me go see my brother."

"Caleb? Why would you want to see him?" Ace asks.

"I haven't seen him since I was six, I- I haven't been able to stop thinking about him, since Conner brought him up. Everyone looked shocked to find out that I have a brother. I feel like I need to see him, you know?"

Ace nods, "Well, the only people who knew what happened was Conner and I. So, it makes sense that you got mad that he shared that with a whole room of people."

"Especially saying that I should be in the psych ward instead of him." I sigh, "That's what hurt the most."

"I'm sorry, I wish I could have helped."

"It's okay."

Ace gives a sympathetic smile before asking, "Why don't you know where your brother is?"

"I was six and a year after he left my parents divorced, as you know since that's when we became friends. So, I guess my mind was in other places." I explain.

"Oh yeah, I remember when we met during-"

"Dodgeball." I say with her.

I look down and laugh, "I missed this." Ace says.

"What?" I ask looking back up at her.

"Our friendship."

"Oh... I've missed it too... but I actually have to go and meet up with Jade right now." I say glancing over to the clock, "Sorry."

Ace shakes her head as I stand up, "It's okay, say hi for me."

"Will do." I smile before walking out of the lounge, giving a small wave in Adrian and Adams direction.

I begin to walk away once I have my knife back, "Maggie wait." Jade grabs hold of my arm. "Who do you think did it?" She asks.
 "Did what?"
 "Killed Kian, who do you think did it?" She asks again.
 I shake my head, "No idea, all I know is he was stabbed three days before I got back, so it can't be me, and things- things just don't add up-" Jade stares at me as if she's waiting for me to say something else, but I don't. "I'm gonna head to class now, thanks for my knife back."

 I stand outside my house; I don't want to go inside. This was another reason I left town, not the main one, but it was still a reason. I couldn't stand having to come home in the fear of having a fight with my drunk dad.
 I open the door reluctantly and walk inside, "Dad?" I call out as I close the door behind me.
 I peer into the living room, my dad nowhere to be seen. I walk through the kitchen and down the hallway, I slowly push open his bedroom door. He isn't there either.

This is perfect for me, not that I don't want to see my dad, but I'd rather not see him at this moment. I'm not in the mood to talk.

Moving into my room, I close the door behind me and throw my bag into my bed. I open my closet and pull out one of the boxes that I saw when I first came back.

It's surprisingly heavy for me, I try to pick it up, but can't, resulting in me having to drag it over to my bed. I sit down and place the box between my legs.

I take my knife and cut the tape that's sealing the box closed. I open the flaps and look inside to see a large pile of papers and photos.

Reaching in I grab the first thing I see. A photo of me, my mom, my dad and my brother. This was taken two weeks before he was sent away. I place the photo beside me and look back into the box, right on top is a folder. Written across the top of the folder is *Swan Lake Mental Institution*.

I place the folder on my lap and slowly open it. There are a bunch of papers clipped together, the one at the very top is a photo of Caleb when he was eight, a small wide-eyed kid with dusty brown hair. I wouldn't even know what he would look like now, I don't even know if I'd recognize him.

Once I stop staring at the photo of my brother, I begin to read the page that is underneath.

In a week we will have a team come down from Los Angeles and take young Caleb Snow. At the bottom is a place where we will need both parents or legal guardian's signatures in order to come and pick up Caleb.

I move the photo of Caleb out of the way to read the top of the page. *We are glad to hear you have chosen our program to help better your son. As you may have read on the web site that our facilities welcome anyone from all around the world. Everyone has their own room and is allowed regular visits if wanted. Swan Lake is to help better the children for as long as they need.*

My eyes move back down to the bottom of the page where my parents had to sign to send my brother away. I look at my dad's signature which looks normal, but as I go to look at my mom's I know it's not hers.

I've forged my mom's signature thousands of times when I was younger so I would be able to go on school field trips. My parents we're always fighting, and I was scared to ask someone to sign the form, so I learned my mom's.

So, I know for a fact that the signature in front of me is not my mom's. It's my dad trying to imitate what my mom's looks like.

I place the folder back into the box and push the box back into my closet. Why didn't my mom sign the paper herself?

CHAPTER TWELVE

Adrian Fisher
Thursday, September 19th, 6:30am

    Most mornings the sun is shining through my bedroom window. Most mornings the sun wakes me up, but this morning my alarm woke me up. I ended up falling asleep at 3 in the morning last night, I knew that I'd have to set my alarm if I wanted to wake up in time.
    For my whole life I've had the same routine every day, wake up, go to the bathroom, shower, come back to my room, make my bed and get dressed. By the time all of that is done it's 7 in the morning.
    I make my way downstairs to the kitchen. To my surprise the kitchen is empty, I shouldn't be surprised though, my parents' study is right beside

my room, and I heard them working for most of the night.

It's the main reason I couldn't get to bed.

"Morning Sweetie." I turn around to see my mom walking into the kitchen.

"Morning, Mom." I smile as I make my way over to sit down at the island.

I watch as my mom makes her way over to the coffee machine, "How was your sleep?"

"It was fine." I wasn't going to tell my mom that she and my dad kept me up most of the night.

My mom begins to make breakfast, I look out the window to the backyard. The pool was emptied last weekend, I don't think I tried to use it once during the summer. My parents were the only ones to use it.

"Uh, where's dad?" I ask, looking back over to my mom.

"He's working in the study." My mom says.

Still? I think.

"Cool, what's he doing?" I question.

"We got lots of harsh feedback on the paper, so you father is trying to clean up that mess." She explains while placing my omelette onto a plate.

"Well, you did put a photo of a dead body in the paper, mom. Did you really think people would be okay with that? Especially Kian's family?"

My mom places the plate down in front of me, "We were just reporting the news, like we always do."

"Doesn't mean you put a photo of a dead

body in the paper for the whole town to see. It's gruesome." I say while I start to eat my omelette.

"Your father and I are going to a dinner meeting tonight; you'll have the house to yourself after 3." She says, changing the subject.

I nod, "Sounds good," I move off the stole and pick up my backpack, "I've got to go pick up Oscar and get to school, I'll see you later."

"You're trying out for the basketball team tomorrow, right?" Oscar asks as I drive away from his house.

"Yeah, but I doubt I'll make the team again this year since I've already been on it two times. I don't even want to be on the team again. I'm only trying out to please my parents."

"I bet you'll make the team, you're a star player." Oscar smiles.

I sigh, "Thank Bud." I turn into the school parking lot unintentionally parking beside Jessica.

"Hi Adrian, and... cousin." Jessica gives Oscar a death stare before looking back over to me with a big smile.

Jessica walks over to my car door and opens it for me, "Uh... thanks." I step out of the car.

"Of course." Jessica smiles.

Oscar walks around the car to stand beside me.

"So, Adrian are you trying out for basketball tomorrow?"

"Yup." I nod keeping my answers short.

Jessica nudges me with her elbow, "I'll be cheering you on from the side lines."

I smile, trying very hard to not show any ounce of my annoyance.

Ever since the dance last Friday I've been having a hard time not thinking about Maggie, especially since Maggie did verbally attack Jessica and it was funny. But not just that, she's everywhere, it's hard not to think about her. But I don't have a crush on her. I only think she's badass. Part of me wishes I had some of her confidence.

Jessica continues to blab on about something to do with cheerleading when my eyes catch onto Maggie walking into the school, she doesn't look happy.

"Adrian?" A hand waves in my face snapping me out of my daze, "Were you listening?" Jessica asks.

I didn't hear a thing she said, "Yeah."

"Adrian and I have to get to class, see you later Jessica." Oscar smiles before grabbing my arm, pulling me towards the school.

"I thought she stopped obsessing over you last year?" Oscar asks as I stop walking, causing him to look over to me.

"No. I just started to avoid her."

"But it's weird that she opened your door, right? Especially since she's my cousin, and aren't guys supposed to open the doors for girls?"

134

I shrug, "It's Jessica, so I don't really know."

I glance over at the clock, "The bells about to ring we should get to class."

Oscar looks over to the clock, "Ah shit, yes we must go!"

Oscar and I have been sitting in the lounge for lunch recently, normally we'd be sitting outside, but the lounge has been eventful.

"Hey." I turn to see Conner as he sits down beside me.

Conner's nose is still broken from when Maggie beat him up on Monday. He's had his nose covered for most of the week, but today it's not. It doesn't look as bad as the bruises under his eyes made it seem, it's only a little swollen now if anything.

"How's your nose healing?" Oscar asks.

"It hurts, but I can't do anything about it." Conner shrugs and shifts his attention towards me, "You're gonna be at tryouts tomorrow, right?"

"Yup." I nod, why do people keep asking me that?

Conner throws his arm over my shoulder, "Adrian Fisher and Conner Martin back on the court for another year." He says while moving his arm out in front of us in a shooting star motion, "I can imagine the headlines when we win."

"It's only high school basketball, Conner."

Conner pulls away from me, "No it is not! This is my future and yours too, now I've got to go to the cafeteria, see you later!"

Conner gets up from the couch and walks away, I glance over to Oscar who is staring at me, "What?"

"Are you not gonna tell him you don't want to be on the team this year?"

"I can't do that to Conner, it's Conner, you know his life is basketball, you saw how he reacted when I said it's just high school basketball."

"But you still want to become a writer, right? If you take the road of basketball, you won't really get to writing." Oscar points out.

"I know, but I haven't even started applying to Universities or Colleges, I just-" I look over to the window to see Maggie standing outside with a group of people. She never seems to worry about anything and lets everything happen as it happens.

I look back over to Oscar, "I'm just gonna let things happen, how they happen."

The time slowly ticks by while sitting in science class. Mr. Gibes has been non-stop talking about drawing atoms. I learned all of this in grade ten, and I almost failed. I haven't understood one word that's come out of his mouth.

I glance over to the clock, only 5 minutes left of class.

"Okay, before we go, tomorrow we will be doing a review for the test we'll be having on Wednesday. So, make sure you bring in all your notes." Mr. Gibes explains.

I keep my eyes on the clock, one more minute until the bell rings and then I can finally leave.

"And can Mr. Fisher and Miss. Snow stay back for a second after class today." Mr. Gibes says.

I shoot my attention to the front of the class, then over to Maggie. We look at each other from over Oscar's shoulders. The bell rings and I don't get to leave.

"I'll see you tomorrow, I'm gonna walk home. Good luck." Oscar whispers to me before leaving the classroom with everyone else.

Mr. Gibes walks over to us and sits down on the table in front of ours, "Miss. Snow, feet off the table."

"The bell rang, you can't tell me what to do anymore." Maggie smiles while tilting her head to the side.

I do have to be honest with myself, Maggie does have a lot of sass at times.

Mr. Gibes rubs his temple before looking over to me, "You are failing this class, and it's only been three weeks so far."

"Yeah..." I lower my head, out of the corner of my eye I can see Maggie looking at me, she seems confused.

"Since we have a test coming up on Wednesday, it will bring up your mark a lot if you pass." Mr. Gibes explains.

I look back up at him, "How am I supposed to pass? I didn't understand a word you said today."

"Miss, Snow will be tutoring you."

"What!?" Maggie says.

Maggie throws her legs off the table and sits up straight, "I am?"

"She is?" I ask at the same time.

"Maggie, you have the highest grade in this class," Mr. Gibes says while turning to face her. Maggie's body tenses up, almost as if she didn't want anyone to know that. "Make sure he's ready to pass this test on Wednesday."

"Why should I?" Maggie asks.

"I'll let you keep your feet up on the table in every class and won't bother you about it." Mr. Gibes says.

Maggie looks over to me, "Fine."

We both get out of the classroom, and I have to practically run down the hallway to catch up with her. She walks way too fast, which is weird because she has really short legs.

"So, when are we doing this?" I ask.

"Well, I can't do it tomorrow or on the weekend because of Kian's funeral." Maggie explains as she pushes the door to the staircase open and starts to, basically run, down the stairs. I forgot that Kian's funeral was this weekend, "And it would be stupid to do it on Monday or Tuesday before the test." Maggie stops walking and turns to look at me, I stop in my tracks trying not to run into her, "How about tonight?" She asks.

"Uh... yeah, sure, that works. My parents will be out of the house... so do you want to come over right now, or?" I ask.

"Sure, it's a good thing I walked to school today." Maggie turns and continues down the stairs. "Oh okay, we're going now." I mumble to myself.

I follow her outside the front of the school, "Do you even know what my car looks like? Or where it is?" I ask.

"It's the white convertible, right?" Maggie glances back at me.

"Yeah, that's the one."

Maggie hops over the car door and into the passenger seat as I calmly unlock the car and open my door.

"You should really put a roof on this during school hours. Someone could easily steal anything you have in here, or even hotwire the car and drive off." Maggie says.

"Uh, yeah I guess that would be smart then."

I drive down the road to my house and glance over to Maggie staring out the window. I never realized how long and curly her hair was until now, with it blowing in the wind. She looks cute.

I pull out front of my house, my parents' car still in the driveway.

"And we're here." I say, time to hope that my parents don't hate Maggie. Maybe this was a bad idea...

CHAPTER THIRTEEN

Maggie Snow
Thursday, September 19th, 2:35pm

  We pull in front of Adrian's house. When looking at his house it's a mansion compared to mine. Two ~~stores~~ stories, a front porch, and a garden that is filled with blooming flowers, and the front lawn is actually green.
  I get out of the car, followed by Adrian. He walks around the back of the car and up the driveway, I follow him up to the porch. His driveway has a cobblestone pattern along with the path up to his porch. He stops at the mailbox by the door and grabs a handful of mail. I don't even have a mailbox.

Adrian opens the front door and lets me walk in first, which I do despite how awkward it feels.

"My parents are still home, but they should be going out soon." Adrian says closing the front door behind him.

"Cool" I say flatly.

As Adrian takes off his shoes, I look around the house, or at least what I can see of it. There's a large spiral staircase in the center of the house. I've always wanted to slide down the railing of one of those.

Adrian walks up beside me, "We can go to the kitchen, my parents are probably in there and will want to meet you."

I nod. I don't understand why they'd want to meet me though, I'm not the most loved person in this town. Not to mention I look like a lost street dog in his house, I do not fit the rich aesthetic.

When we walk into the kitchen, I don't notice his parents right away, instead I notice the pool in his backyard. What I'd give to have a pool in my backyard. What I'd give to have a backyard in general.

Once I stop staring at the backyard, I look to my left to see his parents sitting at an island mumbling to each other.

"Mom." Adrian says, no response.

"Dad?"

"What son?!" His dad asks aggressively.

"I'd like you to meet my friend." Adrian says sheepishly.

Oh, so him and I are friends now? This is information to me. I don't really care either way though. How else is he supposed to introduce me? *"Hi mom and dad this is a girl I met in the café, she also found Kian's dead body, she's pretty weird, and she broke Conner's nose the other day."*

Both his parents turn around, I can tell that they're both stuck up pricks. Not to mention that Adrian gets most of his looks from his dad. He looks nothing like his mom.

"Oh, hello." His mom smiles as she looks me up and down.

I'm obviously not what she expected when she turned around. I bet she's despising my leather jacket right about now. Good thing she hasn't seen the tattoo.

Adrian's dad stands up from the island and walks over to me, he reaches out to shake my hand, I shake it back, "Nice to meet you. I'm Matthew and this is Linda." He smiles while gesturing towards his wife.

"Hi," I smile, "Maggie."

"Are you two going out soon?" Adrian asks.

"Yes, we're just about to leave," Adrian's mom gets up from the island, "But what are you two going to be up to?"

"School project for English." Adrian says without missing a beat.

I obviously know that he's lying, but I don't know why he's lying.

"Okay, sounds good. Have fun then, we'll be back by ten." His dad smiles.

His dad seems nice, much nicer than his mom.

His parents walk past me and out of the kitchen. Once we hear the front door close Adrian lets out a deep breath, that I bet he had been holding since we stepped foot into the kitchen.

Adrian pulls out a chair at the circular table to my right and sits down, I set down my bag and look around.

"What are you doing? You can sit down."

"I know, it's just- your house is really big." I admit before sitting down at the table beside him.

I've always wanted a house like this.

I look over to Adrian, "So lying to your parents? Doesn't seem... rich of you."

"Rich of me?"

"You live on the wealthy side of town and usually kids over here live on a, I must please mommy and daddy loop."

"Well in that case, that's why I lied, to please them." Adrian says.

"But... why lie?" I lean forward on the table, "It's only tutoring."

Adrian hesitated before speaking, "They don't know I suck at science, they made me take it again this year because they think I got a 99% in last year's class."

"Why do they think that?"

Adrian scratches the back of his head, "Uh... well... you see, last year Kian helped me fake my grades, but only for them, only they think I got a

99%, I barely passed last year. If they knew that I failed a class I would be kicked out of the house."

I'm surprised that Adrian would admit that to me, but I guess in his words, we are friends, "Seems like Kian screwed everyone over in this town."

"He didn't screw me over, he helped me."

"Yeah? And what was in it for him?" I ask.

Adrian stays silent, "Exactly."

"Did he screw you over?" Adrian asks.

"In one way, yeah..." I take in a deep breath, "Let's just get started on the tutoring."

Adrian pulls out his notebook, "So I haven't really finished any of the worksheets, since none of them have made any sense."

"Okay... Well, they are very easy once you understand it, so let's start with the first one, and you just tell me what you don't understand, and I'll explain it the best I can."

Adrian nods, "Okay, sounds good." He shuffles his chair closer to me. "So how do I do this?"

"Really? We learned this in grade nine."

"I moved here at the very end of grade nine and my school before sucked and never taught me how to do it properly. My brain hasn't been able to understand it. I'm an English guy." Adrian explains.

I grab a spare piece of paper and begin to draw out an example of how to draw an atom. For me this is one of the easiest things to do once you understand.

"Oh okay, I kind of understand it."

"Good, so if you have any questions or get stumped when answering any of the questions, just ask."

Adrian nods and begins to answer the questions. I reach down into my bag and pull out my notebook. I've got math homework, normally I wouldn't do it until the first five minutes of class, but if I have the spare time to do it now, I might as well. And it's better than sitting in silence not doing anything.

I'm about to start working on my math questions when I feel a tap on my shoulder, I glance beside me to see Adrian staring wide eyed at me. "I'm confused."

I look over to the question that he's on, "There are only 2 electrons, so there would only be two dots on the outer circle." I explain.

Adrian looks down at the paper and sighs, "I'm stupid."

"You're not stupid, it's just not your strong suit."

"But I didn't understand it."

"Are you going to be doing something scientific in the future? No probably not, so you only need to remember how to do it for one second and then you can forget it. School is run to make you feel stupid, but you're not. Trust me."

Adrian nods, "Thank you."

After an hour of working, Adrian calls it off and says it's time for a break. Which I'm completely okay with, and very sure of the fact that he should not have taken science again this year.

Adrian gets up and walks over to the fridge, "Drink?"

"Uh, water?"

Adrian walks back over to the table with two glasses of water and a bag of cheese pretzel bites. They're surprisingly good.

"What, you've never had these before!?" Adrian says in shock.

"No." I shake my head and I crunch down on another one. "You haven't lived with my mom for the past two years; she would never buy chips or snacks. Oh, and if I bought any, she would throw them out."

"That sounds like hell! Is it the reason you moved back, so you could have snacks?" Adrian chuckles.

"Sure, we'll go with that."

"What is the reason you moved back? Oscar explained to me millions of rumours for the reason people thought you left. But what's the reason, why'd you leave? Why'd you come back?" Adrian asks.

"Well, if I told you the mystery would be all gone." I shrug as my body tenses.

"You and your mysteries."

"What can I say? I'm full of them, it only depends on if they get solved or not."

"Speaking of solved," Adrian reaches into the bag of pretzels, "Who do you think killed Kian?"

"Well, if we narrow it down to everyone who knew Kian, the whole town would be a suspect. Kian was like one of those lights that attract flies and just at the right moment he zaps 'em. Everyone in this town was a fly."

"I don't understand what you mean." Adrian says.

I sigh, "Everyone has a reason to want Kian dead, even if they don't know it. He knew small details about everyone."

"What makes you say that?"

"Let's use you as an example, he helped you fake your grades for your parents. I bet if you didn't do something in return for him when the time came, he would have told your parents the grade was fake. Tell me you wouldn't be mad if that had happened."

"Okay, yeah I probably would be mad, but that didn't happen." Adrian says.

"No, not to you, but he could have done something like that for someone else and they didn't do their part when he asked for a favor and then poof they snapped." I wish I was the one to have snapped, "But this is only all theoretical."

"Did he have something on you?" Adrian asks.

"No." I say flatly, it's not a complete lie.

"Then why do you keep talking like he did?"

"Well, he didn't! He was an asshole and I'm the only one who could see through him when everyone else was treating him like some god." I lean back in my chair, "He wasn't a good guy, and everyone is actually lucky that he's dead. He was a horrible person and I had to learn that the hard way and everyone else should have learned it to."

I take in a deep breath, "And someone else must have because... now he's dead." I grab my water and take a sip, "We should get back to tutoring."

Adrian nods, "Uh, yeah, sure."

If I had said something earlier about Kian, he wouldn't be dead, but I believe that everything happens for a reason, so maybe even if I did say something. He would have still ended up dead... somehow.

Adrian offered to give me a ride home, but I declined, I didn't want him seeing my house compared to his house.

"Where have you been?" My dad asks as I step inside. I look over to him sitting on the couch with a beer in hand.

"I was helping someone with science." I take off my jacket and shoes.

"Who?"

"A guy?"

"Are you friends?"

"I guess, yeah, why are you asking?"

He shrugs, "I'm just checking up on you."

"Well, you don't have to, you never did before, so you don't have to start now." I say before walking through the kitchen and down the hallway to my bedroom.

I still haven't brought up to my dad about me finding the papers about my brother. And I didn't think now was the right time.

I sit down on my bed and open my notebook. At the very back I made a page for suspects on who could have killed Kian. I wrote Jade down at the top once I found out she stole by knife. I don't think she'd be capable of killing someone, and if she had a pocketknife to begin with then she wouldn't have taken mine. There is also no way for her to have killed Kian in the time in between us talking at the party, to the time of me finding Kian. Not to mention the report say he was dead three days before being found.

I slowly write down Adrian's name once I cross out Jades. There was a lot said that could make Adrian a suspect, not the mention that Kian did have something in it for him when changing Adrian's grade, I just don't know what.

But I don't know if Adrian is capable of killing either, he doesn't seem like he'd be able to stomach it, but I don't want to rule out the possibility. I still hardly know him.

The only thing I haven't been able to wrap my head around is the letter I got from Kian asking me to come back to town. It got to my house on the day that he died, August 31st three days before I came back home. The worst part is that I don't know if the letter was sent on the 29th of August like it says on the front. The employee at the cafe says that's when he went missing.

Anyone could have killed Kian, and if I've learned anything from this town it's that everyone's putting up a front. Even me.

CHAPTER FOURTEEN

Conner Martin
<u>Friday, September 20th, 7:05am</u>

    Tryouts for the basketball team are today and I need to be ready. My whole life has been leading up to this moment, if I make the team again this year, then I'm set for universities.
    "It's only high school basketball." My mom says.
    "It's not just high school basketball, mom. This could lead me to so many bigger and better things for my life, and career." I explain as I open the fridge and grab out the milk.
    "And we support all of it, even the guys are the station are excited for you," My dad says as he wraps his arm around my mom, "So just try your

best at tryouts today, and you can tell us all about it when you get home from school."

"Don't worry I will." I smile as I pour the milk I grabbed from the fridge into a bowl with some cereal.

I move through the kitchen over to the staircase, "I'll be in my room for a bit."

It's nice to hear that the guys at the station are excited for me. My dad has been working at the Police Station for over a year now, I still don't really know what he does there since he's not a cop, but he told me that he'd keep me posted on anything that he hears about Kian's case.

It's hard to believe that someone murdered him, especially because the last time I saw him was the day before he went missing. Nothing seemed off about him then, but maybe I wasn't paying attention, it's been getting harder and harder for me to focus recently.

Ever since I was younger, I always woke up early and ended up having an hour to spare until school started. I would spend most of the time working on homework or playing video games, but now I can only do one thing at a time.

Once I get up to my room I sit down at my desk and quickly eat my cereal, my leg begins to bounce up and down. I squeeze it with my hand trying to make it stop. I adjust the collar of my shirt and take in the last spoonful of cereal.

I lean back in my desk chair and glance over to my backpack, I shake my head, "You're fine." I mumble out loud of myself. I take a deep breath.

My eyes stay closed as I breath in and out, trying to calm my breath. My hand grips my leg trying to stop it from bouncing.

I abruptly stand up, grab my bag from the floor and run out of my room.

"I'm gonna head off to school now!" I yell to my parents as I run down the stairs.

"But school doesn't start for another half an hour." I hear my mom say.

"I know, but I got to be ready!" I shout as I close the door behind me.

My dad bought me a Jeep last year for my birthday, not really my car of choice, but everyone at school seems to like it.

The ride to school is quick for me, as it is for most people who live in the same area as I do. I pull into the parking lot, not many people have arrived at school yet, which is perfect.

I speed walk into the school and straight to the locker room. I walk over to the small bathroom and place my bag on the counter.

I've been trying my best not to be the first one at school every morning, trying to fight everything, I try my best not to do it in the house with my parents around. I don't want them catching me.

I dig through my bag until I pull out a small zip lock bag from the bottom.

Before opening the bag, I look around to make sure no one else has entered the locker room. I know that I would have heard if someone walked in since the doors creak so loudly, but I'm always cautious.

I open the bag and pull out a small pill, I pop the pill into my mouth and quickly swallow it. I catch a glimpse of myself in the mirror. My nose is healing quickly, my doctor doesn't know how it's happening so quickly, but I know. The only thing I have left is a yellow bruise right across the center of my nose, the rest of it has mostly straightened out.

Right as I put the zip lock bag back into my bag the locker room door opens. I pick up my bag, give a small nod to the guy in the room and walk back out into the hallway.

I notice Adrian and Oscar standing near the vending machine. I've never been able to understand why Adrian hangs out with Oscar, he gives me the creeps.

"Hey boys." I say as I approach them.

"Hey, are you ready for today?" Adrian asks, turning to face me.

"More than ready." I smile.

My leg has stopped bouncing and my muscles feel more tense. I clench my hand together feeling the muscles in my arm tighten.

Oscar starts to talk, and my mind begins to wander. I can't listen to him; his voice is deep and squeaky, and he never talks about anything interesting.

My eyes wander over to Maggie standing at the end of the hallway near the gym with the gang. I don't blame her for breaking my nose, I would say that I deserve it after what I said, especially bringing up her brother. She trusted me with keeping that a secret and then I blurted it out in front of so many people. But I'm not the type to say sorry first. Plus, I don't think that's how our relationship ever worked.

When we were dating, we'd get in a fight, and I'd pretend like nothing happened the next day, a week would pass, then she would bring it up and say sorry. She's always the first to say sorry and somethings don't change.

"Conner were you listening?" Oscar asks.

My eyes move back to look at him, "What?"

"I was telling you that I heard the Coach and the Principal talking about you and Adrian and how you both basically have a guaranteed spot on the team this year, no matter what." Oscar explains.

"I'm still trying out, I'm not gonna risk it on what you *think* you heard."

"Thanks for the information though." Adrian smiles at Oscar. I still really don't understand how they're friends.

"Well, I'm gonna head off to class now, see you later." I pat Adrian on the back before walking off down the hallway.

As I walk down the hallway, I notice Ace standing by her locker with her head down. I've hardly talked to Ace since Maggie left. I was still friends with Kian, but we never hung out at his house much, so I didn't see her often.

I tap on her shoulder, "Hey, are you okay?"

Ace looks up at me, "Uh, yeah, do I not look good?"

"No, you do, I just- you look gloomy."

"No, I'm good. Thanks for asking though."

"Yeah, no problem." I smile before continuing down the hallway.

I tried my best to make that not awkward for the both of us, I know she wasn't telling me the truth, she's clearly hurting since her brother passed. But I don't feel like I have a right to help her.

The hallways are crowded as I make my way to the locker rooms at the end of the day. I push the door open and walk over to Adrian standing in the corner.

"So, you ready?" I ask as I approach him.

Adrian shrugs as he pulls his shirt over his head, "I think so."

"People are gonna be watching tryouts again, right?"

"Yeah, I know Oscar is coming to watch to document for the paper. And I'm positive Jessica said that she and the rest of the cheer team will be there."

I look at him confused, "I thought you stopped talking to Jessica."

"I did, but for some reason she's talking to me again." Adrian sighs.

I laugh, "That's Jessica for you, wouldn't leave me alone the whole time I was with Maggie."

"Can she go back to you please." Adrian says.

"Nah, you can keep her. To clingy for me."

"Come on boys!! Out of the change room tryouts are starting now!!" Coach yells as he comes into the locker room clapping his hands together.

Every year he does this, even before games. He comes into the room, claps his hands together and yells *let's go* at the top of his lungs. I'm surprised it hasn't popped an eardrum yet.

Once we get out to the gym, I notice a small crowd of people sitting in the stands. My eyes scan to see if I can recognize anyone. I can see Oscar sitting in the top corner writing in a notebook, I don't understand why the tryouts have to be documented for the newspaper. My eyes move over to the gym doors where Maggie stands leaning in the doorway.

I lean over to Adrian and ask, "Why is Maggie here."

"I don't know," He shrugs, "Maybe she likes basketball."

"She hates basketball."

"... okay? Maybe she's just here to help Oscar with the paper? I've got no clue man."

Coach blows the whistle which means tryouts are beginning. Everyone gets split into two teams. Luckily, I have Adrian on my team, we work the best together.

Once Coach blows the whistle the game begins. I run down the court passing the ball to one of the newbies. I always like to make sure that I involve them, that way the Coach can see how they react and what type of talent they can give to the team. Plus, I don't want to be seen as a ball hogget like Jacob. God, I hope he doesn't make the team this year.

The kid I passed the ball to ends up getting a shot. I walk over to him and pat him on the back, "That shot will definitely get you in the eyes of the Coach."

I stop and stand beside Adrian, "Helping out the new guys again?" He asks.

"Well, I don't want to be a Jacob now do I?"

"That's fair."

After five more mini games Coach blows the whistle to call us all over. "I'll be posting who made the team on Monday out front of the office. If your name is there you made the team, if not, try again next year."

Everyone begins to head towards the locker room. Adrian and I stand at the back of the group, I look over to the gym doors to see Maggie still standing there.

"I can't believe Maggie stayed to watch the whole thing." I say.

"Maybe, she actually likes basketball now." Adrian suggests while pushing the locker room door open.

"Maggie normally doesn't change her mind if she doesn't like something… but what do I know it's been two years."

"You two dated right?" Adrian asks.

"Yeah, we started dating in the summer before grade nine and then broke up that November, two weeks before she left town." I explain as I pull my gym shirt over my head, "It was like a switch went off."

"What do you mean by a switch?" Adrian asks.

We walk out of the locker room and into the hallway.

"So, she just turned into the Maggie she is now?" Adrian asks.

"Basically, yeah. She told me she was never going to join her dad's gang, and then one day she came to school with a tattoo, was wearing all black and ignored me the whole day. Not to mention she became closed off, and aggressive. I wasn't even allowed to touch her anymore, then I got mad, we got into a fight, and she broke up with me."

"That sounds like it would have sucked." Adrian says.

"It did in the moment, but I'm over it. No more feelings there."

"Cool, well thanks for telling me all that. I'll see you at Kian's funeral on Sunday?" Adrian asks.

I nod as Adrian walks off down the hallway to the back parking lot. I make my way to the front where I parked my car this morning.

Once I get outside, I notice Maggie leaning up against my car.

"What are you doing?" I ask as I approach her.

She stands up straight with her hands in her pockets, "The tryouts were good, I bet you'll make the team." She smiles.

"Thanks?"

Maggie looks down at the ground and takes a deep breath, "I'm sorry for breaking your nose."

I stay silent until she looks up at me, "Thank you... I'm sorry for saying that you killed Kian... and for bringing up your brother. I deserved the punch."

"But not the whole break, and... I'm just sorry." Maggie takes a deep breath and shuffles her feet along the gravel.

"You seem uncomfortable saying sorry." I point out.

"I'm not... I just haven't said sorry to someone that I've cared about in a while, especially someone I've hurt in more ways than one." I take a deep breath as I stare at her, I know she's talking about the breakup, she did say something that was ruthless.

Maggie continues to shuffle her feet around on the ground, "I am really sorry, Conner. I'll explain my reasoning one day. And I regret hurting you, and I wish I never had to, but I can't take it back and I know that. I just hope you can forgive me eventually."

I nod, "I think I will be able to."

Maggie smiles, "Well, I'll let you get in your car now."

"Thank you." I chuckle as Maggie moves out of the way.

"Bye." She says before walking off towards her motorcycle.

I get into my car and watch as she drives out of the parking lot, I throw my bag into the passenger seat and follow the same way she left. The only difference is I'm going to my house.

It was nice of her to apologize to me. I didn't really understand what she was talking about near the end, but I guess it's like she said, she'll explain one day.

I get out of my car and head inside my house, "Conner, honey! Can you come here!" My mom's voice echoes through the house as I step inside.

My body tenses as I slip off my shoes and slowly walk towards the kitchen, I peek my head around the corner before fully walking in, "Is everything okay?"

"Come sit down." My dad says, his face is flat, normally I can read my dad's facial expressions, but this time there's nothing there.

I slowly walk over and sit down at the table, "Am I in trouble?"

"Very." My mom says.

My heartbeat speeds up. Did they go looking through my room after I left this morning? I swear I took everything out of my drawers and that it's all in my backpack, what would they have found?

"What did I do?"

"You got your university acceptance letter today!! You got a scholarship!" My mom smiles while placing the letter in front of me.

It takes a second until I fully register what she just told me, "Wait, what?!"

"You have a full ride that allows you to still do basketball!" My dad explains.

"Wait! This is amazing!!" I jump up from my chair and grab the letter, my eyes skim over it before stopping to look at my parents, "And why would you scare me like that I really thought I was in trouble."

"We knew it would get your attention." My mom explains.

I guess she's right, I normally never get in trouble. At least they didn't find anything in my room.

"Umm... I'm gonna go shower and then I'll come right back down."

"Good, because we're going to make celebration brownies." My mom smiles.

I leave the kitchen with a smile, but once I get to the bathroom my face drops. I turn on the shower and place my bag on the bathroom counter.

As I pull out the zip lock bag full of steroids and glance over to the bathroom door to make sure

I locked it. I turn towards the toilet and dump all the pills inside.

Even though I thought my parents found something in my room they didn't, but the worry is still there that it could happen someday, and now with this full scholarship, I can't get caught with these.

I take a deep breath before flushing them all down.

I watch as a chapter of my life closes, one that should have never been opened in the first place.

CHAPTER FIFTEEN

Ace Turner
Sunday, September 22nd, 9:25am

    This day has snuck up on me, I've been dreading it for the past couple of weeks. Not because it's my brother's funeral, I mean that too, but because of the fact that my mom is doing everything in her power to make it perfect.
    I've tried to tell her that *"No matter how many tissue boxes you get, people will still be a crying mess."* Honestly though, she has a tissue box for every seat and an extra one under the seats. I don't believe that many people will be crying other than family or close friends to Kian.
    The loud banging on my bedroom door wakes me up after snoozing my alarm for the tenth time. "Alec, wake up! Your uncle Ryan will be arriving soon, along with your aunt Lily."

I don't answer, all I do is roll over and face the wall. I hear my bedroom door creek open, "Alec Turner! You get up right now, it's 9:30!"

With that my body is sitting up, "Maybe if you called me by my real name I'd answer!" I yell to my mom.

She takes a step back out of my room, "Just get ready." She says before slamming the door.

New day.

Same Mom.

I slowly get out of my bed and walk over to the door; I place my ear up to it to listen.

"Can you call her Ace, for today at least, she is Ace now, Faith. Not Alec." I hear my dad say.

"I'll try."

A funeral, it's taken a funeral for her to finally try and call me Ace.

I move away from the door and walk over to my window to pull open the curtains. The sun shines right into my eyes, almost blinding me.

Last night when I was doing math homework my mom came into my room with Kian's old clothes. She told me that I had to wear them because I didn't own any black clothes that I could wear for today.

I stare down at the outfit draped over my desk chair. I am not wearing my brother's pants. Luckily for me I have a dark gray skirt that I bought when I first transitioned.

I change into the skirt and my brother's black button up shirt. I tuck the shirt into the skirt and sit down on my bed to pull on a pair of black socks and my bright yellow converse.

Stepping into the hallway my dad looks down at my shoes, "Ace, your shoes."

"What?" I ask looking down at them, "They're the only ones I have."

"Hold on." My dad walks away and when he comes back, he has a pair of his black dress shoes in hand, "I know you won't like these shoes, but at least they're black and will fit."

"Thanks, Dad."

I hope that my dad knows when I say thanks, I'm really thanking him for saving me from the wrath of mom, "Let's go wait downstairs for your aunt and uncle."

I follow my dad downstairs after changing into the new shoes. They do look good with the outfit; I must admit.

My aunt and uncle are from my dad's side of the family. My mom has an older brother who I've never met before. My mom told me that they had a falling out when she and my dad got married, I don't know the full story and I haven't really cared to ask.

A loud knock echoes from the front door into the kitchen, "I'll get it." My dad says.

"How was the ride up?" I hear my dad ask.

"Long." A female voice says, I'm assuming it's my aunt.

I turn to see my dad walk into the kitchen followed by my aunt and then my uncle. My mom gets up and greets them both with a hug.

"Hey kiddo." My uncle Ryan says as he rubs the top of my head messing up my hair.

"Hey." I say as I begin to fix my hair.

"How's the niece doing?" Aunt Lily asks.

"I'm good." I smile.

My aunt nods, "I wish we could see each other under better circumstances."

"Yeah..."

I've never been close with my aunt, she always liked Kian more. So, I bonded with my uncle. He was one of the first people I told about me changing my gender. He even helped me come up with name ideas, I didn't use any of the ones he picked. He said to use Alexandra, but it seemed to close to Alec, and I didn't want to be him anymore.

"What time does the service start?" Aunt Lily asks while turning towards my parents.

"10:30." My mom says.

My uncle sits down beside me, "How've you been?"

I shrug, "Good, I guess."

"I know it's hard, but it gets worse before it gets better, right?"

I nod, "Right."

My attention shifts to my dad, "We should probably get going it's ten now."

My aunt goes in the car with my parents, but I opt to go with my uncle. My uncle and I are the first to leave because my mom is slow, but in the long run it's a good thing.

"So, how's your mom holding up?" My uncle asks.

"Well, she's gotten more untight, not to mention she keeps calling me Alec." I explain. Sometimes I forget that he's my dad's brother when I say stuff like this, but then I try not to worry about it since he's not truly related to my mom, so he won't care that much.

"That sucks, but hey maybe she's trying right?"

"I don't really think so." I sigh.

My uncle rubs my shoulder as we turn the corner into the church parking lot. We got out of the car right as my parents and aunt pull up beside us.

We all walked over to the church together, everything had already been set up the night before by my mom. Kian's body was dropped off this morning though. That's so weird to think about, I'm burying my brother today.

I am glad that my mom decided on a closed casket since I'm being forced to stand beside it as everyone arrives. I don't think I'm prepared for everyone's sorry and morning faces.

At 10:30 people begin to arrive. I expect the whole town to show up, and I think my mom does too. Misthill is a very small town, if someone doesn't show up, I think we'd notice, but if everyone shows up than that means Kian's killer will be in the room.

I watch as people I recognize from school arrive, they're parents say something to mine before they walk away and take their seats. The past ten families have done that.

I watch as Conner walks into the church with his family. His parents go to talk to mine, but he walks straight over to me, "Hey."

"Hey." I reply.

"How you doin?" Conner asks.

"Better." I smile.

"I hope they find out who did this to him." Conner says.

I nod, "Me too."

It's weird to be talking to Conner, we only used to talk when him and Maggie were dating. I know he still hung out with Kian at school, but I never saw him around my house. I guess you could say we used to be friends, but I don't really know.

Conner smiles once more at me, glances towards the casket and walks away to sit with his parents.

I watch as Adrian and Oscar's families walk in together. I've never really talked to either of them, Adrian came near the end of grade nine or beginning of grade ten. I can't really remember; I never paid much attention. But Oscar became friends with him right away, I assume it's because he had no friends. I only talked to him sometimes in grade nine, but that was only when he would talk to Maggie randomly in the hallway or at parties.

"We're so sorry to hear about your brother." Oscar's Mom says.

I nod and smile as both of his parents go to sit down with Adrian's parents who have already found their seats.

"Are you okay?" Adrian asks.

"Yeah," I nod, "Thank you for asking."

"It's sad he's gone." Oscar smiles.

I nod, I never know how to act when people say stuff like that.

Adrian and Oscar walk away and go to sit with their parents. As they do I notice Jade walk into the church. Two younger girls stand on either side of her, they look like twins. I never knew Jade had siblings. But to be fair I don't know much about her. She's said hi to me a couple of times in the hallway and even started a conversation once, this was all since the back-to-school dance.

Each time she talks to me I can feel butterflies rising in my stomach, I don't understand it. I haven't liked her since grade eight, I don't understand why these feeling are coming back now.

Her parents talk to my parents as her and her siblings walk up to me, "Hey." Jade smiles.

"Hey."

I glance down to see the two girls hiding behind Jade's legs, "Who are these two?"

"Oh," Jade turns her head and looks behind her, "They're my sisters, the one with the bun is Jamey, and the one with hair down is Sam."

I lean to the side to see them better, "Well it's nice to meet both of you."

"You too." Sam whispers.

"Uh, how are you feeling, I know today is probably hard." Jade says as she glances towards the casket.

I take a deep breath, "I mean, as best as I can feel."

"Yeah, that makes sense."

"Can we sit now? My legs hurt." Jamey says, pulling on Jade's arm.

"Yes cookies," Jade replies before turning to look at me again. "See you after? Maybe?" I ask.

"Yeah." Jade nods with a smile before walking away to go and sit with her family.

A couple more people arrive before I notice Maggie and her dad walking through the door. Her dad looks exhausted, but I haven't seen him in a long time so maybe that's how he always looked, and I've just forgotten that.

I watch as Maggie and her dad sit down in one of the back seats. Neither of them say anything to each other, they just sit and wait. It's awkward to watch.

I stare at Maggie; it's hard knowing that she's back and that she's here at the funeral. It's hard knowing the reason that she left, and that she never talked to me about it.

My mom walks up to me, "*Ace*, it's time to sit."

I couldn't help, but smile. She called me Ace, "Okay."

I sit down in the first row beside my uncle. My mom stands at the front of the room with a podium in front of her, "Thank you all for coming,"

She takes a deep breath before continuing, "it means a lot."

"I think that these past weeks have been hard on everyone, not just my family. I don't believe that anyone expected something like this to happen in our town, especially to my son."

"He was perfect, he always did his best and always put a smile on everyone's faces, and never did anything to upset anyone."

My mom continues to talk about Kian and some random memories about him. She talked about the first time he ever went swimming and being honest there are much better memories than that one.

"This town is small, I know everyone in this room, everyone. And someone here killed my son." My mom chokes on her words, tears begin to form in her eyes as she glances back at the casket, "Who would do such a thing."

My dad quickly gets up from his seat and stands in front of my mom, "That will be all, thank you all for coming." I watch as my dad turns around and hugs my mom.

Everyone slowly gets up to leave the church. My aunt and uncle stand by the doors talking to people they used to know. I stand off to the side of the church, looking towards the road.

"Uh hey."

I turn to see Maggie walking up beside me.

"Hey."

"Sorry I didn't come and say hi before the reception."

"Oh, it's okay, you didn't have to say hi." I smile.

"I felt like I had to." Maggie smiles before looking down at the ground.

I stare at her, I shouldn't say anything. But I should have said something two years ago. I could have stopped her from leaving.

"Maggie."

She looks up at me, "Yeah."

I take a deep breath, "I know what happened."

"Ace you're gonna have to be more specific a lot of stuff has happened in the past couple of weeks." Maggie chuckles.

"With you and Kian, I know what happened."

Maggie's face drops, her shoulder becomes tense and she's no longer joking around with me, "I don't know what you mean." I watch as she fiddles with her fingers, pulling them back and forth, bending them up and down. I've known her long enough to know that's one thing she does when she's lying or nervous. Somethings don't change.

"Maggie-"

"This was a really nice service for Kian, but I have to go now." Maggie quickly walks away and hops onto her motorcycle.

I was about to walk after her when there was a tap on my shoulder. I spin around to see Jade, "Hey." I let out a deep breath I had been holding.

"Hey, that was a good service." Jade smiles.

"Was it really?" I ask knowing my mom's breakdown at the end wasn't the best.

"I was wondering if you maybe wanted to go to Dark Treasure?" Jade asks, completely dodging my question, "Maybe it'll make the day a little better."

I smile, "Yeah sure, like right now?"

"Yeah, if that works with you?" Jade smiles.

I nod, "It does."

Jade and I start to walk away from the church. I notice that Maggie hasn't left yet. She's sitting on her motorcycle. Staring at the ground.

Maybe I should have kept my mouth shut...

CHAPTER SIXTEEN

Jade Button
Sunday, September 22nd, 11:40am

  It was hard working up the nerve to ask Ace to go to the Cafe with me. It's not like I asked her on a date, I'm only trying to make her day better while also trying to get to know her better. So maybe in my mind it could be a date, but in hers it's probably not.
  I don't understand why I'm so nervous, I hardly get nervous. Normally I'm confident with these sorts of things. And to be honest with myself, I noticed Ace around school every once and a while and always thought she was cute, but I never had the courage to talk to her because normally no one wants to talk to people who are in the gang.

Not to mention no one at school really knows that I'm bisexual, so how do I even go about flirting with Ace. If that is what I'm trying to do.

"Are you good to walk there?" I ask.

Ace nods, "Oh yeah, it's not far."

I watch as Ace glances back towards Maggie, she's done that two times now and all Maggie is doing is sitting on her motorcycle.

"Is everything good with you and Maggie? I saw you two talking before I walked up."

"Uh yeah, I just said something I shouldn't have." Ace looks down at her hands, fiddling back and forth with her fingers.

"Well, everything will work itself out, I hope."

"Yeah, I hope so."

I don't know much about Maggie and Ace's relationship, I only got to know Maggie through the gang, and even then, I'm still not close to her. Plus, I've only started talking to Ace this year, I know nothing about her past. Especially her past with Maggie.

"If you don't mind me asking, why shouldn't you have brought up whatever you ended up saying? Did you have a crush on her a long time ago or something." I chuckle.

Ace giggles, "No I didn't, we were strictly best friends. It was just something I don't think I was supposed to know about, and I don't know if she's going to be mad that I'm only saying something about it now."

I feel my shoulder lower and become less tense, maybe I was a little nervous to hear Ace's answer. What would my reaction have been if she did have a crush on Maggie?

"That sounds tricky, I honestly don't know what to say."

Ace shrugs, "That's okay, you don't have to say anything. We don't even have to talk about it anymore."

"Okay." I nod.

Dark Treasure Cafe is empty except for one worker, I saw at the funeral, but she must have rushed over to work once it was done. I'm surprised that it's actually open.

"Hi, what can I get for you?"

"Just a black coffee for me." Ace smiles.

"I'll have a hot chocolate please." I smile.

Ace turns towards me, "Can I pay?"

"I asked you to come, so I'm paying." Before Ace even has a chance to respond I've placed 10 dollars down on the table.

Once Ace and I get our drinks we sit down at the table in the far corner.

"Thank you for paying." Ace smiles.

"Of course, I wasn't making you pay." I take a sip of my hot chocolate; I always forget how warm it is at first... I burnt my tongue.

"I've never seen anyone drink hot chocolate in September." Ace giggles.

"Hey! I drink hot chocolate during every time of the year, and it's almost October."

Ace smiles, "Okay, fine, that makes sense."

Ace turns to look out the window, I can't help, but notice that Ace's face is completely clear, no pimples, no random scratches or marks. I've noticed it before, but now I'm really noticing it. She looks beautiful.

She looks back over to me, "Your sisters are really cute by the way."

"Thanks."

"How old are they?" Ace asks as she moves to rest her chin in her hand.

"They're only eight."

"Really?! They look like they're ten." Ace says in shock.

"I know right, it's crazy. They're growing too fast, it's kind of scary."

"Why scary?"

I shrug, "Well in my mind they're still my two younger sisters and then within the blink of an eye they're going to be like 15."

"Oh yeah, that makes sense then." Ace smiles.

I lean forward on the table, "I have an idea."

"Okay?"

"Let's play 21 questions."

"Sure, but why?"

"Well, we know each other, but we don't *know* each other. The only thing I feel like I know about you is that you're an amazing singer."

"Oh, well thank you." Ace smiles, I can see her cheeks turn red, but I could be imagining it, "Who's going to ask the first question then?"

"Do you want to?" I ask.

"Sure um," Ace looks down at her drink as she bits her bottom lip, "Oh! If you were to only eat one sweet treat for the rest of your life, what would it be?"

"Chocolate chip cookies without a doubt." I smile.

"Really? Why?"

"Obviously because they're the superior cookie."

"Are you sure? Why not the rainbow chocolate chip cookies, now those are amazing." Ace laughs.

"They're okay, but chocolate chip cookies all the way."

Ace sighs, "Well I'd have the rainbow ones, but it's your turn to ask a question."

"Umm okay... You can only sing one song for the rest of your life, what would it be?"

"Runaway by Aurora." Ace answers.

"That was fast, am I allowed to ask why that song?"

"Yes."

I stare at Ace for a second waiting for the answer, "Okay, then why?" I chuckle.

Ace quickly shakes her head as if she realized I was waiting for an answer, "I can relate to all the words, not to mention it's a very peaceful song." She explains as I take a sip of my hot chocolate.

"I'll have to listen to it sometime then."

"Favourite tv show?" Ace asks.

"Teen wolf." I answer.

"Favourite movie?" I ask.

"Love, Simon." She answers.

I smile, "That's a good movie."

Ace and I begin to ask each other more questions, I find out that she doesn't have a favourite book, but if she were to have one it would be a romance novel.

I quickly flip my phone over to check the time, we've been here for over an hour. I swear that only ten minutes have passed.

"Okay I've got a question." Ace smiles.

"Okay?"

"Why did you join the Hunters gang?"

"Umm, well, I... I never felt like I belonged at home, I felt like an outsider where I live, if you don't know I do live on the wealthy side of town, not where the gang resigns."

"Wait really?! I- I didn't know that."

"Well now you know, but, um the gang helped me find a place where I could be myself and not have to worry about anything, they became more of my family than my actual family. Not that I don't love my sisters, they're awesome, but my mom she's kinda controlling."

"I know what you mean by that, my mom won't even call me Ace."

"Oh shit, I'm sorry to hear that."

"It's okay I deal with it, but I never thought that the gang could be like that, like a second family, or even a first family?"

"Well, they are family." I smile.

Ace smiles at me, "Well, it's your turn to ask a question now."

"How are you?"

"What?"

"Truthfully, how are you? With everything going on, has anyone actually asked you how you are, and have you answered truthfully? Because I would like to know how you are."

"I mean..." Ace pauses and looks out the window, it's started to rain out, "How is someone supposed to feel when their brother dies? Or should I say gets murdered."

"I wouldn't know."

Ace looks back over to me, "No one does, because no one expects it to happen, but then it does and everything gets flipped upside down and you have to start asking yourself questions, and.... I don't know how I'm feeling, I just know it hurts." Ace bits the bottom of her lip, I can tell she's trying to hold back tears.

I grab her hand, "I am so sorry. I can't imagine what you are going through," Ace nods, "But I want you to know that if you ever just need to talk, to spew out random words of emotions because you're sad or angry, or confused, that I will always be here, and I can always listen or give advice. Because I am literally never busy. I can't promise that I'm good at giving advice or comforting people, but I can always try."

A small smile tugs at the corner of Ace's mouth, "Thank you, that means a lot."

Ace and I stare into each other's eyes for what feels like forever, like two strings attaching together at one end, but then a loud blaring ringtone buzzes across the table.

"Uh, sorry that's probably my mom." Ace picks up her phone and places it to her ear, "Yeah.... Okay... Yes... Okay I'll be right home... Okay... Bye."

Ace places her phone back down on the table, "You have to go?"

"Yeah, I'm sorry. Dinner with my aunt and uncle."

"Don't be sorry at all, but I can walk you home, and the rain has slowed down a lot." I smile.

"Sure, I'd like." Ace smiles.

Ace and I walk down the middle of the street, cars hardly pass down here unless they're leaving or coming home.

"I didn't even notice it was dinner time." Ace laughs.

"I know, time went by fast. You had fun, right?"

Ace nods, "Lots of fun, it let me have a break from my mind for a while. Thank you."

"You're welcome, I'm really glad."

We begin to approach Ace's house, "I'll see you at school tomorrow?" Ace asks.

"You bet!" I smile.

Ace nods with a smile on her face as we both stop at the end of her driveway, "Okay, well great... yeah... bye." She quickly turns around and makes her way up her driveway.

"Have a good dinner!" I shout.

She turns around and smiles at me before opening her front door and walks inside.

I head back towards my house. I'm glad that hanging out made her day better. She looked so sad this morning, I'm glad I know her a little bit more now. And now I know I can make her smile.

CHAPTER SEVENTEEN

Maggie Snow
<u>Monday, September 23rd, 11:35am</u>

Timing is everything.
If you don't time something right, everything could go wrong, the same goes for not saying something the right way.
This is especially certain when trying to confront your dad for the reason behind him forging your mom's signature on a paper that sent your brother 1080 miles away.
I pace back and forth in the living room. School started three hours ago, and I never showed up. It would be lunch by this time. I couldn't bring myself to go to school today, not after everything that happened at the funeral. How am I expected to

look at her after she knew what happened and never said anything? *Just forget about it and don't bring it up.* You've done this before.

A small bit of me is wishing I went to school, not because I wanted to, but because it's 11:40 and my dad still isn't awake.

I stop pacing and walk into the kitchen, I grab a glass and fill it to the top with ice cold water. I move down the hallway to my dad's room, stopping in the doorway. I see him sprawled out in a starfish position snoring like a trucker. I walk over to him and pour the water all over his face.

He flings straight up shaking his head, "What!? What happened?!"

He turns to face me, "Why aren't you at school?" He asks as he runs his hand through his wet hair, "And why did you pour water on me?!"

"I need to talk to you."

My dad sits down on the couch with a towel draped around his neck. I throw the papers down onto the coffee table, "Why did you fake mom's signature?!"

I watch as he looks down at the papers for a couple of seconds not saying anything. His whole-body tenses, I swear he's sweating, but it could be the water dripping off his hair. He picks up the paper, it shakes in his hand, he takes his other hand, now holding the paper still with both, "Where- Where did you find these?"

"My closet. You think I just move out and you can shove all your shit in there and not expect me to find it!!"

"I never expected you to come back, Maggie. When you left you didn't even say goodbye, you just left a note and were gone."

I swallow the lump in my throat before kneeling down to the ground so I'm at eye level with my dad, "Why. Why did you fake it?"

"I can't-" He places the papers back down on the coffee table.

"Dad, please. I need to know why you thought this was a good idea, to send him away and to fake mom's signature."

My dad rubs his hands across his face and takes deep breath, "Your brother was dangerous, Maggie. Your mom couldn't see it, but I could, and I knew she wouldn't approve so I had to do it."

"I don't get it though, why did you have to send him so far away!? Why couldn't he have been closer so mom could have visited him! So, I! Could have visited him!"

"Like I said, your brother was dangerous, you may not remember because you were so young." My dad says calmly.

"No, he wasn't, it was my fault!"

"None of what happened was your fault, Maggie. You may not remember because you were six at the time, but he was dangerous, you have to believe that I did this for a good reason, Maggie."

I remember, I remember everything.

I stand up from the ground, "Stop saying my name like I am ten years old! I am seventeen and I should be allowed to know why! I don't understand your mindset as to why you thought this would be a good idea!!"

"You don't have to understand my mindset, but what you do have to do is get to school." My dad stands up from the couch and walks into the kitchen.

I grab the papers off the coffee table, "No! You cannot walk away from this conversation!" I shout as I follow him into the kitchen.

My dad turns around and slams his hands down on the table, "Just drop it, Maggie!! It doesn't matter!"

"You are hiding something from me because I know that Caleb was dangerous, I know that he could hurt people, I know all of that and all of it was my fault! So, what aren't you telling me!!"

He looks away from me, not meeting my eyes. As I got older the more, I realized I was like my dad. Stubborn, avoidant. Things that happened to me brought out those traits, some of the traits I never wanted.

"Is it about mom? Is it about the signature, is that why you're getting mad, I can see it on your face even if you're trying so hard not to yell at me."

He sits down at the table and buries his face into his arm, "Why did you have to do this today? Any other day would have been fine." He mumbles.

I sit down across from him and push the papers towards him, so they touch his arm. He looks up at them, "Your mom found these documents one day, and it's what led to our divorce."

"What?" I stare at my dad in silence waiting for him to say something else, but he doesn't, so I do.

"Did you not say sorry? Did she not know what Caleb was doing?"

"She knew, but she couldn't admit it to herself, she didn't want to believe that her son could do what he was doing. It turned into a big, long fight and it ended with our divorce." He explains.

"Did you ever say sorry?"

"I couldn't, because I was protecting you and your mom from a monster."

"But if you sent him somewhere closer you and mom could have still been together, she could have visited him."

"It's better that he's far away." My dad says flatly.

"It's better? Really dad! Caleb is in some fucking insane asylum!" I point my arm towards the door, "He's probably worse than he ever could have been because his family fucking abandoned him!!"

I stand up from the table waiting for him to say something, but nothing comes out, "I'm going on a walk."

I can sense the blood pooling through my veins as I walk down the driveway. I don't bother to get on my motorcycle and ride somewhere far away, I can't leave yet.

How could my dad hide something like this from me for so long, and not only my dad, my mom too. She had told me that things just weren't working out for them anymore, but now I know it's because of a fucking signature and my dad being unable to think of a different solution.

I approach the end of the street and turn towards a fire hydrant that's beside me. I take my foot and forcefully kick it.

"You know you could get arrested for that, right?" I turn around to see Conner walking up behind me.

"Only if I broke it."

Conner walks closer and takes out of one his earbuds, "Why aren't you at school? And why are you so sweaty?"

Conner places his hands on his hips and takes a deep breath, "I'm on a run, working out, and it was a half day today."

How did I not know it was a half day? It was probably said on the announcements, and I wasn't paying attention.

"You go on runs?"

"I've always gone on runs." Conner says.

I shrug, "Okay."

"Can I ask why you're kicking the fire hydrant?"

"It's been a rough day."

"Want to talk about it?" He asks.

I huff and sit down on the curb, "Not really."

"You sure?" Conner asks as he walks over and sits down on the curb, the fire hydrant in between us. "You do still have your *'I want to say what's on my mind, but I don't want to bother anyone'* Look." Conner mimics my voice.

"Shut up."

"Honestly though, do you want to talk about it?"

My apology in the parking lot on Friday must have worked, because I could never see Conner asking me if I wanted to talk, at least not this version of me.

I sigh, "I just brought up something that I shouldn't have, and I wish I could redo everything, because I fuck everything up."

"That sounds rough... But I've got no idea what you're talking about."

"It doesn't matter. I don't even want to talk about it."

"Then you don't have to." Conner says.

I slowly turn my head and look over to him, "Dude, you literally just wanted me to talk about it!! Don't pull that you can talk about it, but you don't have to talk about it, bullshit!"

Conner puts his hands up in defense, "You're right, I have no say in this. Just don't punch me."

I reach over the fire hydrant and punch Conner's arm.

"Hey! I said don't punch me." Conner laughs.

"At least it wasn't in the face this time."

Conner smiles at me, "I still see the old you."

"The old me?"

"Yeah, the always smiling, pastel colours, hair always in a ponytail. I still see her."

"Well, she's not really here anymore. She had to be buried to survive."

"What do you mean by that?"

"It's just a random quote I saw once. I like it, it- I just like it." I explain.

Conner nods, "Can I ask why you changed so much in the first place?"

I get up from the curb and begin to walk away. "Um! So, are you just gonna walk away and not going to tell me?!" Conner yells.

"Think about the quote and maybe you'll figure it out!!"

Mystic Glass is surprisingly crowded for this time of day. I notice Clark sitting at the bar once I walk in and make my way over to him.

"Hey!! Where were you today?" He asks.

"Half day, no point in showing up." I explain while sitting down beside him on one of the bar stoles.

Clark nods, "That makes sense."

Jade walks over to Clark and I from behind the bar. "You're working an early shift today." I point out.

"Yup... it sucks. Why does everyone in the gang like to get drunk early?"

"Because half of the people getting drunk early are old men in their 60's." I explain.

I don't know when Jade got a job here. It could have been before I left, but also in between the two years that I was gone. She could have even started working here two weeks ago. I don't care to ask though. I don't want to waste my time trying to become friends with her when I'm probably going to leave once I find out who killed Kian. Get my closer and go. I have no clue where yet. Maybe LA, visit Caleb.

"Want a drink?" Jade asks.

I do. I really do, but I know that once I start drinking, it might be hard to stop. Thanks for that dad.

"Just a glass of water."

"Coming right up!" Jade turns around and fills up a glass with water, she turns back around and places it down in front of me, "So did everything work out with Ace?"

"What?"

"Yesterday after the funeral I saw you two talking, she said she brought up something she shouldn't have... I just wanted to know if you two were good."

"We're fine... when did you two have time to talk?"

"After the funeral. We went to Dark Treasure." Jade explains.

"Ohhhh." Clark chimes in.

Jade rolls her eyes, "You don't have to act like we're in Elementary School, it's not the latest gossip or anything."

"You and Ace have been hanging out a lot recently." I say as I take a sip of my water.

Jade shrugs, "I guess, we hung out when doing the back-to-school dance, and we talk in school."

"Well, it sounds like you two went on a date yesterday."

"What? No, it wasn't a date we just were hanging out, I wanted to get her mind off everything." Jade explains.

"Well, that's a shame, she used to have a crush on you." I smirk.

"Wait really?" Jade stares at me, her eyes wide and her interest perked.

"Yeah, but if you two are just friends then nothing will really happen right?"

Jade nods, "Yeah... right... I'm going to go get orders from other people now."

Jade quickly walks away from Clark and I and over to a table in the far corner of the bar. Even if I don't want to be friends with Jade, at least I know I can make her squirm a little bit.

I turn to face Clark, "So want to hang out?"

"Can't I've got to get home." No matter how much I don't want to.

I get up from my chair stretching my back. "Oh okay. Have fun. See you at school tomorrow." Clark smiles.

"Yup." I nod as I walk away from him and out of the bar.

I get into my house and peer into the living room. My dad wasn't there, nor was he in the kitchen, but what did I really expect. When things get thrown at him, he runs... but always comes back.

Once I get to my room I sit down on my bed and run my fingers through my hair. I unzip my boots and as I do so I grab my knife. I lay down in my bed twirling the knife in my fingers.

"Did you ever say sorry?"

The twirling speeds up. The more I think, the faster it goes.

"I couldn't, because I was protecting you and your mom from a monster."

The knife stops mid twirl as I sit up and fling it towards the wall, watching as it smoothly glid into it.

I lay back down looking up at the ceiling.

Maybe everything would have been better if I never brought it up in the first place.

CHAPTER EIGHTEEN

Oscar Adams
Thursday September 26th, 2:10pm

Silence.
I hate it.
The word.
The non-existent sound.
Silence is worse than a noise.
The only thing that ever breaks the silence are the thoughts inside my head. Or in this case the slow ticking of the classroom clock.
Small beads of sweat sit on the back on my neck, making me nervous, which makes me sweat more and that makes me more nervous.
"Adams." Echoes into my ear as I stare forwards.
There it is again, "Adams."

I turn to my right to see Maggie and Adrian both staring down at me.

"You good bud?" Adrian asks, "You were out of it for basically the whole class."

"I was? I must be tired. Sorry." The lump in my throat finally goes down.

"It's all good, but you're still coming to help with the paper, right? We need to come up with next week's issue and do more Kian investigating." Adrian whispers the last part.

"You don't have too though." Maggie adds as she turns around, walking towards the door.

"No, I'm coming! I'll just meet you guys down there."

Adrian nods, "Sounds good."

I put my binder into my bag and fling it over my shoulder. I get up from my seat and rush into the hallway almost running into a group of people, "Sorry." I mumble as I hurry down the hallway.

I rush down the stairs through herds of people almost tripping on the last step. I reach the newspaper and calmly walk inside.

"You got down here fast." Maggie points out as she sits down at the table.

"Yup." I nod.

I place my bag down on the ground before sitting down beside Adrian and across from Maggie.

Adrian claps his hands together, "Okay! So, what's going to be in this next week's issue of the paper. Since we didn't get anything out on Monday for this week."

Maggie leans back in her chair swinging her feet up onto the table, "Well not much happened last week, but we could always write about how stupid it is to have a half day on a Monday."

"Yeah, it's pretty weird." I agree.

"That wouldn't give us much material though." Adrian adds.

Maggie nods, "I guess that makes sense, but what else would we write about."

I pull out a piece of paper and begin to jot down ideas.

"Does the school do anything for Halloween anymore, maybe we could write an early segment about it?" Maggie suggests.

"The only thing the school ever does is have students dress up, and half of the time only 20 students do." Adrian explains.

I tap the pen on the table, "We could do that and add in something about how more people should dress up and we could add in the basketball try out since that hasn't been added in and announce who made the team."

"Oh yeah, Adrian, did you make the team?" Maggie asks.

"Yeah."

"You don't seem excited about that."

Adrian shrugs, "It's just tiring, but we should diffidently do both of those so it's out by Monday."

I jot down the ideas onto the piece of paper.

Halloween

Basketball tryouts and team

"I also overheard a group of grade nine's talking about how they want semi formal to be before Christmas or around exams." Adrian says.

Maggie puts her feet back on the ground and leans forward onto the table resting her head on her hand, "We could do that and basketball? I don't think the Halloween thing is that important, not until closer at least, we need more to write about it."

Semi Formal

"What have you written down so far?" Maggie asks.

I pass the paper to Maggie. I watch as her eyes skim the paper before looking up at me, "Why the fuck does the I in semi have two dots? Is that how you're supposed to spell it?"

"Oh no, it's a habit of mine, I've done it since I was a kid, no clue why."

The back of my neck becomes increasingly itchy suddenly.

"Well, it looks cool." Maggie says as she passes me back the paper. I shift my shoulders trying to get the itch on my neck to go away without me touching it.

"Well should we get writing then?" Adrian asks.

"Yeah." I nod as I give in and begin to scratch the back of my neck.

While Maggie is working on the semi formal issue for the paper, Adrian and I are working on the basketball issue.

Adrian's fingers fly across the keyboard as he types out the notes I wrote about the tryouts.

When Maggie left two years ago Principal Galilean came and asked me if I wanted to take over The Loadstar Daily. I obviously said yes because it gave me time to stay out of the house for when my parents would be fighting, the fighting died down for a bit, but it's picking up again.

Writing has never been my strong suit so when Adrian came to school and wanted to join the paper as an extra activity it was a big weight lifted off my shoulders. We came up with a system for getting things done. He would write and I would tell him what to write and all the ideas. I was always the one to go around school and find out things we could put into the paper. Adrian pointed out to me that we shouldn't turn the school paper into a gossip thing because that could get us suspended for sharing people's secrets. I agreed with him, but I still remember all the secrets that everyone told me, or that I overheard.

"Fuck!"

Adrian and I slowly look over to Maggie.

"Are you okay?" Adrian asks.

"Yeah.... sorry. I took a break from writing, and I was playing a snake game and I just lost... so... yeah." Maggie gives us an awkward thumbs up before turning back to look at her computer.

Adrian looks over to me, "I finished the issue so I'm going to print it and go get it."

"Okay perfect!"

Adrian and I are the perfect team. We complement each other perfectly. I hope that never goes away, I don't know what I'd do.

Adrian gets up and walks out of the paper. Now Maggie and I are left alone, the silence begins to creep in, but I interrupt it, "So, Maggie. How's life?"

Maggie looks over to me, "It's been better."

I know that as soon as she says that my face fills with concern, "Why do you say that?"

"I mean, when isn't my life bad? Sure, good things happen throughout a day, but as a whole it's usually bad. But it's getting better." Maggie explains.

"When was it fully good?" I ask.

Maggie sighs, "I honestly have no clue."

"How more can I help?"

"You don't have to help me, Adams. I can figure it all out on my own. But how's life for you?"

"It's okay."

"And why is that?"

"Parents. They've been fighting."

"Is that why you're so tired?" Maggie asks.

I shrug, "I guess, yeah."

"It'll be worse before it gets better, trust me, my parents are divorced. But it will get better." Maggie smiles.

I nod, "I trust you."

Adrian walks back into the room with a stack full of papers, "Adrian, I just printed mine can you get it for me?" Maggie asks.

"Why didn't you text me that when I was still down there?" Adrian asks as he sets down all the papers onto the table.

"One because I don't have your number, two I don't have an iPhone, I have a flip phone."

"You have a flip phone?!" Adrian and I both say in shock.

"Yes, I know it's crazy, but can you just go get it for me?" Maggie asks.

"I'll go get it." I smile.

I make my way back down the hallway, a stack of papers in my arms. I've never liked the school hallway after hours, it's quiet and you can hear everything, mostly your own footsteps. It feels like you're stuck in a horror movie.

"That was fast." Adrian says as I walk back into the room.

"I tried to be; we want to get this paper together as fast as possible." I smile as I place the papers onto the table.

I feel a slight buzz in my back pocket, I reach back and pull out my phone to see a text from my mom asking me to come home.

"I have to get home. Can you two manage getting the papers together?" I question.

Adrian nods, "We've got it all under control."

"Okay!!" I grab my bag off the floor, "See you two tomorrow." I say as I exit the room and make my way out of the school.

Adrian gave me a ride to school today like he normally does, so that means I have to walk home since he's not leaving yet.

Over the past week it's been easy to tell that it's becoming fall, some trees have slowly begun to change colour and it's windier out.

I stop and look to my left and right before crossing the street. Misthill hardly has any cars driving on the street, but I still want to be cautious because the time that I don't look, will be the time I get hit.

My house isn't far from the school, it's a manageable walk, but it doesn't mean that I enjoy it. I don't know why, but I decided to walk the long way home today. Maybe I'm trying to avoid my parents for as long as possible or maybe I wanted to go for a walk.

My House is big, smaller compared to the others on the street. Along with size it's completely different in style, the whole house is made from brick with a modern white porch. Most of the houses on the street have gone fully modern, but my mom insisted on keeping the vintage looking brick.

"I'm home!" I shout as I walk inside.

"Good," My mom peeks her head out from the kitchen, "Dinner is about to be ready, come sit."

I take my shoes off by the door and walk into the kitchen placing my bag down beside the fridge.

"How was your day?" My mom asks as I walk over to the cupboard to grab out the glasses.

"Normal." I walk over to the table and place the glasses down beside the plates. As my mom has been saying since I was 8, *"You're our little glass man."*, it's my one job in the house, set out the glasses before any meal.

My dad walks into the kitchen, "Is dinner almost ready?"

"Yes." My mom says flatly.

I can feel the tension bouncing off them. I slowly sit down in my seat at the table and stay quiet.

After a couple of minutes my dad comes and sits down at the farthest end of the table. My mom walks over and places all the food down at the table, "Dig in." She smiles as she sits down at the other end of the table across from my dad.

We all start to plate our food. I'm the first to take a bite.

"So, how was the school paper today?" My dad asks as he plops a pile of potatoes onto his plate.

"It was good, Adrian and I are still getting used to having Maggie around, but it's good because we're getting things done faster." I explain.

"Maggie's that girl that randomly left town, right?" My dad asks.

"Uh, yeah. But she's back now." I always forget that more people know that Maggie left town. I forget how small Misthill is sometimes.

I take a bite of the chicken on my plate. The strong taste of salt quickly attacks my tongue and I instantly regret adding so much of it.

"The chicken is too dry." My dad says.

I look up at him.

"Maybe add some salt." I suggest.

"I did. It's too dry."

"Well maybe make it yourself next time." My mom says.

"I was working on important business tonight, which I told you about. I also said I would help you cook dinner, but you went off and did it all yourself." My dad scowls.

I slowly start to slide down my chair.

"We'll I was getting hungry and didn't want to interrupt you and your, *'Important work'*." My mom says in air quotations.

"Are you just angry because I'm the only one in the family that has a job that can provide for us?"

He's clearly forgotten that I have a job.

"Oscar has a job, not just you. And just because I haven't had a job in the last two months doesn't mean I'm not trying to find a new one."

"Well, I don't see you trying hard enough."

"Shut up!" I yell.

My parents look over to me.

"Both of you have been nonstop fighting since the beginning of summer and you guys hate each other so why don't you just get divorced already and end this misery for all of us!"

I look at both of them before getting up from the table and hurrying down the hallway to my room.

The door slams shut behind me as I make my way to sit on my bed. I bury my face in my hands as I hear my door creak open, "Hey-"

"Get out."

"I just want to talk to you about everything going on." My dad says as he steps into my room.

"Everything going on?" I stand up from my bed, "I shouldn't be the one you're talking to, dad! You should be talking to mom! Asking how she feels, trying to fix things!! Because I'm not your wife, and in the long run... I don't really care anymore; I just want you two to stop fighting!"

"Oscar-"

"Get out." I turn around and walk over to my desk, I glance back to see my dad still standing in my room, "Get out!"

I turn back around.

The door shuts behind me.

And the silence fills my ears once more.

CHAPTER NINETEEN

Adrian Fisher
Thursday, September 26th, 4:35pm

      Oscar left a little while ago. He didn't explain why he had to get home. I'm assuming he had to leave for dinner, but normally he would tell me. Maybe he didn't say anything because Maggie is here?
      Sometimes I think he likes Maggie, even though I know that he's gay, but other times he seems uncomfortable around her.
      Maggie and I began to print and staple all the papers together so they could be on the stands by Monday.
      "My hand is cramping." Maggie declares as she dropped the stapler onto the table and turns towards what we've dubbed the murder board.

"Mine is too." I say as I place my stapler onto the table and lean up against the wall behind me.

I stare at Maggie's back; her hair has grown since the first time I met her. I remember that it was just past her shoulders when we sat in the cafe talking for the first time, but now it's lower on her back and wavier than before.

"So... I was talking to Conner last week and he told me you were never going to join the gang."

She turns to look at me, "Yeah."

"Can I ask why you joined?"

She turns to fully face me, "Things just change, that's why. Conner couldn't keep with that change."

I nod slowly, "Oookay."

A small part of me doesn't want to believe her, but the other part of me wants to believe that she's telling the truth.

Maggie turns back around to face the murder board. I walk around the table and stand in front of her crossing my arms. Maybe if I were to dig deeper, I'd get to know if she's telling me the truth or not. I don't exactly know why I want to know so badly, maybe it's as Maggie said in the cafe. *I like the mystery*, maybe I like the mystery too, maybe Maggie is that mystery.

I go to speak, but Maggie cuts me off, "How did you do on the science test yesterday?"

"Umm, I don't know... I think I failed." I say honestly.

"You don't think you passed at all?"

"Nope." I shake my head.

Maggie shrugs, "Well if it means anything, I think you *just* passed, almost failed, but still passed."

"Thanks?"

I don't feel much better about the test than I had before. It doesn't give me much hope.

Maggie turns around and goes back to stapling papers together.

"Did Oscar seem different today? Less talkative?"

Maggie shrugs, "I don't really pay much attention to Adams, but he did tell me when you were gone that his parents have been fighting. It's probably why he said he was so tired and not as talkative today."

"He told you that his parents are fighting?" I ask. Oscar doesn't tell many people about what's going on in his life. He hardly told me anything when we became friends until I saw him crying in the bathroom one day and he finally opened to me about a lot going on in his life.

"Yeah."

"Oh," I walk around to the other side of the table and begin to staple papers together, "I wouldn't have expected him to tell you that."

"People can surprise you." Maggie says while taking a quick glance up at me.

She places the stapler back onto the table and looks up at me.

"Yes...?"

"Can I see your book?"

"What?"

Maggie pointed to the small table behind me where my leather notebook sits, "Your notebook, the leather one. Can I see it?"

"Um. What? No. Why?"

She shrugs, "Why not?"

Maggie slowly makes her way around the table and goes to reach for the book, but I grab it before her. Holding it close to my chest, "No."

"Why?! What are you hiding in that secretive book of yours?" Maggie asks taking a step closer to me, squinting her eyes.

"Why did the conversation turn to this? And nothing important, it's my private book, no one looks in it."

Maggie avoids my question, "I basically know what's in it because when we first met you said there were poems and I want to read one."

"No." The book is still held close to my chest.

"Come on."

"It's not happening."

"I just want to read one, you can pick it for me, and I promise I won't flip any pages." Maggie smiles, one of the most manipulative sneaky smiles I've ever seen on her face.

"I wouldn't ask to read through your private notebook."

"How do you know I have a private notebook?"

I shrug, "I don't know I was just using it as an example, but since you do have one would you let me look through it?"

"No. Not unless I picked."

"Exactly!"

"But I said you could pick what I read!" She shouts with astonishment; I glance down to see her fist beginning to clench.

"It's not happening." I say calmly.

She turns and walks back to her side of the table, "You suck."

"You're just saying that because you didn't get your way." I say as I set my notebook back down on the table.

"What?"

"People talk, Maggie, and to be ~~far~~ fair when you get mad you punch people. I saw you clench your fist just a second ago... you were thinking of punching me. It's obvious, but for some reason you didn't and instead you said a 10-year old's insult."

"Don't believe what everyone says Adrian, only believe what you know, and you still don't know me. But yes, I have punched people, but I don't punch people because I don't get my way. And frankly you do suck because anyone would have shown me that book, but you didn't so it shows you have something to hide." Maggie shrugs.

"Who isn't hiding something? You admitted to that yourself by not showing me your book." I point out.

"I only didn't show you because everything in my book is the same, they aren't poems, news articles, book plots. It's all my thoughts."

"Whereas if someone were to find your notebook laying around and read one of your poems, they would have no clue what it was about. Like I said you still don't know me, and I still don't really know you. The only thing you may know about me is that I can be a stubborn bitch, and I'm fine admitting that." I chuckle at Maggie's words, "So you can sue me for just trying to get to know you a little better."

There's a minute of silence. I feel like a dick for some reason. But I have all the right to not let her read my poems. Besides I haven't wrote any good ones in a while.

"I'm going to get the rest of the papers from the printer." Maggie says before leaving the room.

Somehow this girl can make me regret everything I say yet make me want to say it all again. Her words wrap around my mind, I get lost in thought and I can't comprehend where I am anymore. Every time I've said something she doesn't understand or doesn't necessarily like, I get a glimpse into who she truly is. I strongly believe this Maggie is a front, but I don't know for what.

Everyone keeps saying to me that one day she just came to school, and she was a different person almost, and then within a month she had left. Something must have happened. Things sometimes can't just change without a reason.

I try to think about something else by shifting my focus to the murder board. The same constant thought running through my head.
Who would want to kill Kian?
Who would want to kill Kian?
Who would want to kill Kian?
Who would want to kill Kian?
Why would someone kill Kian?
Why would someone kill Kian?
Maggie walks back into the room with a stack of papers in hand.
"What if it was for power?"
"What was for power?" Maggie asks, placing the papers down on the table.
"Killing Kian, what if someone wanted power."
Maggie stares at me confused, "What are you getting at?"
"You said it yourself that everyone knew who Kian was, he talked to everyone and was nice to everyone. Star basketball player, always center of attention, always getting good grade-"
"He could have been faking his grades, I mean it did help you fake yours." Maggie adds.
"That is a possibility, but when you think about it, Kian had all the power in the town, everyone knew him. If you take him out of the equation the power is up in the air for anyone to take. So, what if someone killed him because they wanted the attention and power Kian had."
"That's very likely." Maggie says as she walks over to her bag, she pulls out her notebook.

She rips out a piece of paper quickly scribbling something down on it.

"What are you writing?"

"Power with a question mark because we don't fully know, it's just a theory. Like most of this murder board."

Maggie grabs a thumb tack and pins the piece of paper onto the board right above the photo of Kian from the newspaper and beside the word pocketknife.

She turns back to look at me, "Three things on the board, we should think about possible killers, maybe tomorrow? Because right now we should finish these papers."

I pull out my phone and look down at the time, "Oh yeah, I guess it is almost six, we should hurry this us." I smile.

Right as I'm about to put my phone back in my pocket it buzzes with a text from my mom, *where are you?* I quickly type back that I'll be home soon.

My Mom isn't much of a worrier, but I think she's been more worried since everything happened with Kian. And I don't blame her, I'd be worried to.

Maggie waits down the hallway as I lock the newspaper's door. I walk up to her, and we begin to walk down the hall together.

It's silent, neither of us saying a word. I know why I'm not talking, it's because I'm tired all of a sudden. But I wonder why she isn't talking, maybe she's tired too?

We get outside the school, "I'll see you tomorrow?" Maggie asks, turning towards me.

"Yeah, unless I get murdered. Then no." I chuckle.

"Some friendly advice, don't get murdered." Maggie smiles. I'm glad she knew I was joking.

"Bye." Maggie says before walking towards her motorcycle.

Once Maggie has left the parking lot I make my way over to my car, she had already said goodbye and I thought it would be awkward if we we're to both walked in the same direction.

I get in my car and lean my head up against the headrest.

My brain begins to settle, and the thoughts begin to slow. This girl makes me think way too much, but I can't stop thinking about her.

CHAPTER TWENTY

Oscar Adams
Tuesday, October 1st, 2:15pm

The stairs flood with students as Maggie, Adrian and I try to make our way downstairs. It's as if at the end of the day everyone is trying to claw their way outside.

Once we reach the bottom of the stairs we shift to stand under the staircase. The sound of everyone making their way down echoes like a herd of elephants.

"So, we'll be in the paper, if you finish work early you should come by." Adrian says, "I think we'll be there for a while."

"I doubt I'll finish up work early, but if I do, I'll come. Especially if Frances is working today, that guy is always in my space."

"Who's Frances?" Maggie asks.

"A guy at my work, he's always trying to flirt with me." I explain.

Maggie shrugs, "At least someone is trying to get with you, anyway," She turns to face Adrian, "I'll meet you down at the paper."

Maggie walks into the crowd of students and vanishes. I watch as Adrian stares in the distance, his cheeks begin to fill with a small blush colour before turning back to me. The colour falling from his cheeks.

"What?" He asks, realizing the way I'm staring at him.

"You're blushing, you like her."

"What no! I've told you this, bud, we're just friends. Even if that."

"You were staring at her all of science class, and even when we got our tests handed back you showed her your grade."

"And that's weird?" Adrian asks, clearly puzzled by what I'm saying.

"It's weird because that's immediately what you did, and normally you hide any science quizzes." I explain.

Adrian shrugs, "Well she helped me study, and besides you have to get to work, and I have to get to the paper."

Adrian begins to walk off into the crowd, "Oh yes! Of course! Go enjoy the time with a girl who could punch you at any second!! I've warned you!" I shout as he disappears into the crowd.

I awkwardly look around before walking outside.

Even with it only being the first of October the wind is sharp and cold, and the trees have already begun to change colours. Bright oranges and yellow line the streets with only small hints of green left.

Mother nature does have a way of making some of the coldest months the most beautiful.

I walk past Dark Treasure Cafe and cut through the parking lot to go in the back doors of Club Azure.

The back room is bright, there's around 10 to 15 lockers with every employee's name on it. I clock in and get into my work shirt. A black top with the word Azure embroidered onto it, we're supposed to wear name tags, but I don't wear mine for privacy purposes. I don't like the thought of random people who hardly come to the club knowing my name.

I walk out into the main area. My eyes take a few moments to adjust to the lighting change.

The windows are tinted so no one can see inside, and the lights are dimmed to the lowest setting. The main light source for the whole club is the endless supply of neon lights, all flashing different colours of blue, red, green and purple.

When I first started working here over a year ago some guy came in not expecting there to be so many flashing lights. It turns out he was epileptic and ended up having a seizure.

Now the door and all the windows have a sign on them warning people about the flashing lights. I honestly don't know why they didn't have signs up before.

"Hello, Oscar." I slowly turn my head to see Frances standing beside me, the lights bouncing off his blond hair.

"Hi... Frances."

"Cleaning the glasses?"

I glance down to the wine glass in my hand, "That is what I am doing."

I take a small step to my right realizing how closer he is to me.

"Do you need help?"

I shake my head, "No, I think I'm good. Do you have drinks to serve?"

"Already served them all."

I glance over Frances's shoulder seeing someone walk through the doors, "Well looks like someone new just entered, I would go get their drink order."

Frances turns to see the person sitting down, "I guess you are correct. But I will talk to you later." He twiddles his fingers as he walks away.

I let out a breath I had been holding. It's not that I don't like Frances, he's a very nice guy, just a little overbearing and in my face.

I go back to cleaning the wine glass in my hand. My Job mostly consists of me cleaning. Cleaning the glasses, cleaning the tables, cleaning the floor if some drunk old lady spills five separate drinks five separate times... that was a bad day.

For most of the day I'm listening to people's conversations.

I turn to clean the back counter when two girls walk up to the bar and sit down, getting served by another employee.

"So, what ended up happening with all the Sharon's?" One of the girls asks, her voice is extremely high pitched.

"She stood me up, like all of them do." The other girl replies.

"You need to delete Tinder, you've only matched with girls named Sharon, and all *five* of them have stood you up."

Five Sharon's!! Did this girl put *only* looking for Sharon's in her description?

"You know what! You're right! I'll do it right now."

I turn and quickly walk away to go and clean a table that a group of middle-aged women just left.

I begin to whip down the table and listen in to a conversation that is beginning behind me.

"How've you been since everything happened?" A guy asks.

"I mean, his family didn't even know about *us*, about *him*." Another guy says.

"It must suck."

"It does, and I never got to say goodbye before he died."

Are they talking about Kian?

I slow my whipping down of the table, "Have you talked to the cops? Maybe something you know could help them find out what happened."

They must be talking about Kian... Right?

"Kian would have wanted you to help find out who did this to him."

Holy shit they are talking about Kian.

I quickly finish cleaning the table and begin to make my way over to the door without being noticed.

"And where are you sneaking off to?" Frances asks, walking up behind me.

"Not the time, Frances, sorry."

"Where are you going?" He asks, crossing his arms.

"I'll be right back, please don't say anything."

Frances stares at me, tilting up his head, "I want something in return."

"Okay, okay, what?"

"A date. Tomorrow night."

"Okay fine."

"I'll see you here at seven tomorrow." Frances says quickly before I dart out the door.

I run across the street, a car slams it's brakes as it almost hits me. The driver blaring their horn, "Sorry!" I shout as I continue running towards the school.

As I'm halfway to the school it begins to rain out. I sprint through the school parking lot and into the school. As I'm making my way down the hallway I almost slip as I'm turning a corner because of how wet my shoes are.

I stop in the doorway of the paper, both Maggie and Adrian turn to stare at me, "Hey bud, you're here! Did you run or something?"

"He was gay."

"Who was?" Maggie asks.

"Kian... Kian was gay." I pant and lean up against the doorway sliding down to the floor as they both stare at me.

CHAPTER TWENTY-ONE

Maggie Snow
Tuesday, October 1st, 4:40pm

     I lean up against the edge of the window seal as Adrian stares intensely at the murder board. "Okay, who would want all the power in the school?" Adrian asks, "Who would gain from that?"
     "Well, first off we shouldn't just think of people in the school."
     "But those are the people who technically were the closest to him." Adrian explains.
     I shrug, "Yeah... I guess... maybe Jessica, she seems like she'd want to be able to control things."
     "Eh, I don't think Jessica would have the guts to do something like that... she's too-"

"Girly, stuck up, already butts her way into everyone's business so why would she need to even more."

"Yeah, exactly that." Adrian chuckles.

I've been enjoying Adrian's company a lot more recently; in some sense I feel like he's bringing out a happier side of me.

A loud crash comes from the door, Adrian and I both look over to see Adams now standing there out of breath.

"Hey bud, you're here! Did you run or something?" Adrian asks.

"He was gay."

I blink, "Who was?"

"Kian... Kian was gay." Adams slides down the door frame out of breath.

Adrian and I both make our way over to him and look down.

"What do you mean Kian was gay?" Adrian asks.

Adrian helps Adams up from the ground and into a chair, "Two guys were talking, and it seemed like one of the guys dated Kian."

"That doesn't mean he's gay. I've seen him with girl, if anything he's bisexual." I point out.

"I'd rather not assume a dead guy's sexuality; I feel like that's not a correct thing to do." Adrian says, looking over to me.

"It doesn't matter right now," Adams says, "What matters is we need to talk to this guy because he could give us information. Maybe this guy even killed Kian, we don't know."

"Like talk to him right now?" Adrian asks.

I quickly scribble bisexual onto the piece of paper and pin it onto the board before flipping it around so no one can see.

"These guys may not be there another time so let go!" Adams says and before I know it, he's on his feet and out the door.

"Bud, we don't have to rush!" Adrian calls after him as he leaves the newspaper.

I glance at Adrian running his hand through his hair before grabbing my bag from the table and following them both.

My mind takes minutes to wrap around everything Adams just said. If Kian had a boyfriend, does that mean he'd know about Kian's past? How horrible he was?

Once we reach outside the rain began to pour down harder than it had before, "I'll take my motorcycle and meet you two there."

Adrian and Adams run towards Adrian's car, "Wait where am I going! Adams, where do you work?!"

"Club Azure!" He shouts as him and Adrian get into the car.

I make my way over to my motorcycle. The seat is covered in water, I take my hand and brush off as much as I can before sitting down. The worst thing to have while on a motorcycle is a wet ass.

We follow Adams into the bar, "Those two guys right over there." Adams discreetly points in their direction, I glance over to see two boys maybe a bit older than us, "I have to get back to work, but I'll be listening nearby."

Adrian turns to face me, "How are we going to approach them? I don't think we can just walk up and be like *hey do you know Kian, we're teens at a high school trying to solve his murder.*"

I look over to the two guys and then back at Adrian, "I have an idea, it may be a long shot. But can I see your phone?"

"Do I get to know this idea and why it involves my phone?"

"Do you trust me?" I ask.

Adrian nods, "Okay, then follow my lead."

Adrian hands me his phone after I make him unlock it. I make my way over to their table with Adrian following behind.

They both look up at us, "Hi, I'm Gala," I look over to Adrian and quickly back over to the two boys, "And this is Freddy, we're currently interning at the Police station and we were told by a witness that they saw Kian Turner come here a couple days before he disappeared and we were wondering if you two are regulars and if you could maybe answer a few questions for us."

The two boys look over to each other, "Uh shouldn't an officer be here with you?" The red-haired boy asked.

"They're doing things a bit different nowadays... So do you mind if we ask a few questions?"

"Sure, take a seat, we do come here regularly." The black-haired boy says.

Once Adrian and I are sitting down I take out his phone and open the voice recording app, "Is it alright if we record everything?"

They both nod and I press the record button.

"So, what are your names?" I question.

"I'm Cal." The boy with the black hair says, "That's Biff." He says pointing to his red-haired friend.

"Are those fake names?" Adrian asks.

"No short forms." Biff says.

I take a deep breath, "Did either of you know Kian personally?"

"I didn't, but Cal did." Biff says, pointing in Cal's direction.

I turn my whole body towards Cal, "Were you two friends? Or just small run-ins with each other?"

Cal's eyes dart back and forth between Adrian and I, "Not exactly."

"What does that mean?" Adrian asks.

"He was... um... he was my boyfriend."

"So, Kian was gay." I exclaim.

"No bisexual, he dated girls in the past." Cal explains.

I rub the thumb on my left hand and clear my throat, "Did his family know about you two?"

"No, no. He wasn't ready to tell them yet, he was mainly worried about his mom knowing, his sister might have known, but I don't fully know."

"Did you ever meet his sister?" Adrian asks.

He shakes his head, "No, I just heard a lot about her, I've seen photos of her, I said a few words to her at the funeral, but she doesn't know who I am."

I glance over to Adrian before he speaks, "When did you two start dating?"

"About five months ago, yeah." Cal nods as if he was confirming what he said was correct.

"You said he has relationships with girls, did he ever say who, exactly?" I question.

"He didn't really talk about them much, when we first met, he did talk about this one girl who would always play hard to get, eventually she ended up leaving or something." Cal explains.

A lump settles in my throat, please don't be telling me he twisted things.

"Do you have a name? Or can you describe what this girl looked like?" Adrian asks.

"I don't know what she looks like, but I do know her first name." Cal stops and looks at the both of us.

"Okay, what is it?" Adrian asks, glancing over to me and back at Cal.

My heartbeat becomes unsteady, slowing down and speeding up. I can no longer tell how loud my breathing is.

"Her name was Maggie, if I remember correctly, the conversation happened a while ago."

Adrian glances towards me trying not to make his confusion obvious. I've never met another Maggie in this town, and I don't think Adrian has either.

My whole body is rigid, I don't know if I can breathe, "He said that... she would play hard to get? Did he say anything else?"

"He said she was always showing off, trying to get his attention and when she had it, she would just push him away. He said that kind of stuff happened at a party once."

I abruptly push away from the table and stand up. I press the stop button on the recording and pass the phone to Adrian, "I have to get going, just remembered something- uh my partner here will finish the interviews.... Goodbye."

I practically run outside, the rain pouring down harder than before. I don't whip off the seat on my motorcycle before getting on and I don't bother to put on my helmet, I just want to be home.

I get inside my house and kick off my boots.

"Finally, you're hom-"

"Not the time dad!" I shout as I hurry down the hallway to my bedroom. I slam the door shut behind me and fall to the ground.

My whole body begins to shake, I bring my knees close to my chest and wrap my arms around them. I try to calm my breathing, but nothing seems to work.

Don't let it in, you don't have to think about it. I tell myself.

A light knock on my door echoes into my room, "Mags?"

I don't reply, I can't reply, "Are you okay? Did something happen?"

I hold my knees closer to my chest, "I'll be in the living room if you need to talk."

I listen as my dad walks back down the hallway.

I take in a deep breath, trying to calm myself.

Why did I have to know?
Why did I have to ask?
Why.
Why.
Why.
Why.
Why.
Why.

I rest my forehead on my knees, I stare down at the zipper on my pants trying to stay focused. Trying to distract myself from the endless overflowing thoughts rushing through my mind.

Finally, a tear hits my leg, and I can't hold it back anymore. They flow from my eyes, all the emotions I've been trying to keep hidden for two years flow out. The night I've been trying to suppress moves to the front of my mind, playing on repeat in my head, never stopping, always going. I'm stuck. I don't want to be stuck, but I'm stuck.

I don't know how to handle this.

CHAPTER TWENTY-TWO

Maggie Snow
<u>Wednesday, October 2nd, 7:30am</u>

I only got an hour of sleep last night.
I didn't get any sleep last night.
It seems harder to remember this time around, like a distant memory that didn't really happen. But I know it happened, I can still feel it.
I slowly walk out of my room and into the bathroom.
I didn't even go into my room, I slept in the bathtub and cried.
I splash cold water on my face, I look up at myself no anger runs through my veins, just pain and hurt. Anguish.

When I splashed my face and looked up at myself, I was angry, angry at everything.

"I got this." I mumble to myself. "I got this." I say again before leaving the bathroom to the kitchen.

"Morning." My dad smiles.

"Morning." I force a smile back as I walk over to the kettle. My whole body is still shaking.

I try to put my focus on the boiling water, the loud rumbling that's echoing in front of me. I rub my hand over my face not being able to focus.

"Are you okay, Mags? I thought I heard you crying last night."

I turn to face my dad, "I wasn't crying, I'm fine. I'm always fine."

"Why were you in the bathroom all night? Were you crying?"

"I wasn't crying, I never cry."

"Are you sure? You know you can always talk to m-"

"Thank you, dad." I smile, "But I'm fine, promise, I'm just gonna get to school."

I walk past him and over to the front door, "You don't want your tea?"

"Uh no. I don't even know why I turned the kettle on in the first place.... I should get going."

"Bye." My dad says before I close the front door behind me.

The air is cold and it's foggy. I should have brought my jacket.

The air was musty, everything felt like it was touching me, and I just wanted to punch something.

I sit down on my motorcycle and don't move; I stare down at the meter for what feels like two hours when in reality it was only two seconds. I finally got enough energy to start the engine and ride off to school.

I had to walk, it was long, I hugged myself my whole way to school.

Once I arrive at school, I make my way inside. I'm earlier than I normally am so I know that I can take my time. I round the corner and stop as I reach the office. I stare towards the lockers near one of the girl's bathrooms.

"Why'd you do that?" My voice hissed as I approached Kian, he looked over to some guys on the basketball team waving them off.

"Do what?" Kian smirked when looking back at me.

"You know what I'm talking about." I was shaking again.

"Be more specific, Maggie, for once in your life." Kian's voice was aggressive.

"You- you-"

"I touched you." Kian said while placing his hand on my shoulder, I flinched away.

"Was it really that bad?"

"You forced- You-" My voice broke off, "I'll tell people what you did."

"Maggie, you won't, you can't even get the words out right now. Not to mention I can easily twist everything, make it look like you were asking for it, make it look like you cheated on Conner. It would even ruin your friendship with Alec."

I took a step back, "You're not telling anyone, Maggie."

"Maggie. Maggie."

I blink and see Jade standing in front of me, "Are you falling asleep in the hallway."

"What?"

"You were just standing here with your eyes closed." Jade explains.

I look around to see people staring at me as they walk by, "How long?"

"A couple of minutes, I was saying your name for a while."

I rub my eyes, "I just need to get to class and sit down."

For two years I thought I had beaten this. For two years I have been a different version of myself. For two years I thought I was free of him, but then I get a letter from him, and I came back. For two years, for two years I thought I was in control of my life.

Why did I have to know what Kian said about me? Why did I have to come back? If I never had, would I still be free of these thoughts, or would they have snuck up on me slowly? Killed me, slowly?

I resist the urge to scream. I resist the urge to say fuck. I resist the urge to punch the wall beside me. I resist the urge to get up from this chair right now and go to the graveyard and scream in Kian's face. I resist the urge to have people think I'm crazy, to have people think I killed him.

I am strong, I tell myself, but *why do I feel so weak*? I reason.

"Maybe Maggie can answer."

I look up from the table, everyone is staring at me, "Huh? Sorry I wasn't paying attention."

"Maybe start paying attention or you're not going to understand the rest of this class."

I nod and slowly shift my eyes back down to the table.

I'm being consumed by my mind again, last time I turned into a strong Maggie. A Maggie that wouldn't care what people said, wouldn't care if people stared. But if I am a strong Maggie when I get knocked down again, how am I supposed to get stronger?

The moments repeat over and over again in my head like a movie. The same words, the same motions, everything is the same. The only difference is it's a memory, and I still can't fight it away.

Lunch came around, the world seems big and empty. I sit alone in the corner of the lounge. Adrian and Adams sit across the room from me, I've caught Adrian looking at me a couple of times, but I don't do anything about it. I don't make a remark back, I don't go over and sit with them. I just sit and stare forwards at the ground.

"Hey." I turn to see Ace sitting down beside me.

"Hi."

"So, I was wondering-" Ace's voice begins to fade away.

"Why did you want me to come here?" I whispered as I stepped into Kian's kitchen.

"You're leaving."

"What? What do you mean I'm leaving?"

"You're leaving town tonight." His voice was harsh.

"What!? No, I am not, you've done enough to me. You can't make me leave my home!" I shouted.

Kian grabbed my arm, "Keep your goddamn voice down." He spat, "You'll go live with your mom. I don't want to see your face in this town again."

"Just because you're realizing what you did to me, doesn't mean you get to throw me out of town. You don't control me." I hissed.

His grip around my arm got tighter, "Maggie, you will leave this town tonight or so help me everyone will know what happened by tomorrow morning. I will ruin your relationship with Alec and make your relationship with Conner worse, hell I'll even ruin your relationship with your family. Even that weird little Oscar kid you're nice to."

"Don't you think this is a little much, Kian! I told you I wouldn't say anything."

"I don't care, I want you out of my sight and out of my house. Get out and leave this town, tonight!"

"Maggie, are you listening?"

236

I blink and Ace comes back into my vision, she's staring at me with a worried expression on her face, "You said you knew."

Ace's mouth parts, I stand up from the couch, "You heard the conversation in the kitchen, you heard everything he said to me, and you didn't do anything." Tears form in the corner of my eyes.

"Maggie-"

"I have to go." I pick up my bag from the ground and rush out from the lounge. As I was leaving, I saw Adrian staring at me from the corner of my eye.

I get into the bathroom and push one of the stall door open, I sit down on the toilet and put my face in my hands.

You're okay.

You're okay.

You are OKAY.

The bell rings, I don't move. I don't go to fourth period, it doesn't matter, I don't think I could move even if I wanted to.

I heard the bathroom door squeak open, "Maggie, are you in here?" Ace's voice echoes to me.

I see her feet approach the bottom of the stall I'm in, "Maggie is that you... I'm so sorry, I should have come downstairs, I just- I didn't understand what was happening, I didn't put all the pieces together until weeks after you left."

I bite down on my bottom lip, "I'm always here if you need to talk, please know that."

I watch as Ace's feet disappear, and the squeak of the bathroom door echoes again as she leaves.

I sit quietly in science class beside Adams. I can feel him staring at me, his eyes are burning into my soul, but I can't manage to say anything to him.

"Hey…" I glance over to him, his eyes soft and kind, "I brought ring pops, do you want one?"

I glance down to see a red ring pop in his hand, "I'm okay, thanks."

"Okay." Adams gives a soft smile before looking forward.

I stare down at my bag on the ground.

I grabbed a small brown bag from the back of my closet, I shoved a small amount of shirts and pants inside along with a small notebook. I walked out to the kitchen and grabbed a napkin from the counter.

I'm moving in with Mom, she already knows, no need to call and check on me- Mags

"Do you know the answer?"

I look over to Adams, "What?"

"Do you know the answer to number five?" Adams asks, glancing down at the paper in front of me, "Oh you haven't even started? This is due tomorrow and it's almost the end of class."

"Um… It's just a worksheet, I don't care about it."

"But you like science, it should be easy for you." Adrian says, poking his head out from behind Adams.

"Like I said, I don't care right now!" I snap. I didn't expect that to come out so harsh.

I quickly look back down to the floor.

Once the bell rings I get up from my chair and practically run from the classroom. I didn't realize how much I wanted to be at home until now.

As I'm walking out of the school towards my motorcycle, I hear my name being called, "Maggie!"

I stop and slowly turn around to see Adrian jogging up to me.

"Yes?" I ask looking around, I can feel everyone's eyes on me. I hate it.

"What happened yesterday? Were you and Kian?"

"No!" Why would he assume that?

"Okay... um, are you okay though?"

"Why wouldn't I be?" I snap.

Adrian scratched the back of his head, "I just- It seemed like everything that guy said really bothered you and-"

"I'm good" I blink back the tears forming in my eyes. I just want to get home.

"It doesn't seem like it though. You don't seem like you today-"

"Why do you care?"

Adrian licks his lips, his eyes darting around, "I- I don't know, I just want to help if something is wrong, you've helped me so much with science and other things, I just- want to return the favour, and I mean-"

"I don't need your help, Adrian, I'm fine."

"But you're not, Maggie. You've been phased out and tense all day, I saw you in the lounge with Ace you weren't even paying attention to anything she said-"

"You're not my boyfriend, Adrian!" I shout, that came out more aggressive than I wanted it to, "I don't even know if we're friends! I don't need you to sympathize for me!"

I turn as quickly as I possibly can.

Once I get on my motorcycle, I look over to see Conner now talking to Adrian.

I don't care that I yelled at him, I don't care if I hurt his feelings. I don't need anyone. All I need is myself, I've gone through this once before and I can do it again.

By myself.

CHAPTER TWENTY-THREE

Conner Martin
<u>Wednesday, October 2nd, 2:20pm</u>

I've been jittery all day. I've gone to biting my lips as a coping mechanism ever since I dumped the pills down the toilet. My mom asked me the other day why I'd started doing that. I didn't know how to reply, I just shrugged.

I walk out of the school to see Maggie walking away from Adrian. She looks angry, the same kind of angry look she had before she left. I wonder what he said to her.

I walk up to him, "Hey, man. Can I talk to you?"

"Yeah sure, what's up."

"Um... not here. Follow me."

Adrian follows me to the side of the school, "Are you okay?"

I stop walking and turn to face him, "No. Not okay. Definitely not okay." I shake my head rapidly.

"Okay, what's going on?"

Adrian is the only person I feel close enough to trust, I don't think he would tell anyone, "I took steroids."

"What!?"

"I know it was stupid of me, but I flushed them all down the toilet. But I think my parents know and I just can't stop shaking and talking and biting my lips." I ramble.

"Okay, okay, first off why do you think your parents know?"

"I flushed them about two weeks ago after I found out I got a full ride to university."

"Well, congrats, but why would that mean that they know?" Adrian asks.

I shrug, "I have no clue, I just have a feeling."

"Well, if they don't bring it up with you, I wouldn't worry about it."

I nod, "Okay, good idea."

"Can I ask how you got steroids?"

"Kian gave them to me."

Adrian's mouth drops open and quickly closes, "That guy really did have leverage on everyone." He mumbles loud enough for me to hear.

"Huh?"

"Uh nothing, but did anyone know Kian gave you the drugs because-"

"I already thought of that, no one knew, I couldn't get blamed for his murder, knives scare the shit out of me anyways." I explain.

"Okay well, if anyone asks why you've been shaky or biting your lips, just say you've been nervous for a test or a basketball game coming up."

I nod, "That's actually really good advice, thanks."

"Of course, but I've got to get going."

"Where?" I question.

"To help a... friend."

"Maggie?"

Is that what was going on when I saw her walking away from him? Was he trying to help her? He helped me so I know he can give good advice, but it's hard to believe that Maggie would listen, it didn't look like she wanted to listen.

"Yeah, Maggie."

"You two are friends now?"

Adrian shrugs, "I don't really know."

"Well good luck, and I guess you won't be coming to the practice then?"

"Shit, completely forget, cover for me?" Adrian smiles.

I nod, "Got you."

My parents pick me up from practice, "How was it?" My mom asks.

"Pretty good, boring without Adrian."

"Why wasn't he there?" My dad asks as he pulls out of the parking lot.

"Had to help a friend."

"Do we know this friend?" My mom asks.

"No."

I couldn't tell them it was Maggie, neither of them were very fond of her after our breakup, especially my mom. I never really knew why she was so mad when Maggie broke up with me, and when I asked, she never told me. But they started to hate her even more after they found out she was the one who punched me in the nose.

I think that it would be bad if they found out Maggie and Adrian were friends, or as he says he doesn't know.

We arrive back at home, and I run inside, "I think I'm gonna head up to bed."

"Are you sure sweetie?" My mom asks.

"Yeah, really tired." I smile, and I feel my whole body wanting to shake again and I don't personally want them to see that.

I jog up to my bedroom, closing the door behind me. A cold breeze hits the back of my neck. I turn around to see my window open, I didn't leave my window open when I left for school, and my parents never come in here.

I walk over and close it shut. I sit down on my bed and begin to take off my shoes right as I'm doing so, I notice a small piece of paper sitting on my desk.

Slowly I get up and reach for it, the top has my name on it in sloppy handwriting. I unfold the piece of paper and stare down at the words written inside. My whole-body freezes as my mind reads over the words again and again.

Watch your back

I look around my room as a shiver travels down my back. I quickly crumple up the piece of paper and throw it into my side table drawer. An unsettling feeling sits in the pit of my stomach. Who is watching me?

CHAPTER TWENTY-FOUR

Adrian Fisher
<u>Wednesday, October 2nd, 4:50pm</u>

For the past two hours I've been sitting in the cafe trying to decide whether or not to talk to Maggie.

I knew something was off the exact moment she had left Club Azure yesterday, something that guy said had to have upset her. It sounded like he was saying that Maggie and Kian were in a relationship, but Maggie said that's not what it was.

I stare out the window of the cafe, the clouds are rolling in, dark and gloomy, I would expect that it's going to rain soon. If I was going to go to talk to Maggie, I'd better do it before the rain starts.

My body is stiff when I finally decide to stand up and make my way out of the cafe to my car. Once I'm outside the sky is covered in full darkness. It's going to start raining any second.

I begin to make my way towards the other side of town, if I'm being honest, I've never been to the other side of town. I don't even know where Maggie lives, but I would assume I'd be able to spot her motorcycle.

I slowly drive down a very twisted street looking in every driveway for Maggie's motorcycle. I slow down as I reach a small blue house with the number *16* beside the door. There's a motorcycle sitting on the side of the road in front of the house. It's clearly Maggie's, I know because one of the handles is covered with dark red tape.

As I turn into the driveway, I realize how unkept the house is, the grass is tall and brown, it's growing over onto the small pathway that leads up to the front door. I almost didn't see it.

Once I step out of my car the rain begins to fall slowly to the ground. As I get up to the front door, I notice the white paint chipping off to show an ugly brown colour. I quickly knock and take a step back.

The rain begins to hit the top of my head harder as the door slowly creaks open. Before Maggie says anything, I notice how tired she looks, even more so since school. Her eyes are red and puffy, and the tip of her nose is a bright shiny rose colour. She looks smaller than normal; I don't know if it's because she's wearing baggier clothes.

"Why are you here?" Maggie's voice is quiet.

"I'm not trying to be your boyfriend, and I know you said that you don't even know if we're friends, but I think that we are, and as your friend I'm checking up on you because that's what friends do." I smile.

"Oh."

I take a deep breath, "Can I come in? It's starting to rain pretty hard out here."

Maggie nods, "Um yeah."

She moves out of the way allowing me to step inside. Right away I notice the scattered beer bottles all over the floor.

"Don't mind the beer bottles, they're my, dads." Maggie explains as she closes the door behind me. Did she read my mind?

"It's okay, I don't mind." I smile.

Maggie shuffles in front of me, "You can sit down if you want."

"I'm okay standing for now." I don't exactly know where I could sit, I'm still standing in the entryway.

"How did you find where I live?" Maggie asks.

"Just drove around looking for your motorcycle." I shrug.

Maggie nods, "Makes sense, uh… do you want a drink?"

"I'm okay, thanks."

Maggie smiles before shuffling into the kitchen, I slowly follow behind her, I watch as she fills up a glass of water taking a slow sip.

"Okay... I don't want to push you to talk, but I can tell something is wrong. Hell, your eyes are so red and puff, it's like you've been non-stop crying, Maggie. What's going on?"

Maggie freezes before slowly placing the cup of water onto the counter. Her head drops, "I- I can't say it."

"What?"

"I can't bring myself to say it out loud."

I throw my hands in the air, "Who am I going to tell?"

"That's not it, I don't care who knows at this point!! I just can't bring myself to say it out loud or I'll fall apart!!" Maggie shouts, but it's not an angry shout, instead it's pain.

I stare into Maggie's hopeless eyes, the ones I always saw filled with mystery, but in the moment, there is no mystery, she's being completely vulnerable in front of me for the first time.

Maggie drops her face into her hands, I walk over and stand in front of her, "You can tell me, Maggie. I won't judge if you fall apart, everyone has their low moments, right?"

Ever since I met Maggie, she was always tough, that's how everyone described her, but this is a completely different person. She looks up at me, tears forming in the corner of her eyes.

"I can't, I know it can't happen again, but I still can't face it."

"I wish I could agree with you, but I don't know what you're talking about unless you tell me."

Maggie takes a deep breath, "We can sit in the living room." She walks around me; I turn and follow her into the next room.

She sits down on an old brown couch; I walk over and sit down beside her immediately sinking into the cushion.

"You can take your time to tell me, you don't need to rush, but I will be here to help and comfort to the best of my ability." I explain.

Maggie stares down at the ground, she's pulling at her thumb before she finally speaks, "I was raped."

A sudden rush of anger runs through my body, an anger I never knew I could feel, "What?! By who?" *I think I know the answer.*

"By Kian, at a party."

I stare at Maggie who is still looking at the ground, fiddling with her fingers. I don't know the right thing to say.

Maggie takes a deep breath, "One blink I was downstairs drunk, dancing with Conner and Ace... the next blink I was upstairs on a bed, no longer drunk with Kian on top of me-"

I cut her off, "Maggie you don't have to go into detail."

"I- I need to get out, even if it's hard to say."

I nod, allowing her to talk, "I screamed and screamed, and no one heard me, Kian just smirked like he'd won something," Maggie was no longer crying, her body was stiff, almost as if she was numb, "He left me in the bedroom, naked, alone and crying... by the time I got downstairs the house was practically empty, and when I got home my dad was asleep. I had no one to talk to and the next morning, Kian laughed it off and said I was asking for it and that I was enjoying it when clearly I wasn't."

"Why the fuck would someone do that?"

"I've asked, millions of times. I still can't find the answer," Maggie looks up at me, the tears forming in her eyes once again, "I had blocked out everything from that night and the following month, for two- two years I hadn't thought about it.... But when those guys, they brought up Kian and how he talked about me-" Maggie looks back down, "Everything came rushing back."

"Is this why you left town?"

Maggie looks back up at me biting the side of her lip, "Kian made me. He controlled me. I couldn't tell anyone, he said he'd ruin all my relationships, saying I was asking for it. Saying I cheated on Conner."

"And you believed him?"

"I didn't know what else to do."

I think back to almost every conversation I've had with Maggie about Kian, almost everything she ever said was hinting at him controlling her, she was silently crying out for help.

"You were trying to tell me, without telling me, when we were studying?"

"I think I was, I don't why. When you asked why I joined the gang- he's the reason, I thought it was the only way to protect myself. I changed who I was, I was angry at everything."

"You did all of this? Because of Kian?" I ask almost in disbelief. The guy I remember to be so kind to everyone, the guy I remember to have a bright flashy smile. How could he hurt someone so much? "Why did you come back if he made you leave?"

"He told me to come back, but when I got here, he was missing. Like fuck he still had a hold my life and he was fucking dead." Maggie sobbed. "What if he hurt other girls, and one of them was stronger than I was and- and just killed him?"

I place my hand on Maggie's shoulder to stop her from shaking, "That's a possibility, but don't think about that right now. And besides you're so strong, Maggie."

"It's all fake. I'm not strong."

"You're going to tell me that you're not strong? I'm not talking about physical strength, Maggie. You spend two years fighting, you spent two years in a mental battle whether you knew it or not, you were fighting everyday just to keep yourself afloat, and if that's not strength then I don't know what is."

Maggie shakes her head.

"Don't shake your head, you're strong, and just because it broke you down now doesn't mean that you're not. What happened to you does not make you weak."

Maggie looks up at me, "But I feel weak."

"You're not, you are the strongest person I know, and if it means anything, if Kian was still alive, I'd go and punch him in the face and then report him to the police, with you standing by my side, strong and proud speaking your truth."

Maggie stares into my eyes, tears running down her cheeks. Without missing a beat she's crying into my chest; I wrap my arms around her and hold her tight. Her whole body shaking in my grasp, I hold her tighter trying to calm her down.

I've never been the best with people's emotions, I never know how to react, and I never know if I'm saying the right thing or not. But I feel like I must have said something right.

Maggie pulls away whipping under her eyes with the sleeve of her sweater, "Sorry I think there are tears on your shirt."

"Don't worry, it'll dry."

"If you can't tell, I hate getting emotional." Maggie says.

"Oh, I can tell."

Maggie shoves me, a slight smile rises.

"I know this is probably a bad question, but are you okay?"

Maggie nods, "I'm better, I shouldn't have bottled it up for long... Thank you for listening."

"I will always listen. You don't have to feel ashamed to talk about it with me, or anyone for that matter."

Maggie smiles, "I think I'll just talk to you about it for now. If I ever need to."

I smile, "Sounds good with me, also I still have a ring pop from Oscar, it's a red one and those aren't my favourite if you want it."

"Yeah, I could go for a ring pop right about now."

I pull it out from my jacket pocket and pass it to her, "Here you go, your majersty?"

"Did you just try and combine mystery with majesty?" Maggie asks as she grabs the ring pop.

"Yeah, I tried, it wasn't the best." I chuckle.

"It was perfect."

Maggie and I sit beside each other in silence, "I can go if you want to be alone."

"No, I'd like it if you stayed, if you'd want to… I don't know if the TV works, but we can try and find a movie… I don't want to be alone right now."

I nod, "I can stay."

Maggie smiles before reaching for the tv remote, turning on the tv. She flips through the channels until she finds a station with a good movie.

"What's this?"

"10 things I hate about you." Maggie says, "It's a love story, I used to watch it a lot."

"Well, I can't wait to watch it then, it must be good if you like it." I smile.

"You do seem like the rom com type."

"What does that mean?"

Maggie shrugs, "Kind, you just seem kind."

The movie reaches its final act. I stare into the tv wondering when it would be a good time to leave. My mom's probably worried as to why I haven't come home yet, but I've surprisingly not gotten any texts.

The couch shifts in weight. I glance to my right to see Maggie leaning on my shoulder curled up in a ball. Her chest rising and falling as her eyes lay shut.

Guess all that cry can really tire a person out.

I move my arm to reach for a blanket, as I do her body slumps down, her head now resting in my lap. A small smile tugs at the sides of my mouth. I lay the blanket across her body.

I don't think I'm going to be leaving any time soon.

I look back up at the tv, continuing to watch the movie as Maggie lays asleep peacefully in my lap.

CHAPTER TWENTY-FIVE

Maggie Snow
Thursday, October 3rd, 7:20am

My whole body is warm, comfortable and warm. I don't want to move. I want to lay in this spot forever, in complete peace and quiet.
"Maggie!"
I jolt awake and roll off the couch falling onto the floor.
"What!" I shout as I sit up from the floor realizing I was inches away from hitting my head on the coffee table.
I blink to see Jade standing in the doorway of the living room. "Why are you here?"
Jade doesn't respond, all she does is shift her eyes towards the couch, I look over to see Adrian

laying asleep. I didn't realize he had stayed the night; I don't remember falling asleep, especially with him on the couch.

I stand up and poke him in the side a couple of times before he wakes up, "What's happening." He mumbles.

I look back over to Jade ignoring his question, "Why are you here?" I ask again.

"Rick is at the Mystic Glass drunk off his ass." Jade explains.

"Okay? Why is that my problem?" I hate how she calls my dad by his name; it makes me uncomfortable; I also hate that she's coming to me about it. What would she do if I wasn't here?

"What time is it?" Adrian mumbles.

Jade sighs, "Why is he here? He goes to our school, right?"

"His name is Adrian, and yes he does. Now why is my dad being drunk *my* problem?" I ask.

"Because I worked last night and he was there, when I came back this morning he was still there in the same spot, but this time crying about how he broke up his family."

"Oh god." I rub my hand across my face.

"Can someone please tell me what time it is?" Adrian asks.

Jade pulls out her phone, "It's seven thirty, okay?"

"We're going to be late for school." Adrian panics as he sits up. I push him back down, "Only by a couple of minutes."

"Can you just meet me at the bar in five minutes to help?" Jade asks.

"Fine, five minutes." I sigh as Jade walks out of my house.

I turn to face Adrian to see him frantically flipping through his phone, "Shit, my parents are going to kill me."

"Well, they'll have to kill you later, because you're coming with me."

"No, I have to get to school, Maggie. I'm sorry." Adrian stands up from the couch and looks down at me.

"No, you're coming with me. I need to talk to you after about why you slept over." I explain.

Adrian stares down at me, "You were upset."

"Doesn't give you a good reason to sleep over *and* cuddle me on the couch." I turn on my heel towards the door and pull on my shoes, I swear I could hear Adrian mumble something about cuddling, I look up to him with my hand on the door handle, "Are you coming?"

He nods reluctantly, "I guess."

I let Adrian walk out the door first.

"Wait, where are we going?"

"Mystic Glass." I say flatly as I pass in front of him.

"What's that?"

I sigh and stop walking, turning towards him, "It's the bar where everyone from the gang hangs out."

I turn back around and head towards the small clearing behind my house that sits beside the bar. Adrian jogs up beside me as I enter through the side doors.

Clark comes running up to both of us with Jade following close behind, "Your dad is in the corner crying and holding a beer bottle." At least Clark calls him my dad.

I glance over his shoulder to see my dad in the exact way he described, "Yeah I see that."

"Who are you?" Clark asks while pointing at Adrian.

"Adrian." He smiles awkwardly.

I look down at the ground and sigh, "Keep each other company I'll go talk to my dad."

I walk over to the corner where my dad is now rocking back and forth repeating, "I'm sorry. I'm sorry. I'm sorry."

"Dad."

No response.

"Dad!!"

He looks up at me, "Oh, Maggie."

I watch as he stumbles to his feet, placing his hands on my shoulders, "I'm so sorry I ruined everything."

"I don't know what I'm doing. I ruined everything with your mom and your brother. I'm so sorry."

"Yeah, you better be." The words flew out of my mouth before I had time to think, he slowly moves his hands from my shoulders, "I am the kid, dad, and when I needed you the most, I couldn't talk to you. I'm the one who is supposed to be getting drunk and making the mistakes, and you're supposed to be the parent, there when I'm crying, not the other way around."

I know it was harsh, but it was the truth. I haven't had my dad as a parent for a long time, especially when I needed him.

"I know."

"Do you know? Like really, do you know?"

"I want to fix things." He says.

"And how are you going to do that? Call mom on the phone? You don't even have a phone? I saw it broken on the ground when I got home from school yesterday."

"I'll find a phone and call your mom."

"Okay, but what about Caleb? Are you going to visit him? Try to call him?"

"I can't."

"Because he's a danger, right? Because it's too hard to face?" I ask.

My dad lowers back to the ground. I crouch down to his level.

"If you put in an effort to fix things that you want to fix, I will burn all of those documents about you sending Caleb away."

"Mag-"

"Will that get you to at least talk to mom again, say sorry? Me burning those stupid papers? Erasing the very moment, you fucked up?"

My dad nods.

"I will only do that if you promise to fix things like you say you want to."

"Okay."

I get up from the ground and begin to walk away. I make my way out of the Mystic Glass and back through the clearing.

"Are you just gonna leave me there after you wanted me to come in the first place!" I hear Adrian yell from behind me.

I slow down as he catches up to me, "Sorry."

"Is your dad, okay?" Adrian asks.

"Yeah, but I've got to burn some stuff. Can you help me?"

"Why?" Adrian stares at me confused.

I don't really know why, I don't know if it would be comforting to have him there, or if I want to find out why he slept over.

"Because I just want your help." I shrug as I walk up the pathway to my front door.

"Maggie, are you trying to avoid everything?" Adrian asks as we step inside.

"No."

He steps in front of me, "Are you positive? Because yesterday you said a lot that you hadn't said out loud before."

I stare into his eyes, there's the kindness I've seen in them since the first day I met him, "Yes I am avoiding things, okay? But it's only because I don't want to handle it all at once, I don't want to heal within a couple of days, because that's not realistic. I need time, but I'm not going to shy away from it anymore. I'm not going to block it out. So, I'll talk about it when I need to. Okay?"

Adrian nods, "Okay."

"Now, can you tell me why you slept over?"

"You said you didn't want to be alone, and you fell asleep on my shoulder and then fell onto my lap, and I didn't want to wake you. I must have fallen asleep. I didn't mean to sleep over. I'm sorry if it bothered you."

It didn't bother me, which is the strange part. "Okay." I nod.

I move past him and down the hallway, I don't know why the end of what he said kind of hurt, I understand that he didn't mean to sleep over, but I don't know, it was comforting... I guess. Everything he said to me last night was comforting.

"Wait, so what are we burning?" Adrian asks while following me down the hallway.

"Stupid files so my dad can get his life together." I explain as we walk into my room.

"Is this your room?"

"Uh yeah, my dad sold my bed frame so that's why there's only a mattress." I open my closet and grab the most important papers from the pile.

"We can go." I say looking back at Adrian.

"Where are we going to burn them?"

"There's a big trash can at the very back of the field at school, I was thinking there."

Adrian and I walk back down the hallway and outside, "I can drive if you want, it's better than walking and plus I have all my stuff in my car."

"Yeah, sure." I nod.

I get into the passenger side of the car, "Am I allowed to ask what these files are?"

"They're about my brother."

"Where is he? I know Conner said something that one day, but-"

"A mental institution..."

The car becomes eerily quiet as Adrian backs out of the driveway. "That must be hard, how long has he been there?"

"Since I was six, he was eight when he left."

"I'm really sorry."

"It's okay," I shrug, "You don't have to be sorry, it's not your fault." *It's mine.* I still feel as though most things are my fault.

The car becomes silent again. It's not like the ride from my house to the school is far so it won't be that painful to sit through, it's five minutes at the most.

The silence is oddly comforting, like it was last night when we were watching the movie. That's probably why I fell asleep so easily, because my mind finally had time to settle down, that along with the fact my eyes were tired as anything and the rain outside was calming.

Adrian and I make our way to the back of the school field. It's probably the middle of second period right now so the possibility of teachers coming outside to find us is very slim.

"Why have I never noticed that this is here?" Adrian asks.

"Probably because you don't do drugs and aren't in the gang." We approach a trash can and I pull a small lighter out from my boot.

"Wait you have a lighter in your boot…. And you also have a knife in your boot…. How big are your boots?" Adrian asks.

"Pretty big."

"Do you smoke?"

"No, I never will, I mainly have the lighter in case of emergency and it's fun to burn things." I smile.

I throw the papers into the trash can except for one. Taking the lighter I light the corner of the piece of paper on fire before setting it into the trash can with the rest of the papers.

Within seconds the whole trash can is bright with reds, oranges and yellows. Adrian and I wait to walk away until it dies down.

"My parents are going to kill me for being late, and not going home last night." Adrian says as we walk back towards the school.

"You can blame it on me, I have a feeling they would believe that I could convince you of doing something bad, like skipping school." I chuckle as I shove my hands into the pockets of my sweater. I didn't realize until now that I was still wearing my sweater and sweatpants.

"I won't blame it on you." Adrian smiles, "Thank you though."

"You should get home though, make sure your parents aren't having a heart attack."

"I left my bag at your house though, I remembered when we were halfway to the school, but didn't want to say anything."

"I thought you said you had everything in your car? But I'll bring it to you tomorrow." I say as we reach the end of the field.

"You don't have to do that, I can drive you home and pick it up, it'll be quick."

"Adrian, I literally cried in your arms yesterday, can you just let me bring it to you tomorrow and you get home."

Adrian stops walking and looks at me, "Fine, but can I give you a ride home at least."

I shake my head, "I should walk home, I need to clear my mind, be alone for a bit."

"Are you sure?"

I nod, "Positive, now you get home."

"Okay, I'll see you tomorrow." Adrian runs off through the back parking lot to his car.

Once I see him pull out of the parking lot I begin to walk home. There is no use in going to school today, especially when I don't have my bag, and I'm still kind of in my pajamas.

I walk back inside to see my dad sitting on the couch watching tv. "They're burned."

He nods, "Thank you, Mags... Whose bag is this."

"A friend's, he stayed the night." I say while grabbing the bag from him.

"He?"

"Yes, he. We're just friends."

I get down the hallway to my room and place Adrian's bag on the ground by my door. I have to fight the urge to go into his bag and read the poems he's written in his notebook.

Instead of grabbing his notebook, I grab mine and sit down on my bed. I open to the end of the book where I've written my suspect list. Right beside Adrian's name I write down (*maybe*).

Something about last night changed how I view him, in a good way. I don't know exactly what changed, but I know I trust him a lot more than I had before. I don't think he would be able to commit murder.

Now this only means I'm further away from finding out the truth, which means I have to stay in town longer than I wanted to.

CHAPTER TWENTY-SIX

Adrian Fisher
Sunday, October 6th, 6:40pm

"Please remember to keep the house clean, and don't make a mess with the popcorn." My mom says as I walk her and my dad to the front door, Oscar following slowly behind.
"We know, mom."
"We should be back tomorrow morning by 10, be safe." My dad says as they walk out of the house.
I close the door behind them and quickly whip around to face Oscar, "Now we wait for Maggie."

"I still don't understand why you invited her to guys' night." Oscar sighs as I walk past him into the kitchen.

I look over my shoulder as he follows me, "Because she didn't have the best week and I think this would cheer her up a bit, plus we can get some investigating in before we start the movie."

"I bet you wouldn't have invited her over if you didn't have a crush on her." Oscar says.

"I don't have a crush on her, how many times do I have to say that." I sigh as I reach the microwave.

I never told Oscar about me sleeping over at Maggie's because I knew that he would have a reaction like this. And so, what if I have a crush on Maggie, would it really be that big of a deal? She is a nice person who has had a hard past. I can't blame her for that, and she's trying to work through everything so she can be a better person to the people around her.

"I will keep saying it until you admit it to yourself."

What if I've already admitted it to myself, but I don't want to admit it to Oscar because I know he'll freak out. I know that Maggie is cute and everything, but would that classify having a crush on her. I mean her personality is awesome.

I put the popcorn in the microwave, "We aren't talking about this for the rest of the night."

"Fine, but if I catch you two flirting, I'm going to say I told you so." Oscar says.

"We're not going to be flirting, now put the chips in the bowl for me." I point over to the chip bag and bowl on the island.

"Fine, but also have we even decided on what movie we're watching yet?"

"I think one of the marvel movies, I could be wrong though." I say as the microwave beeps.

"God people don't know how to drive!" Maggie stumbles into the kitchen with her hands on her hips.

"Why hello to you too, did you close the front door?" I ask.

"Yes, I closed the front door." Maggie rolls her eyes, "But sorry, people need to learn how to drive, I almost got hit two times."

"Are you okay?" Oscar asks, turning to look at Maggie.

"Yeah, but fuck."

"I don't know how to drive and people like that make me nervous too." Oscar says as he picks up the bowl full of chips.

I pour the popcorn into a bowl and walk over to them, "Well you're just in time since the snacks are ready."

We all get comfortable in my living room, it's probably one of the biggest rooms in my house, there's two leather couches and one leather chair with a large flat screen tv. I don't spend a lot of time out here, especially with people, this might be, at most, my 5th time sitting out here since I moved in.

"So what movie are we watching?" Maggie asks as she reaches for the popcorn before stumbling back down into the chair in the corner.

"We haven't picked yet, but we were thinking of doing some investigating beforehand." I explain.

"It's no use, we aren't going to figure it out." Maggie says, throwing a piece of popcorn into her mouth.

"But you're the one that wanted to figure this out." Oscar says.

Now that I'm fully looking at Maggie something does seem off about her. Her pupils look larger than usual, and she did stumble into the kitchen and onto the chair. Maybe she was the bad driver on the road?

Maggie shrugs, "I mean we can still look into it, but we honestly have no leads. We're just shooting in the dark."

"But we can find a lead by talking to those guys from Club Azure again, they seemed to know a lot." I suggest.

"We're not talking to them again!" Maggie snaps, she repositions herself in the chair and looks at Oscar and I, "All they told us was that Kian was bisexual, that really didn't help us."

"Maybe he was with more guys we can talk to." Oscar suggests.

"And we can even talk to Jessica, remember how you said she seemed like she was always trying to get with him." I point out.

"It doesn't seem worth it."

On Friday at school Maggie was staring at the murder board the whole time we were in the newspaper, what happened to make her not want to do this anymore. Does she not want to think about Kian anymore? I can understand if it's part of her healing, but it doesn't seem like it.

"We can just drop it for today and do something else."

Oscar and I look over to each other, "Sure, we'll pick a movie." I smile.

Oscar goes to reach for the remote when the doorbell rings, "Who else did you invite?"

"No one." I get up from the couch and head towards the front door. Maggie and Oscar follow behind me.

I pull the door open to see a crowd of people standing outside my door with Jacob Ross standing at the very front, "Let's get this party started!!" He shouts as everyone storms into my house.

I get pushed into the wall as more people flood into my house. I move my way over to Oscar and Maggie who are standing in the middle of the house.

"I would find beers and more chips, people at parties can get angry sometimes." Maggie smirks.

That's when it clicks, she's been drunk this whole time, "Did you invite these people to my house?!" I shout as music begins to play.

"Guess it's just another mystery." She shouts as she stumbles into the crowd of people.

Oscar and I slowly look over to each other.

"You still like her now?"

"Not the time, bud, not the time."

I believe in everything that I know about Maggie. She would never invite half of the school to my house if she wasn't going through something. She has to be going through something, but this time I'm not so sure it has to do with Kian.

I walk through my dining room, squeezing past people. I've lost track of where Oscar is, the last time I saw him he was at the bottom of the stairs, but then I went to stop someone from touching one of my mom's expensive vases. I've lost track of so much time.

I walk through the kitchen and round the corner bumping into Jade.

"Jade!" I say louder than I anticipated.

She blinks, "Adrian, right?"

"Yeah... umm... have you seen Maggie anywhere?"

"No, why?" She asks.

I scratch the back of my head, "Well you see this is my house, and she kind of threw this party here without me knowing."

Jade chuckles, "Classic."

"Umm well she'd probably be upstairs knowing her, no one really goes up there unless they're couples looking to hook up so she's probably hiding out." Jade explains.

"Okay, thank you so much." I move past Jade.

"Also, she's probably drunk off her ass!" Jade yells after me. I think I already knew that.

I move up the stairs past two people making out, it's very intense, is that what making out is like? I wonder what that would be like.

I shake the thought from my mind and make it up the stairs. I look into every room until I finally reach the guest room. I push the door open slowly to see Maggie sitting on the ground at the end of the bed drinking a beer.

"There you are!"

I walk in and close the door behind me, "You can't just throw a party at my house without permission!!"

Maggie looks up at me, her eyes hanging heavy, "Sorry." She brings the bottle of beer up to her lips taking a long sip.

"Why did you invite everyone here!! To *my* house!" I shout, "If my parents were to come home early, I'd be grounded for life!"

Maggie shrugs, taking another sip of beer before speaking, "I was bored."

"You were bored! How were you bored!? We had a plan to watch movies and investigate Kian's death again! How could you have been bored when we didn't even start doing anything yet!!"

"We have all the time in the world to solve a death until the killer strikes again, that's when we speed up the process." Maggie says, rolling her eyes.

"Yeah, and what happens if it's you or me who gets killed next? What are you going to do then?"

"Well, if I'm the one that dies then I guess I'd be able to beat up Kian in hell right." Maggie chuckles before taking another sip of beer.

I stare at her, my mouth agape, "What... what is going on with you, Maggie. I invited you here tonight so you could have a calm night because I knew you had a bad week. Why are you getting drunk?" I ask lowering my tone.

Maybe yelling wasn't my best approach, but I was angry, things in my house are getting broken and people I've never even talked to are walking around my dad's office.

Maggie looks down at the ground, I walk over and sit down beside her, resting my back up against the footboard of the bed.

"I can't see my brother, my mom called me today to basically yell at me and say that she never wants to see me again, and my dad is still getting drunk, even though he said he would get his act together... not to mention remembering everything that happened with Kian... I just screw everything up."

Well now I feel like a jerk for yelling at her. I watch as Maggie takes another sip of beer.

"You don't screw up everything, Maggie. I haven't seen you screw up one thing since I've met you."

"Really? So, you're going to tell me that letting Kian control half of my life wasn't me screwing up? You're going to tell me that breaking Conner's nose wasn't a screw up?"

I shake my head, "No it wasn't, at least I don't think it was."

"Well, I think it was... I shouldn't have even come here tonight. Your house is falling apart and it's my fault. Again, all my fault."

"It's fine, Maggie."

She finally looks over to me, "How can it be fine, Adrian! You were just yelling at me about it!! But I can't do anything about it now because my actions *always* have horrible consequences."

Maggie takes another sip of beer once she looks away from me, I grab the bottle from her hand, "Okay, no more drinks for the night, and actions? You say that like this has happened before."

"No, I don't mean a party I mean that I'm the fucking reason my family is a shit show because I'm the reason my brother is in that fucking psych ward." Maggie laughs hysterically.

"Okay, how many drinks have you had tonight?"

Maggie continues to laugh, "Maybe 20, I don't remember."

How the hell is she still awake and sitting up right.

"Well, Maggie. I don't think you're the reason your brother is in the psych ward. You can't blame yourself." I say as I finally place the beer down on the ground beside me.

"But it is my fault, because you know how kids like to play games when they're younger, like truth or dare, or make believe, well *I* made a bet with my brother to see who could last the longest being psycho... I didn't last ten minutes, but I woke up the next morning hearing a repeated banging coming from outside. I went to the backyard, and you know what I saw?!" Maggie stares at me, "My brother, smashing in a bird's head in with a rock. When he went back inside, I hid from him, then I buried the bird."

"Maggie-"

"He was eight, and I was only six. I confronted him about it later in the day when our parents were out of the house. He pushed me between the door and the wall and slammed the door into me making me repeatedly hit my head. My parents came home, I said I fell on the ground bruising my face. They didn't believe that."

"If I hadn't made that bet with him, maybe my parents would still be together, maybe what happened with Kian wouldn't have happened because I would have had my brother to protect me."

Maggie looks down at the ground, "Maggie, none of that was your fault, he did that all himself and you can't keep blaming yourself for that, the same thing goes for Kian. It was his choice to do that, and you can't keep blame yourself for it."

Maggie looks back over to me, "You've been too nice to me, Adrian, and I don't deserve that."

"Yes, you do, I told you this. I will be here, if you need to talk. About anything, you don't have to get drunk or throw random parties at my house. If you don't face things, sometimes they'll just get worse."

Maggie takes in a deep breath, "Sometimes I wish I could just snap my fingers and I could redo something, the moment I think everything went wrong in my life."

"Everything happens for a reason, and I mean everything, even if we don't like it. Hell, I didn't want to move here when my parents told me we were, but if I hadn't, I wouldn't have met Oscar, and I- I wouldn't have met you."

"Was meeting me really that special of a thing?"

I nod, "I think so yeah... because meeting new people can make you view things differently, right?"

The whole world slows down around Maggie and I. I can no longer hear the loud pounding of music coming from downstairs, I can no longer feel the floor shaking below me.

My eyes don't shift from Maggie's as we both lean in, our lips connecting. My hand cups the side of her face as I taste the beer on her tongue. To my surprise I don't mind it, it's kind of sweet.

Maggie leans in closer to me, our legs touching as she rests her hand on my chest. The kiss deepens as we both lean in closer; my hand begins to get tangled within her hair.

A loud knock comes for the door before it opens. Maggie and I pull away from one another as music fill my ears once more.

We both look over to see Oscar standing in the doorway, "Hey, bud."

"Uh, someone is trying to use that expensive vase again, but as bong."

"Okay." I get up from the floor. As I'm leaving the room I look back at Maggie, "I'll be right back." I awkwardly smile as I turn to catch up with Oscar.

"Did you see anything?" I ask as I reach Oscar on the stairs.

"Do you mean like? Your first kiss being with Maggie?"

I clear my throat, "Uh, yeah... That. Can we not talk about it right now though?"

"Sure... but I told you so."

I roll my eyes as I walk down the stairs, I grab the vase from the random guy trying to smoke out of it. I walk back up the stairs and put it in my parents' room.

I walk back towards the guest bedroom and open the door, "Maggie?"

She's no longer in the room. I close the door behind me and lean up against it. I feel like I just fucked things up.

How did she get down the stairs without Oscar and I seeing her, and where would she have gone?

And why did that kiss feel so good.

CHAPTER TWENTY-SEVEN

Jade Button
Sunday, October 6th, 7:00pm

    Sitting at my drum set always helps me think, feeling the vibrations run through my veins, the thumping that echoes through my head. It's beautiful.
    When I play everything around me disappears, it's just me and the music alone. No crazy family, no crazy town and no crazy feelings for people I know won't like me back.
    I know what Maggie said, about Ace having a crush on me a while ago. But it's hard to believe. Ace and I are two different people, the only thing we have in common is that we both like playing instruments. But I guess you don't have to have

everything in common with someone you like or there would be nothing to talk about. So, is us being different from one another a good thing?

I hit the snare even harder as my bedroom door opens. I take off my headphones and look over to my mom, "You better be careful, you don't want to break that, it was very expensive."

She walks into my room and places a pile of clothes onto my bed, "It's my drum set, I can hit it however hard I want."

She glances at me before beginning to fold my clothes, "I just didn't think you'd want it broken."

"I can fold my own clothes."

My mom turns around and crosses her arms, "Why are you in such a bad mood? I know you aren't on your cycle because I haven't seen anything in the garbage."

Is she seriously looking in the garbage for pads?

"I'm not in a bad mood."

"Then why were you hitting the drums so hard?"

"Maybe so it creates noise?"

My mom turns back around to fold my clothes again, "Well, what are you doing tonight? Samantha and Jamey wanted to watch a movie."

"What movie?"

"A Tinkerbell movie, Secret of the Wings, I think."

"I'm good. I actually think there's a small party being thrown down the street, I might go."

"A party, Jade? It's a school night."

I roll my eyes, "I've been to parties on school nights before."

"Yes, when you were six, and those were birthday parties, for friends you actually had before you joined *a gang*." My mom says. The disgust in her voice is way too obvious.

"It's not my problem that all of those friends became stuck up bitches that wanted to be on the cheer team while I wanted to be in a band."

My mom spins around, "Jade! Watch your language!"

I stand up from my stool, "I can fold my own clothes, mom. I'm more grown up than you think."

She drops the shirt in her hands onto the ground, "Fine, I will leave, but if you end up going to that party, at least tell me before you go, and don't sneak out the window like you normally do. I would love to know where my daughter is going."

She walks out of my room slamming the door behind her. I walk over and pick up the shirt from the ground.

If only she listened to me for once I wouldn't be sneaking out of the house.

"Jade!" Jamey yells as her and Sam come running over to me once I reach the bottom of the stairs.

"Are you going to watch the movie with us?" Sam asks.

"I'm actually about to go out, but next week I can. Promise." Both their heads drop to the ground. I crouch down so I'm at eye level with them, "You two can tell me all about it in the morning, okay? And show me your favorite scene too."

"Okay..." They both pout.

I stand up and walk towards the door, "I'm going mom!" I yell.

No response, "Can you two tell mom I've gone out if she asks."

I walk outside. Why'd she ask me to tell her if she wasn't even planning to respond.

I walk down to the end of the street where I notice people from school flooding into someone's house. I also notice that a lot of people gave up on getting inside.

It's a smart idea, wait until people stop showing up and then go inside. It's also not bad to stay outside because you can still hear all the music blasting from the house. I'm honestly surprised none of the neighbours have called the cops yet.

I make my way into the house, I've never understood why people crowd around at parties, everyone's drunk and sweaty and people can end up thinking you're Toad from Mario Kart.... Clark did that to me once.

I squeeze through a crowd of people, one of the perks for being short. I head towards what looks like a less crowded room, I glance behind me and when I look forward again, I bump into someone.

"Sorry." I mumble

"Jade!"

I blink, not expecting my name to be yelled in my face. It takes me a second to realize who's standing in front of me, "Adrian, right?"

His hair is ruffled and there looks to be beads of sweat on his face. Is he okay?

"Yeah... Um, have you seen Maggie anywhere?"

"No, why?" I ask, crossing my arms.

Adrian scratches the back of his head, "Well you see this is my house, and she kind of threw this party here without me knowing."

I understand why he's sweating then, and I can't help, but laugh, "Classic."

Adrian stairs at me, waiting for another response.

"Umm well she'd probably be upstairs knowing her, no one really goes up there unless they're couples looking to hook up so she's probably hiding out." I explain.

"Okay, thank you so much." Adrian moves past me towards the staircase.

"Also, she's probably drunk off her ass!!" I shout after him not knowing if he heard me.

I continue my way to the kitchen as an arm gets wrapped around me, I look to my left to see Clark standing beside me with a drunken smirk on his face.

"Hey, Clark."

"I didn't think you were going to show up, I missed you." Clark smiles as he stumbles forward.

"Well, I needed to get out of the house."

"Well, it's good you did," Clark stands with his hands on his hips, "Now, let's get you some vodka." He grabs my hand and pulls me towards the sink.

"Clark, this is water."

Clark begins to giggle like a lunatic before slumping to the ground. I join him on the ground.

"You, okay?"

"Well, my mom yelled at the dog again." He giggles.

"How is your mom?"

"Still sick, and mad a lot, but yesterday she actually remembered my name, and used the colouring book I got her." Clark smiles.

"That's a good thing."

I've known Clark for three years now, he's probably my best friend. I was the first person he ever talked to about his mom and what was going on with her.

"Why'd she yell at the dog though?"

"He wasn't going onto the bed with her." Clark laughs.

"That's an interesting reason to yell, but" I stand up, "Let's get you up and let's go listen to some music... closer to the music."

We walk through the house and into what I think is the living room. I stop in my tracks, "What?" Clark asks.

285

"She's going to regret that." I mumble as I stare forwards to see Ace sitting on Conner's lap, making out with him.

I feel as though bubbles are rising in my chest every time I breathe. I'm suddenly warm and I can now feel my skin touching me.

"I can't hear you!!!" Clark yells right into my ear.

I bring my hand up to my ear covering it, "You go listen to the music, I'm going to stand here!"

Clark walks into the living room and sits down on the ground with a small group of people. I keep my attention focused on Ace and Conner. I've never had a conversation with him, I only know that he's Maggie's ex and play's basketball.

It might be the jealousy getting to me, seeing her making out with someone else, *God, I wish it was me*, but I couldn't stop my feet from moving towards them.

I pull Ace away from Conner, "Time to go." I mumble to myself.

"OH OkAy, byeee." Ace waves at Conner as I pull her through the crowds of people and outside the house.

Ace stumbles down the stairs on the porch, "Where are we going?"

"I'm taking you home."

Ace places her chin on my shoulder, "But I was having fun."

"I doubt you'll like the thought of you making out with Conner when you wake up in the morning."

"Meh." Ace shrugs as she stumbles in front of me.

"Let's keep walking." I say as I link arms with her so she's able to walk straight.

"Okay!!" Ace says in a high pitch voice.

I scratch behind my ear, "I wouldn't have thought you were much of a party girl."

"I'm noT, I just need to let go for one night." Ace says as she unlinks arms with me and skips forward.

"Let go?"

Ace stops and looks at me, "Yeah."

"Let go of what?"

"Liffe! Obviously! My crazy mom and the obvious death of my brother!"

I have a feeling she's not going to have the best time when she wakes up in the morning and that she might think she's less drunk than she is right now.

"Well, drinking doesn't help solve everything, you can't always turn to it to help."

Ace shrugs and walks up beside me, "How are you though, why'd you come to the party."

We both continue to walk down the street, Ace swaying back and forth with every step. I'm scared she's going to fall over and clearly; she doesn't want to talk about things, and I'm not going to force her to, "Just wanted to get out of the house, glad I did or I wouldn't have been able to stop you from making out with Conner."

"And why do you care about who I make out with?" Ace asks, getting close to my face, her eyes squinting. She's so close I can feel her breath on my cheek.

"Well... we're... we're friends... right? Just helping out."

"Thank you!!" Ace gives me a big smile as she wraps her arms around me.

"Skip with me?" Ace grabs my hand pulling me forward.

Both of us are now skipping down the street, Ace giggling like a crazy person.

"How is your family doing?" I ask, which immediately makes the skipping slow back down to a walk.

"Well, the detective keeps coming over to ask us questions, I've answered the same 20 thousand million questions every time she comes, but I don't care, if it helps find who killed Kian, I'm happy."

"Do they have a lead?"

"Nope, cops always take their time, they can't just find the killer in one day."

"Well, if they did, it might end up being the wrong killer, we don't want them to lock the wrong person away." I smile.

We approach Ace's house, and she begins to skip again, "Come on!"

I jog and catch up to her as she skips up her driveway to the front door.

"Thanks for the walk." She turns to me and smiles.

"You're welcome, I wasn't going to make you walk alone." I smile.

Without notice Ace leans in and kisses me, she pulls away, "Thank you, Jade."

"Uh... yeah, you're welcome." I stare in shock as she walks inside her house.

"I have to pee." I hear her say as the door closes.

I slowly turn around and walk back down her driveway. I graze my finger over my lips. She kissed me so fast, I almost forget what it felt like.

I walk into my house; all the lights are turned off. I slowly make my way upstairs.

I glance into my sister's rooms to see them both fast asleep.

"How was the party?" I turn around to see my mom standing in the doorway of her bedroom.

"Good."

"Your sisters say goodnight."

"Well, I'll tell them I said goodnight in the morning." I smile as I head towards my room.

"Sweetheart."

I turn around to look at my mom, "Have a good sleep."

"Yeah," I nod, "You too."

I walk into my room, closing the door behind me.

I lay down on my bed without changing into pajamas. I didn't care tonight, I was comfortable.

And for the first time in what seems like months, I'm going to sleep with a smile on my face.

CHAPTER TWENTY-EIGHT

Maggie Snow
Monday, October 7th, 6:40am

The pounding in my head gets worse as my eyes blink open. I reach and pull the elastic band out of my hair, throwing it onto the table. The headache hurts less, but it's not completely gone.

A yawn escapes my mouth as I stretch and look around to realize that I'm sitting in the newspaper.

How did I get in here? How did I even get into the school?

I reach into my pocket and grab my phone, there's two more hours until school and I'm having a buzzing hangover.

I go to my small list of contacts and call Adrian; I got his number a couple days ago.

"Hello?" A groggy voice answers.

"You and Adams get over to the school now and bring a bagel."

"What... Maggie, it's 6 in the morning, what... Why are you at school?"

"Well, it's almost 7 actually, and just get to the school, and please bring me a bagel."

I hang up the phone in hopes that he won't fall back asleep, and that he'll wake up Adams, and bring me a bagel.

As I lean back in the chair, I realize there's a bunch of small pieces of paper scattered in front of me on the table.

I reach for the papers.

Jessica

Jacob

Cal

The Hunters Gang

From what it looks I went on a suspect spree last night, and the gang now happens to be on my list?

I get up from the chair and walk over to the murder board. I take thumb tacks and pin the pieces of paper in a line at the top of the board.

If we're going with the theory of power, I guess Jacob makes some sense, same with Jessica. But if I'm going with my theory that Kian could have hurt someone else the way he had me, then Jessica can also be an option, or now with the knowledge of him being bisexual, would he be capable of doing that do a guy to?

Cal is only up there because he dated Kian. He could have known something, but didn't tell us. I don't have the nerve to talk to him again and question him more.

But was I so drunk last night that I wrote the gang down? The gang is another form of family, it's there to be a family for people who don't have a family or support. They would never kill someone unless that person crossed someone from the gang... but I guess, Kian technically crossed me, so if someone found out...

That's a very slim chance though, most of the gang didn't even know who Kian was.

I look over as the door slowly opens, Adrian's head peaks in before stepping inside with Adams in toe. They got here faster than I had thought they would. How long was I staring at the board?

"Here's your bagel." Adrian says while placing it down on the table beside me.

"Thanks."

"Why did you need us here so early?" Adams yawns as he rubs his eyes, "I'm not even awake yet."

I sigh as I grab the bagel off the table and start unwrapping it, "I don't know how I got into the school last night. Was the door open when you guys got here?"

"Yes." Adrian nods as he takes a set in the chair beside where I'm standing.

I take a bite of the bagel, it's surprisingly good, "Did you make this?" I ask turning to face Adrian.

"Yes, I did."

"It's good, thank you."

I take another bite, "But…" I chew the rest of the bagel in my mouth before continuing, "I didn't have any bobby pins so I must have picked the lock with my knife."

"Woah, wait, back up. Did you call us here this early so we could help you figure out how you got into the school?" Adrian asks, he's sassier when he's tired.

I shrug, "Possibly, and I wanted a bagel…"

"I woke up from a good dream, because you needed help figuring out how you got into the school last night?!" Adams yells, the temper throws me off in the slightest. I assume he's only yelling because he's still tired, I hadn't realized the bags under his eyes until now.

"Well…. I also wrote down suspects who I think might have killed Kian." I smile in hopes that'll make them less aggravated with me.

Adrian rubs his eyes, "Great." He says flatly.

Maybe waking them up this early in the morning wasn't the greatest choice.

"Wait!!" Adrian and I both look over to Adams, "Why have we never thought of looking in Kian's locker?"

"I don't know dingus, maybe because Kian graduated!"

Adrian shakes his head, "No he didn't, he was coming back for 12b."

"And Kian always had the same locker every year, everyone does. So, it's likely that he'd have something in there that could be useful." Adams explains.

I nod in agreement, "Okay, fine, but wouldn't the police have already searched his locker? And why would he use it over summer?"

"He was using the gym for basketball practice. And I never heard anything about it the police searching the lockers, but it's possible." Adrian shrugs.

"It's still worth the look." Adams says, "I'll go check it out and see if it's open. I'll come back if I find anything."

Before Adrian and I could say another word, Adams was out the door.

I finish my bagel and make my way over to the garbage to throw out the napkin it was wrapped in.

"Maggie... should we talk about last night?" Adrian asks as I turn around.

I had tried to block out the fact that I had thrown a party at his house, I know it wasn't the right thing to do, I know that I shouldn't have done it. But my impulse took over and I couldn't stop myself.

"I know, I shouldn't have thrown the party, I'm sorry."

"Oh no, uh that. I understand why and I understand that you didn't mean to... I was talking, more about the kiss."

"Oh, right... that."

Maybe I had blocked that out of my mind too, but that's probably the clearest thing I remember from last night.

I slowly walk back over to a seat at the table, "What about it? The kiss."

"Why did you kiss me?"

"Why did you kiss me back?" I counter as I sit down.

Adrian stares at me, I wonder what he's thinking, is he trying to figure out what to say. What would the correct response even be? He licks his lips before speaking, "It was in the moment I guess... But why did you kiss me?"

I shrug, "It was just a kiss, I was drunk, obviously. And like you said, it was in the moment."

"But was it just a kiss, Maggie? It didn't seem like just a kiss to me, it seemed like, I don't know I'm sorry if that's not-"

I cut him off, "I can't get hurt again."

"Do you really think I would hurt you?" He asks, his eyes are slightly closed.

Why did him saying that string my heart so much? I hadn't realized it until now, but I trust Adrian a lot. I could be vulnerable with him, but that doesn't mean I enjoyed the feelings, that I understand them, and it doesn't mean I'm not scared of them.

"The people you trust the most can hurt, so can we just... not talk about the kiss."

As Adrian opens his mouth to say something right as Adams bursts through the door.

"Did you run back here?"

"I found a letter." Adams breaths as he holds up a small piece of paper in the air.

"A letter?" I try to keep my breathing steady. I had mentioned to Adrian that Kian was the reason I had come back to town, but I never mentioned how he got in contact with me.

"What does it say?" Adrian asks.

Adams takes a deep breath, "Hey Kian, I'm back in town, if you don't want anyone to know what happened, meet me under the bridge tonight. From Maggie."

They both look over to me, "I did not write that! I wasn't even in town."

"I know." Adrian says quietly to me, I can't tell if Adams heard, "We believe you." he says louder.

"Well at least we know where he was probably murdered, or at least where it started?" Adams glances back down at the letter in his hands.

"Yeah! *That's* the good thing here! If the police had searched his locker, or hadn't yet, they would have and then I would be arrested on the spot!!" I take in a deep breath as Adams walks over and pins the letter onto the murder board.

"How did you get into his locker?" Adrian asks.

"I just tried his basketball jersey number on the combination, it seemed to work." Adams shrugs.

"But all that matters right now is that school is going to start soon and we need to look like we haven't been here since seven in the morning... I had to run back here because I saw teachers arriving." Adams explains, "We should probably get into the hallway and act normal."

"We can go laugh at the hungover kids from last night, if they even decide to show up." I chuckle trying to distract myself from the thoughts about Kian getting a letter from *me*.

Once we leave the newspaper I go in the separate direction of Adrian and Adams.

I notice Clark standing at his locker without the rest of the gang.

"Where is everyone?" I ask.

He looks up at me, "Oh no one else has shown, probably all hungover, but do you want to see my dog?"

"Uh, sure."

Clark turns his phone towards me and on the screen is a small chocolate lab smiling.

"Aw he's so cute, what's his name?"

"*She*, and *her* name is Buggie."

"Well, she's very cute." I smile.

"Hey." I turn to see a half-awake Jade walking up beside me.

"Did you go to that party last night? You look... tired and drunk still."

Jade nods, "Yeah I went, but I hadn't had anything to drink."

A small smile rises on her face as she looks down at the ground.

"Why do you look so tired and why are you smiling like that? I've never seen you smile like that."

In all honesty I don't pay much attention to whether or not Jade smiles, but I'm positive I've never seen her smile like she's standing in front of a bath of puppies that are all licking her face.

"I'm just smiling, can I not smile?"

"You can, it's just a different type of smile."

"Did Adrian end up finding you last night?" Jade asks to change the subject.

"Yeah... Why are you asking?"

"Because he asked me where you were, he seemed pretty mad that you threw a party at his house."

"He didn't seem that mad when he found me."

Jade's eyes widen. "I did not mean to say it in that way!!" I shout.

"Did you two?"

"What no! I didn't mean it like that!"

Clark looks up from his phone, "It did sound like you were insinuating something."

"Seriously, nothing happened, I was drunk, and he just listened to me talk. Is there something so bad about that?" I didn't want to tell either of them about the kiss with Adrian, mainly because I still haven't figured out in my mind why it

299

happened in the first place. Was I just drunk and it was an in the moment thing? Or did I want to kiss him?

"Nothing's bad about it, but why are you now the one smiling like an idiot." Jade smirks.

"OH! So, you admit it, you were smiling like an idiot!"

"Don't turn this back to me!"

"Fine, we'll turn it to Clark then," I turn my head towards Clark, "Were you drunk last night?"

Clark blinks, "Uh, yes."

Jade looks at him in astonishment, "Wait, yeah, how are you not hungover? You could hardly stand last night."

Clark shrugs, "I guess I'm just good at hiding it... and I've also had five things of coffee already."

"Five!?" Jade and I say in unison as the bell rings.

"Well, I'm going to English, enjoy your five cups of coffee."

"I might have my sixth soon!!" Clark yells as I walk down the hallway.

I sit down in English class and realize that I just had a conversation with Jade about our lives... kind of. I mean we've had conversations in the bar, but it's still weird that it's somewhat becoming normal. I wouldn't say that she's my friend and that I'd trust her with all my secrets, but I assume she is trustworthy.

Once class begins my mind begins to fade back to the newspaper and that letter Kian got.

Kian had gone to the bridge because of a letter that was from someone pretending to be me and I came back to town because of a letter that I now can confirm wasn't from him.

Whoever killed Kian had to have known what happened between Kian and I, because why else would they have used me to get him under the bridge, and why else would they have used him to get me back into town.

If this person was able to trick both of us and kill one of us. What else could they be capable of?

CHAPTER TWENTY-NINE

Conner Martin
Friday, October 11th, 11:30am

  I grind my teeth together as I wait in the lounge for everyone to arrive. I've sat in my room almost every night staring at the note I got. I've come to the conclusion that it had to be from whoever killed Kian.
  Who else would send a random anonymous *watch your back* note? But that isn't what I needed to talk to everyone about.
  Adrian and Oscar are the first to arrive. They both sit down on the couch across from where I'm sitting.
  "Why did you need us here?" Adrian asks.

"We need to wait for everyone else before I can explain." My leg bounces up and down.

"Everyone else?" Oscar asks as Jade and Ace walk over to us.

"Oh, so this is like a meeting." Jade says.

"What's going on?" Ace asks as she sits down in the chair beside me, Jade stands behind her leaning to rest on the back of the chair.

"We just have to wait until Maggie is here."

"Can't you just tell us, most of us are here." Jade says.

"No!"

I don't know Jade very well, the only thing I really know about her is her name, and I only know her name because in grade nine that's who Maggie started to hang out with.

Maggie walks into the lounge and stops in her tracks when she realizes everyone else is here. She looks over to me, "Conner, what's going on?"

"Well now that everyone is her-"

"Guess who's back!!" Jessica smiles as she walks up beside Maggie.

"You were gone?" Maggie asks while talking a step sideways away from her.

Jessica keeps smiling ignoring Maggie, "I was in LA for the last couple of weeks visiting someone. Did anyone miss me?"

"Nope." Jade says flatly.

I have the feeling that Maggie and Jade feel the same way towards Jessica, and they're the only one's that'll tell her to fuck off if the time comes to it.

Jessica rolls her eyes before strolling out of the library.

I clear my throat, "Anyways, I asked you all to come here because we all knew and talked to Kian."

"I've never talked to Kian, so why am I here?" Jade asks.

I turn and look at her, "Because you talk to Ace."

"But anyways, yesterday when I was dropping something off for my dad at the police station, I overheard some cops talking about how they are going to start questioning more people about Kian, anyone who has talked to him and hasn't come forward with any information yet, with that I also heard they're going to start questioning people who also talk to Ace."

"Okay, and?" Maggie asks as she sits down on the armrest of the couch.

"And I wanted to warn all of you, I doubt any of us did it, but I know that all of us have talked to Kian, and or Ace."

Maggie's eyebrows raise, "Seriously, you called us all here because you wanted to warn us?"

"Yes, I didn't want any of you to get caught off guard." And that fact that focusing my energy into helping other people has helped me with not trying to get steroids again. The other day I helped an old lady bring her groceries to her car after I saw her drop two of the bags.

"Everyone would have gotten investigated either way." Oscar says sheepishly.

"And I've already been investigated." Maggie adds.

"Okay, okay," I put my hands up in defense, "I was just trying to help out."

"Thank you, I'm glad you told us." Ace smiles.

"Your welcome," I smile, "And there's another thing, I think the police are going to do a sweep of everyone's lockers for any evidence they could find. I don't know why they haven't done it yet, but they're doing it soon."

Maggie, Adrian and Oscar all look at one another.

"What are those looks about?" Jade points out.

"Nothing." Adrian and Oscar say.

"Maggie?" Ace asks.

Maggie's eyes dart to Ace and then to the ground, "It's nothing."

"You're lying, Maggie. You're fiddling with your fingers; you do that whenever you're nervous or lying."

"Then I'm nervous." Maggie moves her hands away from each other and crosses her arms.

"Maggie, what did you find?" Ace asks.

"Wouldn't you want to know?" Maggie asks, something in her tone is angry, but I don't understand why she'd be angry with Ace.

Adrian looks around before leaning forwards, "We found a letter addressed to Kian, it told him to meet under the bridge out of town, we assume that's where he was killed and then maybe floated down the river." He whispers.

I don't know if now would be the right time to mention that I got a note, but this does confirm for me that it's probably from whoever killed Kian.

"And you haven't given it to the cops?" Jade asks.

"My name is signed at the bottom." Maggie says in a harsh whisper. I haven't seen Maggie get nervous in a while, but she clearly is, she's fiddling with her fingers again and she doesn't have the same tough demeanor she's had for a while now.

"Whoever sent Kian that letter wanted it to look like I killed him. But I wasn't even in town when he died, and I don't want to give it to the cops because that would just give them another reason to suspect me. I am the one that found his body, I don't need to look more suspicious."

"So, where's the letter now?" I ask.

"We're keeping it a secret; we don't want anyone finding it and taking it." Oscar says.

"I would give it over to the police and let them do their job." Ace says.

"Really? The cops haven't done their job in a month, they haven't found a single lead and once again you're protecting Kian even after he died. Does it not concern you that I could go to jail just because they'd want to put someone behind bars and move onto the next case?"

Everyone goes silent.

"That's not what I'm saying." Ace says.

"Then what are you saying because you seem to not say a lot of things when you should."

I watch as Oscar slowly sinks back into the couch, and I fully understand why. I don't understand why they're arguing and it's making things uncomfortable for everyone.

Jade clears her throat, "Ace you did say yourself that the police haven't really been doing their jobs, and what difference would it make to tell the cops that he was under the bridge, especially when they already know the murder weapon. But if the police still can't find anything in about a week, the letter should be given to the cops for investigation."

"Okay." Ace says.

"Maggie?" Jade questions.

"Okay, fine, but if I go to jail, I'm blaming you two."

"So, let's just be clear, that if any of us are investigated we don't say anything about the letter." Adrian says.

"Got it." I nod.

Ace just nods, obviously she's still hurting and wants her brother to be avenged. But I don't understand why she and Maggie were arguing. There must be something that happened between the two of them.

"Well, with this talk over. I'm hungry so I'm going to go." Jade says.

"I'm going too." Ace says as she stands up, her and Jade leaving the lounge.

Maggie stares at the ground before realization strikes her face, "Oh shit!!" She gets up quickly and makes her way out of the lounge.

"I'm going to go grab my lunch from my locker." Oscar says getting up from the couch.

"And I need to talk to Maggie." Adrian says.

"Wait, why?"

Adrian stands up, "Uh, just newspaper stuff."

Adrian walks out of the lounge, and I'm now left alone.

I don't feel like that went as well as I had planned in my mind. I expected more thank yous for the warning I gave them all, but instead it turned into a random argument about a letter.

I lean back in my chair and shake my head.

"Can Conner Martin come down to the office, Conner Martin down to the office."

I stand up from the chair, can this day get any better?

I end up getting escorted out of the school by police. Almost everyone is looking at me and I can guess what they're thinking. *Did he kill Kian?*

I get seated in a room and unlike in the movies this room doesn't have a glass window that people can look through. It's just a small room with a small table and a very bright white light.

308

The door behind me opens and a lady walks in. The only thing I can notice about her is her clearly bleached blonde hair; her dark brown roots are sticking out at the top.

"Hi, I'm Detective Lana." She reaches out her hand and I shake it as she sits down across from me.

"It's, Conner, right?" She asks.

I nod, "Yeah."

"I just have a few questions for you, and you can leave at any time."

I nod and watch as she folds her hands together, "So I've been assigned to the Kian Turner case and just last night we did a sweep of the school."

She reaches down and pulls out a small bag placing it on the table. I realize the bag is filled with tiny pills.

"Those are the steroids that we found in your locker. Have you ever taken these?"

"No, what does this have to do with Kian's case?"

From watching multiple crime movies and tv shows, it always works when you deflect a question with another question.

She pulls out a small pile of photos and places them on the table. "This is a photo of you from grade nine," She points and moves her finger to the photo beside it, "And this is a photo of you in the summer and you look drastically different. Care to explain?"

I shrug, "Puberty."

I know she was talking about the muscles I got.

"Puberty doesn't make someone have muscles like that, you have to work out, and even then, it would take longer to get those muscles. Conner you can tell me if you took these steroids, I know you have a scholarship, and I've talked to your dad about it. I can keep you safe, but that isn't going to happen unless you tell me the truth."

"Okay, I took them for a little bit, but last month I threw them out, I haven't had any in weeks. Someone must have put those in my locker, you should be able to check the cameras."

"Funny thing, where your locker sits, the cameras can't reach."

"What!? Aren't they supposed to have cameras that cover every inch of the school?"

"Who gave you steroids in the first place?"

I take a deep breath, "Kian."

"Did he by chance stop giving them to you? So, you killed him?" Detective Lana asks, leaning forwards on the table.

"What! NO! What!? Why would I do that?"

"People with addictions can do crazy things."

"They were steroids!! I wasn't doing them a crazy amount and I would never kill anyone, especially someone who was like a best friend to me."

"Like a best friend, so you two weren't best friends?"

"No, what no, I didn't say it like that!"

"You've become very defensive, Conner." Detective Lana says calmly.

"Wouldn't you if you were being accused of murder?" I ask.

Detective Lana leans back in her chair, "You do understand that if we find any more evidence that points towards you-"

"You won't, because there isn't any and what you have isn't even evidence," I stand up from my seat, "You said I could leave at any time so I'm leaving."

I walk out of the room and down the long hallway until I'm outside the station. I'm glad my dad wasn't working today.

Sitting at the dinner table was awkward. I knew my parents wanted to say something, but were tiptoeing around the topic.

My dad clears his throat, "So, we got a call from the station today."

"What did they say?"

"That you were called in for an investigation! That there were steroids found in your locker!! That Kian gave them to you!" My dad shouts.

I look down at my lap, I don't know what to say. What should I say? Sorry, yeah that's all true? Would that make this situation any better?

"Are you going to say anything?" My mom asks.

I shrug, "What should I say?"

"Is it true?" My dad asks, placing his fork and knife down on his plate.

I nod. I don't think I could tell them in words.

"Why would you do that!! Do you not realize that all of this could ruin your scholarship!?" My mom yells.

"I have stopped taking them, the ones they found in my locker weren't mine. Someone put them there, and besides the Detective said that I would be safe."

My dad huffs as he leans back in his chair, "They say those things to get you to talk son!... Did you do anything to Kian?"

My mouth drops open, "No! God no, Dad! The fact that you even have to ask that."

"Why did you take the steroids from him?"

"To make you guys proud! I was falling behind all the other guys with how strong they were, I know you don't have to be strong for basketball, but I just wanted to be like them and make you guys proud. I know it was stupid, but basketball is basically the only thing I'm good at other than video games and I wanted to keep being good at it."

My parents sit in silence while staring at me. Are they going to say something?

"I'm sorry." I mumble.

"You stopped taking them?" My mom asks.

I nod, "Yes, for a couple of weeks now."

"I'm sorry I disappointed you guys. But I swear the steroids they found in my locker weren't mine."

"We believe you, and you didn't disappoint us... we're just ashamed we didn't notice." My dad says.

"And we'll find a lawyer, just in case someone is trying to frame you. They're not taking our son from us." My mom says.

I nod, "Okay."

The rest of the dinner we sat in silence; it filled the room slowly with the only sound being the echoing clock. It reminds me about the note, *watch your back*, it reminds me about how I might not have much time left until this person comes at me with something more than just drugs.

CHAPTER THIRTY

Ace Turner
Friday, October 11th, 12:00pm

"Well, with this talk over. I'm hungry so I'm going to go." Jade says.

"I'm going too." I quickly get up from the chair and follow Jade out of the lounge.

"What was all that with, Maggie? She seemed annoyed at you."

I shrug, "I don't really think it's my right to say why. Sorry."

Jade has been talking to me every day this week. I can't tell if it's because she wants to talk to me or if it's because she's trying to figure out why I kissed her at that party Sunday.

If she were to ever ask about the kiss, I don't know what I'd say. Most of that night was a blur. I still can't believe I made out with Conner. It's hard to look at him now and not feel awkward, but he doesn't seem to remember it and I'd like to keep it that way.

I have been trying to figure out why I kissed Jade in the first place, the only conclusion that I came up with was that I had such a bottle up of emotions from when I used to like her that it all just came rushing out. And maybe the fact that I kind of sort of like her again...

"Are you okay though?"

Jade and I stop walking and stand against one of the long walls of lockers, "What?"

"Are you okay? I know that conversation might have been difficult for you."

"I mean why wouldn't I be fine? It's not like the whole conversation was about my dead brother." I laugh nervously.

"At least the cops are trying to do something now, right? Even if it is something small, they seem to be trying harder." Jade smiles.

God that smile makes my stomach turn upside down and fly in heart shaped circles.

"That Detective my parents hired doesn't do her job, but to be fair there hasn't been any leads until now with that letter and everything."

I'm not saying Maggie killed Kian. I know she wouldn't do that, and I believe her when she says that she wasn't in town. But it's the closest thing we've got to a lead.

"I wouldn't say that too loud." Jade says.

I let out a sigh, "Am I going crazy?"

"What? No! Why do you think you're going crazy?"

"Am I grieving weird? I feel like I haven't sat down and just grieved for Kian, I just keep going and never stop to think."

Jade places a hand on my shoulder, "I think that's how anyone would react, and there's no set rules for grieving. And trust me, you aren't going crazy."

"I feel like I am."

"It's okay to feel that way, but know that you aren't." Jade moves her arms to her side, "And um, can I ask you something?"

I nod, "Of course."

"Would-"

"Can Conner Martin come down to the office, Conner Martin down to the office."

That can't be good. I've never heard Conner get called down to the office. Not even in elementary school.

"Anyways, would you-"

"Finally, I found you both!" I glance to my right to see Maggie approaching us.

"Yes?" Jade asks with a hint of annoyance in her voice.

"I completely forgot that tomorrow night is Mystic Glasses' karaoke night and my dad signed me up to sing, and I don't have any idea what to do and I kind of want your guys help. Only if you'd want to."

"We'll do it." I smile, I hope Jade is okay with that.

This might be my one way of saying sorry to Maggie. It's not much, but it might go a long way, maybe even get her to forget. It might not make me feel better about everything that happened, but it might help.

"Really?! Sweet, meet me in the music room after school then, and come with a lot of song ideas, and I mean a lot!" Maggie smiles as she walks off down the hallway. It was a smile that I haven't seen since we were younger.

I turn back to Jade, "As I was trying to say?" She takes a deep breath, "Would you want-"

"Hey, did you guys by chance see where Maggie went?"

I slowly turn to see Adrian standing beside me, "Are you serious." I mumble.

"She went that way." Jade says, pointing down the hallway, clearly as annoyed as I am.

"Thanks." Adrian smiles as he moves past us.

I look back to Jade, "I'm going to wait a second before speaking to make sure no one else interrupts us."

I begin to laugh.

"It's not that funny."

I stand up straight and shake my head, "You're right, not funny at all." A smile threatens at the sides of my mouth as I try not to laugh.

"I think you can tell me now." I giggle.

"Well, what I was trying to say before the universe interrupted me, was. Would you like to go on a date?"

"Really!?"

"Yeah… it's fine if you don't want to, I was just thinking that we've been spending time together a lot and I don't know if you've been feeling the connect too, but it's fine if you haven't I just-"

"I want to go on the date." I smile.

I've never seen Jade this flustered, normally she always knows what to say at the right time. She always seems so confident.

"Wait really?"

"I wouldn't have said yes."

"Right, right, yeah. That makes sense." Jade says, nodding to herself.

Once the bell rings I head to my class. As I sit down my head begins to spin. So many things happened all at once, but the main take away from it all is that I get to go on a date with Jade.

Jade and I walk down the road towards my house, "Maggie seemed more agitated than normal, don't you think?"

"Yeah, I guess so. I didn't really seem to notice." Jade shrugs.

"You didn't have to walk me home by the way."

"I wanted to," Jade smiles, "Plus there is a murderer out there somewhere."

"Then shouldn't I be walking you home too?"

Jade ponders the thought for a second before speaking, "No."

"Why not? Because you're in a gang, you've got a tattoo and you're all buff." I giggle as I flex my non-existent muscles. And come to think of it, I don't know where Jade's tattoo is. I know that Maggie's is on her left forearm, but I've never seen Jades.

Jade chuckles, "You're cute."

"Thank you, but that didn't answer my question."

"I don't need you seeing my house."

"Why not? It's probably much bigger and more beautiful than mine."

Jade nods, "It's more my family that makes me nervous."

We reach the end of my driveway, I walk in front of her, "Do you want to come inside?"

"No, it's okay. I should get home before my mom has a fit." Jade smiles.

"Well come over anytime you need, I'd love to be your escape." I smile.

Jade reaches her hand out and tucks my hair behind my ear. She takes a small step closer to me. I can feel my heart flutter as her hand rests on my cheek. Is she going to kiss me this time? Because last time it was an impulsive kiss on my part and caught both of us off guard.

My front door swings open, "Alec Brown Turner! Get in this house right now!" My mom yells.

Jade takes a step away from me, "Looks like you have to go."

"Yeah, I'll text you." I smile before walking up my driveway.

I get up to my front door. My mom standing there with her arms crossed in front of her chest.

"What's wrong?"

"Did you know about this!?" My mom yells.

"How- What- I hardly talked to Kian about his personal life and after Maggie left, I hardly ever talked to Conner. How was I supposed to know Kian was giving him steroids?"

My mom paces back and forth in the living room while my dad sits calmly in his chair.

"How did you not know anything about this!?" My mom yells, it's almost as if she didn't just hear anything I said.

"Because Kian was always the center of focus! I never talk to anyone!!" I shout.

I don't understand why she was yelling at me. Is it because she can't yell at Kian for selling drugs so she's taking it out on me instead?

"Then who was that girl outside?"

"We just started talking at the beginning of the school year, she's my... friend."

My mom stops pacing and crosses her arms, "She looked more than just a 'friend'."

I lean back on the couch and sigh.

"Alec, I want you to stay away from that Conner kid, if he hurt your brother-"

I stand up from the couch, "For God's sake Mom! My name is Ace! And Kian isn't hurt, he's dead! And Conner wouldn't have killed him, I'm positive. So, I'll talk to whoever I want to talk to because this is my life!!"

Before she can say anything else to me, I bolt upstairs to my bedroom.

Saying all of that felt liberating. I've been needing to say it. Kian always used to say to me, *"If you don't start speaking up for yourself, everyone will walk all over you."*

It kind of hurts to think of that now, because it's almost as if he used that power against Maggie in grade nine.

I feel bad for thinking that he'd be proud of me for standing up to our mom, mainly because he took away Maggie's right to speak up, or at least he for sure made her feel like she couldn't.

I get into my room and begin to pace back and forth.

Conner couldn't have killed Kian, he warned us earlier that the police would be investigating people and questioning them. He wouldn't have told us that if he wanted to frame one of us. And Conner wouldn't be capable of that.

One time in the summer before grade nine, Maggie was talking about how she got her period and Conner almost passed out just from the mere mention of blood.

I sit down on my bed.

Everyone is going to know about all of this by Monday. Conner's whole career in basketball could go down the drain. And technically it would all be because of Kian.

Would Kian have threatened Conner the same way he had threatened Maggie?

No, no, Conner couldn't have killed Kian. I'm positive.

But why is my leg bouncing up and down with anticipation.

CHAPTER THIRTY-ONE

Maggie Snow
Friday, October 11th, 12:10pm

    I walk out of the lounge and into the hallway.
    I've been so focused on Kian's case that I completely forgot about the karaoke night.
    Once I spot Ace and Jade down the hallway, I make my way towards them. "Finally, I found you both!"
    "Yes?" Jade asks, I ignore the fact that she sounds like she wants to verbally punch me.
    "I completely forgot that tomorrow night is Mystic Glasses' karaoke night and my dad signed me up to sing, and I don't have any idea what to do

and I kind of want your guy's help. Only if you'd want to."

"We'll do it." Ace smiles.

That was a faster response than I had thought. I assumed that both of them would say no, at least I thought that Jade would say no. After what happened in the lounge, with me basically taking a rip out of Ace, I swore she was going to punch me.

But she doesn't know the situation, she doesn't know all the things Ace could have done to help me that night, Kian made me leave. I have the right to be angry.

"Really?! Sweet, meet me in the music room after school then, and come with a lot of song ideas, and I mean a lot!" I put on my best fake smile as I walk off down the hallway. I tried to hide my nervousness the best that I could.

I stop walking once I reach the vending machine that sits down by the cafeteria. Pulling out a five-dollar bill I slide it into the machine after selecting a pack of gum. I truly can't remember the last time I had gum. Maybe two years? It's all because of my mom's stupid rule of no junk food, and I guess that includes gum.

"Hey." I take a sideways glance over to see Adrian leaning up against the side of the vending machine.

"Hey?" I reach down and grab the gum out from the bottom of the vending machine dispenser.

"Want to go on a date?"

I slowly stand back up and look at him, there is an odd sense of confidence in the way he's standing. His chest seems puffed out a bit and he seems to be leaning in a *I'm trying to look cool* stance.

"Excuse me?"

"Do you. Want to. Go. On. A. Date?" Adrian asks again.

So those were the actual words that came out of his mouth.

"You want to go on a date with me?"

Adrian nods, "Yes."

"Why?"

If this is because of that kiss at the party, I might just scream. I still haven't figured out why I kissed him. But clearly, he figured out why he kissed me back.

"Well, I like you, and I've realized that I have probably liked you for a while now, and um that kiss kind of helped me figure that out."

Of course, it was the kiss.

"And I know you said you didn't want to get hurt again, which I promise I won't do. And all it is, is one date, and if you don't feel anything back then we will just say friends... hopefully."

Adrian gives an awkward smile as he takes a deep breath. I do have to be honest with myself that he is good looking, and he can kiss well. And he has a kind heart, that I believe truly cares for me.

"So, you want to go on a date with me? Even after I punched Conner in the face, could be a number one suspect in a murder, clearly have a messed-up family, and messed up past. Also, the fact that I somehow broke into the school, oh and not to mention that I'm in a gang."

"And all that makes you the person that I want to go on a date with because it makes you who you are, and I'd love to get to know this person more. Plus, the gang isn't actually that scary."

He does have a point there.

"This isn't just because you feel pity for me? Or that I'm a fabulous kisser?"

Adrian chuckles at the last part, "I don't feel pity for you, I mean do, because what you've been through is horrible and that should never happen to someone even though it does, but like that's not the point. I just- I want to get to know you more and I like you, a lot actually."

My heart does an unexpecting cartwheel.

"It's only one date, and if you don't feel anything, which I'm pretty sure you do because you wouldn't have fallen asleep on my shoulder and you probably wouldn't have kissed me, but, if after the one date it's a no, then I would love to just be a really nice friend."

I take a deep breath, "Fine, just one date. But don't bring up that I fell asleep on your shoulder, ever again, please."

I don't really care whether I fell asleep on his shoulder or not, I know I did, but what I don't know is if I drool or snore in my sleep, and I'd rather not find that out. So, it's best if he doesn't bring it up anymore.

"Fine, but let me quickly point out that I didn't hurt you when you were completely vulnerable in front of me. And I wouldn't hurt you, I never will."

"Why are you so nice to me?"

"Because you're nice to me."

I raise my eyebrows, "I am!?"

Adrian smiles, "Well, the nicest that I know you can be, because I know it's probably hard for you to open up to people."

"Fuck. You've seemed to have got me all figured out. Are you sure we need to go on a date? I'm pretty sure you know everything about me." I laugh.

"How about tomorrow?"

"Can't, karaoke night at the Mystic Glass."

"Are you singing?"

"Reluctantly, yes. My dad signed me up. I have to pick a song and sing it."

"Are the words shown somewhere?" Adrian asks.

"Nope."

"Then it's not really karaoke, is it?"

"Not one bit."

"But can you sing?"

I shrug, "I guess."

"What do you mean you guess? You either can or can't, there isn't really an in-between."

"I don't know, I haven't been here for two years."

My hands have suddenly become very clammy.

"What does that have to do with singing?"

I shake my head, "It doesn't matter, the point is I can't do a date tomorrow night. But you can gladly come to see me fail at singing."

"Yeah, I'll come, but I bet you'll be great." Adrian smiles.

I raise my eyebrow, "You know that flattery doesn't always win over a girl, right?"

"But it can." Adrian smirks.

I don't understand where all this confidence is coming from. I mean sure, Adrian is confident, but with certain things he can be awkward, and I would have sworn he'd be awkward about all of this.

Maybe he's not because I've somewhat opened up to him? Maybe I don't look as intimidating as everyone says I am?

But I'm glad I opened up to him, it's given me an odd sense of relief.

"Well anyways, you should bring Adams too, I don't think he's been out in a while, and he'd probably enjoy coming."

"Yeah, sure, but why do you call-"

"You two get to class! The bell rang five minutes ago!" Principal Galilean says.

Adrian turns around, "Oh sorry, we didn't hear it."

Adrian and I walk down the hallway toe in toe. We split and go separate ways; I make my way up the stairs to the second floor and once I reach there it hits me.

I haven't been on a date since I was dating Conner. And I don't even think Conner and I went on an official date, we mostly sat in the park and played soccer, or we were at his house playing video games.

I've never gone on an actual date before.

"So, your dad just signed you up and you didn't have a choice?" Jade asks.

I spin around on the stool and stop when I see her, "That's exactly what happened."

"Wasn't the last time you sang a song in front of people at the grade eight talent show?" Ace asks.

I shiver at the thought, "Yeah. God too many ukuleles."

I wasn't the only one on stage, but was it horrifying to be up there in front of your whole elementary school, yes. It was as if everyone was waiting for me to mess up or fall off the stage.

Jade laughs at little too hard, "I remember that."

I lean forwards and rest my elbows on my knees, "I don't even know what to sing, let alone get up in front of everyone in the gang and sing."

"It's just the gang." Jade says as though it isn't a big deal.

"But this is probably one of the ways my dad is trying to fix things. And if it is, it's a horrible way to fix things."

"How about when you're singing you focus on one thing, it should hopefully make you less nervous." Ace smiles.

"Yeah... I'll try that."

"And if it doesn't work, wear some empowering badass clothes and if no one likes the song then just punch them. I think it's a good solution, for you at least." Jade smiles.

"Well, I'd love to punch many people who are in the gang, but I feel like they could all punch me back ten times harder, so I'll just wear the empowering clothes."

Ace pulls her laptop onto her lap and opens it, "Well let's do some searching for a song then."

An hour passes and we still haven't been able to find a song easy enough for everyone. There have been no easy songs for me to sing, there have been no easy songs for Ace to play an instrument, and there have hardly been any songs for Jade to play the drums well enough.

"Maggie, stop pacing." Ace says.

"Nope, I am going to be constantly pacing back and forth because we're never going to find a song that is easy for all of us."

"I think I found one."

I stop pacing and look over to Jade. She turns Ace's computer towards us so we can see the screen.

"That could definitely work." Ace says looking over to me, "I can easily play all those guitar chords."

"And the drums are super easy." Jade smiles, "Not to mention the singing is beautiful, it'll work perfectly."

I nod, "Okay, sure let's do it."

I don't want to stop and think about another song, if this one works, it works.

Ace gets up from the floor and moves over to the guitar. Jade does the same but goes over to the drums.

I slowly make my way over to one of the mics set up in the room.

"I don't think I'm going to be able to do this."

"I can sing some backup parts; would that help ease your nerves?" Ace asks.

I nod, "Yes, actually it would."

I don't know if Ace realizes how much that means to me. Even if it is only a small way for her to try and say sorry to me, it's working. I hope she realizes that I'm not mad at her specifically, I'm more mad that she didn't come downstairs that night to stop anything she was hearing.

We run through the song a couple of times before we realize that it's almost 6 o'clock.

We walk out of the music room and down the hallway, "So you two will meet me at the bar tomorrow, and be early please, I want to make sure we can run through the song a couple of times."

"We will be there." Ace smiles, "And maybe try and practice the song a couple more times on your own so you aren't so nervous for tomorrow."

"I will."

I turn and head towards the back parking lot while Ace and Jade head for the front entrance.

I had to park in the back today because being late for school means you can't get your usual spot at the front. And running into the backs of people's cars to get them to move isn't always the best idea... trust me I've tried. I don't feel like getting sued again.

Once on my motorcycle I head towards Dark Treasure to get a quick tea before heading home.

After ordering my drink I turn around, almost running into someone.

"Sorry-"

"Maggie?"

It takes me a second to look up and realize who it is, "Detective Lana, right?"

"Yes. I'm actually glad I ran into you, are you able to talk?"

"I actually can't, karaoke night tomorrow and I've got to practice." I smile, I grab my order from the end of the counter, "Another time though."

I slowly back out of the cafe. I turn and push the door open, quickly walking over to my motorcycle. Never was I more in the wrong mindset to be talking to the detective.

Worrying about the karaoke night has honestly messed with my mind so much, not to mention getting asked out on a date today. I feel like for most of this day I've been living outside my body, just observing. There is no possible way for me to answer questions about a murder. I got to get through tomorrow night first, and then possibly yes.

I walk into my house to see my dad kneeling on the ground picking up old beer bottles that have been on the ground since I got back to town.

"Are we expecting someone?" I ask.

He stands up and dusts off his hands, "No, I just thought that getting the house together would be a good first step."

I look around, half of the beer bottles are gone, the carpet looks clean, the pillows on the couch are fluffed, and I can see the coffee tabletop.

"Well, it looks good." I say honestly, "What's next, the kitchen?"

"That and to find you a bed frame. It's not good for your back to be sleeping on a mattress on the ground." My dad says as he walks past me into the kitchen.

"Did someone steal my dad?"

He chuckles, "No, I'm just holding myself to the promise I made you. Also are you ready for karaoke night tomorrow? Everyone in the gang is excited to hear you sing, including me."

"Wait everyone? As in you told everyone I was going to be singing?"

My dad looks back at me as he throws beer bottles into the garbage, "Yeah? Why wouldn't I tell everyone that my daughter is singing? I'm proud of you."

"Well thank you... um, I'm going to go to my room and do some practicing then."

"That's my Mags." My dad smiles as I pass him and walk down the hallway to my room.

I close the door behind me and rest my head against it.

Did the whole world just flip on its head?

CHAPTER THIRTY-TWO

Adrian Fisher
<u>Saturday, October 12th, 7:10pm</u>

    The kitchen is silent as I pop a piece of bread into the toaster.
    My mom walks into the kitchen wearing a pantsuit, a long jacket and high heels. I hardly see my mom dressed up, so it catches me off guard.
    "Are you going out with dad?"
    "Oh no, it's just me, I'm going out with a-friend. What are your plans for tonight?" She asks while digging through her purse.
    "Yeah!! I'm going to a karaoke night, which isn't really a karaoke night, but it's for Maggie." I smile.

My mom shakes her head with disapproval, "I don't know about that girl, Maggie."

"Well, she's really amazing when you get to know her better. I know when you first met her, she probably seemed a bit standoffish, but trust me, she is not like that at all."

"Huh? Interesting, well... have a fun night and stay safe. I have to get going, so I'll see you later." My mom smiles as she leaves the kitchen.

My newly toasted bread pops up from the toaster.

If I'm going to a bar tonight, I most likely won't be drinking. But I'd still like to make sure I have some food in me either way. I really doubt a bar will have snacks for people.

I told Oscar that I would pick him up around 7:30, he was reluctant to come at first, but after I convinced him it was to watch Maggie sing, that she asked me to ask him to come and the fact that it'll only be a couple of hours. He gave in and was surprisingly excited.

Sometimes I don't understand him, but I can't read his mind so I guess I never will.

I quickly eat my toast before walking over to the front door to put on my shoes, "Dad! I'm heading out now! I'll be back later!" I shout.

I wait a second for a response, but nothing.

Making my way down to my car I notice five spots of bird poop on the hood, "You've got to be kidding me." I sigh as I get in the car and make my way to Oscar's house.

I pull in front of his house just as he comes outside and makes his way to the car.

"You ready?" I ask as he sits down.

"I guess... I've never been on the other side of town before so I'm a bit nervous."

I pat his shoulder as I signal back onto the road, "It's not that bad, no need to be nervous, Bud."

We get out of my car and head towards the front doors of the bar. I can already tell how different it looks from when I was in here a week or so ago.

We walk inside, there is a significant amount of people. Most of them being tall buff men that could probably break both Oscar and I with a flick. I'd like to think I have some muscle, but compared to these guys it's practically nothing.

The bar has a couple of neon lights, not as many as Club Azure though. Honestly that place has a crazy amount of neon lights, I don't understand how people can spend hours in there. This bar is much easier to stay in for a long amount of time.

I glance around to see if I can spot Maggie anywhere, but she's nowhere to be seen. To be fair she is short, but I would like to think I'd be able to spot her out, especially since there's hardly any girls in here.

"Hey guys."

"Jesus!" Oscar yelps as we both spin around to see Jade and Ace standing behind us.

I give a small wave, "Hi."

"Have you two seen Maggie anywhere?" Ace asks.

"I'm right here."

I'm the only one to jump as Maggie pops up from behind the bar.

What is with everyone and the jump scares?

"I'm going to fall over, pass out and die." Maggie says.

"Why?" Oscar asks.

"Because I just will." Maggie hops over the bar countertop and stands beside me.

"You're not going to die." Jade says, rolling her eyes.

"You don't know that. My heart could stop at any moment and then I would fall forward onto Clark in the middle of singing."

"Why Clark?" Jade asks.

"Because he said he'd be right in the front row cheering me on, and to be honest it wasn't that comforting."

I glance down at Maggie, taking in what she looks like. Her hair is set in looser curls than normal. Suddenly all the confidence I had yesterday has fizzled out, I feel as though I'm going to melt into a puddle just by looking at Maggie. I understand that she is obviously nervous, but she doesn't seem it. She seemed more confident than ever, which made me suddenly feel less confident in myself.

How am I supposed to impress her when there isn't much I can do to impress.

Ace places her hands on Maggie's shoulders, "Well go get set up, you try and calm yourself down."

Ace grabs Jade's hand and pulls her away into the crowd of people. Maggie looks over to Oscar and I.

"I'm surprised you two actually came."

"Why wouldn't we?" I ask.

Maggie shrugs, "I don't know."

"You'll do great." Oscar smiles at Maggie.

"Your confidence in me sadly isn't helping my nerves, Adams."

"Why are you so nervous?"

Maggie looks over to me, "Because I haven't sung in front of people since grade eight! And that was five years ago, and if you look around there are a bunch of drunk gang members."

I tilt my head, "And? What's wrong with that?"

"They can get mad if they don't enjoy your singing."

"Isn't your dad the gang leader though?"

Maggie sighs, "Yes, but that doesn't always stop angry drunk people from throwing things."

"I'm so confused." Oscar says.

I ignore him, "Just focus on someone, or something, or just close your eyes and sing. Pretend you're in your room alone."

Maggie opens her mouth to say something when a high pitch noise runs through the room.

I look towards the stage to see who I think is Maggie's dad, "Welcome everyone!! We're about to start the karaoke night starting with my daughter Maggie."

My eyes shift back to look at Maggie, she's frozen staring at the stage.

"I think you have to go up now."

She snaps her head towards me, "I know!" She shouts before walking past Oscar and I, making her way up to the stage.

Oscar leans over, "Did you know she could sing?"

"I found out yesterday."

The room is still filled with loud chatter as no one pays attention to what's happening on the stage. I watch as Ace leans over to Maggie and whispers something in her ear before looking back at Jade who is sitting behind a drum set that looks a little too big for her.

Maggie glances over in my direction, I flash a smile and a quick thumbs up before she looks down at the ground.

I believe in her.

The room becomes silent as Ace begins to play the guitar. Maggie takes a deep breath before singing, "I watch the work of my kin bold and boyful. Toying somewhere between love and abuse."

Her voice is low and soft. I can tell that she's nervous, but already one line through she sounds amazing. I don't want to be bias just because I like her, but her voice is beautiful.

She looks at the ground, I've never seen her this nervous before, yet so confident at the same time.

As the chorus comes around Jade begins to play the drums and Maggie begins to sing louder. The confidence in her voice catches me off guard. One second ago she seemed like a shy sheep in a field, but now she's the wolf hunting that same sheep.

I truly didn't believe it, by the way Maggie was talking a second ago it seemed like she wasn't a good singer, or at least a mediocre one. But to my surprise she's good.

I can't pull my eyes away from Maggie as she sings, I've never seen her so calm yet so frantic at the same time.

The song comes to a rest, the drums and guitar fade out along with Maggie's voice. Everyone begins to clap as Maggie practically runs off the stage.

I watch as she dips out the side exit, I lean over to Oscar, "I'll be right back."

Once I reach outside, I see Maggie laying in the middle of the parking lot. Both her arms are out above her head and her legs are spread open. She looks like she's trying to make a snow angel in the pavement.

"Um... what are you doing?"

She glances up at me, "Being happy because I'm done with that."

"Why were you so nervous, you were great!" I smile as I stick my hands in my pockets.

Maggie sits up and looks up at me, "Thank you, I hope you're not just saying that to flatter me... but I have horrible stage fright."

"Well, I mean it, whether it's flattering you or not, I mean it. And seriously!! You have stage fright? The girl who half of the school is afraid of?"

Maggie stands up and dusts off the back of her pants, "People who are scary, still have fears." She explains as she begins to walk away.

"Where are you going?"

She turns around and begins to walk backward, "A walk, you can come if you want."

I look back at the bar, Oscar is waiting inside for me, but what would a couple minutes of waiting do. I look back over to Maggie, "Sure I'll come."

I jog to catch up with her.

"So, when did you develop stage fright? Was it when you were in grade eight?" I ask.

"Yup, the grade eight talent show. Also, when I got a fear of ukuleles."

"Please explain." I laugh.

"Almost everyone used a ukulele in the talent show that year, so the sound became horrible to me. Once summer started, I made Ace throw hers out, she was mad at me for a week." Maggie smiles.

It makes me happy when she smiles, I don't know if she realizes how beautiful it is. And I don't think I have the courage to tell her just yet.

After a couple minutes of silent walking, Maggie turns to me, "So does this count as the date?"

"What?! No, I'm going to take you on a real date, not a walk around town. Besides you're the one who invited me on this walk, so it can't be the date I asked you on."

Maggie nods, "Makes sense, makes sense. But when is this date happening then?"

"Whenever you're free next."

Maggie nods, "Okay."

We walk in silence for a bit longer, just long enough to realize that Maggie is walking at a slow pace, my pace.

"So, how are you feeling since the party? I never asked, but I remember you ranting before kissing me."

"It's weird..." Maggie pauses, "I saw my dad cleaning yesterday, that coffee table in my living room, it's clean. All the beer bottles on the ground, they're gone. It's like he's possessed."

"Well, isn't that a good thing?"

"That he's possessed, I don't think so."

I laugh, "No, that he's actually cleaning, that he's trying."

"Yeah, I guess, it's just weird, those beer bottles were on the ground since I got home a month ago-"

"Really?! It's been a month?"

"I know right!! Hard to believe that you were the first person I talked to when I got back, well besides my dad and Jade for a brief second."

I smile at the memory, "It's crazy."

It's crazy how we met that night, because all I wanted to do was sit in the cafe and write. I didn't even end up writing because I was so interested in who this new girl in town was. But as it turned out she wasn't really a new girl after all.

"Oh, and another fucking weird thing my dad said, he wants to get me a bed frame because it's bad to be sleeping on the ground… He's the one that sold my bed frame to begin with." Maggie rants.

I start laughing.

"What?"

"It's just funny because you're being very passionate about a bed frame." I purse my lips together trying not to laugh.

"Of course, I'm passionate about it!! Because it doesn't make any sense! I know he said he wanted to get his act together, but I didn't think buying me a new bed frame was going to be a part of it, like I don't care that my mattress is on the floor! I've gotten used to it!"

I begin to laugh even harder. Maggie punches me in the arm, "Ow," I wince, "For someone so tiny you have a strong punch."

She punches my arm again, "I'm not that tiny!"

"I'm pretty sure I'm 6 feet." I laugh while looking down at her.

"Yeah, and I'm only 5,7, so I'm not that much shorter."

I shrug, "It's still pretty short."

"Shut up, 6 feet isn't even that tall." Maggie glares.

"Compared to a short person it is."

"You know if this is your way of trying to flirt with me, it's not working, and I may just not go on the date with you anymore." Maggie says.

"Okay, fine I'll stop."

"Dang, you must really want that date." Maggie laughs.

I don't think I've ever heard Maggie truly laugh before; she has the laugh where there isn't really any noise except for the small part where air gets sucked in. It's really cute and makes me laugh.

"Maggie Snow."

"Shit." Maggie mumbles before we both turn around, "Detective Lana, hi. How are you?"

"I'm good. Who's your friend?" She asks.

"Uh," Maggie glances over to me, "This is Adrian."

She reaches out and shakes my hand, "Detective Lana, nice to meet you. What are you two doing out so late?"

"It's a weekend, and we're just going on a walk. Needed some fresh air." Maggie smiles.

"Are you two heading anywhere?"

"Nowhere specific." Maggie says.

"Perfect, could I ask you those questions I wanted to ask yesterday. Inside?"

Maggie and I look to the left of us to see we're standing out front the Police Station. I was having so much fun that I hadn't even noticed how far we had walked.

"Sure." Maggie says with a hint of sourness in her voice.

Detective Lana looks over to me, "Did you know Kian Turner?"

I nod, "Yeah."

She must be the Detective that's working on Kian's case. Honestly not what I pictured.

"Would I be able to ask you both the questions. It'll be quick and then you two and go on with your walk." She smiles.

"Yeah, sure."

Maggie and I follow behind Detective Lana into the Police Station.

I lean over to Maggie and whisper, "Shouldn't we be split up for this?"

She shrugs, "Maybe they're trying something new, but... let me do most of the talking."

We get seated in chairs beside each other while Detective Lana positions herself in the small chair across from us.

Without notice my heartbeat increases and my hands begin to sweat. I don't have anything to be nervous about. So why does it feel like my heart is going to come out of my chest.

CHAPTER THIRTY-THREE

Adrian Fisher
Saturday, October 12th, 8:50pm

 Detective Lana opens a small notebook and looks up at us, "I'm mainly doing follow up questions, so Maggie some of these may seem familiar to what you were asked at the crime scene, but Adrian, I would like you to answer the questions too."
 Maggie and I both nod.
 "So, what was your relationship with Kian?"
 "I was on the basketball team with him." I answer.
 "Friends with his sister."

Detective Lana nods before quickly writing something into the notebook. Her writing is so small I can't read what it says.

"Were there any romantic encounters with Kian?"

"No." Maggie and I both say at the same time.

I'm going to assume that was Maggie's answer the first time she was questioned, and I doubt she'd want to change her answer now. I also assume she wouldn't classify anything that happened with Kian as a romantic encounter.

"Was Kian ever a violent person?"

"No." Maggie and I both answer again.

I know he was a violent person towards Maggie, but he never was towards me. I never saw any violent nature in him.

"Was Kian acting different before he went missing?"

"I wasn't here until the 2nd of September, so I wouldn't know." Maggie says as she leans back in her chair.

I shake my head, "I maybe saw him once during summer, but that was in July I think."

"Maggie, where were you before September 2nd?"

"In British Columbia living with my mom. I can give you her number and you can ask her yourself." Maggie smiles.

It's hard for me to understand how calm Maggie is in this situation. I understand that she's been questioned by the police before, but it's an odd sense of calmness. How can the person who has stage fright not be afraid of the police?

"That won't be necessary, at least not now. But Maggie. What led you down to where Kian was found? It was so far away from where the party was being held."

Maggie shrugs, "I don't like crowds. Needed to step away for some fresh air."

"Now I see that's very similar to what you said in your first interview right after you found Kian's body, but were there any other reasons as to why you would have gone down there?"

"Umm... Well, I just broke up a fight, and I needed fresh air from that because like I said I don't like crowds. And when I was walking back from the river I tripped over Kian's body." Maggie leans forward on her chair; her voice was harsher than it had been this whole time.

I never knew that was how it happened, I knew she found Kian's body, but I didn't know that she tripped over him.

"Adrian, were you at the party too?" Detective Lana asks.

"Yes, I was, but I stayed with the crowd the whole time, until the police showed up and I followed everyone to see what was going on." I explain.

Detective Lana nods while writing down some quick notes in the notebook before looking back up at Maggie.

"Maggie who was fighting. In the fight you broke up?"

"Conner Martin and I'm pretty sure it was Jacob Ross."

"Is Conner known to be a violent person?"

Maggie scoffs, "What? Seriously, no, never, he was just drunk and trying to show off."

"Does he drink often?"

"Not that I know of. I was gone for two years, it was my first full day back in town, and I haven't seen him drink since."

Maggie leans forwards resting her elbows on the table, "Why are you asking so much about Conner?"

Detective Lana closes the notebook and stands, "You two are able to leave now, all the questions are asked."

Maggie and I slowly stand up and make our way out of the room and the Police Station.

Maggie leans over to me once we're outside, "Do they think Conner had something to do with Kian's death?"

I shrug, "It's possible, maybe we can do some investigating?"

"What?"

"Well, I had this idea while we were leaving, since I have a key to the school, maybe we could sneak in? Investigate some stuff in the newspaper?"

Maggie stares at me, her eyes wide open, "You want to sneak into the school?"

"Yeah, why not."

Maggie begins to walk down the street, "Looks like I'm rubbing off on you!! But it wouldn't really be sneaking in since we have a key."

"Hardy har har, it's still technically sneaking in." I say as I walk up beside her.

She links arms with me, "Then let this be the first adventure."

"First adventure of what?"

Maggie smiles, "You being more like me."

I honestly love how excited she is about this.

We stand out front of the school doors. I grab the key out from my wallet and unlock it, pulling the door open, "After you." I smile at Maggie.

"Why thank you."

Maggie steps inside with me following.

"So, what evidence do you think they'd even have on Conner to suspect him?"

"No idea."

I do have an idea though. I don't know if it's possible, but if it is, they could have found out about him taking steroids. Then found out that Kian was the one who gave them to him. It would make him look suspicious in a sense. But could I really see Conner killing someone? I don't even know the answer to that.

I snap back to reality once I realize that Maggie has been talking this whole time.

"Truly if it was Conner, he wouldn't stab someone."

"Agreed." I nod.

Maggie and I both stop in our tracks as we hear something squeaking from down the hallway. She looks back at me, "Did you make that noise?"

I shake my head. How could I have possibly made that high pitch of a noise?

Maggie grabs my hand and pulls me over to the wall right as the squeak happens again. Maggie glances around the wall, quickly looking back at me, "It's the fucking janitor."

"Why is he here on the weekend?" I whisper.

Maggie shrugs.

The noise gets closer when eventually the janitor walks past us with the squeaking cleaning cart. He honestly looks shorter than when I normally see him in the hallways, but it could be the lighting.

Maggie grabs hold of my hand again and pulls me around the corner and into the office. I stand in front of Maggie while she stands with her back against the wall.

We both peek our head out from behind the wall to see the janitor turn the corner.

I take a sigh of relief and look back over to Maggie who is staring at me, "We could probably get to the newspaper now." She says.

"Yeah." I nod.

I glance down at her lips before meeting her eyes again.

"So."

"So?"

Impulse runs throughout me and right as Maggie is about to open her mouth to say something I lean down and kiss her.

Energy shoots through me as she leans deeper into the kiss. I cup the side of her face with my hand. My finger touching her jaw line, I hadn't realized until now how sharp her jaw line was.

My other arm wraps around her waist as her arms wrap around my neck. Her fingers toying with the back of my hair.

This kiss is much different from the first. Mainly because Maggie is sober, and there is more lust to this kiss. The last one was soft and shocking, while this one is rapid.

I feel her smile against my lips before pulling away.

"Second times the charm, right?"

She chuckles, "Let's just get to the paper before the janitor comes back to kick us out."

We get to the paper. Maggie quietly closes the door behind us before flicking on the light.

I walk over to the chalk board and flip it around to show the murder board, I glance over to Maggie, "Should we put Conner's name up?"

"No," She shakes her head, "He isn't capable of that, trust me."

"Yeah, but he would damage his body so..." I trail off.

"I don't follow?"

Shit. I say that out loud.

"It's just an inside joke I've had with him since we met." I completely lie.

I want to date this girl and I'm already lying to her... but it's to protect Conner. You truly never know who could be listening and I don't want to tell Maggie Conner's secret, it's not my secret to tell. Just like how I haven't told anyone about what Kian did to Maggie. That's her choice to make.

I walk around to the other side of the table to stand beside Maggie.

"Why do you have Jessica's name up there? I know you two don't get along and that we've questioned her as a suspect, but still?"

Maggie looks at the board then back at me, "I was drunk the night I wrote it, and it goes along with the whole power theory. She always wants to be in the spotlight, and I have strong memories of her trying to get with Kian. Maybe she did, or he did something to her..."

I can tell in the way that she said it she's hoping for that to be the answer. That he wasn't only a monster to her, that she might have someone to talk to about what happened, someone who knew what she was going through even if it was Jessica. But I can tell she doesn't believe that.

Maggie shrugs, "I don't know. There's just always been something off about her. Maybe it's the fact that she's constantly trying to insert herself into every situation."

"What if it's not even a student that killed Kian." I suggest.

"Kian hardly talked to adults unless it was his parents or the coach."

I lean over, close to her ear and whisper, "What if it was the janitor, and that's what he was doing in the school, plotting his next murder."

Maggie laughs, "Why aren't you always like this?"

"Like what?"

"Like making jokes. Whenever it's just you, me and Adams in here you never make a joke."

I shrug, "I guess I never realized. But I'll try to make more jokes, just to make you laugh."

"That works for me." Maggie smiles.

Maggie looks over to the shelf full of old newspapers, "I looked through all of those when I first came back. I thought there would be something in there to point in the direction of who killed Kian. Clearly I didn't find anything."

I was going to say I know, but then I realized she didn't know I followed her down here the night of the dance.

"Kian was horrible, but I never thought someone would go so far as to kill him." Maggie says.

I'm beginning to think Maggie is thinking out loud.

She looks back over to me, "What's the motive? Why kill him? Did he hurt someone else?"

Maggie asks as if I'm supposed to know, "And why the hell was my name signed on that fucking letter!"

"I sadly can't answer those questions, but would you think that he was murdered... because of you?"

Maggie sighs, "I've been hoping not. Because I really don't want that to be the case. Because I never wanted him dead. Maybe in jail, sure. But dead, no."

Maggie points her finger up in the air, "And another thing, why a pocketknife as the murder weapon? Of all things, could Kian not run or something?"

"Actually no, he couldn't. The coach had put him on a strict rest because he pulled his leg weird, and it needed to heal because of some College try out thing. I remember him telling me about his mom having a strict no running regiment. Only walking or jogging." I explain.

Maggie nods, pondering the though, "So, whoever must have killed him, had to have known that, and I'm not saying that you killed him because then the letter to him wouldn't have made any sense since you didn't know who I was."

I nod, "Thank you for not thinking it's me, and the person could have also gone for his legs first."

Maggie shakes her head, "Actually no, because when I found him all the wounds were waist up. I maybe saw a couple of blood stains on his pants, but no cuts through the jeans he was wearing. It was dark, so I could be wrong, but?"

It gives me chills to think of how much Maggie has probably thought about this. Imagining his body repeatedly, trying to find any clues. I know that Kian hurt her, but at one point they were friends. So, in some way she did lose a friend.

"We'll never truly know until whoever killed him is found." I say.

"It's just annoying because for all we know this person could be walking past us every day."

Maggie sighs, running her hands through her hair before turning to me, "Let's change the subject."

"Okay, to what?"

"Uh, why basketball, why not be a competitive swimmer?"

"Why competitive swimmer?"

She shrugs, "First thing that came to mind."

"Really?! Not soccer or football or tennis even?"

"My brother wanted to be a competitive swimmer when he grew up, and he would have been great at it if... well you know."

I clear my throat, "Well... I actually can't swim."

"Seriously?! But you have a pool in your backyard!"

"The pools for my parents."

"Well, that's weird, but why can't you swim?"

I shrug, "Never learned. My parents never wanted to pay for lessons. They wanted me to focus on school and basketball. They want me to get into a good school and then get a good well-paying job. My whole life is practically planned out for me."

"My future was just going to be me traveling the world on my motorcycle." Maggie smiles.

"That sounds a lot more fun than parents controlling everything."

"That does suck. I'm sorry." Maggie looks down at the ground.

"It's okay, I'm used to it. It's all I've ever known." I smile, "Uh so… what's your brother's name? I don't think you've told me, or I just forgot."

"Caleb… the one and only psychopath."

"How old is he?"

"He might be 20 now, I think? I was 6 when he got taken away and he was 8… and I turn 18 in March so, yeah he'd be 20 right now." Maggie smiles.

I can see how much it hurts her to talk about her brother. Even if she tries to hide it, I can see in the way she smiles. It's the way her eyes look, they aren't fully closed like they are when she's normally smiling,

I change the subject, "Well that's cool, I'll have to get you a present for your birthday in March then."

Maggie shakes her head, "I don't need presents."

"Something small, besides it's still a far ways away."

"Okay... Also, what time is it?"

I pull out my phone from my pocket, "Shit it's 10, and Oscar has texted me 15 times."

"Shit, yeah. We should get back to the bar." Maggie laughs.

Maggie and I slowly walk back up to the bar, it's cleared out a bit from when we were last here a couple hours ago.

As we approach, I see Oscar leaning up against my car with his arms crossed.

"And where did you two go?" Oscar glares at us.

Maggie and I glance over to each other before looking back to him.

"Got investigated by the Detective," Maggie says, "But I should get going. I'll see you two on Monday."

I watch as Maggie walks back into the bar wrapping her arm around some blond guy. I'm pretty sure his name is Clark. I sigh and look back over to Oscar who is practically blasting lasers into my soul.

"What?" I ask while walking over to stand beside him.

"You left me in a bar full of people from a gang!"

"Well, you survived, didn't you?" I ask while opening the car door.

Oscar rolls his eyes before getting into the passenger seat. I drove him home before heading back to my place.

"I'm home!!" I yell as I get inside, locking the door behind me.

No response.

I take off my shoes and quickly run up the stairs to my room. I assume my dad passed out at his desk in the study.

I flop onto my bed right as a cool breeze hits my face. I sit up to see my bedroom window is open. I never leave my window open while I'm out of the house.

I get up and close it, as I do I notice a small piece of paper sitting on the window seal. I pick it up.

Stay away from her

I look around, as if I'm expecting someone to show up behind me. I would assume the *her* is, Maggie.

Maybe all of this has more to do with her than both of us had hoped for.

CHAPTER THIRTY-FOUR

Maggie Snow
Monday, October 14th, 8:00am

"Heads, I get the pencil, tails you get the pencil." Jade says to Clark.
We all stare intensely as Jade flips the coin into the air, it lands on the ground beside the pencil. We all crouch down, "Dang." Clark sighs.
I pat him on the shoulder, "You'll get the floor pencil the next time."
It's hard not to laugh over this fight, it's a pencil on the ground and when are either of them truly going to use it? I know for a fact that neither of them take any notes in any of their classes.

"Can Maggie Snow and Adrian Fisher come down to the office. Maggie Snow and Adrian Fisher down to the office."

Jade and Clark look over to me, "What'd you do now?" Jade asks as we all stand up.

"I actually didn't do anything... but I'll see you guys later."

I walk away from them and down the hallway to the office.

Adrian is already waiting there when I arrive.

I almost let a laugh slip when I see him, he looks like a scared puppy not knowing where to go. I'm going to take a broad guess and say he's never been called down to the office before.

"Just sit out here and wait until Principal Galilean is ready for you." The secretary says as I walk into the office.

I nod and walk over to Adrian.

"Well, Good morning." Adrian smiles.

"Morning. Do you know why we're here?" I ask while taking a seat beside him.

"No idea."

"This is interrupting the coin toss for a pencil battle."

"The, what?"

"Jade and Clark found the pencil on the ground that they both wanted and Jade just won, but Clark is a sore loser, so I bet they're flipping the coin again right now."

"Ah," Adrian nods slowly with confusion before speaking again, "Also I need to tell you-"

"You two!" Adrian and I look to our left to see our Principal glaring at us, "My office now!"

We sit down in the two chairs across from her desk. I look around. I haven't been in here since grade nine when I got in trouble for talking back to a teacher.

The room isn't any different, the walls are still maroon with hints of green throughout the whole room. I swear that Principal Galilean is trying to make it feel like an enchanted forest... it isn't really doing it for me.

Principal Galilean sits down in front of us, intertwining her hands together placing them onto the desk. "Do you two know why you are here?"

"No." I say flatly as I cross my legs and lean back in the chair.

"Well," She turns her computer screen to face us, "Care to explain why the security cameras picked you two up? Sneaking into the school on Saturday?"

I look at the screen to see Adrian and I walking through the front doors of the school. I'm just glad she isn't showing us kissing, that would be awkward.

Adrian and I glance over to each other and then back at the screen.

Principal Galilean clicks the space bar, the footage quickly changing to Adrian and I kissing. I thought too soon...

I stare at myself, it's weird to see yourself kissing. I almost want to critique the way I kiss, but she turns the computer around before I have the chance to do so.

She leans forwards onto the table, "Get explaining."

Adrian opens his mouth to talk, but I cut him off before he can say anything. I already know he's horrible at talking himself out of situations and his parents would most likely kill him if they found out about this.

"I knew Adrian had a key to the school... So, I suggested we go to the newspaper and get some work done, to get a head start.... And what? Two teenagers can't have some fun?"

"Miss Snow you two were trespassing on school property-"

"No, we weren't. We had a key to the school, we didn't break in. We walked in... with a key. A key that you give to students to use, so technically this is all your fault for giving keys to students."

"You blame me for this?" Principal Galilean asks.

I simply nod.

"Students are to use those keys on school hours, not nights on a weekend."

"But if it's not school hours, why would you need a key? All the doors are unlocked. So, we did

364

not break in, we used a key to do work for a school club."

Principal Galilean stares at me, I smirk, "Are we able to leave now?"

"Fine, but I'm leaving you with a warning. Now get to class."

Adrian and I get up and leave the office. Once we're in the hallway Adrian turns to face me.

"That was awesome." He smiles.

I shrugs with pride, "I have a way of talking myself out of things."

"Why'd you cover for me though? I could have taken the hit."

Adrian and I walk further down the hallway, "Adrian, you're a straight A student, you're on the basketball team and I'm fairly positive you've never broken a rule in your life until Saturday night. It's more believable if I take the blame and besides, your parents would have gotten called."

"Well thank you." Adrian smiles.

"No problem, plus I couldn't have your parents murdering you before our chance to go on a date."

Adrian starts to rummage through his bag, "Speaking of date." He holds out a small, folded piece of paper.

"Paper? If you're asking for my number, you know you already have it right?" I laugh.

"Just open it."

I grab the paper from his hand and open it. I read over to the words. "What is this?" I ask while looking up at him.

"It was in my room when I got home on Saturday, someone snuck into my house and left it on my window seal." Adrian explains, "I'm assuming it's from whoever killed Kian."

"They want you to stay away from her. Is her me?"

Adrian nods, "Well that's what I'm assuming it's implying."

"Bullshit! It's a fucking letter and a stupid fake threat if anything. Kian listened to a letter and that got him murdered, if you listen to it, it'll just get you where he is."

"You got a letter too and you listened to it." Adrian says.

"That was different."

"How is it different when you could have gotten murdered too?" Adrian whispers while taking a step closer to me.

I'm not in the mood for an argument about this, especially with someone I'm not even dating, "Just don't listen to it."

"I never said I was going to, but... Conner wasn't at the bar on Saturday, I know he probably didn't know about the karaoke night, but-"

I shake my head, "No, just stop. This isn't Conner's handwriting, and he's your friend, why would he do that? You didn't start thinking it was Conner until the Detective put it in your head. You know him and so do I, he wouldn't kill anyone."

I shove the piece of paper into my pocket while Adrian isn't paying attention, "People can disguise their handwriting."

"But you can't disguise true friendship."
"We don't know-"
"It's not Conner. Okay? I'm not talking about this anymore."
Adrian nods, "Okay, who else could it be then?"
I shrug, "I don't know right now. Why don't you think of things? I've got to get to class."
I walk down the hallway and round the corner. I head towards the back parking lot to my motorcycle.
I don't want to argue, especially with Adrian. He has been the first person in a while that I have been able to talk to about my feelings and I don't want that to stop. I had to walk away, or I was going to say something that would ruin everything.

I walk into Dark Treasure, order tea and grab a seat.
I pull out my notebook, flip to the last pages and begin to write down everything I know so far.
Kian was killed under the bridge
He was stabbed (Pocket Kinfe probably)
I can't be the only one that believes Conner isn't capable of killing someone. Why would Adrian even think that? Is there something he knows that I don't?
Kian and I both got letters, Adrian got a note/letter

This person likes sending letters/notes to people?

Possibly killed Kian for power?

I pull the small note out from my pocket and place it onto the table. That isn't Conner's handwriting, and he wouldn't threaten or kill anyone. He wouldn't have killed Kian; he was his best friend.

I lean back in my chair and look down at my notebook and letter.

Someone's trying to frame Conner?

CHAPTER THIRTY-FIVE

Jade Button
Thursday, October 17th, 3:00pm

    Blossom Park, known for its endless row of blossom trees. Even during fall they look beautiful.
    The Park is just past the school and is the only park in all Misthill. Sometimes I think the park is how the town got its name, because when spring comes around the whole park gets covered in mist and the park has a couple of small hills in it.
    I had to wait outside the office for Ace. She had to meet with the principal before we could go on our date. I don't know why, but I don't mind waiting.
    Ace walks out from the office, "Sorry about that."

"It's fine, we aren't in a rush, are we?"

"No, but I know you were excited to show me where we are going." Ace smiles.

"I am still excited." I smile.

We walk out from the school and head towards Blossom Park, "So why did the principal need to talk to you?"

"I organized the pep rally, and since I'm not going to be there, she wanted to run a couple things by me, so everything was timed perfectly with the basketball game."

"Oh, that's really cool.... I've never been to any of the school pep rallies or basketball games."

Ace's mouth drops open, "Seriously?! Never?"

"Never."

"Do you not like basketball?"

I shrug, "Not my favorite sport, and I bet if I had someone to go to the games with, I would have gone, but no one in the gang really likes basketball... or pep rallies."

"Well then we will just have to go to the next one together." Ace smiles.

"Sounds like a plan."

"Also, where are we going?" Ace asks.

"Well," I stop walking, "We're actually here."

Ace looks away from me to see where I'm looking, her mouth drops open. "How have I never been here before?"

"Most people don't walk down this street, so it's kept pretty secret."

"It's so beautiful." Ace says as she walks ahead of me down the path.

I watch as she looks around her. Her yellow clothes contrast from the soft pink that surrounds us. The leaves are all along the path, every step we take is pink. Ace turns to look at me, "How did you find this place?"

"I would come here when I was five, my mom would always take of photos of me."

This place is one of the only places I still have good memories with my mom. Running around on the grass, playing tag, hide and seek, having picnics. Then my sisters were born, and it was like she instantly became a stuck-up rich lady that had no time to focus on the fun things.

When I think about it, my sisters don't really know who our mom is or was.

Ace and I make our way over to a park bench that sits between two of the trees and looks out at the rest of the park.

I wipe off some of the leaves from the bench before sitting down.

Ace looks around, "They should build a small park here, more people would be able to see how pretty it is."

"But then it would lose all its beauty because people don't know how to pick up their trash."

Ace nods, "Yeah... didn't think of that."

She quickly turns to face me, "Why did you start playing the drums? Like what made you want to start playing?"

"Uh... I guess it was an escape. I could get my anger out easier because I was just aggressively hitting the drums as best I could. Then I realized, oh hey, I can make music."

"Why were you so angry?" Ace asks.

"My family went from just me, my mom and my dad. To me, my twin sisters, my dad and my mom who no longer had any time to pay attention to me."

"Oh," Ace looks down at the ground, "I'm sorry, that's probably not fun, or wasn't fun. Did your dad pay attention?"

"Hardly, he tires, but he's focused on work too."

Ace nods. I doubt she was expecting the conversation to go in this direction.

"Why'd you start singing and playing instruments?" I ask, changing the subject.

"Well, Kian was always the smart one and the one in the spotlight. He could never do wrong in my mom's eyes. Truly I just wanted my mom to be proud of me too, so my dad and I went and got a piano and a guitar." Ace smiles, "I would blast it through the house, and my mom would yell at me to keep it down. I never did, especially when Kian would encourage me to keep doing it. But then I started singing too and I developed a passion for it."

"Your mom doesn't seem like the nicest person, no offense."

"None taken. She was nice when I was younger, but as I grew up and started to make my own choices, she didn't like it that much... and it didn't help that I'm pretty shy, so just over the past month or two I've been actually standing up for myself."

"I'm glad you're finally standing up for yourself, Ace." I smile.

"Thank you, and it's hard, especially when my mom realized I wasn't a boy... Kian was the one that helped keep her a bay. But with him gone, she's only called me Ace once I think and that was at Kian's funeral."

"That really sucks. I'm sorry."

I don't know what else to say. I can't imagine my mom not accepting me. Sure, me and my mom don't have the best relationship, but she still tries her best to understand who I am.

"Yeah, but my dad's the best and he tries to talk to her about it so she can get more used to it, even though it's been like over a year now..."

"Was your dad and Kian close? Like what was Kian like? I never talked to him, and you don't have to answer, I'm just wondering."

"Oh no, it's okay. I can answer."

"Kian and my dad didn't have much of a relationship, I don't really know how to answer that one. But Kian himself was always perfect, if I were to describe his life it would be a magazine cover, showing the best version of himself on the cover. And everyone kind of knew a different Kian, whether he was my brother or the basketball teams star or just the nice guy on the street that smiled at you." Ace pauses and fully turns to look at me.

"But you know with a magazine cover, how there's always secrets being exposed about people, that's what makes you want to get the magazine to read. But with Kian, I don't think anyone knew him. The real him… and I think you are actually lucky to have never talked to him." Ace looks down at her lap, "He wasn't a good person, Jade."

"What do you mean?"

Ace shakes her head, "I don't know, I could just sense that he was going to snap, or that he already had. I was waiting for him to explode. But just because he wasn't a good person doesn't mean he's not still my brother, right? I'm still allowed to miss him."

I grab Ace's hand, "Whoever killed him will be found, I promise. And then you will get the answer to whether or not he was actually good."

She looks up at me and smiles, but something behind her eyes is saying something I can't quite read.

Ace looks back down, "Oh, hi little bug." She says before flicking it off her leg.

I begin to laugh, Ace looks up at me, "What?"

"Nothing, that was just a really cute and funny way to change the subject."

Ace begins to laugh along with me. She laughs harder than I've ever heard her laugh before. Eventually she snorts making us both laugh until we're out of breath.

A cool breeze hits us, sending Ace's hair flying into her face. I'm glad I wore my hair in a low bun today.

"Want to head to the cafe? It'll be warmer there."

"Yes please, I'm starting to regret not wearing a warmer jacket." Ace says as we stand up from the bench holding hands.

"At least the jacket is cute." I smile while admiring the yellow puffy jacket that has a couple of patches on it.

We sit down in the cafe, in the exact same spot we sat after Kian's funeral.

"So," Ace says, resting her chin in her hands, "How are your sisters?"

"Good, Sam is still obsessed with her butterflies and Jamey is still trying to convince my mom to let her join the gang with me."

"Is it working?" Ace asks.

"Not by a long shot. My mom is still making her stick to ballet, which she is good at, but I don't think she's passionate about it anymore."

Normally Jamey would want to show me her dance routines over and over against, but that's stopped happening. I want to help her find a new passion.

"Do you want her to join the gang with you?"

"Not really, not at her age. Maybe when she's older."

My phone begins to buzz on the table.

"Who's calling?" Ace asks.

I flip my phone over, "Just, Maggie. Probably has something to do with the gang. I'll call her back later."

The phone stops ringing, and I look back up at Ace, "So what-" I get cut off by the phone beginning to ring again.

"Is it Maggie again?"

"Yup." I sigh.

"I would answer it. It must be important." Ace says.

I shake my head, "No, I don't need to, she can wait. I'm here wanting to focus on hanging out with you."

Ace nods with a smile, "Okay."

The phone stops ringing and within a second, it's ringing again, "Okay, maybe answer this time." Ace says

I sigh and grab my phone, putting it up to my ear after answering.

"Yes?"

"Are you with Ace?" Maggie asks, it sounds like she's out of breath.

"Yeah... why?"

"You two need to get down to the Police Station. Right now."

"Why?"

There's a long pause, all I can hear is Maggie breathing on the other line, "Maggie why?"

"Conner was just arrested for killing Kian."

CHAPTER THIRTY-SIX

Ace Turner
Thursday, October 17th, 4:30pm

    Everything around me is spinning as Jade and I walk into the Police Station. I spot Maggie leaning up against the wall beside Adrian and Oscar.
    "We have to get to the Police Station."
    "Why?"
    "Conner was just arrested for Kian's murder."
    I walk over to everyone, "What's going on?"
    Maggie looks up at me, her eyes hang low. She looks more pale than normal, and her arms are hugging her waist.
    "Was Conner arrested for Kian's murder?" I ask.

Maggie glances over to Adrian, but doesn't answer my question.

"Is anyone going to answer her?" Jade stands beside me, her hand rests on my back as my breathing quickens.

"They found steroids that Kian allegedly gave Conner." Maggie finally says.

Adrian stands up and shuffles to stand beside Maggie, "They arrested him at the beginning of the basketball game. Apparently, they found the murder weapon in his locker…"

Adrian keeps talking, but ringing fills my ears instead. I can only see his lips moving, but no sound is coming out. My head spins as he speaks more. I'm going to fall over; my heart feels like it's going to bounce out of my chest and onto the ground.

I take a deep breath and center my focus onto Maggie. She licks her lips and takes a step towards me, "It can't be Conner, he wouldn't do something like this. He was Kian's friend and so what if he gave him steroids that doesn't prove anything. Someone must be framing-"

"Stop talking!" I shout, Maggie takes a step back, "You have not been here for two years!! You left both Conner and I! You don't know him anymore! You don't know the dynamic Conner and Kian had; you only know the dynamic you had with both of them alone!! You never know anything that is happening or that has happened, all you do is think about yourself, Maggie!! I don't even know why you came back to town!!" The words fly out of my mouth before I have time to think.

Maggie's mouth parts, but she doesn't say anything. I understand that she is trying to help. But she isn't. All I care about is talking to Conner.

Adrian looks over to Maggie then back to me, "We just need to talk to the Detective and see-"

"No, I need to talk to Conner!"

"Ace, maybe now isn't the best-"

I turn to Jade, I can feel myself shaking, "I need to talk to him." I say as calmly as possible.

Jade stares into my eyes before nodding.

I spin around to see Detective Lana standing by a chair in the corner. I walk over to her and tap her shoulder.

She turns around, "Ace? What are you doing here?"

"I need to talk to Conner. Please."

"I just called your parents about everything; they should be on their way over soon. Maybe you should wait until they get here?"

"No, please. I need to talk to him."

Detective Lana shakes her head, "Ace I don't think you're in the right frame of mind right now."

"Please... Please."

Detective Lana looks around and then sighs, "Okay, but only for a couple of minutes."

I follow her down the long hallway of the Police Station. As we approach the very end, I see Conner sitting in a cell, his leg bouncing up and down.

My heartbeat quickens and my head begins to spin. I feel as though my legs are going to give out from under me.

"I'll give you five minutes to talk to him." Detective Lana says before walking away.

I look at Conner. A jolt of anger runs through me which keeps me standing. Conner looks up at me, "Ace." He scrambles to stand up as he walks over to me. I stare at him through the bars of the small cell. The image of who I thought he was twisting in my mind.

My voice breaks, "How could you?"

"What? You don't actually believe it was me... do you?" The look of hurt washes through Conner's face.

"They found the murder weapon in your locker."

"Someone put it there-"

"Why? Why would someone frame you then!? Give me a good reason and maybe I'll believe you didn't do this! You were his best friend."

"I- I don't know why someone would frame me, probably because I was close to Kian. Because they could set up something believable to frame me. Ace you have to believe me, please. I didn't do this."

"You were my friend."

Conner grabs the bars of the cell, "I still am. Please believe me. I didn't do this."

I blink back the tears forming in my eyes, "Did you write him that letter, pretending to be Maggie?"

He shakes his head, "No, I would never. I got a letter myself. Threatening me, you have to believe me, Ace. Please." Conner's voice cracks.

I stare into his eyes, they're pleading with me, but there's something deep inside of me telling me not to believe him. I don't know what to believe, "I can't believe you."

"Ace."

"I'm sorry, Conner. But you killed my brother."

Conner tries to reach for me, "I didn't, Ace please. You have to believe me."

I begin to walk backwards down the hallway, "I can't." I shake my head.

"Ace! Ace please!"

As I walk back down the endless hallway Conner's voice echoes throughout me. My head begins to pound again, and my legs go numb, but I keep walking. I ignore the loud ringing that shoots through my ears as I make it back to everyone.

Maggie walks up to me, "Are you okay?"

Tears fill my eyes, "I understand you're trying to help, but please don't. I know you don't care about Kian."

I shuffle past her and out of the Police Station.

I walk into my house and look towards the living room to see my mom and dad gathering things into a bag.

My dad turns to look at me, "Ace, good you're here, we got a call from the-"

"I know. Conner killed Kian. I know. I'll be in my room."

I run upstairs and slam my bedroom door behind me. I collapse onto my bed as tears begin to pool out from my eyes. The tear's roll over the bridge of my nose landing onto my pillow making a small puddle.

"Al- Ace?" My mom's voice echoes into my room as the door opens.

"What?"

"Are you okay?"

I roll over to face my mom, "Do I look okay?"

She glances down at the ground before closing my bedroom door, she slowly makes her way over to sit beside me on the bed.

"I'm sorry, that your friend was the one who had done this, to Kian."

All I can do is nod.

I don't need my mom's comfort all of a sudden.

"I'm also sorry that it has taken me so long to understand who you are. I was blinded by Kian's death, but I should have learned to cope another way instead of taking it out on your identity." A tear rolls down the side of my mom's face before she quickly whips it away.

"Thank you." I say, although it doesn't make up for the two years of her not accepting me.

"You're welcome sweety."

My mom and I sit beside each other in silence before I speak, "He's gone."

"I know."

"Why does he have to be gone?" I turn to look at my mom, tears swarming in my eyes.

She shakes her head, "I don't know."

My mom pulls me into a hug as I begin to shake, tears falling from my eyes.

I've been trying to hide myself from the truth. I've been trying to keep myself positive and happy. I've been distracting myself by planning school events and hanging out with Jade. Pretending that none of this ever happened, that it was all a bad dream. Thinking that one day Kian would just walk back through the front door again.

The wave of sadness and loneliness finally rushes into me the way it should have a month ago. Now I feel more alone than I had ever felt when Kian was alive.

"He's gone." I cry. *He's gone.*

CHAPTER THIRTY-SEVEN

Maggie Snow
Friday, October 18th, 7:25pm

By morning everyone knew about Conner. Everyone knew that he had killed Kian. That, Conner Martin, one of Hill High schools star basketball players, was a killer.
No one even stopped to question if it was a lie or not, they just believe, and believe and believe. But what's a word that's hidden inside of believe, *lie*. People need to learn the facts before they believe so quickly. Because everyone in this goddamn town is believing the wrong thing.
I can't be the only person that believes Conner didn't do this.

I walk out of my room and into the kitchen to see my dad sitting at the table with his feet kicked back. I watch as he flips through the newspaper.

"I take it back, I'm glad you punched that Conner kid. He deserves it."

I turn on the kettle ignoring him.

"You're really got to be sick in the head to kill someone. And to think, I thought that kid had a really bright future ahead of him."

The kettle boils louder, and I clench the edge of the countertop, "Truly sickening."

I slam my hands down onto the counter and whirl around to face my dad, "It wasn't him!"

"I know you're in denial because you dated him, but-"

"That is not why!! I know it wasn't him, and half of the proof they have on him is bullshit!! Plus who in their right mind would keep a murder weapon in their fucking locker!!! He's being fucking framed!"

"Well good luck convincing the town otherwise, Mags."

"I will, I will show everyone that Conner is innocent," I walk over to the door and pull on my shoes, "Watch me do it, dad! Watch me find the real murderer in this town!" I grab my bag off the ground and walk out the front door slamming it behind me.

I clench my fist as I get on my motorcycle and make my way towards the school.

All last night is still running through my mind, it's as if it's constantly on replay trying to spot something I hadn't noticed before.

But it's always the same.

The Police walk into the gym right as the basketball game starts. They walk over to Conner who has just passed the ball to another player. They put him in handcuffs. Detective Lana says something, but over all the noise I couldn't hear it. I quickly figured it out though.

I distinctly remember looking over to Adams beside me before the both of us began to push our way through the crowd on bleachers. We ran over to Adrian who was following the Police and Conner.

We arrived at the Police Station, Detective Lana said she couldn't tell us anything, but I overheard her say something about the murder weapon being found in Conner's locker. Then I called Jade. Most of what happened after that was a blur.

I arrive at the school and make my way inside and over to where the gang is standing.

I lean up against a locker and stare down at the ground.

Clark pokes my arm, "You look like you're about to explode."

"Well yeah, the whole town has gone crazy thinking Conner could kill someone, like, honestly!" I kick the locker behind me.

Jade grabs my shoulder and squeezes it tightly, "Stop it."

"Why!?"

Jade looks around, grabs my arm and pulls me down the hallway into the girl's bathroom.

"Everyone was looking at you like you've gone crazy." Jade whispers harshly.

"I don't care what people think of me. I thought you would know this by now!"

A girl walks into the bathroom. Jade and I both turn and glare at her, making her back out into the hall.

I'm still staring at the door as Jade begins to talk, "This is what Ace needs to move on. Her whole family needs this."

I snap my head towards Jade, "Seriously? The real murderer is still out there. I bet you they are planning their next murder as we speak. Conner being in jail isn't going to let Ace and her family rest, it isn't even going to let the town rest, especially if there is another murder!"

"You can do your sleuthing, Maggie. But at least keep it quiet, let everyone in the town think it was Conner if you really don't think it was him."

"But the real killer needs to be found, that is the one everyone should be fearing, not Conner!!" I shout.

"Maggie!!" Her tone almost makes me step back, it felt like a slap in the face. But I stand my ground, "I heard what Ace said to you yesterday, you don't care about Kian, you probably don't even care about Conner so you really should give all of this a rest. You haven't been here for two years, and if anything, this will get you to look suspicious."

I push Jade, "You don't know a goddamn thing about what happened!! Ace was mad and I know she didn't mean what she said, because she knows that I never wished death upon Kian no matter what he did to me!!"

I push my finger into Jade's chest, "I was the one that dated Conner, not you!" I poke her chest again making her step backwards, "He has fears that don't just go away!!" I poke again, "He's not a killer and I will yell it as loud as I need to," I poke one last time before Jade is backed up against the wall, "and I don't give a shit if people think I have gone crazy."

"Kian was a monster, and only I knew what he was capable of. And Conner knew nothing, but someone else must have known who Kian truly was."

Jade shakes her head, "If you really think Conner didn't do it, then you'll be the next one dead, Maggie. You're digging your own grave."

I move as close to Jade as I can, "I don't know if that is a threat, or if you're trying to help me. But I don't need help, and if you get in my way of finding out the truth... the *real* truth. So, help me I will take away the only real family you've ever had, because you forget my dad is the leader of the gang, you're in and with a snap of my fingers you could be kicked out."

I lean in close to her ear, "Mind your own business and I'll mind mine."

All of lunch everyone is talking about Conner killing Kian.

"I can't believe he would do something like this."

"Honestly I thought it was him all along."

"Can you believe he was doing steroids?"

"I heard that he lost his scholarship because of it."

The rest of the day I have to fight the urge not to yell at everyone. Something that Jade said earlier did stick with me, *"if anything this will get you to look suspicious."*

There is already a letter that links me to Kian's death. On top of that I found his body. I don't need to look more suspicious. But at the same time Conner is in jail so anyone the police had on a suspect list is gone.

For all I know someone on their list could have been the real killer. But I don't even know who was on the list. I only know who's on mine, and it doesn't seem promising.

I couldn't sit through science class today, everyone kept talking about Conner including Adrian and Adams. It was oddly painful to hear.

I sit in the newspaper hiding out for all last period.

"I told you she'd be in here." Adrian says as he and Adams walk into the room.

I've hardly talked to Adrian since Monday when he showed me the letter he got. We maybe spoke the on and off words of how you are and how was your day. But nothing more. I guess I was hurt that he had suspected Conner. I'm hurt that everyone does.

I look over to them as they walk into the room, I glance down at the town newspaper on the table, "It's all fake news." I mumble to myself.

Adams clears his throat, "Guess it's time to take down the murder board."

"No!" I yell as I jump up from my chair standing in front of them both, "It wasn't him."

"When we overheard Detective Lana talking, she said that someone gave her an anonymous tip. That is one of the worst ways to find a criminal, why would someone anonymously tell the Police they think Conner killed Kian. The Police are just trying to wrap up this case so it can be done and over with."

"But what if it was him?" Adams asks.

"No! For one he told me yesterday when I went and talked to him that he had stopped taking steroids!! And he wasn't lying because whenever he lies, he laughs!! He would be the worst murderer; you'd find him automatically!!"

"Oh, and let's not forget Conner's fear of anything sharp, and you know what's sharp?! Pocket knives!!" I shout.

"Maybe he lied to you about it?" Adams asks.

"Yeah? So that means he's been planning to kill Kian since like what? Grade eight? That doesn't make so much sense now does it Adams?"

"I don't want to believe it either, Maggie, but he was your ex. It would explain the letter I got." Adrian says.

Adams looks over at him, "You got a letter?"

I tap my foot on the ground trying to control the never-ending stream of anger that is running throughout my blood stream. I stop and look at both boys standing in front of me.

I shake my head, "He's being framed and I'm going to prove it with or without your help."

I push past them both and into the hallway.

"Maggie!" Adrian runs in front of me.

"What?" I ask sternly.

"Where are you going? I want to help, if you're so adamant that Conner didn't kill Kian, I'll believe you."

I walk past him, "I'm going to visit Conner's house. If he's the real killer, then there will be something in his room that says so."

Adrian walks up beside me, "You can't break into their house."

"I'm not going to break in. I'm going to knock on their door and ask if I can have a cup of tea." I smile smugly.

"Well, you're not doing that alone."

"I don't need your help, Adrian."

He stands in front of me again, "I want to help. You don't get your mind set on something for no reason. So, if there is something in Conner's house that can prove he did or didn't kill Kian. I want to help get him out of jail."

My heartbeat slows, "So you trust me?"

Adrian nods, "Of course I do."

"Then we're riding my motorcycle." I say as I walk outside the school.

"Wait what?!"

CHAPTER THIRTY-EIGHT

Adrian Fisher
Friday, October 18th, 2:20pm

Maggie sits down on her motorcycle, "Are you getting on?"

I stare down at the two wheeled death trap. I find motorcycle's awesome, but they've always scared me because of how easy it is to get in an accident, "I think I'll walk."

"You aren't going to die, get on the fucking motorcycle."

"Are you having a bad day-"

Maggie's eyes send daggers my way, "Adrian."

"Okay."

I sit down behind Maggie, luckily, she is small or there probably wouldn't be enough room for the both of us on this seat.

Maggie looks back at me, "I would hold on if I were you."

"Oh yeah." Right as I'm wrapping my hands around her waist, she's already taking off out of the school parking lot.

I have a strong feeling that Maggie is mad at me, mainly because there is a small chance that I do believe Conner could have killed Kian, but that's only because of all the evidence stacked against him.

Maggie pulls into Conners driveway, "You can let go now."

I slowly release my grip from around her waist, "Sorry."

"It's okay."

We both get off the motorcycle, "Are we going in?" I ask.

"Yeah," Maggie nods before looking at me, "Just follow my lead, don't say anything unless they talk to you specifically."

"Okay." I nod. I'm sort of getting used to following Maggie's lead.

The last time I was at Conner's house was at the end of last year for a new year's party, and I might have gone to one of his parties in the summer too. Nothing about the outside of the house has changed, maybe the colour of their garage, but that might be it.

Maggie knocks on the front door taking a step back to stand beside me.

"Why didn't you use the fancy door knocker?"

Maggie glances towards me with a look of confusion on her face, "Because I didn't want to…"

She looks back to the door right as it opens, "Adrian," Conner's mom smiles, but that smile slowly disappears as she looks over to Maggie.

"Maggie… What are you two doing here?"

"We heard about Conner, we just wanted to come and ask you a few questions for the school newspaper."

Conner's mom crosses her arms, "Well now isn't the best time and I don't need more people painting my son as the villain."

"We don't think he killed Kian. We want to prove he's innocent, and we promise it'll only take a couple minutes of your time." Maggie says.

"More promises from you? Weird that you're making them since you couldn't keep them when dating my son."

I feel as if I stepped into the middle of a war and I'm the neutral country that is super confused with what's going on.

"Uh… so can we come in?" I ask with a smile.

Conner's mom sighs, "Okay, I'll put on some tea."

Maggie looks over to me before stepping inside, there's a smirk that lays across her face. I wonder what she's thinking.

"The house is a little messy. Conner's lawyer was just here, and his dad just left for work." His mom explains as I close the door behind me.

I peer into the living room to see papers scattered across the coffee table.

I walk up beside Maggie as she sits down at the island across from Conner's mom. I stay standing.

"Did you know Conner was taking steroids?"

"Yes, Harry and I found out a couple of days ago." She says as she turns on the kettle.

Maggie leans forwards on the island, "Is Conner still scared of sharp objects, like knives?"

"Of course, he is, won't even touch one."

Maggie looks over to me, her whole face screaming. *I told you so*. It's cute to see how proud she is of herself.

"I don't think Conner would be capable of killing Kian, because of that fact alone, not to mention his fear of blood. The evidence they have against him is faulty and-"

"Maggie, I know all of this, what are you trying to do?"

"Can we look in his room? We think there might be something in there that could prove he's innocent and if we find anything we promise to show you." Maggie fiddles with her thumb, she's lying or nervous.

Conner's mom looks at the ground before looking back up at us, "You promise that you're wanting to help my son?"

"It's the promise I know I won't break."

She nods, "Go on up then, I'll finish making tea."

Maggie and I make our way up to Conner's room. Maggie stops in the doorway, "You, okay?"

"His room hasn't changed at all."

Maggie goes right towards his desk and pulls open a drawer, she begins to lift a pile of books out.

"Why are you looking their first?" I whisper.

"If he was hiding anything, it would be in here, there's a secret compartment at the bottom of this drawer. He used to hide tons of things here." Maggie explains.

"Spooky." I mumble.

Maggie pulls something from the drawer, "Seriously." She mumbles as she places it onto the top of the desk. I realize it's a condom… but only the wrapper. Why the hell would he be hiding that? Just throw it out?!

Maggie stops before quickly pulling something out of the drawer and placing it in her pocket. She puts everything back inside and stands up.

"Did you find something?" I ask.

She nods slightly, "Let's go."

I follow her quickly down the stairs, "We're sorry we didn't find anything. But my dad called so we've got to get going."

"Bye. Sorry we couldn't stay for tea." I smile at Conner's mom before following Maggie out the door.

"What did you find?" I whisper to her as she sits on her motorcycle.

"Just get on."

I get on behind her and wrap my arms around her waist tightly. She backs out of the driveway and drives down the street. We arrive at the cafe and make our way inside. We grab a table. The one in the very back corner. The place we first met.

The cafe isn't as busy as I thought it would be at this time.

Maggie pulls a small piece of paper out of her pocket and places it on the table in front of me, "There's proof it couldn't be him."

"Watch your back." I mumble to myself as I stare down at the piece of paper.

"He got a letter or note whatever you want to call it. He got one too, this proves he didn't kill Kian. Especially because the note was in his secret compartment."

I look up at Maggie, "Should we give it to the cops then?"

"No, we need more evidence against it not being him. Because they'd ask us a ton of questions which would lead to us having to give them all the other letters and then it would point back to me. This note Conner got, needs to stay between us for now, until we have something more to prove it wasn't him." Maggie whispers.

I nod, "Okay that makes sense, but should we tell Oscar?"

"Adams is awesome and all, but I can only trust you right now, okay?"

"Okay." I nod. I feel kind of honored.

"Okay, good. I'm also going to go get a drink now, I'll be back." Maggie gets up and walks over to the counter.

There are so many sides to Maggie, sometimes it's hard to figure her out. I never know if she's going to laugh, cry, punch someone or yell.

Maggie comes back with a drink and a cookie.

"You got a cookie?"

"Yeah, I thought you might want it. I heard you talking to Adams in science class yesterday about craving one of the cafes cookies, I never knew if you got one yesterday or not."

Maggie slides me the cookie, "Oh! Thank you."

I pull the cookie out from the bag and take a bite as Maggie looks out the window, "So… you and Conner's mom don't seem to get along that well."

Maggie sighs, "Yeah… that's my fault."

"Is it to do with promises or? She kept going on about that." I'm mainly asking out of my own curiosity.

"When Conner and I started dating he wasn't in the best place mentally. I made a promise to his mom that I wouldn't break his heart. You can guess what happened next."

"Yeah…" I nod. Kian happened and screwed that whole promise up. "Is that why you're so determined to prove Conner's innocence?"

"Partly yes, but also because no one should get years in jail for a murder they didn't commit,"

Maggie sighs, "Stupid person and their stupid anonymous tip."

"Wait! What if the person to give the anonymous tip was the person who killed Kian?"

"Well obviously, that's what I've been thinking this whole time. Unless two people killed Kian, then that's a whole different story."

"I doubt two people killed him."

Maggie nods and takes a sip of her drink and looks out the window. "All of this is so stupid," She looks over to me, "I bet right now if I wasn't here, I'd be having a fight with my mom about school."

"Why school?"

"I hated the school I went to, everyone was so judging, and they all thought they were higher than everyone else, like they were royalty." Maggie shakes her head, "I would skip school, everyday just to avoid those people."

"Did you date anyone while you were there?"

"No, *everyone* thought they were royalty, and I was the weird kid, just because I wore black and had a motorcycle. Not to mention they called me emo."

"Really?"

"Yup, it's fucking stupid!" Maggie laughs, "God I wish I punched half of those people, or all of them for that matter. If any of them ever moved here, they would have a rude awakening to the world. Not everything is sunshine and rainbows."

"Well, if it ever was, Kian would still be alive."

"Bingo."

Maggie leans back in her chair and looks out the window, "Do you think he knew?"

"What do you mean?"

"Do you think Kian knew he was going to die? When he got under the bridge do you think he knew what was going to happen? Did he know who killed him?"

"I'd rather not know the answer to that actually."

"Was ready to die? I shouldn't even be wondering these things."

I shrug, "Why not. It's okay to be curious as long as it doesn't hurt anyone."

Maggie looks over to me, "But I don't want to be curious. I want to be mad at him, I want to be glad that he's gone. But deep down I just wanted him in jail for what he did. It hurt what Ace said to me yesterday."

"What did she say again?"

"She said that I don't care about Kian. But it hurt because I did care for him, and just because of what he did to me... Fuck it was horrible, but I'm still allowed to comfort my friend, aren't I? I was putting my feelings aside to try and be there for her."

I grab a hold of Maggie's hand, "You have a really big heart, even if you try not to. But don't take what Ace said to heart, because she was hurting. Just like how you were hurting when Kian hurt you, and you probably said things you didn't mean, or even wanted to say."

A small smile reaches Maggie's lips as she looks down at the table blinking rapidly, she takes a deep breath before standing up.

"Did I say something wrong?"

"No, you said everything right." She walks over to me, placing her hand on my shoulder, "I guess I'm not a mystery to you anymore. You know how I work and how I view the world. I'll see you on Monday, Adrian." Maggie smiles before walking out of the cafe.

I watch as she gets on her motorcycle and drives off down the street. I lean back in my chair; a smile sits on my lips.

Wait.

How am I going to get home!?

"Thanks for picking me up." I say as I get in the passenger seat of my dad's car.

"Why were you stuck at the cafe in the first place?" My dad asks as he backs out of the parking lot.

"My ride left me."

"Who was your ride?"

"Uh... Maggie."

"You've been hanging out with that girl a lot recently."

I nod, "I guess I have."

"Do you like her?"

"Yeah, I do, a lot actually. But don't tell mom."

He nods, "I won't, but some advice, girls' hearts are fragile, so be careful with it."

I will be. I want to make sure she doesn't have to worry about her heart being hurt, because I know she'll do the same for my heart.

Once in my room I open my notebook. I finally have inspiration to write again.

CHAPTER THIRTY-NINE

Maggie Snow
<u>Thursday, October 24th, 7:00am</u>

It's been a week since Conner was arrested. Adrian and I are the only people who know for sure that it wasn't him who killed Kian.

Now when I drive down the streets there isn't an eerie shiver that goes down my neck. The town feels like how it did when I was a kid. Happy, peaceful, quiet. Everything that it will truly be once the real killer is found.

As I walk out of my room I get hit with the strong scent of bacon. I make my way to the kitchen to see my dad moving from the oven to the fridge. Bacon and eggs are being cooked on the stove.

"What's going on?"

"Oh," He turns to look at me while grabbing the milk out of the fridge, "I thought I would make breakfast today, I've noticed that most mornings you run out of the house without having anything to eat and that's not the healthiest thing. So, sit down, breakfast is almost ready."

I slowly pull the chair out from the table and sit down as my dad places a cup of tea in front of me. "Thanks," I smile.

I look around the kitchen, "Did you do more cleaning?"

"Yeah! I did a bit more cleaning last night, and maybe today we can look online for a bedframe? Or you can take Caleb's old one."

I haven't heard my dad say his name in so long, "Uh... I'd rather a new one if that's okay."

"Of course!" My dad nods while placing a plate full of eggs, toast and bacon in front of me.

He sits down across from me and begins to eat right away, "So what are your plans for the day?" He asks, mouth full of eggs.

"Uh, the usual, school, working at the paper for the school. I think I'm hanging out with Adrian later."

"Adrian? A boy?"

I nod, "Yeah, he's a boy...?"

"Do you like him?"

I shrug, "I don't know." I *do* know, but I don't want to talk about boys with my dad.

"What are you up to today?" I ask.

"Well, I think I'm going to clean the house more, I've got a shift at the Mystic Glass later and I was thinking of applying for another job so we can get more money. I think you should get a job too, Mags."

I clear my throat, "Uh yeah... I'll look into it."

"Good, now eat up you don't want to be late for school and you've got to have a full stomach." My dad smiles as he takes a sip of orange juice.

I didn't even know we had orange juice... Did he go grocery shopping?

I pull into the school parking lot. My dad forced me to wear a jacket today because we're "*in the thick of fall now and it's getting super cold out*" I didn't have a jacket so he forced me to wear his. It's surprisingly warm except for that small hole that's blowing wind down the back of my neck.

I walk over to my locker and shove the jacket inside. I pull my bag back over my shoulder and close my locker. "Holy shit!" I jump as I notice Adrian standing beside me.

"Hi." He smiles.

"You! Ah! You need to stop doing that!!" I hit him in the arm.

He smiles, "I've done this every morning for a week now you should be used to it."

"Well, I'm not." I glare.

"Sooo..." Adrian smiles.

"So what?"

Adrian leans up against one of the lockers, "Technically yesterday you said I could ask you again tomorrow. So, it's tomorrow and we still haven't gone on that date yet."

I haven't been wanting to keep pushing the date back, but I don't know if now is the best time to go on a date. Sure, the rest of the town thinks since Conner is behind bars the town is safe, but it isn't. But I can't keep pushing this date back or Adrian will one day stop asking, and that's not what I want.

"Okay, what day were you thinking?"

"Saturday?" Adrian smiles.

"That should work."

Adrian's smile beams as we begin to walk down the hallway.

"Are you okay though? You seem a little shaken up."

"My dad made breakfast today."

"Okay? Isn't that a good thing?"

I shrug, "Yes, it is, but he hasn't made breakfast, well a good breakfast since I was 8. And that was because he was forced to make breakfast because Ace had slept over... oh and he's cleaning the house again."

"All of that is a good thing though."

I sigh, "Yeah... it's just weird."

"Hey guys." Adams smiles as he walks up beside me.

"Hey."

Adams starts walking backwards in front of us, "I just overheard that the Christmas dance might get canceled this year due to budget cuts. That should go in the paper, don't you think?"

I glance over to Adrian quickly, "Uh maybe we put that in the paper mid-November? It is still October, so Christmas is a bit away."

Adams nods, "Well whenever, but it should go in the paper."

"Sounds like a great plan." Adrian smiles.

My eyes shift down the hallway to see the gang standing together. Jade glances at me before looking away. I haven't talked to her since last week in the bathroom. To be fair I don't really want to talk to her to begin with, but I feel like I should say sorry, I had no right to say certain things to her.

"Um... I'll see you two later." I walk away from Adrian and Adams down the hallway.

"Hey."

Jade looks over to me, "Hey."

"You were right, I couldn't find anything that proved Conner didn't kill Kian. I'm sorry for the things I said to you." Part of that was a lie, but that's okay. At least I said sorry.

"Thank you. Now everyone can be at peace, right?" Jade smiles smugly.

"Right." I smile. I can't wait to punch that smile off her face when I find the real killer.

The warning bell rings, "Well. I'll see you all later."

I stare out the window of the newspaper. It started to rain during last period and hasn't stopped for a second since. My motorcycle is going to be soaked.

"Maggie, didn't you say something at the beginning of the year about every killer striking twice?" Adrian asks.

I turn around, "Yeah I did. It's basically if it wasn't a one off killing for no reason they'll most likely kill again, normally it would have something in common to do with the first killing. Like a guy goes around and kills every female with red hair, that would be a pattern, right?"

"So, if we maybe figure out if the killing was for one specific reason we can figure out if they'll kill more people? Find the pattern basically?" Adrian asks.

I nod, "But it'll be hard to find a pattern based off of only one killing, and like I've said, it could have just been a one and done kind of thing."

"What if this killer wants to be different?" Adams asks. I almost forgot he was here; he's been so quiet recently. Adrian had mentioned to me that his parents might be going through a divorce, so I understand why he's less talkative.

"Different how?" I ask.

Adams shrugs, "I don't know, what if they don't want to follow a pattern, but keep killing people. What happens then?"

"Then, we're probably fucked."

"Oh, yay. Well, I'm going to go get some water now." Adams says sheepishly as he walks out of the newspaper.

I look back out the window at the rain. It hits the ground with such anger. Can rain have emotions? I think it was proven that trees have feelings so why wouldn't rain be able to have feelings?

"Why do you keep looking out the window?" Adrian asks.

"I like the rain, it's peaceful to watch, sometimes annoying, but peaceful." I explain.

Ever since last week I feel as though I can say anything to Adrian, and he won't judge me. I find it confusing that I'm still having a hard time trying to admit to myself that I like him.

For every reason I like him there is something that is telling me no, and it's all because of Kian. I know Adrian is a good guy, but Kian was a good guy in my eyes once, and then he ended up dead. I shouldn't even be comparing Adrian and Kian to each other. I never dated Kian, I dated Conner. Kian was just the asshole that ruined what I had with Conner. If anything, I should be comparing Adrian and Conner, and when I think of that, they aren't that far different.

I turn to look at Adrian, "So, what are we doing on this date?"

"What if I want it to be a surprise?"

"Okay, fine, but are you picking me up then?"

He nods, "Yes I'll pick you up."

"Is there anything specific I should wear?"

"No... just anything you're comfortable in."

I nod, "Sounds good then."

Adams walks back into the room, "Okay should we-"

My phone begins to ring, "Ah, sorry it's my dad... Hello?"

"Hey, can you come home now?"

"Uh sure, is everything okay?"

"Yeah... just get home."

The call ends. I look over to Adrian and Adams, "Sorry guys. My dad needs me home. Can you two work on the paper alone?"

"Yeah, we got it." Adrian smiles.

"Great." I smile. I grab my bag off the ground and make my way to my locker to grab my dad's jacket. Once outside the rain pours down onto me. Luckily the jacket has a hood and is long enough to cover my butt when sitting on my motorcycle, so it doesn't get too wet.

I quickly run into my house, "Dad, why'd you need me home?" I shout as I close the front door behind me.

"Maggie."

"Yes."

I turn around, pulling the hood from off my head, "Mom?"

"Hi." She smiles as she slowly gets up from the couch, she walks over and pulls me into a hug.

"What- What are you doing here?" I ask as I reluctantly hug her back.

"Your dad called me, and long story short I got on a bus and came here." She smiles.

"Oh." That explains the clean house, the jobs, the breakfast...

"I'm sorry about everything I said on the phone. I shouldn't have said it."

I nod and give a fake smile.

The last time I talked to my mom was over the phone and long story short, she ended up telling me that she didn't want anything to do with me anymore and that I wasn't a good daughter. Kind of got crushed and ended up throwing a party at Adrian's... not my brightest moment.

We all sit down in the living room. I haven't seen my parents together since I was seven. The day my mom left is still a blur in my mind.

Did my dad know she was coming back to town after he had called her?

I guess I'm happy that my mom is back, but it's weird to see her in this house again.

I watch as my parents talk as if the past 12 years never happened, as if everything is okay between them. I don't understand how they can act like none of the past happened.

But I guess that's what I've been doing with Kian... I've been trying to forget everything that happened. It's what I've done for two years.

Maybe my parents talked everything through over the phone?

I stand up from the chair, "Uh... I have to go... I'll be back."

"I just got here. Where are you going?" My mom asks.

"I forgot something at school. I'll be quick." I say as I grab my dad's jacket from the closet and leave the house.

Slowly I make my way to the cemetery on my motorcycle. With it raining out the roads are slippery, but I need to talk to Kian... even if he can't talk back.

I make my way over to Kian's gravestone. I stare down at it as rain pours down on me.

"You were a dick you know that... Why me? I'd never wish what you did to me upon anyone else, but why did you pick me to do that to?"

I stare down at his name; I know I won't get the response I need. I know I won't get the closure that I need, but I can still try.

"You were a horrible person... but you didn't deserve to die. You just needed to go to jail. Even if it was only for a year..."

I swallow the lump in my throat, "I know you weren't the one to send me that letter, I've pieced that together by now. But if you were and we actually talked I would have punched you in the face and then told everyone what you did to me!"

My fists sit in balls as I try not to dig my nails into the palm of my hand, "I would have ruined everything you worked so hard for; your life would lose all its control just like mine had."

"Who fucking killed you and why did they have to drag me into it!!! Why does it involve my name, me!!" Tears fall from my eyes as I begin to laugh, "I'm yelling at a fucking gravestone… I'm yelling at a fucking gravestone"

I bite my bottom lip and take a deep breath, "You had your secrets Kian, you lied a lot. I know a lot of those secrets now, and I'm not going to let you control me anymore. I never should have let your control me, but I was scared, and you used that as power, but you truly never had any power over me. You just made me believe that you did."

Rain pours down on to me, "Only I'm in control, and I'm never forgetting that."

CHAPTER FORTY

Ace Turner
Friday, October 25th, 7:30am

A faint knock on my bedroom door echoes through my room. I squint my eyes open, but don't roll over.

"Sweetie, there's some pancakes downstairs if you want them." My dad says through the door.

I don't respond.

The door creaks open, "Ace?"

I don't turn around to face him. I keep staring forwards at my yellow wall, "I'm not hungry, dad."

"Okay, when are you going to go back to school?"

"I don't know." I mumble.

"Okay, but I'm going to bring you up some pancakes and syrup because you do need to eat."

I don't hear my door close, but I do hear my dad leave the room. I pull my blanket up closer to my chin and wrap my arms tighter around my stuffed bunny.

What feels like an hour passes before I hear my dad walk back into my room, "The pancakes are on your desk when you're ready for them."

"Maybe you should try and shower today?"

My last shower was last week Thursday morning before school. I showered for my date with Jade. She's tired texting me to see how I am, but I haven't been responding, I'm pretty sure my phone is dead now. I haven't left my room for a week, except for when I have to go to the bathroom.

"I might." I mumble.

"I'll be downstairs if you need me. Your mom is going out." This time I hear the door close when he leaves.

I roll over and lay on my back. I stare up at the ceiling at the small glowing star that sits between the records, I put the star up there when I was seven. It doesn't even glow anymore.

I shift my eyes over to the window. The sun is peeking through the clouds, sending a soft orange glow around my whole room. Mornings like these make the trees in fall look more yellow and orange.

The sun makes me feel the smallest bit alive, it's the only thing keeping me in reality.

The sun comes out from behind the clouds, it brightens my room. I turn my head towards the wall, my whole body rolling with it. I close my eyes and drift back to sleep.

My body jolts awake to the soft banging coming from my door.

"Ace, one of your friends from school is here." My dad calls through the door.

It's probably past two now then. School must be out.

"They're going to come in, okay?"

I don't respond.

I hear the door slowly open and then close, "Hey." A quiet whisper echoes in my ears. It's Jade.

"Your room looks really nice."

"Thanks." I mumble.

She's never been in my room before. I don't know if now would be a great time for her to be in here or not.

"Ace," There's a brief pause before she continues, "You haven't been at school in a week... you hate missing school. And you haven't answered any of my texts."

"Yeah..."

"Are you okay?"

How am I supposed to respond to that?

"Right, probably not... um that was a bad question to ask."

I can feel her staring at me, but I can't bring myself to roll over. I don't know what I look like, and I don't want her seeing me like this.

"Have you been out of the house?"

"No." I mumble.

"You should go outside. The sun is good for you."

I get plenty of sun in my room.

I feel the bed shift, "Okay, get up."

I don't respond.

"Ace get up."

I can't respond. I'm being a burden.

"Get up, we're going to the cafe."

I pull the blanket closer to me.

"You can't just ignore me."

I don't want to ignore you...

I feel Jade stand back up. Without notice my blanket gets thrown off me. I spin around to look at Jade, "What was that for?" I ask in a low whisper.

"Go have a shower, get dressed. I'm not allowing you to get stuck in this. I need you to live for you. I'll be downstairs waiting."

"Jade-"

"I have my bike outside, and I've got Uno and even rainbow chocolate chip cookies. Your favourite."

I slowly sit up from my bed. The first time I have for a while. Jade grabs my hand and helps me stand up.

"Get showered and dressed. Wear something comfortable. I'll meet you downstairs." Jade nods and waits.

I nod back.

Jade leaves my room, but leaves the door open behind her. I look over to my desk to see the pancakes my dad has brought me earlier. I turn back towards my bed. I want to crawl back into the it, curl up in a ball under the blankets and forget about the world around me.

But I can't. Jade is waiting for me downstairs. I don't want to leave her down there with my dad for long or he'll talk her ear off.

And she got me my favourite cookies.

I grab a towel from my closest and walk across the hallway to the bathroom. As I get into the shower, I let the hot water run down my back, it feels nice, but I still wish I was in my bed. It's more comfortable, it's safe.

I get back into my room and open my closest door. For once I don't want to reach for my usual yellow clothes. I grab a pair of gray sweatpants and an old light blue t-shirt from the back of my closet.

Once I'm dressed, I pull my hair up into the best bun I can. I didn't want to blow dry my hair so it's still soaking wet.

I make my way downstairs; laughter floats up to my ears as I round the corner to see Jade and my dad laughing.

Jade looks at me and smiles, "Outfit looks hella comfy."

I nod, "It is."

Jade gets out of the chair and walks over beside me, "Well we will get going. It was nice meeting you."

"It was nice meeting you too, Jade." My dad smiles.

I wave to my dad before following Jade out of my house, "Your dad got your bike out for you."

"Okay." I smile the best I can.

We walk over to our bikes; they are pretty much the same except for colour. Mine is yellow and hers is an orange, brown colour.

As we ride down the street the wind hits my cheeks, it's cold, but not freezing; I'm suddenly regretting not drying my hair. I can feel my mom yelling at me about how I'm going to get sick. And in that case, I don't really care because if I'm sick that means I get to spend more time in my bed.

We grab a table near the cafe's entrance.

Jade passes me the Uno cards to deal out while she goes to get us drinks.

"Here is your coffee." Jade smiles as she places it down in front of me.

"Thanks."

Jade grabs the rainbow chocolate chip cookies out of her bag and places them on the table.

"Thank you for the cookies."

"Of course, I know they're your favourite and it was the last box. So, they must be good right." Jade smiles.

I nod, "Right"

Jade picks up the cards I dealt out for her, "Shall we play?"

"Yeah."

"Uno."

"How do you keep winning?! Honestly if I knew you were this good, I would have brought a different card game." Jade huffs placing down a card.

I place down my final card, "I win."

"How did you-"

"Strategy." I smile.

There isn't really a strategy... It's just luck.

"Teach me."

"I can't, because then you'll win. You have to come up with your own way to win."

Jade rolls her eyes, "Okay, well we're not playing anymore."

She reaches for all the cards and begins to put them back in the box.

"I never pegged you for a sore loser."

"Hey! I'm not- Why- Why would you- No I'm not." Jade rambles.

"Mhm, sure."

I look over to the clock, "I should probably get going... It's getting late."

Jade turns and looks at the clock, "It's only five."

I clear my throat, "Yeah- I just- Yeah I'm really tired."

"Okay, well we're hanging out tomorrow."

I stare at Jade, puzzled. I don't remember us having plans to hangout, "We are?"

"Yup. My sisters and I are having a movie marathon day and they wanted me to invite you."

"I don't know-"

"Ace, you can't stay in your house forever. I know you're sad, but-"

"You don't get it, Jade! I never realized that he was actually gone until Conner got arrested. I don't know what made up fantasy world I was living in, but he's not coming back, and I don't know how to deal with it."

Jade grabs my hands, "I know it must be hard. And I know I don't and can't understand how you are feeling right now. But life goes on, and you are going to have an amazing life that Kian will be able to watch from the afterlife. You need to live for yourself."

I look down at the table, "But it's hard."

"That makes sense, but I can be here to help you. I can help you get out of the house. If you want my help... I don't want to see the bright happy amazing kind girl that I have fallen for get lost."

What if I am already lost?

"You are stronger than all of this, Ace."

I look up at Jade, my eyes watery. "Thank you, I'll try to remember that."

Jade walks me up to my front door, "I'll come and pick you up tomorrow at 1, okay?"

"Okay, thank you." I smile.

I open the door and wave bye to Jade before walking inside. I glance into the living room to see my dad sitting in his chair. I walk into the living room and sit down on the couch.

"Did you have fun?"

"Yeah." I nod.

I look up at my dad, "Could we maybe watch some Gossip Girl tonight?"

"Yeah! Of course, we haven't done that in a while." My dad smiles.

A long time ago I walked into my parents' room to see my dad watching Gossip Girl. I promised him that I wouldn't tell mom or Kian about it as long as I was allowed to watch it with him.

My dad turns on the tv and I get up to get some popcorn. As I pass the stairs, I want to run up and crawl back into my bed. But I don't, because I am strong, just like Jade said. And I will go day by day and second by second to make sure I can live my life. I can't stop living just because one horrible thing happened. I won't stop living because one horrible thing happened.

CHAPTER FORTY-ONE

Adrian Fisher
<u>Saturday, October 26th, 1:00pm</u>

    Only one more hour until I have to go pick up Maggie. I'm nervous, really nervous. I've changed my shirt five times because I've sweat so much in the other ones. I've had to keep reminding myself that we've hung out alone before, so what's the difference now? I guess labeling it as a date is what's making me nervous.
    I walk into the kitchen to see my mom and dad whispering aggressively to one another in the corner. It's the sixth time this week that I've seen them doing that.
    My mom looks over to me, "What's with you wearing hoodies recently?"

"Um... because it's fall?"

I walk past both of them and open the cupboard, I turn and look back at them, "Everything good? You two are staring at me weird..."

"Everything is fine. I have to get back to work." My dad says as he moves away from my mom and out of the kitchen.

I assume I walked in on one of their many arguments, they've been doing that a lot lately and it's always in the kitchen, and it's always whispering in front of the sink. I'm nervous that one time I'm going to walk into the kitchen, and someone is going to be headfirst in the sink with water pouring over top of them.

I'd rather not bring up that I know they're fighting with one another because I know I'll end up in the middle of it, and I'll be the one trying to fix everything and that's not something I want to deal with.

"Are you going out today?" My mom asks as she opens the fridge.

"Yeah, I'm going out with Maggie... on a date."

My mom slowly turns to face me, "Oh... why?"

"Because I like her, and I asked her on a date. Why else would I go on a date with her?"

"You... Asked her on the date?" My mom's smile is unpleasant as she stares at me.

I nod, "Yes."

"I didn't think she was your type..."

"You don't know my type."

I don't think I have a type. I guess now I would say that my type is Maggie.

"Well, I just didn't think you'd like a girl that dresses... the way she does..."

I tilt my head, "What?"

"She's just... very showy."

"Mom, have you seen what the other girls wear at my school? If anything, Maggie is one of the least showy people."

"Yeah, but she wears those bra things." My mom says while doing a weird hand gesture in front of her chest.

"And normally at school she wears a jacket over it, and it's fall now. Besides, she can wear whatever she wants..." I really don't understand the big deal.

My mom sighs, "Just have fun." She turns around to face the fridge.

I slowly shuffle my way out of the kitchen before she explodes in my face. I wasn't even able to grab the pretzels I wanted.

I pull into Maggie's driveway. I'm about to get out of the car when her front door opens, and she walks out. Her hair hangs over her shoulders in her normal tight curls, and she's wearing jeans without rips in them and a long sleeve shirt. She looks beautiful.

She gives me a small smile before quickly turning towards the door, "Shut up!" She yells, slamming the door behind her.

She quickly gets into the passenger seat and slumps down.

"What was that about?"

"Just drive please." Maggie says. I can feel the awkwardness radiating off her, even if I don't know why she's feeling awkward.

I pull into a parking spot at the cafe.

"I expected it to be this place." Maggie smiles.

"Really?"

Maggie nods, "It's literally the only place in town that people can go on a date. We don't really have restaurants here."

Maggie gets out of the car, and I follow her action as we both walk into the cafe.

We walk up to the counter and order our drinks, "I'll pay for mine." Maggie says.

I slide a 20-dollar bill onto the counter, "No, I asked you out. I'm paying."

We grab our drinks and sit down in the far back corner.

"We need to put a sign on this table saying it's ours because we sit here so often." I smile.

"I like that idea. Next time we'll bring a reserved sign and stick it on the window." Maggie laughs.

I rest my elbow on the table, "So what was the yelling about when I picked you up?"

"The whole day my mom wouldn't stop asking questions about you."

"Your mom is in town?"

"Yeah, did I not tell you?"

I shake my head, Maggie shrugs, "Anyway, she just won't stop asking me questions, anytime I did something she would ask me something. Then followed by that question she'd ask something about you and how we met or what you're like and when she'll meet you. She asked me why my hair was in a bun before I decided to wear it down. It's like she forgot what I was like."

"I can understand the other questions, but you hardly wear your hair in a bun."

"I normally wear it after showering to let the curl's sit. But she's been back since Thursday and her and my dad are acting like they never got divorced. I have to go out for brunch with them tomorrow, I think I'm going to die."

"You'll survive."

"I hope so. It'll just be awkward." Maggie says before taking a sip of her tea and looking out the window.

"I understand that, but um I would also like to say that you do look really good today."

Maggie looks back at me and smiles, "Thank you, I tried."

I lean in and whisper, "I changed my shirt five times before picking you up because of how much I was sweating."

"Seriously?!" Maggie laughs.

"Yeah." I laugh along with her.

"Also! What's your favourite colour?"

"Uh... turquoise why?"

"It's normally the first question people ask each other when getting to know each other. But we've known each other for basically two months now and I still didn't know." She explains.

I guess she is right, we haven't really asked each other those basic questions, "Oh, well in that case. What's your favourite colour?"

"Purple." Maggie smiles.

"Really, but you never wear purple."

Maggie shrugs, "And you never wear turquoise, but it's still your favourite colour."

"Fair point. Fair point." I smile, "And if we're going on a trend of questions people ask each other when they first meet. Then what's your favourite animal?"

"Cat's, hands down."

I really thought Maggie would be a dog person, but now that she says cat, I can see it.

"I like birds." I smile.

"Really? I wouldn't see you as a bird person."

"Most people don't, but I like all the different colours they come in." I explain.

"That's cool." Maggie smiles.

I look out the window and then back to Maggie. I stand up and grab my tea. Reaching out my empty hand for Maggie's.

"What are you doing?"

"Come on, we're going to our next location."

"Oh! So, there's two locations."

Maggie grabs my hand, and we make our way outside. I begin to walk in the other direction of my car, "Are we not driving there?"

"Nope, we're just going on a walk... so I guess you could say the whole town is our next location."

Maggie and I begin to walk down the street. I'm surprised that most people aren't out on walks today, especially because the next couple of days are going to be full of rain.

"Okay, I've been waiting to ask you something for a while now."

"Okay?"

"Why do you call Oscar by his last name? I've never once heard you call him Oscar."

Maggie laughs and looks down at the ground, "It's actually pretty weird-"

"Weird is good." I smile.

"Okay well, in grade nine at a party Adams got really drunk and I mean really drunk. I was upstairs. I was tired and wanted to go home, but Conner wanted me to stay. That's when Adams came bursting through the door crying."

"Really? I've never seen him cry, or drink really."

"Yeah, it wasn't that pretty, but he sat down beside me crying and just started talking. I was the first person he talked about him being gay." Maggie smiles, "But then he just started rambling on about how he hates his name."

"He hates his name?" I'm shocked by this. He's never once mentioned this to me.

"He said it reminds him of an orange cat and that sucks apparently because he doesn't have orange hair so his name can't sound like he's an orange cat." Maggie gives a small giggle, "But that night I promised him that no matter what I would call him by his last name, because then at least one person isn't calling him Oscar."

"That's really nice of you." I smile.

"I couldn't tell you how quickly his face lit up after I said that. He pulled me into the biggest hug before running out of the room." Maggie smiles, "I was the only person nice to him before he met you."

I look down at the ground, I wish I would have known he doesn't like his name, or I would have called him Adams too, but I won't step over that boundary unless he asks me to. "It's really nice that you kept calling him Adams after you came back."

Maggie smiles, "I made a promise to him. I wasn't going to break it."

Maggie and I head back towards my house. Once we got back to the car I asked if she wanted to watch a movie back at my place. I'm oddly more nervous for that than anything else. I think it's because of my mom.

I slowly open my front door and let Maggie inside first, "We can go up to my room, I've got a tv in there and it will save us from my mom." I whisper.

Maggie looks back at me, "You have a tv in your room?"

"Yeah."

We slowly walk up the stairs and make our way to my room. Maggie stops in the doorway and looks around, "How is your room so big?"

I shrug, "Just the way it was built, I guess?" I sit down on my bed and look over to Maggie again, she's still standing in the doorway looking around.

"You can come and sit down."

She looks over to me and moves her arms around, almost like she's swatting away a swarm of flies, "I'm getting there... Do you want me to close the door?"

"Sure, leave it a crack open though."

Maggie nods, closes the door a little bit and walks over to sit down beside me.

"Are you okay?"

"Yes? Just nervous, kind of."

"You, nervous? Really?"

Maggie laughs and looks down at her hands in her lap, "Yes, really."

I nudge her arm, "Well you don't have to be nervous. Let's pick a movie."

Maggie moves to the other side of my bed so she's sitting beside me. We both have our backs resting on my headboard as we stare at the tv.

I flick through the channels.

"Oh, what about this one?" I look over to Maggie to see her already staring at me.

"Huh?" She blinks.

"Were you staring at me?"

"No." Maggie shakes her head.

"Yes! You were staring at me!"

"No, I wasn't. I looked towards you before you looked at me." Maggie tries to hide the smile creeping up on her lips.

I lean closer to her, I glance down at her lips then her eyes, "You're lying."

Maggie smiles, "I'm not lying." She lifts her hand and sticks out her pinky finger, "Promise."

"Seriously." I laugh.

Maggie smiles and leans in closer, "I'm not lying."

I lift my hand and interlock my pinky with hers before leaning in and kissing her. She kisses me back; I can feel her smile against my lips.

My ears perk up when I hear a creek in the floorboard. Maggie and I pull away from each other so quickly that I accidentally push her off the bed.

I turn around to see my mom walk into my room.

"Hey, Mom." I smile.

"Hi.... Hi Maggie.... Nice to see you again... on the floor?"

I glance over to Maggie, she sends me a quick glare before looking over to my mom, "Hi." She waves.

"Why are you on the floor?" My mom asks, giving a judging look.

"It's comfortable."

My mom nods and turns her attention back to me, "I just came to tell you that I'll be going out, your father will still be home."

"Okay. Have fun." I smile as she leaves the room, closing the door behind her.

I look back over to Maggie to see her getting up from the floor, "You really had to push me on the ground?!" She punches me in the arm.

I clench my arm, "Ow, I didn't mean to, why are you so strong?"

Maggie punches my arm again, "Ow, why?!"

"Because I felt like it." She sits down on the bed beside me and crosses her arms.

"I didn't mean to push you off the bed." I laugh.

She looks over to me, "I know, but it still hurt."

"I'm sorry." I slightly nod and hold back my laughter because it was truthfully funny to see her roll off the bed. I'm glad she didn't hit her head though.

I pull into Maggie's driveway. She turns to me, "Thanks for the ride home."

"Of course," I smile, "Good luck with your parents inside."

Maggie huffs, "Thanks for reminding me."

She gets out of the car and makes her way halfway up the trail to her house before turning around, "We're going to have to go on another date soon... It was a lot of fun." She smiles before turning back around, walking inside her house.

    I back out of her driveway and make my way home. It was nice having most of the day to hang out with Maggie, we didn't have to worry about Kian, or anything to do with school. It was nice to spend time with her.

    I hope we get to go on that next date by Monday, but I might be hoping for too much.

CHAPTER FORTY-TWO

Oscar Adams
<u>Tuesday, October 29th, 7:35am</u>

  Yelling echoes up into my room. It's been like this for the past two weeks. My parents won't stop yelling at each other in attempts to figure out who's going to move out. They haven't gotten far, and I haven't gotten any silence.
  I look out my window to see Adrian waiting out front of my house.
  I grab my backpack from the floor and leave my room. I reach the bottom of the stairs and peek out from behind the wall. My parents are in the kitchen, and I don't want to get noticed by them.

I step out from behind the wall, "Oscar! Come here!" My mom yells as soon as she spots me.

"Yes?" I don't turn around in hopes I can leave quickly.

"Tell your father he should be the one to leave." She says.

"You should not be bringing our son into this!! You should be the one to leave because you are the one causing all of these problems in the first place!" My dad yells.

They've both caused these problems.

"Oh, grow up!"

Slowly I step towards the front door and open it. I jog over to Adrian's car and get in.

"What took you so long?" Adrian asks as he pulls away from my house.

The harsh wind automatically smacks me in the face, I can't understand how Adrian is able to drive a convertible all year round.

"Parents." I sigh.

"Are they still fighting?" Adrian asks.

"They have been straight for the past two weeks!! They can't figure out who's going to be the one moving out, I think they should have figured that out before finalizing the divorce," I sigh again, "We should hangout tonight though, it'll help keep me distracted."

"I definitely would Bud, but I'm hanging out with Maggie tonight. I'm free tomorrow though." Adrian says while pulling into the school parking lot.

"Oh, okay. Tomorrow works well... You and Maggie have been hanging out a lot recently."

"Yeah... I honestly think I'll be asking her to be my girlfriend soon. Even though we technically only had our first day on the weekend, but when it feels right it's right." Adrian smiles as he gets out of the car.

I nod, feeling a pull in my chest, "Right."

I get out of the car and run up beside him, "You never told me you went on a date with her..."

"I didn't?"

"No, no you didn't." The sinking feeling in my chest deepens and tightens as we walk towards the school.

Adrian shrugs, "Well you know now."

"Is tonight another date?"

"I guess so, but we're just hanging out at her house, so I don't really know for sure."

I pull open the school door and follow inside after Adrian, "Well it should be fun."

We walk down the hallway to Adrian's locker. It's hard for me to understand how he can hang out with Maggie so much and neglect his best friend. We've hardly hung out this month, but that's not the reason my whole body is beginning to sweat.

"Hey guys." I turn around to see Maggie leaning up against the locker beside Adrian's.

"Hey." Adrian smiles.

"Hi."

I feel awkward third wheeling right now, even if I'm not really third wheeling, it still feels like I am. There's not much I can do to stop that right now.

Maggie and Adrian begin to have a conversation, leaving me out of it completely. They laugh with one another; I don't feel welcome in the conversation, so I walk away.

As I'm halfway down the hallway I turn around to see if they've noticed I'm gone. They haven't. They're taking me away from them and I'm going to be the only one that gets hurt in the end. I don't want to be alone again.

Adrian runs up to me in the lounge, "Where'd you go this morning?"

"I had to go to the bathroom."

I wasn't in the mood to talk to anyone else today. The day started off terrible and it's going to continue that way. I just need silence.

"Oh okay, well I was thinking for tomorrow we could maybe come here and play some basketball in the back of the school? Like we did in the summer that one time." Adrian smiles.

"Yeah, sure." I nod while Adrian sits down beside me.

"Why aren't you with Maggie for lunch?"

"Because we always sit together for lunch. Plus, I can never find her, she practically disappears."

"She's probably with the gang..."

"Oh yeah that would make sense." Adrian says before taking a bite into a carrot.

My eyes shift away from Adrian and over to Jessica who is headed in our direction. Adrian looks up from the carrot and over to Jessica who is now sitting in the chair across from us.

"Hi Adrian..." Jessica shifts her eyes to me, "Cousin."

"Hey." Adrian says.

I nod awkwardly. Jessica and I have never been close, our families always wanted us to be the cousins that were best friends, but we're too different for that to happen.

"What are we talking about?" Jessica asks.

"Basketball."

"Oh fun, it's so awesome when our school gets the ball in the net, but so annoying when the star player turns out to be a murderer."

I nod slowly, "Yes... so annoying."

"Did you guys know he killed Kian?" Jessica asks.

Adrian looks over to me and then back towards Jessica, "What no, why would you think we did?"

"Because you two were friends with him."

I wouldn't really say I was friends with Conner. We're more like two people who are mutules because we're both friends with Adrian, so we try to be civil with one another.

"Anyhow, what are you doing tonight?" Jessica smiles at Adrian.

"Hanging out with Maggie."

Jessica rolls her eyes, "Why?"

"Because I want to?"

I stand up from the couch, "I have to go to the bathroom."

I quickly walk away from them both. I don't want to see Jessica pining after Adrian for the hundredth time, it's kind of sad.

All of science class Maggie and Adrian are talking through me. I really wish I could switch seats at this moment, but Mr. Gibes would yell at me, and I don't want to get yelled at today. So, I can deal with the constant talking through my ears.

I walk out the school doors behind Maggie and Adrian.

I watch as they get into Adrian's car and drive down the street. I don't know how they can trust them so much. They've only known them for a month.

As I begin to make my way home, dark storm clouds roll in from above. Adrian was supposed to give me a ride home.

I walk up my driveway right as the rain begins. My dad walks out of the house carrying a small box.

"Are you the one leaving?"

He nods, "Yeah, your mom is staying. She says you can visit in a month to see me."

"Okay." I smile.

I walk inside my house. I'm expecting it to be half empty, but it looks the same. Turns out my dad didn't have as many things in the house as I thought he had.

If my mom was the one to be moving out, the house would look completely different right now.

Once I'm in my room I sit down on my bed and stare at my tv. I don't want to turn on my Xbox to play any video games. I need the silence right now.

The silence I have been wanting for weeks.
The silence that I need so I can think.

CHAPTER FORTY-THREE

Maggie Snow
Tuesday, October 29th, 2:20pm

"Seriously, she asked you out?"
"Yeah, and it was really awkward even before Oscar left. I know there has to be someone in the school that would want to date her, but ever since I moved to town, I've only ever seen her try to get with me." Adrian explains.
"That's kind of weird..." But I can understand why Jessica would want to date Adrian. He's smart, and polite to everyone and one of the only nice guys in the whole school.
Adrian pulls his car into my driveway.
"Why didn't you take your motorcycle today?"

I roll my eyes, "Because my mom didn't want me to. She says with everything going on in the town right now she doesn't want me getting in an accident... I have literally had my motorcycle since I left town in grade nine and now, she's telling me not to ride it?"

"Well, that is interesting... Will I have to meet her today?"

I nod, "Yes. Sadly." I hop over the car door as Adrian gets out calmly.

I am nervous for him to meet my mom, I don't know what she's going to say, if she's going to ask millions of questions. I don't want her to make Adrian feel uncomfortable.

We slowly walk up to my house. Adrian's hand grazes mine before I reach for the front door and push it open.

"Mags!!!" My dad yells right as we step inside.

"Yes?"

"We ordered you a bed frame." My mom smiles.

I glance over to Adrian, "Oh, that's great, thanks." I shyly point up to Adrian, "This is Adrian, he's going to be hanging out for the night. We'll be in my room if you need us."

My mom stands up from the couch and walks over to us, "I'm Juliet, Maggie's mom. Nice to meet you." My mom reaches out her hand to shake Adrian's.

He shakes her hand, "Nice to meet you too."

"How'd you two end up meeting?"

445

"Uh lockers are beside each other and we've got science class together." I smile. I didn't feel like explaining that I met Adrian in the cafe on my first night back in town. That would turn into a spiral of questions.

"Oh, that's fun!! Well, if you two need anything just come out and get it." My mom smiles. She's acting like this is her house when clearly, it's dad's. She hasn't lived here for 12 years.

I quickly shuffle Adrian down the hallway to my bedroom. I close the door behind me and take a deep breath.

"Our lockers aren't even close to each other." Adrian laughs.

"I know, I know, but it was easier to say that than we met at the cafe on the first night I was back in town. Did you want her to ask you thousands of questions?"

Adrian shrugs, "I guess you're right."

I walk around Adrian and sit down on my bed, he turns and looks down at me, "I know my bedroom is much smaller than yours and that my room doesn't have as much stuff in it as yours does, but... you can still sit down."

He sits down beside me, "I like your room, Maggie."

"Really? Are you not excited about my new bed frame then? Because it'll add so much height to my bed it won't even be recognizable."

I lay back on my bed, "Are you being sarcastic?" He asks, looking back at me.

"Very." I smile.

"Is getting a bed frame not a good thing though? I swear we've had this conversation before."

I sit back up, "It is a good thing, but I've gotten used to my bed being on the ground. I enjoy it."

"Well in the future you can have your bed on the ground all you want." Adrian smiles.

I shove him lightly with my arm, "Also changing the subject drastically, but did Adams seem off today?"

"Not to me, why?"

"I don't know, he just seemed quieter."

"Isn't he always quiet?"

"Yes, he is, but he seemed more quiet than normal. Like in science class he hardly said a word."

Adrian shrugs, "I guess that's unlike him, but his parents just got divorced and have been fighting so that's probably why."

"But wouldn't he talk to you about that so he could feel better?"

"He did on the car ride to school for a little bit, and I'm hanging out with him tomorrow, so it'll take his mind off things, but we don't really talk about that kind of stuff. Every once and a while we do, but not often." He explains.

"Guys are weird with not being able to talk about their emotions."

"Says you who didn't talk about yours for two years... Shit... I'm sorry I shouldn't have said that."

No, he shouldn't have, "It's okay..."

Adrian shakes his head, "No, it's not okay, I shouldn't have ever said that, because I understand why it was hard for you to talk about your emotions. Guys just get raised to not talk about their emotions a lot, so... I just shouldn't have said that."

"Thank you."

Adrian pulls me into a hug, "I'm really sorry."

I know he is I can tell that he's sorry. Doesn't mean it didn't hurt though, but it's not that big of a deal. I can forgive him; it wasn't a big fuck up.

"I'll think before I speak next time I promise, and before I try to make a joke that won't be funny."

I pull away from the hug, "You know how you can repay me?"

"How?"

"Let me look in your notebook." I smile.

"My answer still hasn't changed for that."

"Oh, come on!! I literally basically only talk to you and Adams about stuff so who would I tell? I only want to read one thing."

Adrian shakes his head, "I'm sorry it's not happening, I will repay you with anything else."

I fall backwards on my bed, "Ugh, fine... then I'd just want another hug."

I hadn't realized it, but that was one of the first time's Adrian and I hugged, it felt nice.

He lays down beside me and pulls me into another hug. "You're the perfect hugging size. You fit in my arms perfectly."

I look up at him, "Then you'll have to hug me more often."

This is nice, really nice. I haven't been hugged in a long time, a real meaningful hug. I needed this.

Adrian closes his computer, "There are no good shows to watch right now."

"We'll have to check for something new every day."

"I guess we will."

I sit up and look at Adrian, "Do you ever want to stop trying to figure out who killed Kian?"

"I haven't really thought about stopping, why?"

I shake my head, "I don't know, but do you ever think we could just turn in everything that we know into the cops, and they'll do the rest?"

I've been thinking about this a lot recently. Maybe because we've hit a dead end and I don't know where to go next. Maybe the cops would see something that we haven't been able to see.

"Maggie, that would get you to be the prime suspect. You said that yourself. We both know you didn't do anything, but the police don't know that."

"But what are we going to do if we find this person? If we find out who killed Kian. Are we going to call the cops and let them deal with it? They'll have thousands of questions. Are we going to go after this person? Once again the cops would have thousands of questions."

Adrian grabs my hand, "Maggie-"

"We don't know how strong this person is. I mean they stabbed someone to death, so they have to be pretty strong. But-"

"Maggie, why is this worrying you so much?"

"Because we've never actually thought of the possibility of finding this person and what will happen when we do. I don't want anyone else to get hurt, I don't want you getting hurt."

"I can't promise that no one is going to get hurt. But we are safe, if this person hasn't come after us now, they aren't going to." Adrian says.

"No," I shake my head, "Your name isn't on the bottom of a letter addressed to Kian. This person, whoever killed him, obviously wanted me back in town for some reason. What says they aren't going to hurt me?"

Adrian places his hand on my cheek, "Because we will be vigilant no matter what, no one is going to hurt you. Okay? There is no need to worry."

"This is something about me that you don't know, but me and worrying are best friends."

Adrian looks in my eyes, "But please don't worry, just be vigilant, and I will be too. So, neither of us get hurt, and we'll make sure that no one else in the town gets hurt."

I nod, "Okay."

Adrian and I sneak past the living room and outside.

"Oh wow, looks like rain is going to be coming again soon." I say while looking up at the sky.

Adrian gets in his car. I rest my elbows on the door, "Thanks for hanging out tonight."

"Thank you for having me over. I'm sorry if it wasn't the best time."

"It was great, I'm sorry for worrying."

Adrian places his finger on my nose, "Well stop worrying, because we're both safe, I have a good feeling."

"Well boys' instincts are normally terrible."

"Ouch," Adrian places his hand over his heart, "I would say my instincts are very well rounded."

"Okay, I will believe you. Now I would get going, it's going to start to rain soon." I smile.

I lean in and kiss Adrian, "I'll see you tomorrow." I say against his lips before pulling away.

I jog up to my house and watch as Adrian drives away.

Right as I move back inside my house, I can hear the rain begin. My mom walks into view, "Would you like a tea?"

"Uh sure." I smile.

I follow her into the kitchen, "Your dad is sleeping on the couch tonight."

"He normally does, that's nothing new."

My mom turns on the kettle, "I wouldn't think you'd be interested in a guy like Adrian."

"What do you mean?"

"He doesn't seem like your type." She says as she takes mugs from the cupboard.

I sit down at the table, "I don't really have a type.... I just like who I like."

"He seems like a nice kid."

"He is." I smile.

I grab my tea and head to my room. The rain is pouring down onto the house, it's peaceful. I place my tea on the ground beside my bed and lay in the spot where Adrian and I were laying, it's still warm.

He told me not to worry, I've been trying not to worry every moment I've been back in town. I don't want to worry. I never want to worry. I want to be strong. I want to feel and look strong. But it's hard when someone is out there framing your friend for a murder they didn't commit and lurking in the shadows sending people letters and notes. I never wanted to admit it to myself, but I'm scared, and all I can do is worry about what will happen.

CHAPTER FORTY-FOUR

Maggie Snow
<u>Wednesday, October 30th, 11:30am</u>

I shake my head, "Okay, no. Are you crazy?"
Clark is sitting on the ground in front of me in the lounge, staring at me with wide eyes, "I just want you to sing at my birthday because you did so well at karaoke night."
"But do you know how nervous I was?"
"Please? It's not until the end of November so you'll have time to think about it. I'll even ask Jade to sing with you." Clark flashes me a wide hopeful smile.
"Fine I'll think about it, and I don't think Jade can sing, but speaking of Jade where is she

today?" I ask as Clark gets up from the ground and sits down beside me.

"She hasn't been here for the past couple of days at lunch. I think she's been going to visit Ace."

"Huh." I don't know how to feel about Ace and Jade hanging out a lot. They started hanging out in September and I'm positive something is going on between them. It's not that I wouldn't be happy for them. I would be, it's just that Ace was my best friend, part of me still feels like she is, and I don't want her getting hurt.

I stand up from the chair and make my way out of the lounge away from Clark. I get to the hallway and move towards the water fountain. I hardly drink water to begin with, but I'm surprisingly thirsty.

I lean down and take a sip of water from the fountain. I swear that whoever created the water fountain truthfully wanted to see what the weirdest position people could drink water in was.

"Maggie Snow."

I pull away from the fountain and whip the excess water off my face. That's another thing about the creator of the water fountain, why would they create something that makes water go everywhere?

Jessica stands in front of me with her arms crossed, "What do you want Jessica?"

"For you to leave Adrian alone. He's supposed to be with me and not someone from a gang." She glares.

Her voice is already annoying me, and she's only been here for a second.

"Okay, first off, Adrian and I aren't really together, we've only been on a couple of dates. Secondly, Adrian doesn't like you and he never will."

Jessica takes a step closer to me, "You haven't been here for two years. You don't know him like I do."

Why do people always bring up that I wasn't in town for two years during arguments? It doesn't affect me that much.

"Fine, that's a fair point. But that doesn't mean anything, just because I met him when I came back to town does not change that he doesn't like you."

"Stop seeing him."

"Jessica, I'm going to try to be nice here and give you some advice. You've been to LA, there are probably so many cute guys there that are willing to date you, stop pining after a guy that clearly isn't interested in you."

Jessica shakes her head, "I don't understand what all these guys see in you, first Conner, then Kian and now Adrian. You're not even nice to them."

My heart skips, "What did you say?"

"You're not even nice to them."

"No about Kian."

"You obviously were always playing hard to get with Kian. He came to me one day in grade nine asking if I knew anything. He knew you were with Conner, but he still thought you might like him."

I take a step away from Jessica trying to keep my temper, "Jessica, you have not been my friend for a long time, why the hell would Kian go to you asking that? And what the hell did you tell him?"

Jessica shrugs, "I don't know why he came and asked me, he must have seen us in the hallway one day. But I told him you were playing hard to get and to just go for it. Why the hell does any of this matter?"

Was Jessica the reason everything happened with Kian?

I close my eyes and take a deep breath, "I am going to refrain from telling you what you probably caused by telling him that. But I never liked Kian. You don't deserve any of my kindness, you may not know what you caused by saying that to him, but you're the reason my life got so fucked up."

I step closer to her making sure to breathe. I don't want to punch her no matter how much my body is telling me to, "Stay out of anything to do with my life, or I promise you I will not hold back from punching you. Oh, and Adrian will never ever like you, not as long as I'm here."

My fist clenches as I walk away from Jessica. I now know she could not have killed Kian, because she seemed oblivious to what she had said to him. In her mind she was probably trying to break up Conner and I, but instead she unleashed a drunk and stupid Kian who took too much of a liking to the control he had gained.

I round the corner running into Adams, "Hey."

"Hi."

"Do you know where Adrian is?" I ask.

"I think he had to talk to Mr. Gibes about something, why?"

I would assume he's talking to Mr. Gibes about the test we had last week. Adrian was very adamant with the fact that he was sure he didn't pass. I tried my best to convince him that he had passed, but now I'm thinking I could have been wrong.

"Oh, okay. I just needed to talk to him."

"You can talk to me." Adams smiles as we begin to walk down the hallway together.

Adams doesn't know anything that happened with Kian. Adrian is the only one that knows about all of it, and Ace had pieced it together, but doesn't know the full story.

"What do you do when you find out something that changes a certain situation, and you don't know if it's for the better or for the worse. And you don't know if you should be angry or scream and cry."

"Umm...."

"Sorry... I know it's cryptic."

"Maybe you could write it all down? So, it's out of your mind and on paper." Adams suggests.

I nod, "I might actually do that. Thank you, Adams. Also, Adrian told me about your parents, I'm sorry to hear."

"Oh thanks." He shifts his eyes to the ground.

"Are you okay?"

He nods, "Oh yeah, all good. I've been through tougher battles. But are you okay, Maggie?"

"I don't know, but I think that's okay. I don't always have to be okay." I smile.

"Well, I think you should constantly be okay, and happy." Adams smiles before parting in the other direction.

It's quiet in the newspaper today. Adrian and Adams took some time to hangout after school. I don't blame them, trying to figure out a murder, days on end with barely any time to breath can get boring. Especially when you haven't gotten anywhere, and everything feels like a dead end.

I rip Jessica's name down from the board and crumple it into a ball.

I don't believe she killed Kian. I really don't think she could have killed him. There was no reason, and no reason for me to be dragged into it. She would have had to known something that happened between Kian and I and I'm positive that she didn't know anything. She just made the wrong comment to the wrong person. Causing a horrible butterfly effect.

Sitting in the chair I lean back and stare down at the crumpled piece of paper. I'll take Adams advice and write everything out later tonight.

So, who could have killed Kian?

Could Kian have hurt someone else, and this person got revenge? Why bring me and my name into the letter? Who wanted me back in town? If they were trying to frame me for anything they wouldn't have framed Conner.

I shift my view over to the window. It's been raining on and off for a week. It's now that weird in between area of fall, the one where all the leaves have fallen and since it's rained all the leaves are stuck to the ground, making everything muddy.

I stand up and walk over to the murder board. I pull the town newspaper off the board, my eyes skim over the page.

Due to recent events regarding the death of teen boy, Kian Turner. The autopsy report has come back saying that there was foul play in his death, ruling his death a homicide. The autopsy shows that Kian was murdered 3 days before being found in the woods.... This caused his death to be due to loss of blood.

I look up from the paper. Who would have the strength to repeatedly stab someone? I once read somewhere that if someone has gone through something that makes them extremely angry, they can experience a crazy amount of strength even if they aren't strong. Maybe that's what happened?

I feel as if I'm grasping at straws now.

My phone begins to ring, making me jump backwards. I place my hand over my heart as I answer the phone, "Hello?"

"Hey, it's Jade."

"Oh, what's up?"

"Could you come over to Ace's, I'm trying to get her out of bed, but she won't budge and I kind of need your help."

"Yeah, sure I'll be right over."

"Okay, good. See you soon."

I hang up the phone and place it on the table.

I haven't talked to or seen Ace since Conner was arrested. But she needs to talk to me at some point.

The school hallways are empty. As I walk all I can hear are my own footsteps. School hallways are always creepy when empty, it's not that I'm scared to be alone, I'm more scared that I'm *not* alone. And a school is the best place to sneak up on someone.

I quickly make my way over to my motorcycle. I had parked it under a tree today so the seat wouldn't get wet from all the rain.

I haven't been in Ace's house since Kian made me leave. I'm truly nervous to see if anything has changed inside. I wonder if they still have that ugly green couch that Ace and I would play Mario Kart on.

I knock on the front door.

The last time I was here Ace's mom was being a bitch. I'm not really in the mood to deal with that again. It was enough to keep my emotions in check with Jessica today, which I'm glad I did. I'm proud of myself for that.

The door opens, "Maggie, hello. Jade told me you were coming." Ace's dad smiles. It's a familiar smile that I had forgotten about, but it is welcoming.

I step inside, most things are the same. They still have that old cuckoo clock Ace's aunt gave her.

"How are you?"

"I'm good, you?" I ask.

"We've been better. But the girls are upstairs you can head on up." He smiles.

I nod as I take a quick glance into the living room, the couch is a light gray. It's sad that they got rid of the green one. There were so many memories on the couch, especially the time when I hit Kian in the face with the Wii controller by accident. Now I really wish I wasn't an accident.

If he was still alive, I'd hit him with every object in sight.

If he was still alive, I wouldn't be in town right now.

I reach the top of the stairs and turn to the left to see Ace laying in her bed and Jade standing at the end of the bed hitting Ace's foot while repeatedly the saying "get up".

Jade turns around to see me, "Finally you're here. Ace and I were supposed to go to the Mystic Glass today, but now she doesn't want to leave her room."

I walk into the room and over to Ace. I stare down at her.

"Why don't you want to go?"

"I'm tired." Ace mumbles into the pillow.

Jade rolls her eyes, "You've been saying that every day, and every day I get you out of the house."

Without a second thought I pull the pillow out from under her head.

"Hey!!" Ace sits up and glares at me. I've never seen her glare before, at least I don't think I have, but it's hard for me to hold back my laugh. She doesn't look intimidating at all.

"Get!" I hit her in the face with the pillow, "Up!"

"What the-"

"Get up! Get up! Get up!" I shout as I repeatedly hit her in the face with a pillow.

Jade moves me away from Ace, "I'm not getting up!!" Ace shouts back at me.

"Maybe hitting her in the face with a pillow isn't the best approach." Jade raises her eyes brows and purses her lips.

So, what, maybe it's not, but it still felt good to get some of my anger out. It's not like I was swinging the pillow hard.

"Ace, you need to get up!! I've hardly seen you at school. I haven't seen you at school."

"Well, that's because I've been tired. And I didn't get any sleep last night, so I don't want to go out!" Ace yells back at me.

Jade spins around, "That's a lie you fell asleep on facetime at 10 last night!"

So, they've been facetiming?

"I'm still tired!! And I don't even want to go to a bar." Ace says.

"You don't have to get a drink, you can literally just get water, or a pop. Just to get out of the house." Jade says.

"If I go, will you stop asking me to go places?" Ace asks.

Jade and I glance over to one another then back to Ace, "We'll stop asking if you promise to come back to school." I say.

Ace sighs, "Fine, I'll try."

"I'll be here tomorrow morning to pick you up for school right away." Jade says, "Now get out of that bed we're going to the bar."

CHAPTER FORTY-FIVE

Ace Turner
Wednesday, October 30th, 3:20pm

      Maggie and Jade go downstairs to wait for me.
      I grab a hoodie from my closet and don't bother to change out of my sweatpants. If I'm going to be going to school tomorrow that's when I'll pick a better outfit.
      It was weird to see Maggie in my room, she hasn't been in my room since grade nine. It was also weird to see her after I had yelled at her in the Police Station. I can hardly remember what said, but I know I feel bad about it.
      I run downstairs to the living room where Maggie and Jade are standing talking to my dad. My mom has been out of the house a lot recently,

throwing herself into work to try and keep busy. To me that shows how different my mom and I are.

My dad's laugh roars through the house, I have no idea who made him laugh. But I'm not too worried about it.

Maggie looks over to me with a small smile, "Ready to go?"

"You're coming with us?"

She shrugs, "Yeah why not, haven't really hung out with anyone, but Adrian in a while."

We get outside, Jade and I head towards our bikes while Maggie goes to her motorcycle.

"I'll meet you two there and grab us a spot at the bar away from people." Maggie says before taking off down the street.

Jade and I ride slowly don't the street. It's finally stopped raining outside, but there are still puddles all over the road. I swear that this town needs to fill in all the potholes, there are way too many.

I watch as Jade rides through the puddle, the water splashing up to her feet, "Your feet are going to be cold now." I say as I ride up beside her.

"My shoes are pretty waterproof."

"Well, I'm not risking my shoes getting wet." I say as I dodge the puddle in front of me.

Jade glances down at my feet, "I mean, no one would want those bright yellow shoes to get muddy and wet."

I smile as we round the corner.

We pull into the parking lot beside Maggie's motorcycle. I hop off my bike and follow Jade inside.

I haven't been here since karaoke night when the whole place was filled with so many people, it was hard to move around. This time the bar looks different, less lively, more peaceful and welcoming.

"It's not so busy." I mumble.

"Wednesdays are the down days." Jade smiles at me as we head over to where Maggie is sitting.

"Wow, you two actually got here pretty fast." Maggie says in shock.

I sit down beside her and Jade sits on my left. "We can be speedy." I smile.

"Well, I got all of us cream sodas, I think it's best if none of us drink." Maggie explains.

Jade leans forwards on the bar and looks past me over to Maggie, "That makes sense, and it probably a good idea. I've never ridden my bike drunk before."

I look around the bar. I didn't have much time to look around the last time I was here since it was so crowded. The main thing I see behind the bar is a bunch of cups and different types of beer and liquor. When I shift my eyes up there is a chalkboard with sloppy handwriting, I seriously can't read any of it.

I take a sip of the cream soda as Maggie and Jade begin to talk about something. I heard the word led pip and began to zone out. At first, I thought they were talking about the game Clue, but they obviously weren't.

"All of us should try to have a movie night one night. Just all three of us." Maggie suggests, "All three of us hardly hangout."

"That's because you're always hanging out with Adrian and Oscar." Jade says.

"Well, I have more classes with them and work on the paper with them. I literally can't help but hang out with them." Maggie says.

"I thought you said you've been hanging out with Adrian a lot recently." I point out.

"Yeah, what's going on between you two?" Jade says.

"What, nothing." Maggie tries to hold in an obvious smile.

"Stop lying and tell us." I demand, "You are one of the people who dragged me out here, so I better get to know some gossip."

And it'll help me feel better about whatever I had said to you. I must have been in a blind fit of rage that I blocked it out.

"Fine, we went on a date and have hung out a couple of times and have kissed a couple of times too." Maggie's shoulders hover close to her ears.

"Ohhhh, tell us more." Jade laughs.

"There isn't much more, I don't know. He makes me happy, and I feel safe around him."

I'm glad she can feel safe.

"How was the date? What'd you guys do?" I ask.

"It was good, we went to the cafe and then on a walk and then hung out at his house for a bit." Maggie smiles.

I smile, "I'm really happy for you."

I remember when Maggie and Conner started dating. We were sitting in my room when she told me, and we both screamed. The comparison to now is so much different, I hardly know anything about her life.

"What about you guys? What's going on between you two?" Maggie asks.

"Uh, can I ask you guys something?" I ask to completely dodge the question Maggie just asked, I honestly don't know how to answer that question. I don't really know what's going on between Jade and I. I mean yes, we did go on a date, but that doesn't mean we're dating.

"Um, sure." Maggie says.

"If you were Kian, where would you go almost every night?" I ask.

It's been on my mind the past couple of days, I had completely forgotten that Kian used to go out every night during summer, I never knew where he was going. Maybe it has something to do with why he got killed and why Conner killed him. I still have hope that he didn't kill him, but not much.

Jade shrugs, "No clue, why are you asking?"

"During summer I would always hear him sneaking out of the house at night. I asked him about it one time and he told me not to worry about it. Then within the next couple of weeks he went missing and I feel like it's partly my fault that I didn't say anything to my parents... maybe he wouldn't be dead."

"Holy shit!" Maggie drops down from the bar stole and mumbles something to herself.

"You good?" Jade asks.

"Uh yeah, I just remembered something really important," Maggie looks over to me, "Thank you, thank you. I'm going to figure this out, I promise."

Maggie turns around and sprints out of the bar, I look over to Jade, "Do you know what that was about?"

Jade sighs, "She doesn't think Conner killed Kian. She thinks he's being framed, and I told her to stop looking into this so you could be a peace, but clearly she hasn't."

"But what if he is being framed? I mean I obviously sparked something in her mind. She probably knows more than either of us do... to be fair we hardly know anything."

I haven't wanted to know anything.

"Let's just not talk about it, we can leave it to the cops, or Maggie for that matter." Jade says, I can feel her annoyance radiating off her.

"Do you have any idea of where he would have been sneaking out to though?"

"Maybe a secret relationship? Or just wanted to practice basketball without people watching?" Jade suggests.

I nod, "Those would make sense probably."

I pick up my cream soda and take a sip before looking back towards Jade, "What is going on between us, Jade?"

"What do you mean?"

I straighten my shoulders, *be confident.* I tell myself, "Well we went on a date, and I kissed you while drunk and we've been hanging out a lot. I would like to know what's going on between us so I know whether or not I should protect my heart."

Jade grabs my hand, "I really like you, Ace. A lot, and you don't need to protect your heart because it's not going to get hurt."

"You like me?" I ask as if I didn't already know that. She did ask me on a date, but who knows maybe she could have stopped liking me after that.

Jade nods, "Yes."

Before I have the chance to say anything back Jade's lips are on mine. This time I know what I'm doing, I understand the kiss and I'm not drunk. My lips are tingling at Jade's touch.

We pull away from one another, "Ah wow okay, ah." I giggle.

"Are you okay?" Jade laughs.

"That was. Wow." I smile awkwardly down at the ground.

"Would you like to be my girlfriend, Ace?"

I look up at her, "Yes, very much, yes." My head is nodding up and down.

Jade smiles, "You're too damn cute."

Heat rises on my cheeks; I look back down at the ground hoping my hair falls in front of my them to cover the blushing.

My first girlfriend, wow.

Jade and I pull into my driveway with our bikes.

"I think my dad is out." I sigh.

"Would you like me to stay?" Jade asks.

"If you would like to. I mean I'd rather not be home alone."

Jade nods with a smile as she follows me inside.

We head up towards my bedroom, "I do want to say sorry for how messy my room is." For some reason I feel more self-conscious about my room, I wasn't before, but now I want it to look nice and clean for her.

"It's fine, my room is messy all the time too. We can help each other clean sometime." Jade laughs.

We lay down on my bed with my laptop propped at our feet on a pillow. We put on this first movie we saw; I can't even remember what it's called now. I'm too focused on trying to lay on Jade's shoulder. I slowly move closer to her until my head is finally resting on it. Her hand interlocks with mine.

For the first time this week I don't feel like I'm falling. I feel as though I'm being lifted, and I'm glad for that.

CHAPTER FORTY-SIX

Maggie Snow
Friday, November 1st, 5:10pm

I've gone to Club Azure five times in the past two days and every single time Cal wasn't there. He could be the key to finding out who killed Kian.

I pace back and forth in my room trying to find the right moment to leave. I'm parents are going to start asking questions if I keep going out randomly and coming back 15 minutes later.

Last weekend my mom had asked me to stop risking things. I don't know how she found out I was trying to solve this, but I can't risk her knowing that I still am.

I crack my bedroom door open and pier out. I can't see the living room from my room, so I don't even know what I'm looking for.

I grab my notebook from the ground and leave my room slowly creeping down the hallway. If I'm going to leave, I have to do it before it's too late.

Both my parents are sitting on the couch in the living room. They've been watching the same show for the past week. I slowly walk past the living room and put my hand on the door handle, "Maggie."

"Where are you going?" My mom asks.

I stand in the door frame of the living room entrance, "I'm going to meet up with Adrian at the cafe, we're going to work on the school paper for a little bit. Want me to bring back any tea?" I smile hoping she can't sniff out my lie.

"Sure, that would be nice. Just normal tea for the both of us, two milk and one sugar." My mom smiles.

I nod, "Sounds good."

I run out of my house to my motorcycle. Now I have to spend a longer time out if Cal isn't at Club Azure. I mean at least I'd get to sit in the cafe for a bit.

I pull into the parking lot beside Club Azure. The neon sign is glowing. The only reason I can see the light coming from it is because the sun is resting behind the trees.

I get off my motorcycle and take a deep breath before walking inside.

It's hard to see inside the club because of the neon flashing lights and tinted windows. I'm always surprised when it's less of a club and more of a hangout spot. When I hear the world club, I expect a DJ and lots of people dancing, but there is none of that.

I squint my eyes as I scan the room. They stop when I see a black-haired guy sitting in the corner. I know it's Cal because of the way the neon lights are bringing out the blue in his eyes. It was the first thing I noticed about him when I met him.

"Bingo." I mumble to myself.

I make my way over to where he is sitting. Tonight, he is sitting alone, which means there's a higher chance of getting him to talk.

"Uh, Hi. It's Cal, right? My friend and I talked to you a couple of weeks ago."

Cal looks up at me, "Oh yeah, Gala? Right?"

I forgot I used a fake name, "Yeah, uh can I sit?"

"Sure." He nods.

I sit down across from him and rest my notebook in my lap.

"I hope that some of the things I told you helped catch that Conner kid."

"It actually isn't him; he's being framed."

Cal tilts his head, "I thought they had proof against him?"

"It was a tip off, he's being accused because the police found drugs in his locker that Kian had given to him and now, he's being framed, someone also planted the murder weapon in his locker." I explain.

"Oh shit, is that why you're back? To ask me more questions? Is the internship still going well?"

I adjust my body and lean forwards, "Um, actually there is no internship. I'm not even of age to do that if there is one... I'm in high school, my name isn't Gala, it's Maggie Snow. Conner is my friend, and I don't want him to be stuck in jail for something he didn't do."

I suck in a breath hoping this guy doesn't completely flip out of me.

Cal points at me, "Wait you're Maggie?"

"Yeah."

"Shit, I'm so sorry about the last time you were here, if I had known I wouldn't have said anything I didn't mean to stir up any memories-"

I shake my head, "You don't have to be sorry. I was the one that lied about who I was. I don't think you fully know what happened between Kian and I."

"What did happen if you don't mind me asking?"

I take a deep breath, you've got this, you can say it out loud, speak the truth, "Kian raped me."

Cal sits back in his chair in disbelief, "I am so sorry."

"There is nothing for you to be sorry about, but thank you, but this isn't why I came here. I need your help; I need you to tell me anything you know."

"I'm really sorry, Maggie. I told you everything the last time you were here."

"Can I ask random questions that might trigger a memory?"

Cal nods, "Of course go ahead."

He's calmer than I expected him to be, but I guess I did drop a bombshell on him about Kian that he probably wasn't expecting. He probably doesn't know how to act.

"How many times would Kian come in here a week?"

"Maybe three or four times."

I nod and write that down in my notebook, "Did he ever talk about anyone other than me, in a weird way or mean or rude or?"

"He talked about a lot of people, but mostly you if I am being honest. I do know he felt sorry, he never told me why or happened, but he was sorry."

I don't know if it means anything to me now.

"Could anyone have overheard these conversations?" I ask.

"Possibly, but I doubt it. The music is always pretty loud in here, so it'd be hard to overhear someone's conversation unless you were specifically trying to listen to it." Cal explains.

"Was there anyone who was regularly in here, a worker or customer, maybe a girl?"

"I don't see many girls here, working or as a customer, but there was always this one guy that I saw working while Kian and I were here. He was pretty cute actually."

"Do you know his name?" I ask.

"He never wore a name tag, which I know it's convenient right?"

"Can you describe him to me then? He might have overheard something you two were talking about. I think I might be connected to all of this, so if I know who this person is it'd be helpful."

"Okay, yeah, um I'm pretty sure he had blue or green eyes. It's hard to tell with the lighting in here. He was a white male for sure and had brown hair. In this lighting it was dark, though almost black, but I'm pretty sure it was brown." Cal explains.

"Was there any specific hairstyle or facial features to help narrow it down?"

"Curly hair, I think some freckles too."

"Um, okay, can you stand up for me. Like where height wise would he be beside you?" I ask.

Cal and I both stand up, Cal is around Adrian's height, maybe a little taller. Cal moves his hand to his nose level.

"Okay so around here on me then?" I ask while moving my hand to the height.

Cal nods, "Probably yeah, I haven't seen the guy in here in a while though. So, I could be wrong."

Cal and I both sit back down, "So you are positive blue-green eyes, and brown curly hair?"

"As positive as I can be."

I nod, "Okay um, well I do know someone that looks like that, but I don't know if they could be capable of killing someone... I'll do more digging and investigate everything. Thank you for your help."

"You're welcome." Cal smiles.

I stand up from the chair, "And I can tell that you did really care for Kian. I'll let you know if I find anything out."

"Thank you, and I'm so sorry for what he did to you. I think if he could, he would take it back."

I nod with a smile and without another word I leave the club.

The sky is much darker now, the sun has practically disappeared, and storm clouds are rolling in.

I sit down on my motorcycle and stare down at the ground. I only know one person in this whole town who has curly hair.

I slowly get up from my motorcycle and head towards the cafe to get the tea for my mom and dad.

Slowly I move into the cafe, "Maggie?"

I look to my right to see Adrian and Adams sitting at a table.

"Uh hi."

My eyes are fixed on Adams, he smiles at me. His eyes are blue, I had never noticed… and he works at the club. He's the one that overheard Cal and his friend talking in the first place.

"What are you doing here?" Adrian asks as I walk up beside him.

No, it can't be him, "Uh just getting drinks for my mom and dad."

"Aw if you weren't we were going to ask you to stay and sit with us." Adams smiles, it's such a kind smile.

It can't be him; I need to find more proof. Just like how I proved it wasn't Conner I can prove it's not Adams. None of the people I am friends with can be capable of something like this.

"I'll sit next time, promise. But I've got to go get the drinks now."

I walk up to the counter and order the tea for my parents and quickly walk to the other end to grab the drink. I stop once more back at Adrian and Adams table, "So I'll see you two on Monday?"

"Yup!" Adams nods.

"Yeah, can I call you later tonight? There's this new movie I wanted to tell you about that I think we should watch." Adrian smiles.

I nod, "Yeah sure... uh bye!"

I make my way over to my motorcycle. Cal must have gotten the description wrong. I will make sure that no one I care about is a killer and that no one will get hurt. I can prove it's not Adams.

But why now am I remembering what everyone has been saying to me since I got back to town. *You've been gone for two years, Maggie... people can change.*

CHAPTER FORTY-SEVEN

Maggie Snow
Monday, November 4th, 7:10am

I walk into the kitchen rubbing my eyes.
"Morning sleepy head, we could hear you up last night, what were you doing?" My mom asks.
"Homework." I lie. I can't tell my mom that I was up most of the night trying to prove that another one of my friends is innocent.
"For what class?" My dad asks while passing me a cup of tea.
"Science, all about atoms." I laugh awkwardly, I didn't mean for there to be a pun.
A yawn escapes my mouth, "I'm not really hungry this morning. I think I'm going to head to school now."

I grab my bag and walk over to the door, "But I made pan-" My mom gets cut off as I close the door behind me.

I get on my motorcycle and ride down the street.

The fresh air feels nice, but I can tell it's going to rain again soon. It was raining all night and the whole weekend. It's lucky that it's not raining right now.

I open my locker.

"You're here early." Adrian says while leaning on the locker beside mine.

I'm relieved to see him today, "Yeah... I needed to get out of the house."

"Parents going crazy again?"

"Something like that." I smile.

Adrian looks around before looking back at me, "Well there was actually something I wanted to ask you so I'm glad you're here."

"What are you wanting to ask?"

"Well, I was just wondering if you'd want to be my girlfriend, like officially, since yeah." Adrian smiles.

A sense of relief gets lifted from my shoulders, "I will gladly be your girlfriend."

Adrian pumps his fists in the air making me laugh.

"Hey guys, what are we laughing about?" Adams asks as he walks up beside me.

Adrian wraps his arm around Adams, "You are looking at my new girlfriend." He says with a smile.

"Oh wow, congrats." Adams says.

"Thanks."

Why do I want to take a step away from him, he couldn't have done anything. I've just gotten in my own head and I'm overthinking everything. It's not Adams.

"It's weird to see you at school so early." Adams says.

"Yeah, just trying something different."

All of science class I'm trying my hardest not to stare at Adams. Most of my weekend was spend trying to remember everything from the murder board to prove it's not him. There is no reason it could be, Adams and Kian hardly talked.

My. Gibes walks around the classroom handing out a worksheet. I glance down at it once it's in front of me, but all I can focus on is proving it's not Adams.

Adams helped me at the beginning of the year so I wouldn't get sent down to the office. He helped me the other day and gave me advice. He's always been kind and awkward, but he always does the right thing.... He couldn't have killed Kian.

I look over to Adams who is writing on the worksheet.

"Hey."

He looks up at me, "Hi?"

"What did you do all summer?"

"Uh, I mostly worked, why? What did you do?" Adams asks.

"I was just wondering since I wasn't here during summer, and I mostly stayed inside and slept." I laugh, hoping he doesn't notice how uncomfortable I am.

If he had worked most of the summer, there is a chance he overheard a conversation Cal and Kian had.

I pull out a pencil and begin to work on the worksheet. The whole time my heart feels as though it's going to burst from my chest screaming.

I follow Adrian and Adams down the stairs once class is over.

"Why are you being the slow walker today?" Adrian turns around and asks.

"I'm just really tired today, didn't get much sleep." I say as we turn into the newspaper.

I sit down at the table, "Oscar and I are going to be going to the cafe to get drinks, do you want to come?" Adrian asks, "We'll be right back."

"I thought you were going to teach me how to drive for a bit?" Adams asks.

"Shit yes, we might be a bit longer, but do you still want to come?" Adrian asks.

"No, Maggie should keep working. We'll be really quick anyways." Adams smiles at me.

"Yeah, yeah, Adams is right. You two go, I'm good here." I smile as they walk out of the room.

I twist the back of my hair and pull on it. Maybe I should have said something to Adrian about what Cal had said, maybe he would be able to tell me it's not possible, be able to convince me more, and if there is the slim chance that it is Adams then Adrian would be safer knowing what I know.

I stand up and flip the board over to show the murder board, my eyes drift over to the note I wrote. *Bisexual*

It still shocks me that Kian was bisexual. I understand why he didn't tell anyone, if he had seen how his mom treated Ace, I would be scared to come out too.

I look down at the ground.

Adams wanted to help solve the murder. Was that to throw us off track?

I look up again and grab the letter that was sent to Kian. Adams was the one that found it that morning after the party, at any moment while he was gone, he could have put those drugs in Conners locker to get the police to investigate him.

I shift my eyes down to the letter. I never actually read it myself. Adams read it to Adrian and I.

Hey Kian, i'm back in town, if you don't want anyone to know what happened, meet me under the bridge tonight. From Maggie.

Wait, the I's.

"Why the fuck does the I in semi have two dots? Is that how you're supposed to spell it?"

"Oh no, it's a habit of mine, I've done it since I was a kid, no clue why."

I turn around and place the letter on the table. That can't be a coincidence can it? I grab my bag from the floor and pull out my notebook. I haven't looked back at the letter I got since I came to town. I hadn't even thought about looking at it since that first night.

Dear Maggïe, come back to town, ï want to talk. From Kïan.

I place the letter onto the table, and step backwards almost tripping over my foot.

No.

I won't believe it.

No.

Adams, kind, shy, scared, awkward Adams. He couldn't have, he wouldn't-

Shit.

I rummage through my bag looking for my phone, "Where the hell is the damn thing!"

I have to call Adrian. Something doesn't sit right with me, why was Oscar so adamant with me staying at the paper.

I stick my hand into one of the back pockets and pull out my phone. There is still the chance that I'm wrong. That this is just a weird coincidence that two people in town dot their I's two times, or it was just sloppy writing.

My gut says otherwise though.

I pace back and forth as the phone rings.

"Come on, pick up." I mumble to myself.

The call ends, "Shit." I dial the number again and wait for an answer. I try my hardest not to shake back and forth as the humming of the phone echoes in my ear.

Please pick up.

The phone beeps, there's breathing, "Adrian."

CHAPTER FORTY-EIGHT

Maggie Snow
Monday, November 4th, 2:35pm

"Adrian."
"No, it's Oscar. Adrian is getting our drinks, is everything alright?"
I tap my foot up and down on the ground, "Can you bring the phone to Adrian please."
"He's inside getting our drinks."
"Oscar-" My voice cracks.
"Is everything okay, Maggie?"
I stay silent, trying to control my breathing. All I can hear is Oscar's breathing on the other end. It's sharp.
"I know what you did."

"I don't know what you're talking about." He says, his voice is calm. Normally it's jittery, he doesn't sound nervous about his words.

"You killed him, right?" The silence is pulling at my skin, "Kian."

He stays silent, but I can hear him breathing, loud, it's a consistent sound. "It was for a good reason." Oscar says softly. Why the hell does he still sound so kind?

"Oscar-"

"I have to go take care of some business with Adrian now."

"What does that mean?"

"It will be better this way, I promise, Maggie."

The phone goes silent, "Oscar?"

I pull the phone away from my ear, "Shit! What the hell! Fuck!"

My hands slam down on the table, I close my eyes.

"Think." I mumble to myself, what would Oscar do? What is he going to do?

If he's going to try and hurt Adrian, where would he go?

"Well... I actually can't swim."

Adrian can't swim, the bridge is the only place that has the river below it.

Without a second thought I run out of the newspaper and down the hallway. I don't know what Oscar could have meant when he said he had to take care of some business with Adrian, but it doesn't sound like a good thing.

I reach for my pocket to grab my phone, "Shit." I glance back in the direction towards the newspaper. There isn't time for me to run back and grab it.

I round the corner to the main entrance of the school. Jade and Ace are sitting on a small bench.

"Are you okay?" Ace asks once she notices me.

"I need you two to call the police, get them to go to the bridge." I say out of breath.

"What why?" Jade asks.

"Because Oscar killed Kian and I think he's about to do the same with Adrian!" I say louder than intended to before running out of the school.

I run over to my motorcycle and feel my pockets for my keys, "You've got to be kidding me!!"

What else could go wrong at this moment?

The bridge isn't far from the school, I can run there.

I bolt out of the school parking lot and into the street. Cars hardly come in and out of town at this time, so the bridge won't be busy. The streets aren't busy either.

My foot hammers down into a puddle. The water splashing up on my leg. The wind rushes up against my body, I wish I had brought my jacket. I really should have taken some time to think before rushing out of the newspaper.

I run past the road that leads down to a dead end. The road where everyone parked their cars during the back-to-school party. The road that was filled with police cars after I had called about finding Kian's body. That feels like a year ago, when it was only two months ago.

I approach the bridge and see Adrian and Oscar standing by the railing. My heart feels like it's going to fall out of my chest right now.

"Adrian!" My voice cracks.

They both turn to look at me, "Maggie? What are you doing here? Did you run?"

"Can you come over here please." I can't answer his questions, I don't want to panic him.

I glance over to Oscar standing behind him. His eyes are focused on Adrian, he hasn't taken a second look at me.

It's as if time slows down as I watch Oscar pull out a gun from behind him, pointing it at the back of Adrian's head. A small click echoes through the air.

Adrian turns around and takes a quick step backwards, "Woah, Bud. What the fuck! Why do you have a gun!?"

"Oscar killed Kian." I say as calmly as I can as I take a step towards them both.

Oscar points the gun at the railing and then over to Adrian, "Get over to the railing."

Adrian's face goes pale as he slowly makes his way over to the railing, "Lean against it."

"Bud-"

"Do it!" Oscar screams.

I've never heard him yell before; it's off putting.

Adrian turns around to face Oscar, his hands are up in the air as he rests his back up against the old rusting rails.

"Oscar, please put the gun down, you don't have to do this." I say as I take another step closer. My hands are out in front of me.

I glance over to Adrian; his eyes are fixed on Oscar.

Oscar looks over to me, "But I do, he's just like Kian and soon he'll take you away. Just like Kian had."

He looks back over to Adrian, still holding him at gunpoint. The railings that Adrian are leaning on are too old, if Adrian makes the slightest movement, he could fall through them.

I glance over to the river below, it's rapid, and if Adrian can't swim, he'll definitely drown. I think that's what Oscar is counting on.

Oscar moves closer to Adrian, grabbing the collar of his shirt while keeping the gun pointed at Adrian's head.

"You don't have to do this. We can go to the police and say that everything was an accident. I believe that it was."

Oscar whips his head towards me, "You think all of that was an accident!? Why would that be an accident, Maggie!! I did all of this for you! So, you could come back to town and live your life how it was supposed to be lived before Kian had ever hurt you!!"

But I never wanted anyone dead.

"Did you not care about how Ace and her family would feel? Did you not care about how it would impact them?"

"The only person I care about is you! Because you were the only person who has ever cared for me."

I take a deep breath, "Then if you care about me, please let Adrian go."

Oscar smiles, "You're right, I should let him go."

Within the blink of an eye Oscar lets go of Adrian's shirt and pushes him through the railing. He throws the gun into the water and runs in the opposite direction down the bridge.

I run over to Adrian, by some sort of luck Adrian grabbed the ledge of the bridge before being able to fall. I grab his arms and help pull him back up to the ground.

"Are you okay?"

"Yeah." Adrian breathes rapidly, "Are you okay?"

"Yes, but." I look over to see Oscar still running, "The police should be here soon, stay here and wait for them, I'm going to make sure Oscar doesn't go far."

"What Maggie! No!"

Before Adrian can hold me back, I'm up and running after Oscar.

"Oscar stop!!" I shout.

Oscar stops running off to the side of the trees.

"The cops are coming and will be here soon. There is no use running." I take a step closer to him, "I understand you were angry at Kian."

"Kian needed to die."

"He didn't, maybe he just needed to go to jail."

I never wanted anyone to die, I never wanted Kian to die no matter what he did to me. Most people in my situation might have wanted him dead, but in my heart, I don't wish that upon anyone. I just wanted him to go to jail and for people to know what had happened to me.

"Everyone has hurt you Maggie, everyone and all you have ever been, was kind to them. Conner hurt you when he brought up your brother in front of everyone!! That's when I knew he needed to be framed for Kian's murder."

I shake my head, "Oscar-"

"It was easy to frame him for you Maggie, Kian talked so much while he was at the club. I knew that Conner was taking steroids, so I put a big stash in his locker to get the police to investigate him. Then the night of the karaoke I hid the murder weapon in his locker. I dressed up as the janitor and snuck into the school."

Oscar's eyes are wide, "I did all of this for you, Maggie. To get everyone who has ever hurt you out of your life so you can be happy, so you won't leave town again. And I already know that Adrian was going to hurt you and that's why I had to get rid of him."

He doesn't know that Adrian is safe, he thinks he's dead.

"I didn't want any of this."

"Yes, you did!!" His voice is harsh, making me take a step backwards, "Kian raped you, he deserved to die!! Conner brought up your brother in front of so many people!! Adrian will do all the same to you!!"

"Kian made you leave town!! He forced you not to tell anyone! He was a horrible person to you, and he drove my only friend out of town, the only person who was ever nice to me!!"

"But Adrian is your friend too."

Why aren't the police here yet? What's taking them so long? Please tell me that Ace and Jade did call them. I don't know how much longer I can keep him distracted.

Oscar clenches his fists up in the air and screams, "Don't you understand!! Be grateful, I saved you!! I reunited you with everyone that actually cares about you and got rid of everyone that didn't give a shit!"

I shake my head, "Oscar I didn't want any of this." I say firmly.

"Yes, you did!" He shouts and begins to walk around in circles, "Why aren't you happy? I did all of this so you could be happy!"

"Oscar-"

Something switches in his brain, he stops walking and stares at me, his eyes are fixed on mine and not moving. "God!! Stop calling me that! You never really cared for me did you!!"

"Of course, I care about you, Oscar. That's why I need you to calm down."

"Stop calling me Oscar!!" He charges at me pushing me to the ground. He kneels, slamming my head into the ground.

"You know what! Maybe you are the mean bitch everyone said you were in grade nine, and maybe Kian was the cause of it, but maybe he was the one that brought it out of you, and it was always there, but no one could see it. Truthfully everyone in this town is shit. Truthfully no one has ever cared about me, not even you!!"

Oscar's hands wrap around my neck, "I helped you come back to town, and this is what I get!! I don't even get a thank you!"

"Os- Osc-" I chock. I try a pull his hands away from my neck.

"You were never my friend!"

His grip tightens.

"You never cared about me!"

My vision blurs and my ears begin to ring. I can see Oscar's mouth moving, but I can't hear a word he is saying. I can see five different versions of him.

My eyes shift to the right of his body to see a flash of red and blue. My hearing cuts back in for a second, "Police! Hands in the air!"

Oscar keeps his hands at my neck. I was losing more air by the second and everything was becoming dizzy. It takes a second before Oscar is getting pulled off me.

I cough and take in gasps of air.

I feel two familiar arms wrap around me, "You're okay, everything's okay." A familiar voice repeats as they hold me in their arms, my vision begins to come back.

"Everything's okay." Adrian says, "Everything is okay now."

Red and blue lights flash in front of us. Police and paramedics surround us. It feels hard to breathe even though Oscar's hands are gone from around my neck.

CHAPTER FORTY-NINE

Adrian Fisher
Tuesday, November 5th, 8:30am

The hospital cafeteria is quiet this early in the morning. I sit across from Ace and Jade. They're both holding small cups of tea from the coffee shop just outside the hospital.

"How are you feeling?" Ace asks.

"I'm pretty tired, hospital chairs aren't the most comfortable things to sleep in, plus the doctor said I have a sprained wrist, so that hurts a bit."

"I bet Maggie would have been fine in the hospital alone." Jade mumbles loud enough for Ace and I to hear.

Ace shoves Jade, "Sorry."

I couldn't leave Maggie alone in the hospital last night, her parents hadn't arrived yet, and the doctor said that when Oscar had hit her head on the ground it's possible that she could have a concussion.

"What even happened?" Jade asks.

"Um, Oscar pushed me off the ledge for what I've gathered is because I was going to hurt Maggie? Which I wasn't, so… but anyways I grabbed the ledge of the bridge before I could fall, spraining my wrist. Maggie helped me up, told me to wait for the police and then ran after Oscar."

I rub the back of my neck, "I should have gone to help her, I shouldn't have left her alone."

"That's not your fault, everyone was confused. Maggie seemed to be the only one that knew what was going on. Jade and I were confused when she asked us to call the police and told us about Oscar quickly. It's not your fault that she got hurt." Ace says.

"I still feel bad."

"Yeah, well don't! It's Oscar's fault that any of this happened in the first place." Jade crosses her arms and leans back in the chair.

I nod. It's still hard to wrap my head around the fact that my best friend tried to kill me yesterday. Where did he even get the gun? How was he strong enough to kill Kian?

"I should get back up to her room. See if she's awake yet." I stand up from the chair.

"Okay, we'll be up soon." Ace smiles, "Should we bring up tea for her?"

"Yeah, she'll probably like that."

"Would you like one too?"

I shake my head, "I'm okay, not that hungry or thirsty. Thanks though."

I walk away from the table and down the hallway to where the elevators are. The doors open and I step inside. It's so early the hospital is eerily quiet, especially in the elevator.

I get off the elevator on the third floor and walk down to Maggie's room.

Maggie's room is small with a large window covering half of the wall. Everything is covered in a light pale blue, and smells like hand sanitizer.

"Where's Oscar?" Maggie asks as soon as I step in the room, it's weird to hear her say his name.

I close the door behind me and walk over to the chair beside the bed and sit down.

Maggie looks paler than she normally is, and the bags under her eyes are darker than normal. I don't understand why she looks so sick even though she isn't. Maybe she's just tired.

"He's being held at the police station, but he hasn't confessed to anything yet. He says he needs to know that you're okay first." I don't know why, but when I say that out loud it gives me chills.

"Seriously? Yesterday it was like he was blinded by rage and now he wants to know if I'm, okay?"

"Yeah, I don't really understand it."

Maggie sighs, "Yeah and not the mention that the only hospital is two hours away from town.

They really need to get a closer one, I don't even understand why I had to come here."

"Because your head got slammed against the ground and you were strangled, the doctor said you might have a concussion, remember?"

"Yes, I remember, it's just annoying." Maggie looks down at her hands, "Have you heard anything from my parents?"

I shake my head, "No, but they probably had to take the bus here. They'll probably be here soon."

Maggie nods slowly.

"How did you know it was Oscar?" I ask, I was wanting to ask last night, but the doctors had told me that she had to rest.

She looks up at me, "We never looked at the letter Kian got, since Oscar read it to us. All the I's on the letter were dotted twice, same with the one I got. The only person I knew who did that was him... Plus I talked to that Cal guy again and he helped."

"Why didn't you say anything to me?"

Maggie shrugs, "He's your best friend, I wanted to be 100 precent sure that it was or wasn't him before I said anything. Once I was sure about it, I called you and Oscar answered, that's how I knew you guys were at the bridge. I remembered you couldn't swim and if he knew that, it was one of your biggest weaknesses."

I grab her hand, "He kept saying he killed Kian for me. That he framed Conner for me, that he was going to kill you for me. I never wanted any of that."

Maggie looks into my eyes, they're greener than they've ever been, and glossy, almost as if she's trying not to cry.

"I know you didn't. But don't blame yourself please."

It makes sense that Oscar was mad, Maggie had told me that she was the only one he ever really trusted before he met me. I understand that he would be mad when he found out why she left, but I never thought he could kill someone.

"Why did you run after him yesterday? You could have died."

"You could have died too."

"But why'd you risk your life running after him? We were both safe once you pulled me up from the bridge."

"I needed answers, and I thought I could calm him down. And I wasn't just going to let him run away after trying to kill you, you are literally the only person I have been able to open up to after two years."

I hold her hand tighter, "But you could have died, Maggie."

Maggie shakes her head, "But I didn't."

"I said I would keep us safe. I said that we would be vigilant."

"Neither of us could have predicted yesterday to happen. You can't blame yourself, just like how I won't blame myself."

I lean forwards and kiss her forehead.

"Once we're out of the hospital I'll explain the full story to everyone. I think the police are wanting me to explain everything again too." Maggie says.

"Yeah, we kind of need to know what the hell happened." I turn around to see Jade and Ace standing in the doorway.

"How are you feeling?" Ace asks as she walks over and passes Maggie a tea.

"I've felt much better, it doesn't help that this bed is the most uncomfortable thing in the world, and my neck hurts." Maggie takes a sip of her tea.

"So, I guess you were right about it not being Conner." Jade says as she leans up against the wall.

Maggie smiles, "Will you now believe me next time I have a gut instinct?"

"I said you were right, not that you were always going to be right." Jade rolls her eyes.

"Maybe we should get you up and walk around the hospital?" Ace asks.

"Eh, I'd rather not walk around the hospital with my ass hanging out of this gown." Maggie chuckles.

"Too much information." Jade says.

"Hey! I should get a free pass. I almost died."

I shake my head, "I don't think that warrants a free pass, it was funny though."

"Why thank you, at least I can be funny."

"What is there to be funny about right now!" All of us slowly turn our heads towards the door to see Maggie's mom standing there with her arms crossed and her dad standing behind her.

Maggie's mom walks into the room and stands at the end of the hospital bed, "What were you thinking!? I had asked you to be safe!"

I look around the room not knowing what to do. I make eye contact with Ace who looks just as uncomfortable as I am.

"We are leaving Misthill once you get out of this hospital!"

"You can leave. I'm staying, I'd rather be in the town where I have friends instead of the one where everyone glares at me." Maggie says.

"And Oscar is probably going to jail, so there is no reason for Maggie to leave since the town will be safe." I say.

Maggie's mom looks over to me, "You should want the best for Maggie."

"He does know the best for me mom, he has since I met him. Now if you don't mind, I would like to talk to my friends alone, the doctor says that stress can cause my head to hurt, and right now you're stressing me out."

I was in the room when the doctor was talking about Maggie yesterday, and he said nothing of that sort. But I'm not going to say anything. I know it seemed like she was wanting to see her parents, but I don't think she was expecting her mom to come in screaming at her to leave town.

"Of course, we will go talk to the doctor to see when you're able to leave the hospital. Feel better, Mags." Her dad smiles before grabbing her mom's arm pulling her out of the room.

Ace and Jade left the hospital an hour ago and Maggie's mom headed back to town on the bus a couple minutes ago. Her dad is staying the night with her.

"You don't have to stay here, you should probably get home, your parents might be getting worried." Maggie says.

"I called them last night, they know I'm safe. I'm happy to stay."

"Thank you, but I think you should go home, sleep in your own bed tonight. I've got my dad here. I'll be okay." Maggie smiles.

"Are you sure?"

"I'm positive, plus I'll be back in town in no time."

"I'll call you when I get home then."

"Actually, my phone and all my stuff is still at the school. I kind of just dropped everything and ran to the bridge."

I nod, "Want me to bring it here to you tomorrow?"

"No, it's okay, I can live without my phone. Just make sure my notebook stays safe, and all the proof is still in the newspaper." Maggie explains.

"I will make sure it all stays safe."

I stand up and lean down giving Maggie a kiss, "Want to know one good thing that came out of yesterday?" Maggie asks.

"Sure."

"You asked me to be your girlfriend."

I smile, "Yes I did do that."

I had fully forgotten that that happened yesterday, I remember I spent most of the morning psyching myself up to ask her.

"Thank you."

"You don't have to thank me."

"I know but thank you for just being you."

"You're welcome, now get some rest. You look tired."

Maggie rolls her eyes, she looks less pale than earlier, but still super tired. "I'll try."

I walk out of the room, closing the door behind me.

I know that Maggie is going to be okay, she's one of the strongest people I know. She can survive a hospital stay. All thought it is still hard to imagine everything that happened yesterday. All of it has burled together. I know that it did happen, but it still feels as though it was a dream.

"I'm home" I yell as I walk through the front door of my house.

My mom comes rushing out of the kitchen with my dad in tow. She pulls me into a tight hug, "Thank God you're okay, we were so worried."

"How is Maggie?" My dad asks.

"She'll be okay." I smile. Yesterday morning before school, I had told my dad I was going to ask Maggie to be my girlfriend, he was excited for me. I haven't told my mom yet.

"I knew that Oscar was different from the start of your friendship with him."

"I wouldn't say different is the word, mom. He killed someone and tried to kill me and Maggie."

Oscar isn't *different*, he's a murderer and has been lying to me for months. He's no longer my friend.

"I'm going to go upstairs to rest." I move past my parents and head upstairs.

I sit down on my bed and look out the window.

To think that the first guy I had ever made friends with, in this town would turn out to be a murderer is not something I could have fathomed.

He had sent me a letter asking me to stay away from Maggie. Does that mean he didn't want to hurt me and that was just a warning? How did I not recognize the handwriting?

Oscar had been adamant since Maggie came back to town that I didn't like her. He was trying to keep her safe. Did he really think I would hurt her? He couldn't have known Maggie and I would end up together, was he being cautious?

I want to ask him all these questions, but I don't know if I'll ever be able to face him again. He was my best friend, but did I ever truly know who he was. Everything he told me about his parents, everything I had told him. Was he ever my best friend?

CHAPTER FIFTY

Maggie Snow
Saturday, November 9th, 1:45pm

    I step outside for the first time in five days. The air has gotten much colder since Monday. Ace is riding the bus home with me; she's visited me every day in the hospital since Tuesday.
    "Ready to get on this bus and go home?" She asks as we stand at the bus stop.
    "A fun two hours on the bus and then we've got to talk to the Police... and Oscar."
    "You don't have to talk to him if you don't want to. I know I haven't because I don't want to yell or cry in front of him, I don't want to give him that satisfaction."
    "No, I need to talk to him, if I don't, I'll keep putting it off. And your brother died because of me, I feel somewhat responsible."

Ace shakes her head, "It wasn't your fault. It was because of a mistake Kian made."

"But he didn't deserve to die, I just wanted him in jail."

I don't know if I should tell Ace about what Jessica said to me last week, how she also had some part to play in all of this.

"But after you're done talking to him, we'll go to the cafe and meet up with Adrian and Jade, and you'll tell us everything that happened." Ace smiles.

"Are you coming to the Police Station with me?"

"Of course! I'm not going to leave you."

"Are you sure it won't be too much?"

Ace shakes her head, "It won't be. And I let you down once by not standing by your side, I'm not going to do it again."

I don't think she knows how much that means to me.

I straighten out my shoulders, I need to keep my confident self on while talking to Oscar today. He still hasn't confessed to anything, I need to make sure that he talks today, says what the police need to hear to be able to put him behind bars.

Ace and I walk onto the bus and grab two seats. We try our best to sit as comfortably as possible, but that's hard to do on a bus. Time to spend two hours that'll feel more like five while sitting in these rock-hard seats.

Ace and I stand outside the Police Station, "So do we just walk in?"

Ace shrugs, "I'd think so."

I pull open the door letting Ace walk in first.

"What are you two doing here?" Detective Lana asks right as we step inside.

"Um. I'd like to talk to Oscar."

"He's not allowed any visitors right now."

"But he hasn't confessed to anything yet, I can get him to confess. I can get him to talk." I say.

She shakes her head, "I don't think it's the best idea for you to be talking to him. The last time we saw you he was on top of you with his hands around your neck."

"Yes, I don't need a reminder. Please let me talk to him."

"I can't-"

"We know that he won't talk until he knows that Maggie is safe, so just let her talk to him!" Ace shouts.

I have the urge to applaud her, I've never seen her be that straightforward before. I feel like a proud older sister.

Detective Lana takes a deep breath, "Fine. Follow me."

Ace waits in the main entrance while I follow Detective Lana down the hallway.

"We have cameras in the hallway so if he confesses anything we'll be able to hear it. You only have five minutes." She tells me before walking away.

I stand in front of a small cell. Oscar is sitting on a bench in the same clothes he was wearing on Monday. His hair is messy and straighter than normal.

He looks up, "Maggie." He rushes to his feet and over to the bars of the cell. I take a small step backwards.

"I'm so glad you're okay. You have to tell them what happened, you have to get me out of here. I was helping the world; I was helping you." He whispers. There's desperation in his eyes.

"You strangled me, you tried to kill Adrian! You killed Kian and you want me to help you get out!"

He grips the bars of the cell, "We're friends, that's what friends do."

"You strangled me."

"I never meant to. I was confused."

"Were you confused when you killed Kian?"

Oscar shakes his head rapidly, "I did that for you. For your safety. He took you away from me, he took my only friend away from me."

"Kian should have gone to jail for what he did. He didn't need to die."

I'm not worried about saying any of this out loud. On Monday I explained everything to the police. Every detail.

"You're a monster."

"No! Kian was the monster! He would have hurt someone else again, he would have found you and hurt you again!!" Oscar shouts.

"Then both of you are monsters."

"I'm not a monster, Maggie. I did all of this for you-"

"Stop saying that! I never wanted any of this shit to happen!! You did none of this for me, you did all of it for you just so I could be back in town!! None of this was for me!"

"Friends don't yell at each other." Oscar says calmly.

"Well friends don't strangle or try to kill each other either. So, I guess you got a pretty twisted sense of friendship."

Before Oscar can say anything else I'm already off down the hallway.

"Are you okay?" Ace asks as I walk up to her, "I heard yelling."

"I'm just angry."

Ace nods, "I understand that. I'm angry too."

"Ace? Maggie?"

I turn around to see Conner standing behind me, "Conner!"

Without blinking Ace and I quickly pull Conner into a hug, "I'm sorry that I thought it was you." I hear Ace mumble.

In this small little circle of a hug, I feel safe. All three of us haven't been alone together since grade nine. This feels nice.

We pull out of the hug.

"What are you doing here?" I ask.

"I got let out of jail two hours ago, I had to come here to sign some papers. No one explained what happened to me, just that I was free to go." Conner explains.

He looks different than when I last saw him. There's stubble on his face and a couple of bruises on his arms, and cuts on his hands. But what did I expect him to look like when he got out of jail, a new shiny rock?

"Well, you've missed a lot." I say.

"Oscar killed Kian and framed you for it." Ace says.

"What the fuck!?"

That is the right response he should have. Most people have had that response because no one expected it.

"We're going to the Cafe to meet up with Adrian and Jade right now... I'm going to explain everything. You can come." I smile. I really hope that he will come.

"Gladly, I need to be around non-scary humans."

I laugh, "Well we definitely aren't scary humans."

We walk into the cafe and spot Adrian and Jade sitting in the back corner.

I grab an extra chair as we make our way over to them, "We picked someone up on our way over." I say as I sit down beside Adrian.

"Hell man, did you get stronger?" Adrian asks as him and Conner latch their hands together before Conner sits down.

"I probably did." Conner chuckles.

"How'd it go with Oscar?" Jade asks as Ace pulls out a box of rainbow chocolate chip cookies from her bag.

"He wanted me to get him out of jail."

"Are you joking?" Adrian asks.

I shake my head, "I wish I was."

"Wait, so can you explain everything, since I'm really confused. How did you find out it was Oscar?" Conner asks.

"I fully pieced everything together while I was in the hospital-"

"You were in the hospital?!" Conner shouts, people from other tables look over to us, "Sorry." He mumbles.

"Yeah, that's part of the long story." Adrian says.

"Which, we all still need explaining on how you figured it all out." Jade says.

"Would you like me to start from the beginning?" I ask.

"Well obviously." Jade says while grabbing a cookie.

I begin to tell them everything that happened in grade nine. I tell Jade and Conner for the first-time what Kian had done; I include what I had figured out about Jessica telling Kian. How I figure that all of this was a butterfly effect. I tell them how Kian made me leave town, and then I tell them the story about Oscar wanting me to call him Adams.

Moving the explanation to two years later when I got the letter from who I thought was Kian, but it was actually Oscar. I explained that I came back to town because I was scared. Then I tell them about Cal, and how Kian was bisexual and dating him, that's where he was sneaking off during the night. Oscar had overheard Kian talking about me and pieced together what had happened, he was angry and took everything into his own hands. I explain that he was mad because in his eyes Kian took away his only friend.

I explain why Oscar decided to frame Conner, and how he did it.

"I'm going to make sure I know who's around me when I talk about something secret from now on." Conner says.

I continue to explain why he wanted to kill Adrian, and then why he had strangled me. I explain that Oscar had done all this because he wanted me back in town, that he had done all of this so I could live my life without people hurting me.

"But I think hurting is a part of life. Because if you don't get hurt or sad, you'll never know how it feels to be happy. Oscar was wrong with everything he did, and he only did it because he wanted his friend."

"Please tell me you aren't still going to be his friend." Jade says.

"No, I'm not, he can make new friends in jail."

The table becomes silent, no one knows what to say.

"Maybe we should make sure that any other secrets are out in the open right now." I say.

"What do you mean?" Adrian asks.

I shrug, "Let's think of this moment as a re-start, we get anything we need off our chests, so it doesn't come back to hurt us later."

"I mean I guess I lied about where I live. I literally live a house down from Adrian." Jade says.

"What you do!? Why'd you lie about that?" Adrian asks.

Jade shrugs, "I didn't want to be known as a rich kid."

"I think everyone knows what my big secret was." Conner says.

"I didn't really have any, but I mean I did know what happened with Maggie and Kian. I heard Kian telling Maggie to leave town and I didn't do anything to stop it from happening." Ace says.

"And I forgive you for that."

"You do?"

I nod, "I wouldn't have known what to do in that situation either."

"Kian helped me fake my science grades." Adrian smiles awkwardly.

Jade scoffs, "That's lame."

"So is lying about what side of town you live on." Adrian says.

"Maggie, do you have anything else you'd want to get off your chest?" Ace asks.

"Uh, when I first came back to town and found Kian. I told myself that after I found out who killed him, I was going to leave, just go travel on my motorcycle."

"Are you still going to do that?" Adrian asks.

I look over to him, his whole face has the word worried written on it, "No, I can wait to do that until I graduate. There's no rush to go anywhere."

Ace claps her hands together.

"Let's make a promise that none of us will lie to each other so no one ends up dead in a forest and then goes crazy." Jade smiles.

Conner nods, "Agreed, and no one else goes to jail."

"Sticking together no matter what." Adrian smiles.

Ace nods, "Yes, I don't want anyone else dying."

I chuckle, "I think everyone can agree to that one."

Everyone nods together.

"Good because I think I need a tea and a calm day for once." I smile.

"A calm day forever." Ace says.

I point at her, "Very true."

Adrian stands up from the table, "All get all of us drinks, what does everyone what?"

"I'm coming to order with you." Conner says.

I look over to the window, the first time I stepped foot in the place was two months ago, I was dreading being back, but I've never been happier that I came back. And that I'm here with the people I trust.

The police had kept it a secret about Oscar being arrested, but I was ready for the news about him to spread across town like a wildfire. I was ready for everyone in town to know the truth about what happened.

Two years had passed since I stepped foot into Misthill.

Two years had passed since I had been home.

"I like the mystery."

"What happened to you does not make you weak."

"I guess I'm not a mystery to you anymore."

I have finally found my home again.

AUTHOR'S NOTE

In most books these are called acknowledgements, but I wanted to call it an author's note. A note to say thank you to people and say a thank you to this book. I started writing this book when I was in grade ten, and as one does, I originally uploaded this whole book onto Wattpad, because that was my only way to share my work with the world. Then a year later near the end of grade eleven I started to write a 3rd draft of the book, and this is the version of the book you've just read. The book that has been published.

This book sits so deep in my heart because it's the kind of book I had always wanted to write, but never had the best idea or courage to. Then one day I finally did it and I am so happy and proud that I did. I have fallen in love with the world I have created and all the characters, maybe one day I will revisit them in a new story.

Throughout the book I sprinkled small bits of advice my mom has given me over the past couple of years, some of the advice or sayings in the book were more me talking to my past self, telling me I am strong, and I am the one in control. My goal was to help people know that no matter what you are going through you will get through it and you are strong, and as Adrian said to Maggie "What happened to you does not make you weak."

I would like to give a thank you to my best friend Antigone for helping me with this book over the past three years. When I started writing the book, I would throw all my ideas at her, and she helped me plan out the book and edit it. She was as much involved in this book as I was. Another thanks to all my friends, family and my boyfriend who have listened to me ramble about this book for years. And one final thank you to the reader for sitting through the book that means so much to me. I hope it has helped you in some way or inspired you to write a book yourself.

Thank you.